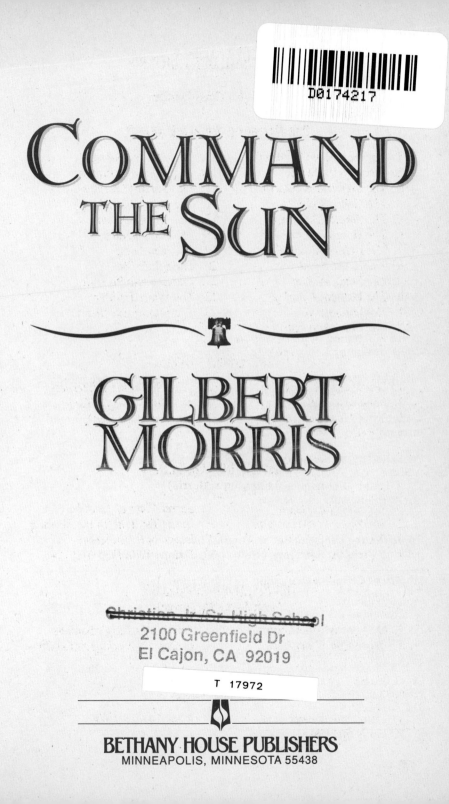

COMMAND THE SUN

GILBERT MORRIS

Christian Jr./Sr. High School
2100 Greenfield Dr
El Cajon, CA 92019

T 17972

BETHANY HOUSE PUBLISHERS
MINNEAPOLIS, MINNESOTA 55438

D0174217

Command the Sun
Copyright © 2000
Gilbert Morris

Cover illustration by Chris Ellison
Cover design by Lookout Design Group

All rights reserved. No part of this publication may be reproduced, stored in a retrieval system, or transmitted in any form or by any means—electronic, mechanical, photocopying, recording, or otherwise—without the prior written permission of the publisher and copyright owners.

Published by Bethany House Publishers
A Ministry of Bethany Fellowship International
11400 Hampshire Avenue South
Minneapolis, Minnesota 55438
www.bethanyhouse.com

Printed in the United States of America by
Bethany Press International, Minneapolis, Minnesota 55438

Library of Congress Cataloging-in-Publication Data

Morris, Gilbert.
    Command the sun / by Gilbert Morris.
        p.   cm. — (The Liberty Bell ; bk. 7)
    ISBN 1–55661–571–X
        1. United States—History—Revolution, 1775–1783—Fiction.
2. Inheritance and succession—Great Britain—Fiction. 3. Nobility—Great Britain—Fiction. I. Title.
PS3563.O8742 C57   2000
813'.54—dc21   99–050484
                                                                              CIP

To Daniel Jones—a good son.

Some sons are of blood, but
some are simply given to a man.
I am so proud of you!

GILBERT MORRIS spent ten years as a pastor before becoming Professor of English at Ouachita Baptist University in Arkansas and earning a Ph.D. at the University of Arkansas. During the summers of 1984 and 1985, he did postgraduate work at the University of London. A prolific writer, he has had over twenty-five scholarly articles and two hundred poems published in various periodicals, and over the past years, he has had more than seventy novels published. His family includes three grown children, and he and his wife live in Alabama.

CONTENTS

PART FOUR
The Victors

The Liberty Bell

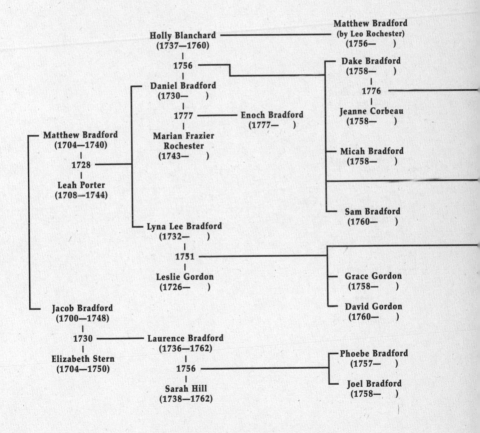

Matthew Bradford
(1704—1740)
|
1728
|
Leah Porter
(1708—1744)

Matthew Bradford
(by Leo Rochester)
(1756—   )

Holly Blanchard
(1737—1760)
|
1756

Dake Bradford
(1758—   )
|
1776

Daniel Bradford
(1730—   )
|
1777 ———— Enoch Bradford
(1777—   )
|
Marian Frazier
Rochester
(1743—   )

Jeanne Corbeau
(1758—   )

Micah Bradford
(1758—   )

Lyna Lee Bradford
(1732—   )
|
1751

Sam Bradford
(1760—   )

Leslie Gordon
(1726—   )

Grace Gordon
(1758—   )

David Gordon
(1760—   )

Jacob Bradford
(1700—1748)
|
1730 ———— Laurence Bradford
(1736—1762)
|
Elizabeth Stern   1756
(1704—1750) |
Sarah Hill
(1738—1762)

Phoebe Bradford
(1757—   )

Joel Bradford
(1758—   )

The Liberty Bell Family Tree is continued on the next page ➔

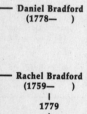

Daniel Bradford
(1778—   )

Rachel Bradford
(1759—   )
|
1779
|
Jacob Steiner
(1751—   )

Clive Gordon
(1753—   )
|
1778
|
Katherine Yancy
(1755—   )

PART ONE

THE PRODIGAL

1

An Old Flame

MAY HAD COME TO BOSTON like a storybook spring. The grass was greener than emerald, the trees dotted the countryside with pink, white, and scarlet blossoms, and the fields exhaled an earthy fragrance as farmers in the surrounding area broke the land with their plowshares. The year 1779 promised to be a gentle one, at least as far as the weather was concerned.

The church that sat back from the dusty road was an old one, and its white spire rose to a needlepoint beneath the white clouds floating above, fleecy and somnambulant. They looked like flocks of sheep drifting across the blue canopy of the sky. The churchyard itself was filled with carriages and buggies, and several men had taken up station underneath a towering chestnut tree, smoking clay pipes as they waited.

Tom Hankins, a tall lanky individual with a scraggly reddish beard and a full head of hair to match, had been the most talkative of the group. Hankins had a pair of sharp gray eyes, and occasionally laughter went up from the other men at one of his remarks. None of them were dressed for a service, wearing instead the plain garb of workingmen—homespun shirts and trousers, scuffed boots, and broad-brimmed hats to keep off the hot sun.

Hankins interrupted himself, squinting toward the east, then said, "Who's that comin' in such a hurry?"

The other four men looked casually in the direction of Hankins' glance, and Farrell Simms, a short chunky individual with a round red face, squinted, then said, "Can't make him out, but he sure is comin' like the devil was after him."

The group waited until the rider pulled up in front of the church, watching as he flung himself off the horse.

"Why, I'll be jiggered. It's Matthew!"

13

"Which Matthew?" Simms asked.

"Matthew Bradford, sure as you're born."

"Better not call him that. It's Sir Matthew Rochester now."

Hankins shot him a withering look. "He may have taken on that title, but he's just Matthew to me. I'm right surprised he's come. I thought he was in Virginia at that new property of his, lording over everybody."

"Guess he come back for his sister's wedding."

Suddenly Hankins said, "I'll go hold his horse. That ought to be worth a couple of shillings." He moved away from the group under the tree and approached the rider rapidly. His eyes studied the man who had dismounted, and he hesitated for a moment and then said, "Well, Matthew—or, Sir Matthew, I suppose it'll have to be now."

Matthew Rochester turned quickly. He was not accustomed to his new name yet, and his face flushed slightly. He was an inch under six feet, very slender, with a strong, wiry build. His brown hair, tossed with the breeze, fell across his forehead as he removed his hat and turned a pair of cornflower blue eyes on the speaker and smiled. "Hello, Tom. I guess you don't have to bother about the *sir*." He put out his hand and gave Hankins a firm grip.

Matthew Rochester was dressed in a very stylish outfit. He had on a dark green velvet coat with turned-back cuffs and large gold buttons, black velvet breeches, a white silk shirt with a cravat around his neck, a tan silk waistcoat, white silk stockings, and black leather shoes.

"You're mighty late. Almost missed the wedding."

"I know." He glanced at his horse, which was lathered from the hard ride, and shook his head with disgust. "I had a horse break down on me. Had to buy another one. Now he's done in."

"Appears like he is. You'd better get on inside. You'll miss the wedding if you don't hurry."

"Can you take care of my horse, Tom?"

"You know it," Hankins nodded. He took the lines and said, "I'll walk him up and down until he cools off, then give him just a sip or two. He'll be all right."

Matthew Rochester grinned and reached inside his pocket. Pulling out a coin, he handed it to the other, saying, "I appreciate it, Tom."

"No trouble at all. You get on inside, now." But just before Matthew turned, he asked, "What do you think about your sister marrying this German fellow?"

Matthew turned and looked at the man. He knew it had caused quite a bit of talk that his sister, Rachel, had chosen to marry Jacob Steiner. Steiner had come over from Europe as a Hessian to fight against George

Washington's forces. He had been wounded and escaped, then had been found almost dead by Rachel Bradford. She had nursed him back to health, keeping him hidden all the time in the loft of the old barn behind the house. The two had fallen in love, and after Steiner had enlisted under Washington, they had agreed to marry.

"I think he's a good man. What are people saying?"

"Oh, you know how people talk. But everybody trusts Miss Rachel. If she'll take him, I'll say he's a good enough fellow."

Hankins moved back as the young man entered the church, then began walking the horse. "Come on, boy. You've had a rough day." He was immediately surrounded by his pipe-smoking cronies, who wanted to know everything. He said loftily, "Sir Matthew and I don't tell everything we know. Here, Farrell, you walk this horse. Take it easy with him, now. He's a fine animal."

Matthew stepped inside the church door and looked for a place to put his hat. He saw a series of pegs on the wall, but all of them were filled, so he simply held the tricorn in his hand. The outer part of the church was a small foyer, and he hesitated to go in, knowing that he would be the object of many curious eyes. As he stood there the door opened, and his younger brother Sam came bursting out.

"Well, Matthew," he said, "you made it!"

Sam Bradford had auburn hair and piercing blue eyes. He was only five ten but strongly built, and he came over at once and gave Matthew a hug. He was an emotional man and showed his affection, or his anger, very quickly.

"Where have you been?" he demanded. "You're about to miss everything!"

"My horse broke down on me, Sam. Is it crowded inside?"

"Jammed like pickles in a barrel," Sam grinned. "I think everybody in the county is here, but I'll put you right down at the front even if you have to stand up."

"No. I'll go up in the balcony. I'd rather not make a splash."

"You'd better hurry, then. I'd go with you, but I'm supposed to stay here in case some latecomers show up. Don't know where I'd put 'em, though."

"I'll see you after the ceremony." Matthew turned and climbed the staircase that led to the small balcony. He entered through a door and saw that it was already crowded. Sweeping the scene, he found one seat. He was aware of whispers and heard his name mentioned but ignored it. "Pardon me," he said as he made his way down the narrow aisle to the empty seat. He started to sit down, but then he saw the woman who was sitting next to him. For one moment, he felt as if he had been hit in the stomach. Then he caught himself and eased himself down. "Hello, Abigail," he whispered.

Abigail Howland sat very still. She was an attractive young woman with a wealth of brown hair, hazel eyes, and a beautiful oval-shaped face. She was wearing a simple dress made of a light gray linen. White lace decorated the round neck and encircled the three-quarter-length sleeves. The bodice was buttoned up the front with tiny white buttons, and the skirt was full and fell to her ankles. Her hands suddenly turned pale as she squeezed the hymnbook in her lap.

"Hello, Matthew," she said quietly.

Matthew was aware that people were watching and listening and could say only, "I'm a little late." He turned his eyes deliberately away from her and fixed them on the scene below, noting his father, Daniel, and his stepmother, Marian, sitting in the first row. Marian was holding Enoch, the one-year-old baby that she and his father had adopted. The sight held Matthew's attention for a moment, but he was painfully conscious of Abigail Howland's presence beside him.

This woman had once been the center of his world. He had been passionately in love with her, and the memories forced themselves into his mind. He blankly watched as the pastor and Jacob Steiner, wearing a Continental uniform, emerged at the front of the church and Rachel began walking down the aisle. But all Matthew could think of was the betrayal he had known at Abigail's hands. It had cut him to the heart more deeply than anything in life, and he now tried to shove those memories back, but they simply would not leave. They had never left, he realized with desperation, although he had tried everything to forget her. He had been simply Matthew Bradford then, a struggling artist with some talent, but now he was Sir Matthew Rochester, having inherited the entire estate and title of his father, Sir Leo Rochester. Nevertheless, Sir Matthew was as conscious of Abigail Howland's beauty as he had been as a younger man.

He listened as the pastor, Reverend Martin Williams, led the couple through the ceremony, and he was filled with pride at the sight of his sister standing in the front of the church. Next to Abigail, Rachel was the most beautiful woman Matthew knew, and she looked almost angelic in her white gown with her stunning red hair and green eyes. The two of them had been very close all of their lives, and now as he saw her giving herself to this tall soldier from so far away a twinge of mixed joy and sadness filled his heart. It had been difficult for him to give up his name and to assume a new identity. In fact, as he sat there watching

16

and listening to Jacob and Rachel exchange their vows, he was suddenly besieged with doubts. *Maybe I shouldn't have taken the title. After all, I was happy enough as a Bradford.*

This thought brought his eyes around to Daniel Bradford, and he admired the handsome profile that he knew so well. Bradford was a strong man with wheat-colored hair and eyebrows and fair skin with a slight tan. He had always looked like a Viking to Matthew, the most imaginative of the Bradfords, and now he studied the face of the only man he had ever thought of as a father. It had come as a shock to discover that Daniel was not his real father, but rather Sir Leo Rochester. When Rochester had cast off Matthew's mother, Daniel married her and cared for her until she died, and he had never made one iota of difference between Matthew and his other children. Matthew felt a sudden warmth as he gazed at the face of his true father, and regret filled him that he had turned away and chosen another name.

Desperately, Matthew forced these troubling thoughts out of his mind and followed the words of the couple on the floor below. He could not help but think that at one time he had thought he would be saying these same words to the woman who sat beside him. He did not turn to look at her but was still intensely aware of her presence. He caught the faint violet scent that he always associated with her and had to restrain himself to keep from turning to look at her.

Finally the ceremony was over, and as Abigail stood, Matthew followed suit. "We were all afraid you wouldn't come."

"Well, of course I would come! I got held up on the way. A horse broke down on me." As the two stood waiting to come down from the balcony, Matthew saw that Abigail had changed very little. She was not a large woman in her demeanor, but there was strength in her figure and also etched on her face. He did notice a change in her demeanor from the earlier days. A while back, she had come to ask his forgiveness for betraying him, claiming that she had found God. Matthew had been hurt so badly that he had turned angrily away and spurned her plea for forgiveness. Now, however, he saw something in her that had been lacking in the younger Abigail. He could not say exactly what it was. A sense of peace, even joy, glowed in her delicate expression, although she had endured a difficult life. Her mother was ill, and they had little or no money.

"We'd better go down," she said with a faint smile.

As they made their way downstairs, Matthew tried to pull himself together. When they reached the first floor, the crowd was so thick they could not move. Everyone was leaving, and the sound of laughter and

17

talking filled the church. Matthew kept back so that he would not be seen by everyone.

Abigail hesitated. She did not know whether to leave or not, and finally she chose to stand beside Matthew and say, "I think they're going to be very happy."

"I don't know Jacob very well."

"He's a fine man—the most gifted musician I've ever heard. Why, he plays the violin as well as you paint, Matthew."

Matthew ducked his head. "There's more to marriage than playing a fiddle—or dabbling with paint."

"Yes. I know."

Something in her tone caught at him, and he turned to face her. They were so close that he could see the tiny flecks of gold in her eyes and the small laugh lines, almost invisible, at the corners of her eyes. He waited for her to say more, but when she did not, he asked, "Are you thinking of marrying?"

"No." The answer was short, and she added no more to it.

"Well, it's a strange marriage. They're so different."

And then Abigail looked him directly in the eyes and said, "Love can make things work, Matthew."

He paused, knowing there was more to her remark than he could immediately apprehend. Finally, he looked away and shrugged. "I suppose you're right."

And then Sam came up and tugged him by the arm. "Everyone's waiting for you, Matthew. We're going to have refreshments. Come along."

"Will you be joining us?" Matthew asked Abigail.

"No. It's just for family, I think."

Matthew allowed himself to be towed along by his exuberant brother, but he caught one glance of Abigail Howland just before they turned out of the foyer. She was standing watching him, her face still, her lips soft and vulnerable, and again he noticed this new and unfamiliar gentleness in her. Then he turned and followed Sam, only half listening as the young man babbled on about his latest adventures.

☙   ☙   ☙

The new bride and bridegroom left for a brief honeymoon, and as the days passed, Matthew found himself having difficulty adjusting to his new role. *Sir Matthew Rochester.* Still, he could see no difference whatsoever in the attitude of his father or of his stepmother, Marian. They fussed over him and insisted that he stay with them as always.

The following Thursday evening, Marian invited Clive Gordon with his new bride, Katherine, along with Matthew, Sam, and Keturah to dinner. Keturah Burns was a young woman the Bradford family had taken in, and Sam was desperately in love with her.

Matthew finished dressing, then gave himself a casual glance in the mirror. He had spent a great deal of money on clothes, for his inheritance from Leo Rochester was more than he could have imagined. He had gone to Virginia to look over his new holdings there, and it had been exciting for a time. Now, however, as he studied himself in the mirror, he murmured, "Fine clothes, but I'm not such a fine man."

The clothes he had donned were indeed fine. He had on the latest fashion, a double-breasted coat of black-and-gray-striped fabric that was cut away in front. The white silk shirt underneath had ruffles at the cuffs and collar, and the waistcoat was made of a solid gray fabric and buttoned with tiny silver buttons. His white fitted breeches ended just below the knees, where white silk stockings began leading down to black leather shoes with bright silver buckles.

Matthew, however, felt like an impostor. He hesitated for a moment, then with a sudden wave of disgust said, "I can't wear this rig!" Stripping off the clothes, he put on a simple brown suit, then went downstairs. He found Marian waiting for him at the foot of the stairs.

"The others are already here." Slipping her arm around his, she said, "Come along."

Matthew followed her into the drawing room, where he found Clive Gordon and his new bride, Katherine. Clive was his cousin, the son of his father's sister, Lyna Lee Bradford Gordon. His father, Leslie Gordon, was a colonel in the army of King George, which presented some problems. The Bradfords were devout patriots, and Leslie Gordon had been a dedicated soldier in the army of England all of his life. However, Clive was not a military man but a skilled physician. He had fallen in love with a young colonist and, after sorting out their difficulties, had married her. Now the two of them came forward to greet Matthew.

"Matthew, you're looking wonderful," Clive grinned. "How's it feel to be Sir Matthew?"

"Just like it felt to *not* be Sir Matthew. You look beautiful, Katherine."

Katherine Gordon was radiant, a strong young woman with beautiful brown hair. She took Matthew's hand, and her grip was as strong as any man's. "I'm not going to call you Sir Matthew."

"Good!" Matthew grinned. "Having a title was exciting for about a week, but now I wish sometimes I'd never heard of it."

"Never heard of it! Just give it to me. Sir Sam sounds pretty good."

Everyone turned and grinned at Sam. He was an outspoken young man, perhaps best known for his inventions, some of which worked, but most of which were dramatic failures. He was standing very close to Keturah Burns, as he usually was. He turned to her and said, "Keturah, you'll have to be careful about how you address Sir Matthew. You know how these English lords are. Proud as peacocks!"

Keturah Burns was a striking young lady with an oval face and dark brown hair cut fashionably short. She had large, startling, widely spaced light blue eyes, thick dark lashes, and arched black brows. Though she was short of stature, she was slim and somehow gave the impression of stateliness. Now she smiled and said, "It's good to see you, Matthew."

Matthew had always felt close to Keturah. After finding out that he was not a Bradford by birth, he identified with this young woman. She had had a rough life, living with her mother, who was a camp follower. Micah Bradford had rescued her from a grim fate. He had brought her home, and the family had opened their arms and taken her in. Sam had fallen in love with her almost at once, but Keturah had resisted his attempts to court her.

"Come along," Marian said. "Everything's ready."

They filed into the dining room, a large room with wall-to-wall green carpet. The walls were covered with bold green-and-gold mica diamond-shaped wallpaper. Two floor-length mullioned windows with gold curtains held back with green ties were on one side. Along another wall was a large verde and marble fireplace with a mahogany fire screen, and a pair of silver two-light candelabras flanked each side. The walls were adorned with girandole above the sideboard and paintings from China. The table was massive, made out of mahogany, and now was covered with a fine white damask tablecloth and set with sparkling crystal and shimmering silver. The food was on the table: roasted venison, roasted goose with a bread sauce, baked spinach with cream and butter beaten in, fresh biscuits that were slathered with rich butter, potatoes boiled in a sauce of butter, salt, pepper, and milk, and for dessert, cheese and peach flummery.

Daniel Bradford's eyes went to Matthew and filled with pride for his son, but he was also concerned. He had assured Matthew that changing his name to Rochester posed no problem. Still, he knew that Matthew was a troubled young man who was far from God, and his heart went out to him. He listened as Matthew described the property in Virginia.

After a while Matthew hesitated, then announced, "I sold the place in Virginia."

Everyone turned to stare at him. "You sold the Rochester holdings there? Why did you do that?" Marian asked. She was holding Enoch, and her face was radiant as she held the son she never thought she'd have. "I thought you were going to stay there and run it."

"That was also my understanding, Matthew," Daniel said. "What changed your mind?"

"I'm just not cut out to run a plantation," Matthew explained uncomfortably.

"Well, what will you do?" Clive asked. "Are you going to stay here?"

"No. I'm going to travel. Perhaps go back to England to study art a bit more."

"I'd hate to see you do that," Daniel Bradford said quickly. "Why don't you settle down here? We need to spend more time together, son."

The use of the word "son" warmed Matthew, and he knew that Daniel was totally sincere. "Perhaps later," he said. "I'll be moving around quite a bit."

After the meal was over, the men retired to the study and talked about the progress of the Revolution. It was not going well for the army of George Washington. There had been minor victories for the colonists. General Anthony Wayne had captured Stony Point, and Light Horse Henry Lee had captured Paulus Hook in New Jersey, but Washington's army itself was severely handicapped by lack of money and equipment. The British had sent the largest land army in history to retake the Colonies, but the British generals had been utterly confused. They could win battles, but they could not win the war. This was unfamiliar territory, and Washington's men would simply fade away into the hills, leaving the British to retire to Philadelphia or New York. Then a new army would be raised by the American general, and the fighting would start over again.

Finally Clive was alone with Matthew, and he stirred uneasily, saying, "You know, there's something I'd like to ask you, Matthew. A favor, if you will."

"A favor? Why, certainly," Matthew said with surprise. Clive Gordon was a tall man, lean and long in the arms and legs, with reddish hair and blue eyes. He was an excellent doctor, and Matthew knew that Daniel was glad that his nephew had come over on the side of the colonists. "What is it, Clive?"

"Well, I'm worried about my sister, Grace. I know she is very unhappy. I guess new marriages turn out that way sometimes, but Morrison is having difficulty."

Grace Gordon had married a man named Stephen Morrison, a New

York businessman. He had taken her to South Carolina, where he had invested all of his money in a plantation.

"I don't know him very well," Matthew said. "Actually, I know Jubal much better."

Jubal Morrison, Stephen's brother, had courted Rachel for a time, and Matthew liked him very much. He knew that Jubal and Sam had gone into the privateering business with little success.

"What seems to be the problem, Clive?"

"He has good property there, so I understand from Jubal, but then he bought a place next to his, thinking to enlarge his operation." Clive hesitated, then laughed shortly. "Well, he overextended himself and can't keep up the payments. He says it's a wonderful place, and it's bound to get more valuable all the time."

"What does he need?"

"He needs someone to lend him money, and of course, the plantation would stand as security."

"I don't know much about farming, but if you think it's a good investment, Clive, I'll be glad to help."

Relief washed over Clive Gordon's face. "That's good news, Matthew. Are you sure, now? I don't know much about the situation."

Matthew smiled. "I just sold out in Virginia, and I've got more money than I need. Some of it needs to be reinvested. Why don't we go to the bank tomorrow and get the papers drawn up?"

Clive came over and took Matthew's hand. "Matthew, you don't know what this will mean to Grace."

"Don't mention it," Matthew said. He looked down at the floor for a moment, and there was an odd note in his voice as he said, "You know, Clive, money doesn't mean as much as I thought it would." He hesitated for another moment and then said so quietly that Clive almost missed it, "And neither does being Sir Matthew Rochester. . . ."

2

A Man Needs a Place

"I'M WORRIED ABOUT MATTHEW, Marian."

Marian, who was trying to get Enoch to eat the warm mush she had fixed for him, looked up and studied her husband. His brow was lined, and he was slumped deeply in his favorite chair staring at the wall thoughtfully. She had come to love this man very deeply and knew when something was bothering him. Leo Rochester, her first husband, had been an arrogant, cruel man and had abused her, showing no love whatsoever. When she had married Daniel Bradford after Leo's death, it had been like coming home to a peaceful harbor. Now, putting down the spoon, she began to rock Enoch. "What's the problem?"

"Well, it could be that he's just gotten too much all at once. I mean, one day he's just plain Matthew Bradford—and the next he's Sir Matthew Rochester with plenty of money and a title and all that goes with it."

"Matthew's very level-headed. I don't think he'll let it affect him."

"Maybe not, but he has been unhappy for a long time."

"You don't think it's because he found out that you're not his real father?"

"No, I don't think it's that. We've talked about that several times."

"What is it, then?"

Daniel shifted in his chair and brought his eyes around to gaze at Marian and Enoch. A smile came to his lips, and he did not answer her question at once. "You look beautiful. Nothing more a man likes than to see his wife and son. He's a fine boy."

"Enoch Bradford, you're going to be a man of God," Marian said, squeezing him. Enoch protested with a loud cry and waved his chubby fists around, striking himself in the eye with one, then went to sleep with an abruptness that always surprised Marian. "I don't know how

23

he does that," she said. "I wish I could go to sleep that easily."

"If you didn't have any more worries than he did, you probably could." Daniel came over to sit beside her on the horsehide-covered couch and put his arm around her, drawing her close. "It was a lucky day for me when you said 'I do.' "

"Good for me, too, Daniel."

The two sat there for a time, silent and content. Finally Daniel sighed, moved his arm, and stood up. "I don't know what it is, but I suspect Matthew's problem has something to do with Abigail Howland."

Marian looked up. This husband of hers surprised her from time to time. "I didn't think you'd notice that."

"I'm thickheaded about things like this, but it's pretty obvious. You think he still cares for her?"

"Yes, I do. I don't believe he ever stopped."

"I never could get out of him exactly what happened, but it had something to do with Leo."

"Actually . . . Leo told me, but I've never mentioned it."

Daniel raised his eyebrows. "What was it?"

"He hired Abigail to get Matthew to marry her. He wanted an heir of his own blood. Abigail agreed to do it, but then she found the Lord and couldn't deceive him anymore. When she told Matthew what she had done, he grew very bitter. And the bad thing is, I think she really had learned to care for him."

"She's a fine young woman. She had a rather shady background, but so did some of the rest of us."

"I wish he wouldn't go back to England."

"I do, too, but he's determined."

"He's leaving tomorrow?"

"Yes. No matter what I say, he just won't stay here."

"I think it's partly because of the war. He's never been as dedicated to the Revolution as the rest of the family."

"No, he hasn't, but there are a lot of people in this country who feel that way. Not all of them are evil either. We're English at heart, some of us, and it's hard to turn against all that heritage."

"Well, maybe he won't stay long," Marian said.

"I hope not."

"Where is he now?"

"He went out for a walk somewhere. He's done that almost every day—and he hasn't painted either. He's always been so keen on painting, but now it seems he just can't get back into it."

Marian rose with the baby in her arms. "I'm going to put Enoch to bed." She stopped long enough to turn to Daniel, saying, "Don't worry about it, dear. God will bring him through. We'll just keep on praying for him."

"Yes. That's what we'll do."

❦　　❦　　❦

Matthew glanced overhead, studying the gulls that circled high above the harbor. He had never liked gulls. They were quarrelsome creatures with raucous voices and none of the beauty of other birds. Now as he watched them gliding about, he was glad for something to take his mind off of his problems. He had been restless ever since he had been back in Boston, and now that he was ready to leave for England, things had not changed.

As he ambled slowly along the shore, he looked out at the ships that filled the harbor. The tall masts rose up like skeletons, with the yardarms stretched across them and all the sails furled. Overhead the sky was an oyster gray as darkness settled down to blanket the harbor. From time to time he would stop to pick up a shell, examining its textures and curves in the waning light, then tossing it into the gentle waves.

Matthew Rochester was more introspective than his half brothers, especially Dake. They were men of action, and he was more prone to retreat into his own thoughts. Now as he moved along he tried to simply enjoy the evening, drinking in the smell and sounds of the sea. He loved the lapping sounds of the waves as they broke over the shore, emitting tiny whispers and leaving a white lacy covering of bubbles. There was something invigorating about it, and for a moment, he envied the sailors who spent their lives on the high sea. But he knew that he was not cut out for that. Life on board a vessel was difficult, at times almost unbearable. He had visited enough naval vessels to know that sailors, except for the officers, led terribly hard lives.

He bent down and dipped his hand in the salty water. It was warm. A moment later a school of bright silvery fish suddenly broke the surface. He stood and watched as the last rays of the sun transformed their scales into sparkling diamonds. It was a beautiful sight, and he wondered, as always when he saw something like this, if he could capture it on a canvas. Painting had been such a large part of his life, but now it seemed he had lost his inspiration. It just wasn't there, and he had given up for the time being.

Finally the sun, a huge crimson orb, sank into the ocean, and he turned and slowly walked back toward Boston. He had the unfortunate habit of mulling over his past life and seeing nothing but all the foolish mistakes he had made. Now, as it all played out before him, he thought about his decision to return to England.

"I'm probably making another mistake," he muttered. Then his lips twisted wryly. "But I've made so many it won't matter."

He did not want to go home—for what reason he could not fathom. Neither did he care about going to a tavern. Loneliness had plagued him in Virginia, although he had been surrounded by people. He had not cared for any of them, and as he slowly walked back toward Boston, he felt the need for talk. An impulse came to him, and for a time he fought it off. When it would not go away, he said, "I'll say good-bye to Abigail." He knew seeing her would be unpleasant for him, but every time he thought of her, and even more so when he came into her presence, he was reminded that a part of him still could not turn her loose. "What difference does it make?" he said. He turned and walked more rapidly along and, despite himself, looked forward to seeing her again.

🛡   🛡   🛡

Abigail Howland sat beside her mother's bed reading aloud. She had a pleasant voice and had spent many hours reading to Esther, who was past reading herself.

Looking down, Abigail saw that her mother's eyes were closed, and she shut the book. She knew with a pained certainty that her mother would not live long. The shadows on Esther's thin face had grown deeper, and every day she seemed to slip away from earth a little bit more.

Rising quietly, Abigail pulled the covers up, then slipped out of the room. She went to the kitchen, made a pot of tea, and then setting it on a caddie, she carried it into the drawing room. The salty smell of the sea wafted through the windows, and she could hear the staccato sound of horses' steel-shod shoes as they moved along the road. Sitting down, she looked around the small room, and a flash of gratitude welled up inside her. *I love this house. It was so kind of Mrs. Denham to give it to Mother and me. I don't know where we'd be if she hadn't. . . .*

Esther Denham had been a good friend to Mrs. Howland and her daughter. Though she had been in ill health, she had taken them in when they had no place to go. In her will she had left all of her property, which was not a great deal, to Abigail and her mother. It had been like a gift from heaven, and Abigail had never ceased being grateful for the woman's kindness.

Sipping the tea slowly, Abigail sat looking at the picture on the wall.

It had been painted by Matthew—his gift to Mrs. Denham. It was a simple landscape, a cottage set on a moor at dusk with a line of cows coming home, driven by a lean herdsman. It was a good painting, and Abigail never looked at it without thinking of Matthew.

Finally she closed her eyes, lay back, and rested. She had not slept well for the past few days, for her mother had had bad nights. Now Abigail simply sat still and for a time prayed that her mother's pain would be eased.

Abigail Howland had recently grown very close to God. She had been wild as a young woman, profligate in all ways, and had thrown her virtue away carelessly. When Christ had come into her life, the change was dramatic, nurtured by her childlike faith and trust. Now she simply did what she always did, which was to ask God for the needs of the day and thank Him for His many blessings. She had learned that being thankful was, in her mind, the first duty of a Christian. Others stressed the usual deeds—going to church, helping the poor—and Abigail gladly did all of these. But in her study of the Scriptures it had struck her how many times the word "thanksgiving" had appeared.

A new thought had come to her earlier in the day, and she picked up her Bible and turned to the Book of Deuteronomy. She had been studying this book lately, and now she turned to the twenty-eighth chapter and read quietly. It was a list of the blessings and the cursings that would come upon the children of Israel if they disobeyed God after being delivered out of Egypt. The cursings seemed very strong to her, but she read them all carefully. In the first verses of that chapter it talked about the blessings that God would bestow on His people if they would follow Him. She ran her finger down the line of verses and finally stopped at verse forty-seven. She read it aloud. "Because thou servedst not the Lord thy God with joyfulness, and with gladness of heart, for the abundance of all things."

The verse seemed to imprint itself on her heart, for in it God said that the greatest crime of the Israelites, even more than idolatry, was their lack of thanksgiving. Giving thanks had always been a theme for her, and even now she bowed her head and prayed aloud in a quiet voice. "Lord, I want to serve you with joyfulness and gladness of heart. I want to thank you constantly for the abundance of all things that you have given me." She continued to pray, naming all the good things God had brought into her life. Sometimes the problems of her life tried to intrude in her prayer, and resolutely she shoved them away. She had learned one lesson well—one could do absolutely nothing to change the past. For a time after becoming converted, she had spent hours weeping

27

and mourning over her past misdeeds—especially how she had deceived Matthew Bradford. But finally she had learned that there was no going back. She had learned to rely on the words of the apostle Paul, "Forgetting those things which are behind, and reaching forth unto those things which are before, I press toward the mark for the prize of the high calling of God in Christ Jesus."

So now she sat there, the only sounds in the room her own voice as she occasionally read aloud and the rhythmic ticking of the ormolu clock on the mantel.

She had dozed off into that twilight zone between wakefulness and light sleep when suddenly a knock startled her. She sat up immediately, looked around uncertainly, then rose and went to the door. It was unusual for visitors to come calling this late. She opened the door and, for one moment, stood there with surprise washing across her face. "Why, Matthew . . ." she said.

"Abigail," Matthew said and then hesitated. "I was just passing by and thought I might stop to say good-bye."

"Why, come in," she said. She stepped back and allowed him to pass, then closed the door. "I just made tea."

He followed her into the small drawing room and at her direction took a seat. "Sit right there. I've got some cake that I made."

"No need for that."

"No, it's no trouble. Mother and I can never eat all of it."

Actually Abigail wanted something to do in order to settle her mind. His unexpected late visit had taken her off guard. As she went about cutting the cake and putting the slices on small china saucers, she managed to calm herself. She went back into the living room, put the cake down on the caddie, and sat down. "It's lemon cake. I hope you like it."

Matthew tasted the cake and nodded. "Delicious. You're a good cook, Abigail. How's your mother?"

"Not very well." Abigail hesitated, then said, "She can't live long, Matthew."

Her honest admission shocked Matthew. He had heard this was likely, but Abigail's forthright statement shook him for a moment. "I'm so sorry," he murmured. "Is there nothing that can be done? Doctors—medicine?"

"No, it's her time to go. She knows it, and actually she's anxious. I've never been around anyone dying, Matthew. Every day she slips away a little bit. She grows weaker physically, but her spirit is still bright in her heart."

"What does she talk about?"

"Oh, about when I was a little girl—and about when she was a little girl. I wish I'd been a better daughter to her, but it's too late for that now."

Matthew hardly knew what to say. He picked up his cup and sipped the tea to occupy himself, then said, "It's not good for you to be all alone here. Don't you have any other family?"

"Not really. I have an uncle somewhere in Pennsylvania, but there's been no communication. We don't even know where he is now." Abigail suddenly said, "Are you painting much now, Matthew?"

"No, not at all."

"Well, that's a shame. You should keep it up."

"I've always made fun of painters who said they couldn't paint, that they didn't have any inspiration. I thought they were just lazy, but I'm beginning to see what some of them have tried to tell me. I sit down before a canvas, I get the paints ready, get the brush in my hand—and then I just *sit* there. I've never had that happen to me before."

"I'm sorry to hear that. You always painted so quickly and so well and always threw yourself into it. You have great talent."

"I'm not sure of that."

"Well, I am," Abigail said. "Look at the picture there. That's a masterpiece."

Matthew looked up at the landscape on the wall over the hearth. "I was proud of that one and thought it was one of the best paintings I'd ever done. That's why I wanted Mrs. Denham to have it."

"She thought the world of you, Matthew, and of that painting."

"She was a dear lady. I know you miss her."

"Yes, I do."

The breeze came through the window, stirring the curtains, and Matthew turned to face Abigail. He studied her eyes, and he remembered the time when they had held a great deal of laughter. Now it was not laughter so much as an abiding peace. Her eyes were wide-spaced and very attractive. Her lips were full and self-possessed, and a summer darkness lay over her skin. He admired the smooth shading of her complexion.

As he sat there, the warmth of her personality drew him. Though she had wounded him deeply, he was still moved by her beauty.

"I'm leaving at dawn," he said.

"What about your plantation in Virginia?"

"I sold it. I didn't feel at home there."

"I didn't think you would. You should stay closer to your family, Matthew. You're all so close." Abigail dropped her eyes. "You don't know what it's like not to have a family that cares for you." Then she shook herself. "I'm sorry. I didn't mean to complain."

For a while the two sat there, and then finally he rose, saying, "Well, I just wanted to say good-bye."

Abigail rose with him and led the way to the door. When she turned to him, he was reluctant to leave. The moonlight threw its silver beams on her face, and suddenly a recklessness came to him. He had loved this woman once and knew that deep down he still did. He suddenly reached forward and put his arm around her. He kissed her and found that she neither came to him nor did she hold back. Still, her warmth and the fire that he knew lay within her stirred him, and he finally stepped back.

"Time has passed for all that," Abigail said quietly.

"You loved me once—or so I thought." Abigail did not answer, and the bitterness rose within him. "But you were paid to love me, weren't you?"

Abigail remained quiet. She had already apologized for her deceitful behavior and knew that nothing she could say would take away his bitterness. Only God himself could do that, as He had done for her.

Matthew quickly felt ashamed of himself. "I'm sorry. I don't know why I said that. I don't really even know why I came here."

"God be with you and keep you, Matthew."

The simple words stirred Matthew. Something about Abigail reminded him of his stepmother, Marian. She possessed the same strength and richness, and he said impulsively, "Abigail, it's going to be hard when your mother goes. If you need anything at all, write to me." He took a card out of his pocket. "My name's on there and my address."

"Thank you, Matthew," Abigail said. She took the card, knowing that she would never call upon him. "I trust that you'll have a safe voyage and that you'll find what you're looking for."

Once again Matthew was torn between this woman's attraction and the past memories that had turned bitter in him. "I loved you once more than I thought a man could love a woman," he said, his lips twisted and his eyes troubled.

"We can never be together, Matthew," Abigail said. Then she said what she had never spoken to him. "You are not a forgiving man, and I could never live with a man who was bitter in his spirit. I treated you shamefully, and I'm so sorry. But we can't change the past. Good-bye, Matthew. God be with you."

🔔　　🔔　　🔔

Matthew walked up the gangplank of the *Matilda*. After talking to the boatswain, he turned and went to his cabin, arranged his personal belongings, then returned to the deck. For a long time he listened to the cries of the sailors and watched them as they cast off the mooring lines. They loosed the sails and the wind caught them, billowing them out. The ship began to stir.

He stood there as the great vessel eased out of the harbor, and finally, when the boatswain had all full sails lowered, the *Matilda* sprang ahead, and he held on to the rail as the ship came to life.

Matthew looked back at the shore with a great sadness. *I've done the wrong thing—again!* The thought came almost as clearly as a spoken word. He shook his head and stared down at the water that turned a bubbling froth as the prow of the *Matilda* cut its way through the waves.

Abruptly an impulse came—so strong that it almost took his breath. He felt he should go at once to the captain and ask to be put ashore. At least put him off the ship in a small boat—anything!

The impulse grew in him, but he gritted his teeth and held on to the rail. Lifting his eyes, he saw the shores of Boston fading. He stood there fighting within himself until the shore became a thin gray line on the distant horizon.

Finally Matthew took a deep breath and loosed his grip on the rail. "I can't go back. Whatever's there, I've lost it," he muttered. He turned and walked slowly along the deck with his head down. Overhead a single bird with an enormous wingspread circled the top mast. Matthew glanced up and watched the albatross, silent and ghostly. The bird uttered a single hoarse cry, then turned and faded away into the skeins of fog that hovered over the sea.

3

STELLA

LONG SLANTING BEAMS of angular light reached down through overhead windows, illuminating the large room where Matthew stood before a canvas smeared with fresh paint. He was intensely aware of the babble of voices, for the art students at Derek Laurence's studio were a rowdy lot at best. Glancing around, he saw that everyone else seemed to be busy with their paintings. His eyes caught a movement over in the corner, where a tall, skinny artist named Jacques Frenot was being shoved away by a woman. Matthew caught her sharp words.

"Stay away and keep your hands off me!" and then Frenot's coarse laughter rose above the hubbub of voices.

The room was stifling, for July had come to London bringing hot weather with it. Matthew pulled a soggy handkerchief from his pocket and mopped his face with it, then tossed it down again on the table where his paints lay scattered around. He dipped the brush into the cerulean blue, then poised it over the canvas. Holding his breath, he made a stroke and then uttered, "Blast!"

Disgusted with the stroke, he tried to straighten it up but only managed to make it worse. He was tired and had worked hard since ten o'clock that morning. Now he found that his hand was unsteady. He had been gripping the brush too hard, he knew that. He always did so when he was having trouble painting, and now he stepped back and stared at the mediocre painting.

I should have stayed in Boston!

The words were not spoken, but he was utterly weary with his fruitless efforts. He had been in England now for three weeks—settling in, finding a place, and wandering around London to reacquaint himself with the city. The day he had arrived he had gone at once to Laurence's studio and made arrangements to study with him. Now he thought

33

back over his activities of the last few weeks, and it seemed to him that he had been living in an endless and pointless cycle. He had gone to a tailor and purchased more clothes, which he did not need, and then dined every night at London's expensive restaurants. Several times he had attended the theater but did not like any of the performances that he saw.

Now, even as he stood there studying the painting, he knew that the dark mood that had fallen upon him ever since leaving Boston was not going to go away so easily. He suddenly recalled the image of the albatross circling the *Matilda* as she pulled away from Boston Harbor. He had been troubled by the bird—it seemed to portend a dark future—and had had several nightmares about it.

He sighed and thought once again of home and family. He had traveled a great deal in the past few years, but somehow all that travel had lost its charm, and now he wished he were back in Boston—that he could see his brothers and Rachel and his father and stepmother. As fond memories of home filled his mind, Matthew was aware that he was pushing thoughts of Abigail to the back of his mind. Deep down he knew that she had left an impression on his mind and spirit that he could never erase. He had done everything he could to try to forget their relationship, but she was like a melody once heard that could never be forgotten, coming back to his mind time and again. Sometimes he would see a woman walking down the street, and some quality about her would remind him of Abigail. Or he would hear a voice like hers. Sometimes a phrase used by someone would evoke a conversation that he had shared with her.

"Well, what have we got here?"

Matthew was jolted from his inner wanderings by a voice right at his shoulder. He started slightly and turned to face the man who had come to stand behind him. "Don't sneak up on a fellow like that, Derek!"

"Guilty conscience. That's what you've got." Derek Laurence was a muscular man of fifty with a full brown beard streaked with white and a pair of piercing brown eyes. His smock was smeared with old paint dried to a crust and with new paint that seemed to glow under the bright sunlight. He had hands like a butcher, not like an artist, but he was one of the finest painters in England. Unfortunately he spent money so fast, he was forced to give lessons to keep up with his extravagant lifestyle. He had taught Matthew a great deal on his previous visit here, and now he planted himself firmly before the canvas, setting his feet as if he were about to charge the square.

Matthew said nothing but his heart sank. He studied Laurence's face, which revealed very little. In the process of learning how to satisfy rich and extremely untalented would-be artists, Laurence had learned never to let his true feelings show. He had told Matthew once that it was all he could do to keep from outright laughter at some of the pitiful efforts of his students, but he had learned to smile and make some polite comment.

But he did not smile now. He swiveled around and locked his hands behind his back. Rocking back and forth on his heels, he studied Matthew and said nothing for a long time.

"Well, what do you think, Derek?" Matthew said. Then with a sneer, "Rotten, isn't it?"

"Not up to your usual standard."

Matthew allowed a bitter laugh to escape his lips. "I know what that means," he said. "You never insult the work of a paying customer."

"It's not bad." Laurence turned again to look at the painting. "The proportion isn't as good as I have come to expect from you. That's one thing you've always been able to do, lay it out on the canvas, whatever the subject."

"I know it. This is the fourth time I've tried to catch that. I just can't do it."

"Maybe you ought to try another scene. Sometimes a painting goes sour, and all you can do is walk away. Maybe you could come back to it later."

"I don't know. I'm just about to give up."

Derek Laurence was astute and discerning, and in all his dealings with men and women, he had encountered most types. He stood there studying the young man for whom he had developed a genuine affection. He liked Matthew despite himself, for he was totally opposed to the Revolution. He thought the colonists were ungrateful, and his favorite quotation was taken from Doctor Johnson: "The Americans are all criminals and should be grateful for anything we give them short of hanging."

Still, he had learned to admire Matthew on the young man's previous visit. The two had gone out together and sampled the night life of London, and Derek had been surprised at Matthew's refusal to carouse with him. He had come to respect him, however, and he had been pleased when Matthew had suddenly appeared a few days earlier and had announced his intention of picking up his study of art again. Now he looked at the painting and shook his head. "A new title and a pile of money didn't improve your painting, did it?"

"It's ruined it, Derek. I don't know what's the matter with me."

"Well, I don't think money's the problem."

"I'm not sure about that. There's something about cause and effect. I get all this money, I get a title, and suddenly I can't paint anymore."

Derek grinned, his mouth a broad slash across his pale face. "I can tell you what it is."

"Well, tell me, then."

"Artists have to suffer to gain inspiration." He reached out and punched Matthew's chest with paint-stained fingers. His forefinger was covered with green paint, and the middle finger had yellow dabs all around it. He prodded Matthew hard, and a mischievous light danced in his dark eyes. "That's your trouble. When you came here before to study, you were suffering. Now all your problems are solved. You've got money and a title, you can have any woman you want, any suit you like, live anywhere you take a notion. You're not suffering enough, my friend."

Matthew could not help but grin. "What do you recommend?"

"Why, it's simple! Give me all your money, and you go starve somewhere in an attic. I guarantee you it will make a Michelangelo out of you."

Matthew laughed suddenly. Derek had always had the ability to raise his spirits. "You're a fool," he said. "I'm not giving you anything."

"I'll tell you what. Maybe you're too close to all this. Sometimes it's good to turn away from painting for a while and do something else."

Matthew did not tell Laurence that he had been trying to paint for some time and then had quit for two months. Instead, he said, "That may be the case."

But Laurence had caught a flicker in the eyes of the young man. "I don't think that's really it." He became serious suddenly and said, "I've seen painters go bad. You know, strange as it may seem, this gift of painting comes and goes. It's happened to me. I've had streaks when I couldn't paint a decent picture if my life depended on it."

"Have you really?"

"Oh yes, and most good painters have, but I can always smear paint on the canvas. What you've got here," he pointed to the still life, "is good. Lots of fellows would give their right arm to be able to do as well, but it's not what you're capable of."

The two men stood there, and Laurence spoke on and on about the art of painting. Matthew said little, for he had learned to admire the deep wisdom in this Englishman. He finally nodded and said, "I think I'll just throw this away and start all over again. Start fresh, I think."

"But not today. It's too late." Laurence waved his hand toward the ceiling. "The sun's fading already. You can't paint without light. I'll tell you what. I'm invited to a party tonight given by a rich, stupid man, Sir Giles Moore. We won't have to put up with his talk much, but there'll be plenty of free whiskey and beautiful women to dance with. Come along with me. We'll get roaring drunk together. That may put you back into the mood of painting."

"I doubt it, Derek." Actually he dreaded spending another evening alone at the theater, and he enjoyed Derek Laurence's company. He had never heard of Sir Giles Moore, but he knew from past experience that Laurence was a master at integrating himself with the rich and the famous. "All right," he finally said. "Let's make a night of it."

"Good," Derek replied. "You come by my place, and we'll go together."

🛠   🛠   🛠

Matthew dressed carefully for the evening, thinking, *Be a shame to waste all these expensive clothes.* He chose a suit of dark blue luxuriant velvet with a small spotted design that added to its richness. A white linen shirt peeked out at the neck of his buttoned waistcoat, and white ruffles flowed from beneath the turned-up cuffs of the long coat. His breeches were tight-fitting and ended below the knees with white stockings showing off his well-formed calves. He caught himself admiring his image in the mirror and said, "You look stunning, Sir Matthew Rochester."

He shrugged sardonically and said, "Thank you. Now that we've got that settled, on to the ball."

Leaving his apartment, Matthew made his way across London to Derek's house, a large brownstone on the west side of the city. Derek was ready, and the two got into a carriage. Derek talked incessantly during their short journey.

The ball was being held in a magnificent home on the Thames. When the carriage pulled up and the two men got out, the ornate and imposing structure took Matthew's breath away. The house was a massive three-story building made out of gray stone with large three-over-three windows on all floors and with two large bay windows on each end. The roof was steep and edged with intricately carved wood cornices hanging on the edges, and the main entrance protruded off the front of the house about ten feet, approximately six feet wide. Two massive stone columns supported the black tile roof, and the walk was made of the same stone as the house.

"Pretty nice old shack, eh, Matthew?" Derek nudged his friend with his elbow.

"How did he make his money?"

"He didn't. He inherited it. His father didn't make it either. He stole it."

Matthew smiled at this. "You mean he was a highwayman?" he asked as they mounted the stairs and were greeted by livery footmen.

"Oh no. He was a banker, but they all steal their money in one way or another. Come on inside."

The two men entered, and the sound of music immediately enveloped them. The door opened up into a large, brightly lit foyer with white walls, white-and-gold swirled marble floors, intricately carved woodwork around each door, and winding stairways on each side of the room. There were candles lit and hung in gold sconces on the walls, gilded mirrors reflected the light of the candles, and crystal figures decorated every nook on the furniture, which was polished to a brilliance that Matthew had never seen before.

But the foyer was nothing compared to the ballroom itself. This room was large, oval in shape with large white pillars encircling the entire room. The walls were painted a bright white, and each detailed cornice, ceiling trim, and doorway had been delicately painted in gold. The ceiling was high, and each section had a different scene etched in gold. Large crystal chandeliers glistened with the flickering candle-light. Chairs covered in brilliant colors of blue and gold and red had been placed around the outside walls of the room, and many of the guests were sitting there conversing and laughing. Others were dancing to the soft music of a small orchestra, and brilliant color flashed before their eyes as dresses of red, blue, yellow, green, and purple whooshed around the floor. The light caught on the silk material of some and sent a shimmer through the room. Pictures of French scenery adorned the walls, and between the many floor-length windows, all of which were covered in crimson red velvet, were sconces with candles burning brightly. A huge fireplace of marble and verde dominated one wall, and the mantel was covered with silver candlesticks, candelabras, and silver boxes of all shapes and sizes. Tables were covered with white damask tablecloths, silver trays of food, cut crystal glasses, and the best china Matthew had ever seen.

As Matthew expected, Derek seemed to know everyone. The two of them moved around the perimeter of the ballroom. Derek greeted all of the women with a wide smile and a deep bow, often kissing their hands.

He introduced Matthew to them and said, "If you see any of them you like, just let me know," Derek said.

"Some of them may not be available."

"Don't be a fool. Every woman's available."

"You're wrong there, Derek."

Derek Laurence turned suddenly and studied his friend. A lively gavotte was sending the dancers around in circles, and he ignored them for a moment. "You really believe that, don't you?"

"Yes, I do. I've known many."

"I hope you always keep that viewpoint. Fortunately I'm not of that opinion."

"Don't you think any man or woman could be totally honest and loyal, Derek?"

"I think many would try, but there's a breaking point in all of us, Matthew. Some men and some women never find out what the breaking point is. They go on and they think they're totally incorruptible. But it's only because they haven't been hit with the right temptation."

"You're a cynical scoundrel!"

"Why, certainly! I have been since I was twelve years old. Come along. Let's refresh ourselves."

The evening went by quickly, and Matthew danced with many women, most of whose names he could not remember. He was introduced to several famous people whose pictures he had seen and whom he knew by reputation. One of them was the earl of Chatsworth, a power in British government. He had studied Matthew and asked him bluntly, "When are your kinsmen going to give up that useless war over in the Colonies?"

Matthew simply answered, "Not as soon as you would like, my Lord."

The earl grinned. "You must be a politician yourself. I can't make it out," he continued. "We run battle after battle, and all we get is urgent requests for more reinforcements. The cabinet's going crazy trying to figure out what our generals are doing over there. Have you got any ideas?"

"Well, I'm not a military man, sir, but my father keeps up with these things. He knows General Washington very well and served with him when he was a younger man."

"And what does he say?" the earl demanded.

Matthew hesitated for a moment, then said, "My father says that the British army has never fought a war like this. They're trying to fight it as they would fight a war in England."

"And what does that mean?"

"He says that in Europe when two countries fight, if one of them can take the other's capital city, then the war is over. It's about territory, but that obviously won't work in America. Your armies took our capital, so we moved it to another city, Philadelphia. Then you captured that one, but the war's still not over because the heads of the government simply moved to yet another place. My father says this can go on until your people are sick of it."

The earl stared at him. "Many of us are sick of it already. We don't understand how half-trained, half-starved troops can beat the best soldiers of His Majesty's army."

Matthew noticed that several men had gathered to listen, and he began to feel ill at ease. More than once he proclaimed, "I am not a military man or a politician. I am merely an artist. I can only repeat what others have said. General Washington can retreat back into the mountains and force your supply lines to be ever longer. You can win on the coast because of your magnificent navy, but you can never win an inland war because General Washington refuses to fight according to European battle tactics."

"Exactly what I've been trying to tell His Majesty," the earl snapped. "Well, it will be over one day, I suppose."

The earl drifted away, and Derek said, "That'll give the old boy something to chew on. As a matter of fact, most Englishmen *are* sick of the war. Pitt and Burke and half a dozen others of the leadership in both houses are standing up and demanding that it be brought to an end."

"Do you think the king will listen?"

"When was the last time you ever heard of a king named George listening to anybody? The Hanoverians are all stubborn German fools, and George III is determined to win this war at any cost."

As the two men talked, Derek finally tired of politics and brought the subject around to women again.

During the course of the evening, Matthew had been drinking more than usual. He did not drink much from each glass, but there were so many glasses, and as time went on he became more and more conscious of the effect of the wines.

Now Derek suddenly said, "There. I see one of my rich victims."

"Victim! What do you mean?"

"I paint for rich people, Matthew. There's no money in painting for poor people. They can't pay for it. You see that fellow there? With the blond woman?"

Matthew spotted a man and a woman talking together a short distance away. "Who are they?" he asked.

"His name is Claude Aumont."

"Is he an Englishman?"

"No. He's Swiss, I think, although he stays in France now."

"Is that his wife?"

"Oh no. That's his niece, his brother's daughter. He came to the studio the other day and asked me to paint her portrait, and I need the money."

"You always need money," Matthew grinned. He took another drink and said, "How rich is he?"

"Nobody knows. He's sort of a mystery man. He's in with all the financiers here in London, and also in Paris and Germany. They're kind of a club, you know. It's international—the men who handle the really big funds. Nobody really knows about Aumont. But I know one thing. I'm going to fleece him."

Laurence led the way over to where the two were standing, and the man turned at once. He was not a tall man but had a sturdy build. Matthew judged him to be somewhere close to fifty, but it was hard to tell, for Aumont had a smooth, unlined face. He wore a wig, so it was impossible to tell if his hair was gray or not. His clothing was very stylish, made of brown velvet woven in the lightest design with black floral sprigs. His coat fell below his knees, and the brass buttons on the sleeves and down the front glinted under the lights from all the candles. The waistcoat was buttoned to the neck, and the breeches were tight fitting, fastened below the knees with jeweled buttons. He wore a white linen shirt, white silk stockings, and black leather shoes with a silver buckle. He had a stoic face with dark eyes that revealed very little.

"May I introduce you to my American friend, Sir Matthew Rochester."

When Matthew was introduced, Aumont smiled and bowed but did not offer his hand. "I am pleased to meet you, sir."

"It's a pleasure, Mr. Aumont."

"May I introduce my niece, Miss Stella Aumont. She is my brother's daughter."

Matthew bowed to the woman, who curtsied slightly. She was a beautiful woman with long blond hair, green eyes, and an excellent figure.

"I'm happy to meet you, Miss Aumont."

"The pleasure is mine, sir. You are an American, then?"

"Yes. From Boston."

Miss Aumont studied him and then smiled. "And you must be a painter, I take it."

"I am a dabbler, Miss Aumont, taking lessons from Mr. Laurence here."

Laurence suddenly laughed.

Aumont spoke up then. "And have you decided to do the portrait, Laurence?"

"Yes, I have decided. It will be my pleasure. I am going to ask too much for it, of course."

A flicker of humor touched Aumont's eyes. "I do not doubt it for a moment."

"Well, since we are doing business, Aumont, I will have to warn you. Beware of Sir Matthew here. He will take all your money in cards and then laugh at you when you have nothing left."

"I would be most interested in having him try." Aumont smiled slightly as he studied Matthew carefully. "Perhaps we could engage in a game later on."

"I'm afraid I don't play cards very well, sir," Matthew said.

"Well, he does one thing well," Laurence said and winked broadly. "He's a very devil with women, Miss Aumont. Left a trail of broken hearts all over the Colonies."

Matthew protested. "Derek, stop telling these awful lies!"

Stella, however, was amused. "I will risk it. I haven't had my heart broken by a colonist yet. Would you ask me to dance, sir?"

"Yes, of course. It would be an honor."

The two moved off, and Aumont said, "He's actually quite civilized for an American, but then, he does have a title."

"The title is new. Sir Leo Rochester was his father."

"I don't believe I know that name." Aumont listened as Laurence gave him the details. "Is he coming to settle in England?"

"He seems to be uncertain. He sold all of his property in Virginia and is looking about for a venture. He only took the title and the estate recently."

"Well, a handsome young man with a fortune should have no trouble finding a place here or anywhere else."

Matthew was only thinking of the woman in his arms. He was not a good dancer, but she, somehow, had a way of making him seem to be. As they moved about the polished floor, he was conscious of her figure, of her glowing complexion, of the dancing green eyes that laughed up at him.

"So you are a painter?"

"Well, there's some question about that."

"You must be a good painter if Derek Laurence takes you on as a pupil."

Matthew laughed. "That's where you're wrong, Miss Stella. He takes rich pupils, good or bad. It's not how well they can paint but how heavy their purse is."

"I have heard that about Mr. Laurence. Tell me more about your painting."

Matthew found that she was an easy woman to talk to and was sorry when the dance came to an end. He took her back to her uncle, and she asked, "Where is Mr. Laurence?"

Aumont laughed and said, "I'm afraid he's off on the chase. He's a refreshing fellow. He asked me to point out a plain young woman with a large fortune, and when I did he was off like a shot."

"I don't think he's as bad as he pretends, Uncle Claude."

"Well, in any case," Aumont said, "he's going to do your portrait. I'm not easily shocked, my dear, but when he named his price I nearly choked on my drink. My word! He doesn't mind demanding payment for his services."

At that moment a small man, fashionably dressed, came up and claimed Stella for the next dance. As the two moved out to the middle of the ballroom, Aumont said, "That's the son of the earl of Winton."

"Is he?"

"Yes. He's become quite a bore to Stella, I'm afraid. The fool has nothing but money."

Matthew laughed. He found the remark amusing. "Nothing but money? Most people would find that a strange way of putting it."

"Well, perhaps I put it badly. Perhaps I should say if he didn't have twenty thousand pounds a year, he would be quite a bore."

Matthew laughed and found Aumont an engaging man. He was soon asked about the Revolution as he wandered around the ballroom with Aumont and found himself being invited on the following day to join him at a club for a game of cards.

"Nothing serious," Aumont said quickly. "Just for companionship."

Matthew was not sure of his intention. He knew that men with large fortunes usually did things for money, not for companionship. But he liked the man, and besides, he was interested in Aumont's niece. "I'll be happy to meet you, sir."

He danced twice more with Stella, and finally when Aumont announced they were leaving, Derek said, "I'll be at your home at ten to start the painting, Miss Aumont."

"Why don't you come along with him, Sir Matthew? You can tell this fellow what he's doing wrong."

Matthew accepted the invitation and said, "He's never admitted to doing anything wrong. Perhaps I'd better."

"Come along by all means," Aumont said. "Then you and I can go out to the club later."

Matthew agreed, and as the pair left, Derek grinned. "You see, Matthew, you *are* a devil with women, just as I said. Half the young bucks in London must be chasing around after that woman."

"You don't know that."

"I know she's beautiful and has a rich relative. Those are the only two qualifications necessary. As a matter of fact, only one of those is really necessary." He laughed. "Stick with me, Sir Rochester, and I'll teach you a thing or two about women. My usual fee, of course." Derek continued to tease Matthew as the two left the ball and got into the carriage.

Matthew was already looking forward to the visit. He had found himself enjoying life for the first time in a long time and knew he had to see Stella Aumont again. "You'll need me to give you a few pointers on that portrait of Miss Stella, Derek. My usual fee, of course. . . ."

4

AN UNHAPPY WIFE

"YOU LOOK DOWNRIGHT FOOLISH, Daniel. Get up off the floor."

Daniel Bradford, sprawled out on the floor holding Enoch on his chest, grinned up at his wife. There was a smile on her face, and he knew that she was not really upset.

"Never interrupt a man when he's playing with his son. We have things to talk about, haven't we, Enoch?"

Enoch giggled and squealed as Daniel held him high in the air at arm's length. He was a cheerful little boy, and as Daniel rolled over and came to his feet holding the child, he said, "He's got a sweeter nature than any of the other boys."

"Really, Daniel?" Marian asked. "Are you just saying that?"

"Not a bit of it. They were all cantankerous, every one of them. Matthew, Dake, Micah, and Sam. Rachel was sweet and easy to raise. Like you." He suddenly reached over and with his free arm gathered her in. He kissed her soundly, and she shoved at him, her eyes dancing.

"Leave me alone!"

"Impossible! How could a full-blooded man leave a beautiful woman like you alone?"

Marian Bradford could never resist her husband when he was in a teasing mood. He was the center of her life, and now that Enoch had come, she felt full and complete. No one would ever know how she had longed for a child, and though God had not given her one of her own, this child had been suddenly and miraculously brought into her life. Marian thought for a moment of his parents, both dead, and how she pledged to both of them to raise Enoch as well as she possibly could.

Sitting down on the couch, Marian said, "Is there any other word about Jubal?"

"Just that he's been captured by the British." A troubled look swept across Bradford's face, and he came over and sat down. He balanced the baby on his knee and touched his round cheeks with a forefinger. "It was a close thing. Jubal saved the rest of the men."

"How did he manage to do that?"

"Well, that little boat that they owned had a crew of ten and one small cannon in the bow. They rounded the cape and suddenly came face-to-face with a British frigate. There was no chance, really, to run, but all the men knew what it's like in a British prison—especially on one of those hulks, those ships made into prisons. So Jubal beached the vessel and then took over the cannon. It was just a popgun, but it kept the boarding party away until Sam and the others had a chance to escape. Then Jubal took a bullet, Sam says, and went down. But it was only a flesh wound. Sam stayed long enough to see that, then he had to run to get away himself."

"It broke Sam's heart to lose that ship. He was convinced that it was going to make him and Jubal rich."

"Well," Daniel said heavily, "it's always a risk, and I'm worried for Jubal. He's a fine man, and his chances of surviving in a British hulk aren't good. They are terrible places."

"I know. Katherine Yancy—I mean, Katherine Gordon now—told me how awful they are. Her father and her uncle were prisoners on one of them. She said men are cooped up like animals in damp, wet quarters and left to die."

"Sam's pretty down about it. He thinks a lot about Jubal, and so do I. I'm going to see if there's any chance we can have him exchanged. Of course, the British aren't noted for their flexibility."

"It's a little bit in the family now, isn't it, though?" Marian said.

Jubal Morrison's brother, Stephen, had married Grace Gordon, the daughter of Daniel's only sister, Lyna. Now that Jubal was part of the family, Daniel knew that he would be hearing from Lyna, asking him to do what he could. Now he said, "Maybe Lyna's husband, Leslie, can do something for him. After all, he's a colonel in the British army."

"Oh, I forgot! A letter came from your sister just this morning." Marian got up, went across to the walnut table underneath the tall window, and came back with an envelope. "Let me hold Enoch while you read it."

Daniel opened the letter and scanned it, then said, "Listen to this, Marian." He read the contents, which were very surprising.

Dear Daniel, I know this will come as somewhat of a shock to you, as it has to us, but Leslie has been ordered back to England.

Neither of us was expecting anything like this, but, of course, orders are orders. He leaves tomorrow on the *Phoenix*. There's no room for women on a warship, so I will have to follow later. It seems he's going to be training new officers at Sandhurst.

David has been accepted at Cambridge, so he must return to England very soon as well. We are torn between the disappointment at leaving you, Daniel, and the joy of going home again. Granted, we don't see much of one another these days, but soon this horrible war will be over and we can visit freely.

The matter that bears heavily on my heart is Grace. I have told you and Marian before that her marriage has been unhappy. I can say now, knowing that it will go no further, that it is very obvious that she has married the wrong man. Grace was always a sweet-tempered girl, rather romantic, and she acted impetuously. Stephen Morrison has many good qualities, but I have discovered that he does not know how to be a good husband. Grace is a woman who needs a lot of affection, and evidently Stephen does not have the ability nor the inclination to provide this.

She is expecting now, as I think I told you, and David and I are planning to visit her before we join Leslie at Sandhurst. She is so unhappy, and I simply must see her before we leave.

Daniel read the rest of the letter, giving the details of their departure, then handed it slowly to Marian. She shook her head. "It doesn't sound promising."

"No, and Grace is a fine young woman. I've only met her a few times, but I've been very impressed with her."

"Lyna's very concerned, and I don't blame her. Why did they go to South Carolina in the first place?"

"Her husband sold out all of his interest in New York. With all the political unrest, he thought things were uncertain there, which they certainly are with the British sitting on top of it. It's been burned down once, so he bought a plantation in South Carolina."

"Was Jubal involved with it?"

"No. The two of them split their inheritance. Jubal put all his into the ship, and now that's gone. I know that Stephen was disappointed that Jubal wouldn't go with him to the South. Well, he certainly can't go with him now. Not unless we can get him out of that prison."

Marian slowly reread the letter. Finally she looked up with troubled eyes. "It's terrible for a woman to have a husband who doesn't care for her."

Daniel knew she was speaking of her own first marriage to Leo

Rochester, who had been a brute and had shown nothing of love for anyone, not even his wife. He said carefully, "He's a young man. He can change."

"Of course he can," Marian said. She was trying to remember everything she could about Grace's husband, but their meeting had been very brief, and neither she nor Daniel knew a great deal about him. She did know, however, that Lyna was a good judge of character, and that this was a very serious matter, one that troubled her deeply. She handed the letter back, saying, "It's going to be hard on her, separated by an ocean from her only daughter, who's having a child."

"Yes, it is." Daniel took the letter and gnawed at his lip. "I wish I could do something, but I don't know that I can." He had a thought and said, "I do know one thing. Clive told me before he left that Matthew had financed some sort of land connected with Stephen Morrison's place. I don't know much about the details. I don't think Matthew was very interested in it, but he wanted to help Clive."

At that moment Enoch began to make his presence known, and the two of them rose. "I'll write Lyna," Daniel said. "I wish she could come here before she leaves, but if she's going to South Carolina, I doubt she'll be able to."

🔔　　🔔　　🔔

Lyna Lee Gordon, in her midforties, was still an attractive woman. She was tall, almost five eight, with hair the color of dark honey. Her gray-green eyes were set in an oval face, and she had clean wide-edged lips and fair smooth skin. Now as she sat across from Grace, her daughter, she thought suddenly, *She looks so much like me. She always has.*

Indeed, Grace did have the same dark-honey-colored hair and gray-green eyes. She was not as tall as her mother, and now as Lyna studied her, she saw lines in the face of her daughter that had not been there at earlier times. *She doesn't look well,* Lyna thought, but she did not let this thought show in her expression.

"Well, now. You're going to make an old grandmother out of me. Do you know what your father said?"

Grace Morrison had been fiercely glad to see her mother and her younger brother. She had never known what real loneliness was until she had come to South Carolina, with its flat plains broken by ridges and hills and swamps. She had come with some hope that Stephen would put their marriage together, that somehow things would change. But they had not. Marriage had been the biggest disappointment of her life, for as the Bradfords knew, she was a woman who needed affection,

48

needed to know she was loved. Stephen, despite being a poet, could not seem to provide this, and she had languished in the rambling plantation house while he was gone riding and traveling on the business of managing a large plantation—an occupation for which he had little aptitude.

"What did he say?"

"He said, 'I don't mind being a grandfather, but I hate being married to a grandmother!' "

Now Grace brightened and tried to put cheer in her voice as she said, "I'm so glad you came, Mother! I've been so lonely for you."

"I'm glad, too. I just wish we didn't have to go back to England. Perhaps I can stay here with you until the baby is born."

"No. You'll have to go back. Who would take care of Father?" Grace smiled. She knew that her father and mother had that rare kind of marriage that she had heard once described by a learned man as symbiotic. She had asked what it meant, and he had explained that it meant a relationship where two organisms were interdependent—where they mutually benefited each other. When she had said, "That's like my parents," the biologist had laughed. "There should be more marriages like that. Most are merely parasitic."

Now Grace moved stiffly, and some of the pain that she felt must have shown in her face.

"Are you uncomfortable, Grace?" Lyna asked quickly.

"Oh, I suppose no more so than most expectant mothers. Weren't you uncomfortable when you had me and David?"

"Oh yes. I suppose all of us mothers have to put up with that." Lyna was very concerned about her daughter. Despite her swollen body, she had lost weight, and her face and upper arms were now painfully thin. She was sick and obviously not eating properly. Lyna asked, "Do you have a good doctor here?"

For a moment Grace hesitated. "There's a good doctor in Charleston, but that's too far to go."

"Well, where is the next closest doctor?"

"There's a man about forty miles from here in Millerville. He rides a circuit this way from time to time."

"Forty miles! But when the baby comes it would take him a day to get here."

"I know. I've been worried about it, but Stephen says that when the time comes, he'll have me taken to Charleston, perhaps, for the baby to be born."

Lyna took little comfort from this. She knew that Stephen was basically a thoughtless man. It seemed that he could think of only one thing at a time, and now the plantation and making a success of it were foremost in his mind. Since their arrival, Stephen had been a whirlwind, taking David all over the plantation, proud to show him what was happening. But Lyna would have preferred that he show this kind of attention to his wife.

The two women sat there, and Lyna began to gently draw out from Grace the affairs of life. She finally came around to the subject of the plantation.

"Is Stephen content being a planter?"

Grace hesitated slightly and then said defensively, "Well, of course, it's new to him, and anyone entering into a new profession has to learn new skills. . . ."

"I would not have picked him to be a planter," Lyna said. "I mean, he's a businessman and a poet. A man of the city."

"Stephen says he can learn, and there's a great deal that could be made of this place. He purchased an enormous amount of land very cheaply."

"Why was it so cheap?"

"Because of the war, I suppose. Everything is so unsettled. Did you know that many of the farmers in South Carolina, and people in the cities, too, are sympathetic to the Crown?"

"I knew there were many loyalists here."

"Of course, but there are just as many families who are determined to win their freedom."

"That must be very uncomfortable."

"It is. Terribly so. There are raids constantly. Sometimes the British come through and burn the houses of the patriots, and then there are bands of armed men, loosely organized, who will retaliate and burn the homes of the Tories."

"How do you two stand?"

"Stephen has made it plain that he is not sympathetic to the Revolution."

Lyna bit her lip, for she had the firm conviction that the colonists would win their cause. She wondered what would happen to Stephen and her daughter if the patriots won the war. She knew from firsthand experience what a subjected people had to go through. She mentioned none of this, however, to her daughter but asked, "Well, what about the running of the plantation? Is it difficult?"

"Yes. It's very difficult for people not raised to it."

"Does Stephen have good help?"

"Well, the overseer is a man called Simon Taws. Everyone says he is a good farmer, but I don't like him."

"What's the matter with him?"

"Oh, I don't want to complain, but he's brutal. He treats the slaves miserably, beats them, and he even killed one."

"I think slavery's a terrible business! I wish it were outlawed," Lyna said.

"So do I. Stephen says Taws has told him that slaves are able to stand the climate here, but that white men would perish. He says that many of them already have. They can't take the heat and the climate."

Lyna continued to listen, and soon a picture formed in her mind, and it was not an attractive one. Her daughter was here in a strange country amid people she did not understand. To make it worse, her husband was not thoughtful, and their lives were on the razor's edge, their survival dependent upon the results of a very uncertain war.

The two women talked for some time, and finally Lyna leaned over and took her daughter's hand. "How is it with you, Grace?" she asked gently.

The question seemed to pierce Grace's heart. Her lips trembled and tears came to her eyes. She sobbed, and when Lyna reached out, she fell into her mother's arms. "Oh, Mother, he doesn't love me—and he doesn't want the baby!"

Lyna held Grace close, stroking her back, as she tried to comfort her daughter. She spoke gentle words, but her eyes burned fiercely at the helplessness of the situation. Her daughter was trapped in a miserable life, and there was nothing she could do.

🏺　　🏺　　🏺

David was not a good rider, and as a matter of fact, neither was Stephen Morrison. The two of them had been riding for two days over the plantation, and David was chafed and sore from the constant and unfamiliar exercise. David was more of a scholar than an outdoorsman, and he would much rather have stayed at the house, but his mother had instructed him to spend as much time with Stephen as possible. David knew she wanted to get some sort of opinion from him regarding the man her daughter had married.

Now as they rode along through the groves of huge cypress and tupelo trees, David thought how different the country was from Boston and from England. Although it was now September, the heat was terrible. It was like being in an oven as the pale sun overhead beat down upon the open sandy swells. David surveyed the surrounding dense groves of scrub pines and undergrowth of gallberry and yellow jasmine. He did not like the landscape. It was low and swampy and seemed to him to be unhealthy. David wanted to ask his brother-in-law why he had chosen to bury himself in this country.

Stephen Morrison, however, was busy explaining to David the plans he had for the plantation. They had all been drawn out on paper, of course, in a study in New York. Yet somehow it had never occurred to Stephen that one could not simply draw up a lifestyle on a piece of paper. It had come as a shock to him when he had arrived in South Carolina, for he had come in the heat of summer and had almost passed out. For Grace it had been even worse. She had spent her life in New England, and to be transplanted to the savannas of South Carolina overwhelmed her.

As the two rode over the hills, finally Morrison drew up, and David pulled his own horse to a stop. "Over there is where we're going to put in the new fields. That's the new property I bought last year." He looked embarrassed and said, "Your cousin, Sir Matthew, had to handle the financing, but he'll make money on the deal."

David stretched in the saddle, easing his aching muscles, then brought his gaze around. "It's too bad Jubal couldn't have come down here with you."

"He should have! Then he wouldn't be in some prison hulk somewhere rotting away!" Stephen snapped. He had a narrow, thin, aristocratic face. He was not at all like his brother, Jubal, whom David liked very much. Jubal was a down-to-earth, strongly built man who enjoyed life's adventures, while his brother was artistic and fancied himself a man of business. In truth he was neither a good poet nor a good businessman, but he had convinced himself that he was both.

Finally they turned back toward home. After riding for an hour, Stephen said, "Look. There's Taws with the hands working."

David rose in his stirrups. "Something seems to be going on."

Stephen's vision was poor, and he said, "Well, come along and we'll see."

As they drew near, a shock ran through David. A slave was staked out on the ground, and Simon Taws was lashing him mercilessly. Taws was a brute of a man with tow-colored hair and cold light blue eyes. He glanced up and saw the two men approaching but gave the man another dozen strokes. The man's back was torn to ribbons, but Taws jerked him to his feet and said, "Now, don't let me hear another word out of you or you'll get worse! Get to work!"

David wanted to protest, for he could see that the man was badly wounded, but it was not his place to interfere.

Stephen Morrison was distressed by the incident. "I say, Taws, that's rather severe, isn't it?"

Taws grinned. "You don't know these slaves like I do, Mr. Morrison. You give 'em an inch, and they'll take over. Why, if I didn't keep 'em scared, they'd revolt. No question about it."

As the three men stood there, it was obvious to David that Taws had no respect at all for the owner of the plantation. He spoke roughly, and there was a sneer in his voice when he responded to Morrison's questions.

David thought, *You'd be better off to get rid of this one. He may know farming, but he's not a good man to have around.*

Taws suddenly stiffened and turned. His eyes narrowed, and the other two men followed his gaze. "Better get out of here," he said and quickly ran to his horse, leaving the workers in the fields as he tore away at top speed.

"What's that about?" David asked with astonishment.

Stephen Morrison's face was pale. "It's the partisans, I think."

"Partisans? What's that?"

"A military band, not really part of the army, but they raid. Some are Tories and some are not."

"Well, what do they do?" David demanded, watching the group as they approached at a fast pace.

"They can be very unpleasant. The partisans burned down several loyalist houses last month, but the king's troops have been here lately, so they've been in hiding. I think, though, that this is one of them."

The horsemen pulled up to a stop, and David examined them swiftly. They were all wearing old and worn-out homespun clothes, and each man carried a musket across his saddle. They were sunburned men, rough and with a dangerous look about them.

The leader pulled up in front of Stephen and David, and one of his followers, a tall rawboned man wearing a white straw hat pushed back on his head, grinned. "There's a couple of Tories if I ever seen 'em, Cap'n. What do you say we give 'em a taste of the cat and then burn 'em out?"

The leader did not answer but shook his head, at which the man instantly fell silent. He dismounted and came over to stand before Morrison and Gordon. "I'm Colonel Francis Marion," he said quietly. His gaze took both men in. "What are your names?"

Morrison said quickly, "I'm Stephen Morrison, Colonel. And this is my brother-in-law, Mr. Gordon."

David was studying the man carefully. He was below middle stature and his body was well set, but he seemed to have an injured leg. He had a remarkably steady countenance and an aquiline nose, and his chin projected stubbornly. His forehead was high and large, and his eyes were his most prominent feature. They were black and intense. He was dressed in a close, round-bodied crimson jacket of some sort of coarse material, and he wore a leather cap with a silver crescent on the front inscribed with the words *Liberty or Death*.

Colonel Marion studied them, and for a moment it seemed that their fate hung in the balance. Stephen knew more than David about the violence that could explode almost without warning in these parts. The men behind Marion were a restless band, and at a word from their captain, they would not hesitate to string both of them to a tree and then burn down the plantation.

Marion did not move for a long time, then he said, "British soldiers have been burning the homes of patriots, Mr. Morrison. They burned down Albert Door's house and killed one of Mr. Door's relatives, an older man. He tried to defend the place."

"I'm sorry to hear of it, Colonel Marion," Morrison said quickly. "As you know, I try not to take part in politics."

Francis Marion's eyes were guileless, and his voice was soft as a summer's breeze. "We would all like to stay out of politics, but it seems that's impossible, Mr. Morrison."

"I'm sorry for it. That's all I can say."

"I think you are, sir, but not all loyalists are as gentle as you are."

The tall rawboned man said, "Ought to hang 'em both, Captain. They shot that old man—and him seventy years old."

"That'll be enough, Taylor. We'll get the men who did it. Good day, sir."

A feeling of relief washed through Morrison and Gordon as the small leader mounted his horse. He nodded and then led his group off at a gallop.

"That was a close one," David said. "If the colonel had given the word, we'd both be hanging from a tree."

"Marion's quite a fellow. I'd never met him before, but they say he's giving the British all kinds of problems."

"The men don't look like soldiers."

"They're not. They're farmers and planters. They never stay together, but somehow when Marion gives the word, they gather to do his bidding. Sometimes two or three hundred of them—enough to cut the supply lines and capture isolated outposts."

"I'm surprised our forces here let that go on."

Morrison grinned faintly and said, "They've tried hard enough to catch him, but they've never been able to. When your soldiers get close, the men just divide up and fade away into the swamps."

"What about killing this man?"

Morrison gave an impatient snort. "You need to get back to your father and tell him that the military's doing itself no good here. They burn the patriots out, and they don't always know who's a patriot and who's a Tory. All they know is that we're all Americans. Many who are loyal to the Crown are understandably turned against the British."

None of the leadership of the British forces could seem to grasp the situation. It was an opinion firmly held in London, especially by the king, that there were so many loyalists in Georgia and the Carolinas that with the proper support they would all rise up and stifle the patriots. But the officers could not control the troops, who often attacked homes of those who had been faithful to the Crown, ignoring their protests, and many had been killed.

Now Morrison shook his head. "I'll be glad when this war is over. It can't last long."

David Gordon had listened to his father and to others and knew that the patience of the British people was growing very thin, and that it would not take much to set the machinery in motion to simply give up on the expensive war in the Colonies. However, he said nothing as the two men turned and headed back toward the house.

⚜   ⚜   ⚜

Lyna embraced her daughter and held her tightly. "I wish I didn't have to go," she whispered. "It's so hard."

Grace clung to her mother, bit her lip, and then blinked the tears back. "It'll be all right, Mother. I'll write you as soon as the baby's born."

David was shaking hands with Morrison, and he turned to embrace his sister. "Don't worry, sis. It'll be fine. God will be with you." Grace had always been very close to David, and now she clung to him fiercely. David whispered, "Why don't you come to England with us until the war's over?"

"I can't do that. My husband's here, and my child will be born here."

It was a difficult parting, and as David and Lyna rode away in the coach, it grieved Lyna's heart, and David's as well, to see Grace standing there forlornly, waving a tearful good-bye. Lyna wished that Stephen would sense her distress and move over and put his arm around her, but he did not. He simply waved.

"I wish we didn't have to leave," Lyna said.

"You don't have to, Mother," David said quickly. "You can stay until the baby's born. Father will understand."

But Lyna had already thought through all of this. She felt she must go back to be with her husband. They had been separated often, but somehow she knew she needed to be with him now. "We'll just have to pray, David."

"All right, Mother. Stephen's a good enough fellow. He just doesn't understand women very well."

"No. And he doesn't understand this country very well. It's a powder keg, David." She had heard of the encounter with Francis Marion, and it had terrified her. Now she said, "Why, they could be burned out and butchered at any moment."

"It's like a fight within a family. They are all colonists, but they are dreadfully separated," David said.

The coach rolled on, throwing up a fine line of dust as it carried them away from the plantation. Lyna wanted to cry, but she knew it would not help ease the ache she felt in her heart for her daughter. She clamped her teeth together and prayed, *Lord, you'll have to handle this situation. It's too much for me to bear.*

5

THE WEST INDIES AFFAIR

THE ROOM IN WHICH THE card game took place was large and ornately furnished. It had a very high ceiling, the walls were papered in a dark green and red diamond-shaped design, and the floor was made of highly polished dark oak. Six tables filled the room, each occupied by six men sitting in dark mahogany chairs covered with dark green velvet seat cushions. The walls were decorated with pictures of men in gilded frames, none of whom Matthew recognized, and a huge fireplace of mahogany and brass dominated one wall.

The five men with whom he was playing cards were all important, rich, and powerful, and a sudden gust of satisfaction filled him. Glancing over at Claude Aumont at his right hand, Matthew smiled and thought, *Claude moves in high circles, and I could learn to do the same thing*.

As usual, some of the talk had to do with the war, and James Merrill, a short heavyset man with thick jowls and a pair of steady gray eyes, initiated the subject. He was, Claude had informed Matthew, immensely wealthy from investments on the Continent.

"And so this fellow, Washington—he seems to be doing better than anyone would expect," Merrill said. He studied his cards, played one of them, and then turned his sharp eyes back on Matthew. "Your friends over there, they really expect to win, do they?"

"Some of them do, Mr. Merrill," Matthew shrugged. He had explained the situation, as far as he knew it, over and over again, for the English were openly divided on the question of the war. "I believe the leaders of the Revolution hope that England will just play out."

"Just give up? Never!" A tall stringy individual dressed in a snuff brown suit snorted. His name was Jeffrey Tamms. He now stared at Matthew with an air of open antagonism and shook his head. "The British Empire wasn't built by giving up, sir!"

"I know that's true, Mr. Tamms," Matthew said apologetically. "It's just the talk that goes around back in the Colonies."

Claude Aumont deftly diverted the conversation. "I'm sure we're not going to settle the American problem at this table. I'll take two cards."

When the hand was played, Matthew discovered he had lost over fifty pounds. It gave him a shock, but he let nothing show on his face. Fifty pounds was nothing to these men, he understood. However, he thought ruefully of the losses he had incurred over the past two weeks. He had spent a great deal of time at the card table with Aumont, and though he had won at times, overall his losses were tremendous. *I've got to stop this*, he thought. *I'm just no cardplayer.*

The talk flowed around the table, and most of it Matthew did not understand. These men moved in a different world, and they spoke of stocks and bonds and ventures using terms he could not at all grasp. He lost two more hands, won a small pot, and then in the middle of the next hand Tamms said, "The West Indies venture is looking good."

Bennett at once turned to him. "Shut your mouth, Tamms!"

A silence ran around the table, and Matthew was puzzled by the awkward silence. His eyes moved from face to face, and he tried to understand what was going on. *What's so special about the West Indies venture?* he wondered.

Tamms looked confused, like a man who had made a mistake, and it was Bennett who said, "Let's get on with the game."

The game went on for another hour, and after it broke up, Claude said, "Let's go take a break before we go home, Matthew."

"I think I could use one," Matthew said ruefully. "I'm paying pretty high for my card-playing lessons."

"Your luck is bound to change. It always does. Come along."

They made their way to a tavern and took a seat at a table over in the angle of the large room. There were only a few people there, and after they had ordered their drinks and received them, Aumont said, "I'm surprised you would give up an evening with Stella to go out with me."

Matthew grinned, saying at once, "I didn't do it on purpose, Claude. She said she was tired and needed to stay in."

"You two have been keeping a pretty fast pace."

Matthew was disturbed. He wondered if this was some sort of displeasure at his attention to Stella. A quick look told him, however, that Aumont was amused, and he said, "She's a lovely young woman, Claude."

"Yes. Indeed she is. When I was your age, I was exactly the same. A pretty face and off I went. Could think of nothing else."

The two drank their wine and relaxed as Claude did most of the talking. He had been everywhere, it seemed, and done things most people only dreamed of doing. He knew scores of important people and could tell amusing anecdotes about his encounters with them.

Finally Claude leaned back and studied his companion with an intent gaze. "What do you plan to do with your life?" he asked.

"Well, not make a living playing cards," he grinned ruefully. "I'm not cut out for that."

"Certainly not. No man wants to make a living gambling. It's a gentleman's pleasure, but those who make a living at it are nothing." He sipped his drink, then shrugged. "As I understand it, you've come into your title and the estate recently."

"Yes. That's true."

"What did you do before then? Tell me again."

Matthew found himself telling Claude about his life, leaving out certain parts of it, and finally he said, "So I never had any money. I struggled as an artist. I had some success but not a great deal. And suddenly now all this has been thrust upon me."

"Well, as Shakespeare said, 'Some men are born great, some men achieve greatness, and some have greatness thrust upon them.' It looks as though the latter were true of you."

"I don't feel that way, Claude. As a matter of fact, I'm a little confused." Matthew hesitated, then sipped from his drink again. "All I ever wanted to do was paint, but somehow since I came into the title, I haven't been able to do that. I've tried, but it just doesn't seem to be there."

"I can understand that. A big change in your life is bound to set you off a little bit. It's like stepping into a hole you didn't know was there—and it jars you and breaks the whole rhythm of your walk."

"That's exactly it!" Matthew said eagerly. "I've been jarred, and now I don't know what to do." He turned the glass around, held it up to the light, and then put it down. "I've been very happy lately with your friendship."

"And with Stella?"

"Yes." Matthew flushed. "Of course."

"Don't be ashamed of it, my boy. It's very natural. She's a lovely young woman and you're a full-blooded young man. That's as it should be."

"But what am I going to do? I don't know enough to go into business."

"Why, you don't have to know a great deal to do that."

Matthew looked at his friend with surprise. "I don't understand that. Surely you have to have a grasp of the principles of business."

"Do you know the percentage of business failures in this country? Over fifty percent. Half the people who go into business fail at it."

"Well, that's not very encouraging," Matthew muttered. He studied Aumont and saw something lurking in the man's sharp eyes. "What are you getting at, Claude?"

"There are only two elements to a successful business life."

"What are they?"

"No one knows." Aumont laughed then, humor sparkling in his eyes. "I'm just teasing you. Very few people know, but I'm going to share them with you. It's not really giving away much because most people can't lay hold on the two elements."

"What two elements make for a successful career in business?"

"Money and timing."

"I know about money, but what do you mean by timing?"

"I mean that from time to time an opportunity comes along. It doesn't last long, and it never comes again. It's like that line from Shakespeare. How does it go?" He leaned back and closed his eyes then quoted: " 'There is a tide in the affairs of men, which taken at the flood, leads on to victory. Omitted, all the voyage of their life is bound in shallows and in miseries.' " He opened his eyes and said, "That's been my motto. A tide in the affairs of men. I was as poor as a church mouse when I grew up, Matthew. We didn't have two pence to rub together, but then a deal came along and I somehow knew that it was going to be successful. I gathered all the money I could get—begged, borrowed, and even stole some of it—and put in every penny. And it came through."

"What was the deal?"

"It doesn't matter. It'll never come along again. Since then there have been four ventures like that, each one larger than the last. And each one took every penny I had, I might add. My word, I gambled everything!"

"That might not be a good idea for a fellow like me," Matthew said. "I'm not a very good gambler."

"No, you're not. You're an artist, and it seems that that part of a man's brain takes up all the space otherwise used for business, money, and things like that. Perhaps that's why there aren't very many rich artists."

"You might be right. I don't know of any."

"They don't think of the main chance. They're thinking of the next painting or the one they're working on. Their whole life is tied up in it. Isn't that true?"

"Yes, it is. So I guess that leaves out a business career for me."

Claude signaled for another bottle, waited until it came, then poured the two glasses half full. Taking his own, he sipped at it, then put it down. His eyes were almost burning, and there was an intentness in him as he said, "You don't necessarily have to know a great deal. You just have to know someone who does."

Instantly Matthew understood that his friend was making some sort of offer. He studied Claude Aumont's face and asked, "Do you mean that you might give me some help in a venture?"

"That would not be difficult. There are many things going on, mostly small things. I could help you, but you would have to put your life into it. That's the way it is with men who trifle with small ventures. They constantly have to be redoing it. What I'm talking about is that one financial risk that would set a man up for life."

"But you have found, what, five of those things?"

"Well, only three that big," Aumont admitted. "But that's my life. That's what I do. I could have retired years ago, but I like the excitement. I'm a gambler, as you know."

"Well, I'm not."

"Of course not. What you need is one affair, one investment, one plunge into the world of finance and business. Make your money and get out."

Matthew leaned forward, his face intent. "You're saying that there is such a thing?"

"I'm bound not to speak of it," Aumont said quickly.

Suddenly Matthew remembered the embarrassing moment at the table when Tamms had mentioned a certain deal. "Is it the West Indies business?" he said.

Aumont was startled. He slapped his hand on the table and shook his head, his eyes growing angry. "That fool Tamms! I'd like to shoot him!"

"Then there is something big going on in the West Indies."

Aumont leaned forward and looked down at the table. He did not move for a long time, and finally he lifted his eyes and said, "You're a good fellow, Matthew, and I like you, but I must ask you never to repeat what you heard at that table tonight."

"Of course, if you ask it."

"There's a good man." Relief washed across Aumont's face, and he finished off his drink, then poured another. He held it in his hand, then said, "Well, why not," as if speaking to an invisible companion. "Look. There is something big that's going to happen. All of us at the table tonight are in on it. It was Bennett who put it together, and I knew as soon as he asked me to come in and explained it to me that this was going to be the biggest venture I'd ever been in on."

"Can you tell me anything about it?"

"I can tell you, but you must vow that you will never reveal a word of it."

"I don't know anyone here, Claude. You know that. I'm not a businessman, but I know how to keep my word. I'll never mention anything about what you say."

"All right. Here it is. I don't think you're aware—most people aren't—that sugar is a treasure greater than spices. You'll remember from your history that the early explorers went searching for spices. That's how most of these lands got discovered."

"Yes. I read about that."

"Well, the spices were important. Indeed they still are, but it's sugar that's the rage right now. England and every other country has a desire for the sweetening on the tongue as a regular article of diet. Every nation has to have it, and do you know where sugar comes from?"

Matthew suddenly saw where his friend was headed. "The West Indies."

"Right. Ever since the craze for sugar has been going on, nations have been fighting over those prized islands where the tall canes grow, and planters there have become immensely rich. Why, I remember when William Pitt was prime minister. He saw a planter's carriage with magnificent horses and fittings made of silver and gold, much handsomer than his own. He said, 'Sugar, eh? All that from sugar?' "

"I don't know a thing about how sugar is grown."

"Well, neither did I, but as soon as Bennett came with his proposition, I made it my business to find out. It's relatively uncomplicated. The cane has to be cut, then it has to be hauled to a mill. When it gets to the mill, it is worked through a series of rollers, all by hand, of course. That extracts the juice. When they get the juice they put it into boilers and build fires under it. That reduces it to crystals. It takes several boilings to make it white, although some of it is left dark for other products. It's then packed in molds shaped like loaves."

"I didn't know any of that."

"Not many do. Most people just pay a high price for sugar and never think about where it comes from."

"Is it hard to grow?"

"Hard on those who grow it," Aumont said grimly. "The natives, who are called Caribs, couldn't take the hard labor under that sun, so they started importing slaves from Africa. That makes the slave trade almost as lucrative as the sugar trade. I thought about getting into that, but acquiring and selling slaves is unpleasant—and risky."

For over an hour Matthew sat listening to Claude Aumont. He knew, apparently, everything about trade, and not just sugar and slaves, but other commodities too. Finally Claude said, "Sugar. That's where my friends and I intend to make our fortunes. They all have wealth, of course, but this is bigger than anything we've ever done."

"What will you do? Buy a plantation down there?"

"No. That's much too risky. In the first place, this war has played havoc with the sugar trade. We have the French swarming around the West Indies, as well as some American war vessels, so we can't just go in and do what we please." Leaning forward, he lowered his voice. "Bennett and the rest of us have been buying up all the raw sugar that could be had. Now we're in the process of buying ships to go down. We intend to take all the sugar off of that island—every grain of it."

The enormity of the venture drew Matthew's breath. He could not answer for a moment and finally said, "That's some undertaking, Claude."

"It is the biggest I've ever tried. But if it works, don't you see, Matthew, we will have all the sugar that's been produced over the past two years! It will be on our ships. We will bring it all back to England, store it in warehouses, and sit on it. Anyone who wants sugar will have to come to us."

All of this, of course, was a new world to Matthew. He was not able to take it all in. After a few moments, he said, "Well, isn't there a big risk involved?"

"There's always a risk involved with business, Matthew. I weighed it all before I got into it, and now I've invested every penny I have. If it goes down, I'll be broke. But if it succeeds, as I'm confident it will, the world's my oyster."

Matthew hesitated only for a second. "I'd like to get in on it if I could."

"I don't see how I could do that, much as I'd like to. I would have to talk to all of my friends."

"Talk to them," Matthew urged. "If the Revolution fails in America,

I'll have to help my family there. That'll take money."

"One thing. All of us are putting our eggs in one basket. We'd expect anyone else to do the same. What could you raise? Every penny, Matthew?"

For the next twenty minutes he went over his financial record with Claude, and finally he drew a line under a figure and said, "That would be if I liquidated everything."

"Are you sure you want to do this? It is a gamble."

"But you think it's safe enough that you're trying it."

"That's true, but I've been through this before. I want you to think it over. Come back and see me tomorrow. It's going to take place very quickly—and when I say quickly, I mean within a week. The big item is the purchase of the ships, and credit won't do. We have to have the cash."

"All right. I'll come back tomorrow and let you know."

The two parted, and Matthew took a carriage back to his rooms. He moved the scheme around in his mind and tossed restlessly on his bed, but when the next day came, he arose and looked up Claude at once.

"I'm ready to go in with you if your friends will agree."

"I've talked with all but one of them. They were a little reluctant, but I think we can make it happen. But it's got to be quick. Get the money as soon as you can. It'll have to go in with ours. This is going to take every pound each of us has."

"I'll start today. It shouldn't take long."

🔔   🔔   🔔

The evening had been cut short, for Stella had been bored with the entertainment. They had gone to the theater, and within twenty minutes, she had said, "Come, let's leave. This is terrible."

Matthew did not like the production either and said, "Let's go somewhere else."

"No. I've got to go home. I have a headache. I don't feel at all well."

"Oh, I'm sorry," Matthew said. "Why didn't you tell me?"

"It got worse with that awful play."

As they left the theater, Matthew helped her into the carriage. Shortly thereafter they were in front of her door. He put his arms out, and she came to him and kissed him. He had drunk too much, and he said, "Please let me come inside, Stella."

Stella whispered, "Not tonight, Matthew. Not tonight. I really feel much worse."

"Stella, I think you know how I feel about you."

Putting her hand on his cheek, she said, "You're a sweet young man, but we'll talk about it later."

But Matthew was not satisfied with being put off. "I want to marry you, Stella."

"Do you? Well, you'll have to court me properly, then."

"No. I mean it. I'll be able to take care of you properly."

"I didn't know your paintings were selling that well."

"It's not that. It's the affair I'm in with your uncle, the West Indies business."

Stella's eyes flew open. "Matthew!" she whispered in alarm. She put her hand over his lips and said, "Don't ever say that! Weren't you sworn to secrecy? My uncle is very strict about his business affairs."

Matthew removed her hand and said with some confusion, "But you're his family. He's your uncle. Surely it wouldn't hurt to say it to you."

"Never say anything to anyone, especially to a woman, about this! You promise me?"

"Of course. I wouldn't think of doing anything else."

He tried to kiss her again, but she laughed and pushed him away. "You're a naughty boy," she said, "and I don't feel well tonight. Good night."

He kissed her one more time, then she pulled away and stepped inside the door.

Dissatisfied with himself and unhappy that she had not shown more interest in his proposal, Matthew did not want to go back to his rooms. He went to one of the clubs where he had been introduced by Claude. For over an hour he drank and played cards, then finally left. On his way home he stopped in at a tavern and was surprised to see Derek Laurence sitting at a table alone. He went over to him and said, "Hello, Derek."

"Matthew. Sit down. I'm meeting a lady here shortly, so you'll have to leave when she comes."

"A rich young lady, I suppose."

"Not this one, but she has other—advantages." The artist grinned, and the two men sat there drinking for a while. Matthew was burning to tell Derek Laurence about his investment, but the warnings of both Claude and Stella weighed heavily on his mind. The woman did not show up, and an hour later, the two men were still drinking. By now Matthew was much the worse for it. His speech was growing thick.

Derek grinned at him. "You're talking like a drunk trying to pronounce every syllable of every word."

"Well, I have had too much to drink."

Derek studied his young friend. "Let me give you a word of warning."

"What warning?"

"Be careful about Stella Aumont."

Matthew stared at him and said harshly, "What do you mean? What are you saying, Derek?"

"I'm only saying that you're a young man, and young men are susceptible to seductive young women."

"You're the one who's always saying to find a rich woman and marry her."

"I can't say any more. Maybe I've said too much already." Derek rose and continued, "I guess I've been stood up. I guess she's not coming. I'll see you later, Matthew."

Matthew sat there, his mind reeling, and finally he rose to his feet and followed Derek outside. He caught up with him and pulled him around. "I don't like what you're insinuating, Derek! I'm in love with Stella, and I'm going to marry her."

"Don't be a fool! She won't marry you."

"Why not?"

"You don't have enough money, for one thing."

And then Matthew lost it. His mind was working slowly, and he said loudly, "I will have money! I'm in a deal with her uncle. I'm going to have more money than you ever heard of!"

Laurence's eyes narrowed. "Matthew, I wish I'd never introduced you to the Aumonts. They're sharks, and they're always looking for little fish to gobble up."

"He's my friend, Derek."

"He's no one's friend but his own, and the woman is not what she appears to be."

If he had not been half drunk, Matthew would never have done it. But he was angry, and he struck out, intending to hit Derek in the face with his fist. Instead, he found his wrist clamped in an iron grip, and Derek held him pinioned there. "Matthew," he said, "you're drunk."

"I'm not so drunk I don't know what you said! I thought you were my friend!"

"I want to be your friend, but I can't talk to you when you're drunk. Tomorrow we'll talk. Come to my house early."

Matthew jerked his wrist back. "I know what's the matter with you! You're just jealous because I've gotten close to Claude, and I'm going to make a fortune, and I got a woman you couldn't have!" He turned and walked off, his back stiff with anger.

Derek Laurence stared at the young man as he walked away and compassion filled his eyes. "You fool," he whispered. "You poor fool!"

6

THE WALLS COME TUMBLING DOWN

WINTER HAD SWEPT OVER LONDON, the snow transforming the sharp, angular houses into soft curves, making the whole city beautiful. As Matthew walked down the street, tiny snowflakes that were beginning to fall bit at his face and stuck on his eyelashes. He tugged his coat tighter about him and thought about how he had loved the snow when he was a boy. Now as he moved along, a strange silence had fallen upon London. The snow formed a soft cushion in the street so that the hooves of the horses did not ring metallically against the cobblestones. The very air seemed to be muffled, the voices of people muted and far away. Everywhere the pristine beauty of the snow clothed the brownstone buildings as with white ermine.

Matthew stopped at the Aumont house and carefully ascended the steps. The snow had not been swept away, and his feet sank into the softness of it. Knocking on the door, he waited impatiently. He had not seen either of the Aumonts for three days now, which was the longest break since he had met them. He had come each day, but Jenkins, the butler, had informed him that his master and Miss Aumont were not at home, and he was not at liberty to disclose their whereabouts.

The door opened and Jenkins presented his stone face. "Good day, Sir Matthew."

"Hello, Jenkins. Is Mr. Aumont at home?"

"I'm afraid not, sir."

"Miss Aumont?"

"Neither is she here, I'm afraid."

"Well, where are they, Jenkins?"

"I couldn't say, sir." His face had all the qualities of the sphinx and revealed just as little.

"It's very important that I see one of them. Couldn't you give me at least a hint?"

"I'm afraid not, sir. They did not give me that information when they left. I expect they've gone out of town for a few days. Perhaps the snow has kept them from returning."

A wild impulse to shove past Jenkins and go running into the house came to Matthew. He could not believe that they had left without leaving word for him, but Claude had said, "Things will be going very quickly. We have all the money now, and we are making arrangements for shipping the sugar. I'll be very busy for the next few days."

Stella had been equally evasive. She had said, "I may go see one of my friends for a few days. Uncle's going to be busy."

"Well, I'm not going to be busy," Matthew had said, and she had only smiled and patted his cheek. "Be patient. We'll be together soon enough."

Matthew saw that it was useless to ask anything more of Jenkins, so he grunted, turned, and made his way down the steps. He had nowhere else to go except to the club. He went there hoping to see Tamms or one of the other members of the group that was planning the coup, but at this time of day the club was practically vacant. He drank alone, ate, got into a card game that bored him, and finally left.

As he walked the streets, he could think of no place to go except the studio. He had not seen Derek since the two had quarreled, and he felt badly about it. "I may as well go apologize to him. After all, I was pretty well drunk. Maybe he didn't mean what he said."

When he arrived at the studio, he found the artist giving a lesson to a young woman with obviously little talent. You would not have known it, however, from Derek's smooth conversation and encouraging words to the aspiring young artist. His eyes had picked up Matthew as soon as he had entered, but he had not looked back. Matthew felt very uncomfortable and was about to leave when finally Derek came over.

"Hello, Matthew. I haven't seen you lately."

"No. I guess I've been busy." This was not true, and he said forthrightly, "Look, Derek, I was drunk the other night. I'm sorry I was such a bore."

"I've forgotten all about it. Why don't you take off your coat and do a little painting?"

Matthew felt very little like painting, but he also had no place else to go. "All right," he said. "I don't have a smock."

70

"Oh, I've got several. Come along. Time you went to work."

The next three mornings, Matthew went to the Aumont house only to receive the same news: "The Aumonts are not here." Then he spent the rest of each day painting. His work was not good, but he at least could talk with Derek, and it was something to do. Neither of them mentioned the Aumonts until the third day, when Derek said, "I ran across Claude Aumont. He paid me for the painting of his niece."

"Where did you see him?" Matthew asked swiftly.

"Why, he and his niece have rooms in the Convoy House."

"What's that? The Convoy House."

"Oh, it's more or less a place where wealthy people stay."

"Where is it?"

"Over on the west side. Not far from the museum."

Immediately Matthew pulled off his smock and cleaned the paint off of his hands. He said, "I've got to go, Derek. I'll see you later."

Derek watched him go and shook his head. "Poor devil. I suspect he's about to be dropped by Miss Stella Aumont."

☙   ☙   ☙

Matthew found the Convoy House without any trouble. He asked a porter who was cleaning where the Aumonts were and was told, "On the second floor, east wing."

Matthew climbed the steps eagerly. There were only two apartments off the lavishly furnished hallway. He knocked on the door, and after some time, Claude Aumont himself opened it.

"Claude, where have you been? I've looked everywhere for you."

"Oh, Matthew," Aumont said. "Why, I've been out of town." He hesitated, then said, "You'd better come inside."

Matthew stepped inside and looked around. "Is Stella here?"

"No. She's staying with a friend out in the country."

Matthew took off his coat and tossed it on a chair, followed by his hat. "I've been to your house every day. Why didn't you leave word for me?"

Aumont did not answer. He said, "Sit down, Matthew. I'm afraid I've got some rather shocking news."

A cold hand seemed to close around Matthew's throat. He sat down, and it was good there was a chair, for he felt a sudden weakness in his legs. "What's the matter? Is it Stella?" His first thought was that she was engaged to marry someone else.

"No. It isn't Stella," Aumont said. He went over to stand beside the mantel and reached up and touched the satinwood clock. He traced the circle of the delicate glass, then turned, and his face and his eyes were unreadable. "I hate to be the bearer of bad tidings. Back in the old days when a messenger brought bad news, the primitive tribes would kill the messenger."

"What is it, Claude? Tell me."

"It's our venture."

"The West Indies venture?"

"Yes. That's why I haven't gotten in touch with you. We've been trying to salvage something."

"But what is it?"

Aumont did not move. He dropped his head for a moment, and when he looked up, his lips were drawn tight. "It's all gone, Matthew."

"What do you mean all gone? What happened?"

"We bought the ships and they loaded the sugar, but as they left the harbor they were attacked by French warships. They were captured, every one of them. The French have it all."

Matthew could not think of a single word to say. It was as if he were paralyzed. Finally he licked his lips and said, "But surely there's something to be done."

"I'm afraid not. The French have the ships, they have the sugar, and we're at war with them. They're not going to give it back to us, Matthew. The spoils of war."

"But is it all gone? Did you spend it all?"

"Every penny. As I told you, it took it all for the venture."

"But what about my money? I put everything into it!"

"We're all in poor shape. I'm having to sell all my holdings, the house included. I'm staying here on credit. I'm broke, Matthew. We all are, or nearly so."

"But what am I going to do?"

"I can't tell you. I don't know what I myself will do. I'm going to have to start over."

"What about Stella?"

"She's taking it badly, I'm afraid. She's always had everything she wanted, and now we've had to sell her jewelry, her clothes—that's why she's staying with a friend. We had a terrible argument about it. She's very upset with me. I'm upset with myself."

"Upset!" Matthew said. "You're upset! We're ruined and you're *upset*?"

Claude Aumont stood there silently. Matthew rose and went over to stand before him, and Aumont said, "I can't say anything else. It was a gamble, and when you gamble you sometimes lose." He put his hand on Matthew's shoulder. "I'll tell you what. I'll see if I can get enough out of what's left to buy your passage home if that's what you want to do. It might be best. There'll only be bitter memories if you stay here."

Matthew could not speak. Everything had fallen apart, and the walls had come tumbling down. He stood there unable to think.

"Go on back home, and I'll see what I can do. Try to keep a stiff upper lip."

Matthew turned and left without a word.

When he was outside he walked the streets of London without seeing anything. Finally he went home to his apartment and sat down, his appetite gone and fear tearing him to pieces. Surely this wasn't happening! He paced the rooms for hours and finally threw himself on the bed fully dressed. Even then he slept fitfully and awoke the next morning engulfed by a dark shadow of fear.

⚑　　　⚑　　　⚑

"Derek, what are you doing here?"

Derek Laurence stood outside Matthew's door and did not answer for a moment. The unkempt man standing before him was not the Matthew he knew. "Can I come in for a minute?"

"Yes. You might as well."

The room Derek Laurence stepped into actually was no more than ten feet square. There was a single bed and a washstand and a rickety table. A few clothes dangled from nails in the wall, and an unpleasant odor of boiling cabbage and sweat hung in the air.

"I've been looking for you," Laurence said.

"You didn't expect to find me here, did you?"

"I heard about what happened."

"Who told you?"

"I think one of Aumont's friends talked a little bit too much. He thought it was a good joke taking an American for all he was worth."

Matthew could not even answer. He had not shaved for several days, and he had not eaten in two days. It had been a quick descent. He had given Aumont everything but his watch and his ring and his clothes, and these he had sold to keep his apartment. But with even this money running short, he had been asked to leave the apartment, taking this small room on the third floor of a run-down tenement. He had tried to get in touch with Aumont but had failed. Now he said hoarsely, "Not a pretty sight, am I?"

"I've been down on my luck a time or two, Matthew. You'll pull out of it."

73

"No. I don't think I will."

"Come on, Matthew. You're not the first man to make a blunder, to trust the wrong people."

"Do you think they took me, then?"

"Of course they did. I tried to warn you that he was too sharp for you."

"What about Stella?"

"Forget about her."

Matthew stood there, the strain of the whole ordeal overwhelming him. He could not get away from the embarrassment and the humiliation of having made such a fool of himself. He sat down abruptly on the bed and put his head in his hands. "I've been such a fool, Derek. Such an absolute, blithering fool!"

Derek sat down on the bed and put his arm around Matthew's shoulders. "Well, that's the first step—admitting you're a fool. Now the second step is to get up and do something about it."

"What am I going to do?"

"You're going to get cleaned up and start painting again. I think we can sell some of your work."

"You've forgotten. I can't paint."

"I'll work with you until you can, and you need to get out of this place. Come and stay with me."

"That's good of you, Derek, but I just don't have the heart for it. It's all gone."

Derek hesitated, then said, "Look. Maybe you ought to go home. I'll lend you the money. You can paint there as well as here, probably better. You can send your paintings back, and I'll sell them for you."

Matthew's throat was suddenly thick. Here was a man he had insulted, a tough man of the world, but he had a heart. His voice was weak as he said, "That's very kind of you."

"I'll look around for a cheap passage. Here's a few pounds. Get yourself cleaned up. Best to get away. You've got talent, Matthew. Why, you'll come back in a few years the most famous painter in America." Derek slapped him on the shoulder and said, "Come by the studio later."

🔔　　　🔔　　　🔔

Matthew followed Derek's advice. He went and got his clothes cleaned, shaved, and resigned himself to returning home. He dreaded telling his family that he had wasted his inheritance and made a complete fool out of himself. For a time he walked the streets, and then the humiliation brought anger. "I'm going to meet him face-to-face and tell him what I think of him! It won't help any, but I'll get it off my chest."

He went back to the Convoy House, and when he knocked on the door, it was Stella who opened it. She looked startled and then said, "Why—Matthew!" Then she quickly said, "My uncle's not here."

"Where is he?" Matthew said bluntly.

"I think he's at the club playing cards."

"You're not going to invite me in?" Matthew said, aware that she had no intention of doing so.

"No. I think it might not be proper."

"Proper! That's a laugh! You're nothing but a strumpet!" His eyes suddenly blazed, and Stella stepped back.

"If I scream," she said, "you'll be arrested. Get out of here!"

"You were in on it from the beginning."

And then Stella laughed. "Of course I was. You don't think he's really my uncle, do you?"

At that moment it all became clear. He knew that the two were lovers using the uncle and niece charade as a ploy for gullible men such as himself.

"You make fine bait, Stella. I'll give you that. I ought to pay you off." He lunged forward and grabbed her throat and began to squeeze. Stella could not utter a word, and her hands beat at him frantically. He felt her gasping for air and saw the terror in her eyes, and then when her eyes began to flutter, he released her. She dropped to the floor gagging, and he said, "You got off lightly. Now I'll have a word with your 'uncle.' I don't think he'll be so lucky."

He left the Convoy and went at once to the club. Fury was building up in him. The sight of Stella and the memory of how she had tricked him and led him on, when all the time she was laughing at him, brought a sense of boiling anger such as he had never known. He reached the club, walked inside, and ignored the greeting of the manager. Walking into the card room, he saw Claude Aumont sitting at the table all the way across the room. Aumont's attention was on the cards in his hand. He was laughing, and the men at the table laughed with him.

At the sight of him, white-hot fury consumed Matthew. It was a fierce emotion, something so alien to him that it almost made him weak. He stiffened himself and stalked across the room. When he reached the table, without pausing, he reached down and grabbed Aumont by the lapels and jerked him to his feet. His hands moved swiftly as he slapped him on the right cheek, then the left, and then shoved him away.

A gasp went up from the men sitting at the table, and Matthew said loudly, "Aumont, you're a liar, a thief, and a yellow dog with no courage!"

A dead silence settled on the room. Aumont reached into his pocket, pulled out a handkerchief, and touched his cheeks, which showed the outline of Matthew's fingers. His eyes were fastened on Matthew, and he said, "I'll have satisfaction for this!"

"Send your man to see Laurence."

"The choice of weapons is mine."

"Anything you want. You're a cowardly swindler, and I intend to see that you're stopped."

Matthew turned and walked out of the room. He could feel eyes boring into his back, and as he left he knew that he had let his anger lead him into a foolish action. Somehow he did not care. *He may kill me, but not before I get a bullet into him*, he thought.

🔔   🔔   🔔

A cold wind cut into Matthew like a knife. He was wearing only a thin coat, and as he stood beside Derek Laurence in the barren woods, he shivered and tried to conceal it.

"It's not too late to get out of this duel," Laurence said. Derek was wearing a heavy wool coat, but his face was pinched with the cold. He had argued against the duel ever since Matthew had told him what had happened.

"I'll get someone else, Derek, if you won't help me," Matthew had said adamantly.

Now Derek stared across the field at the men who were waiting for them. "Look," he said. "What difference does it make if people here say you are a coward? Go back to America. You think anyone here will care? Do you think Aumont will care? He'd like to get out of this as much as you would."

"No. I'm going through with it."

Laurence shook his head in dismay. "I've asked around. He's been called out several times. He killed one man. You don't have any practice with guns."

"I know. My brothers would be good at it. I just never liked guns. But this is something I must do."

A tall man wearing a tall silk hat dispatched himself from the group and came over. "My name is Smith. I am acting for Mr. Aumont."

"My name is Laurence. I'm acting for Sir Matthew."

"If you would care to come and examine the weapons, I think we're all ready."

76

Laurence shot a despairing glance at Matthew, who shook his head stubbornly. "All right," he sighed.

Matthew stood alone as the two men went over the weapons. Finally he got a signal from Laurence and advanced. He felt light-headed but sensed no fear. He had been afraid up until he had arrived on the scene, but now he was like a man in a dream. He fixed his eyes on Claude Aumont's cold, pale features as the instructions were given, and strangely enough the burning, fierce anger that had so racked him was gone. He had made the challenge, and he had to play out his role.

He felt the coldness of the butt as he was handed the dueling pistol, and the tall man was saying, "You will stand back to back. You will count off ten paces at my signal, then you will turn and fire. Is that clear?"

Both men nodded, and Matthew moved over to the center of the clearing. Aumont did not speak, nor did he. Standing with his back toward the man, the scene became more and more surreal. Overhead the sky was gray. A lone bird far in the distance sailed gracefully over a copse. The sun was white, as though it had been rebuked by God, and there was no warmth in it.

"One—two—"

Matthew held the pistol at his side. He knew that it was cocked and ready to fire, for Laurence had seen to that. But the count seemed to go on forever. He was conscious of a dog barking in the distance far away, frail and thin, and then it faded into silence so that the only sound was that of the man counting off the steps. "Eight—nine—ten—" Matthew had no training and knew only to turn. His weapon was at his side, and as he turned, he saw that Aumont had already whirled and his weapon was pointed right at his heart. He felt a sudden, overwhelming despair and thought, *I'm going to be killed!* His own arm came up, very slowly, it seemed, and he heard the explosion of Aumont's pistol. A hand pushed at his chest, and as he fell over backward, he heard his own weapon explode. But he lay on the ground, thinking, *It doesn't hurt!*

A face appeared over him, and Laurence said, "You're not going to die." He probed at the wound and said, "It's high in the chest, but it missed the heart."

"What about Aumont?"

"Not a scratch."

Matthew closed his eyes and felt hands touching him. The doctor was there and he heard his voice, but then he faded away, slipping into unconsciousness as he was lifted and moved from the field.

T   T   T

"I think it's too early for you to make this voyage. You're not over your wound yet, Matthew."

Turning toward his friend who stood at the rail beside him, Matthew felt a deep affection. It was the middle of January, and he had stayed with Laurence while he recuperated. The wound had been painful but not dangerous, and Laurence had had the best physician in London taking care of him.

Now he laid his hand on Laurence's shoulder and smiled. "I think I would have died if it hadn't been for you."

"Oh, don't talk nonsense! But it's too soon for you to travel. Wait another month. You don't have your strength back yet."

At that moment a boatswain came by yelling at the top of his lungs, "All visitors ashore! All visitors ashore!"

"You go on, Derek. I'll write you when I get to Boston."

Derek Laurence chewed his lip. He knew that Matthew was not physically ready for the long trip, but his young friend would not be talked out of it. "All right," he said. "God bless you."

A look of surprise washed over Matthew's face. "It's the first time you've ever mentioned God, to me at least."

Embarrassment showed itself in Laurence's face. "I suppose so. You know, Matthew, when we were out there on that field and you went down, I realized how frail we all are. I thought you were going to die, and I realized it could just as easily have been me. So for the first time in my life I've come to see that there's more in this world than just chasing women and money."

Matthew felt touched by his friend's confession. He knew it came hard for the painter. "I felt about the same thing. Let me tell you this, Derek. I was bitter, as you can imagine, when I was done in by Aumont and Stella, but then you came along and took care of me as if I were your brother. And I know, as long as there are a few people like you around, I can survive the rest."

"All visitors ashore!"

"Good-bye, dear friend. I'll write to you."

Matthew watched as Derek left the ship. He saw him turn and stand there until the *Monarch* edged away from the dock slowly as the wind caught her sails. Matthew began to cough, sending pain into the bullet wound high in his chest. *Got to get out of this wind*, he thought. He did not stay to watch the London docks fade away but went to his cabin. It was plain and small, but he had insisted on the bare minimum. He

78

knew he would have to pay Laurence back for the money he had spent on him.

Lying down on the bed, he closed his eyes. He knew that he was still sick and weak. His wound had not completely healed, and the fever that had attacked him still came at times.

He thought of home, and the shame of what he had done weighed heavily upon him. *I don't see how I can ever tell them what happened to me. What a fool I was*, he thought. He lay there for a long time and then finally drifted off into a fitful sleep.

❉ ❉ ❉

"Captain, I don't think that sick passenger is going to make it. The one in the small cabin in the stern."

"What's his name?"

"Well, it's kind of confusing. The fellow that bought the passage told me it was Rochester, but he says it's Bradford. In any case, I don't think he's going to make it, Rochester or Bradford."

"What's wrong with him?"

"I don't know, sir. He's bad sick."

The voyage was half over, and the boatswain had become aware that the pale-faced American was not in good health. They had no doctor on board, so he had asked one of the officers, who had a little medical training, to go by and see him. It was then that they discovered he had been shot and was not recovering well.

"Well, he was shot, you know, Captain, and them wounds sometimes go bad."

"What does Evans say?"

"He says there's nothing he can do. There ain't no bullet in there, but it's gotten infected. Evans thinks he's comin' down with pneumonia."

Captain Simms shrugged. He had a ship to run, and the passengers were no concern of his. "Bad luck for him," he said.

"What'll we do, sir?"

"Have Evans keep an eye on him, and you do the same. If he makes it, that's good. If he doesn't, there's nothing we can do."

The boatswain nodded. "Right, sir. I'll see to it."

❉ ❉ ❉

The *Monarch* plunged on through heavy seas. The cold penetrated the whole ship and made the passage miserable. Down in his tiny room, Matthew Bradford grew steadily worse. He had made up his mind

79

never to use the name Rochester again. It had a hateful sound to him and was the mark of his failure. Now as the ship rose and fell, he struggled against the cold, unable to eat, and burning with fever.

At one point he felt that death was near, and he almost welcomed it. He lay there sick and weak, miserable, with no joy in his spirit whatsoever, and in desperation, he uttered up a prayer. "Lord, if this is all there is to life, take me now. I can't bear the thought of anything more."

Overhead the sun put out its pale beams. The *Monarch* creaked and shivered in the freezing seas. The sailors worked the lines, and the officers charted the course, but Matthew Bradford was oblivious to the activities of the ship.

PART TWO

—

STROKE OF FATE

7

EVIL TIDINGS

AS SAM HURRIED ALONG THE WALK that led to the house, he tried to shake off the bad mood that had fallen upon him. His whole life had been wrapped up in the ship that he and Jubal Morrison had built and used, with some success, to raid British shipping vessels. Sam had thrown all his energy, which was considerable, into that venture. He had admired Jubal Morrison as much as any man—except for his own father—and now the thought of Jubal rotting away in a dank, stinking hulk was a constant pain to him.

The snow crunched underneath his feet. Ordinarily during this season, Sam was happy and spent a great deal of time making simple gifts for his family. But this year he had not been able to get himself into the spirit of it. He had become silent, even morose, to the point that his family had almost lost their patience with him. He was the youngest of the Bradfords and the favorite of everyone, but he had not yet learned to control his temper. He also had never had a problem face him such as he confronted these past few days.

Pausing on the stoop, he stomped his feet and scraped them on the iron contrivance he had made for just this purpose. He was an inventor of sorts and had a bright future in that field of endeavor. As he turned, however, he was not thinking of careers or of Christmas or of gifts, and his face was set in a sullen cast.

Stepping inside the house, he pulled off his heavy wool coat and hung it on the rack, along with his fur cap. As he did so, the sound of laughter came to him from somewhere in the house, and he straightened up, for he recognized Keturah's voice. If there was one bright spot in Sam's life, it was the affection he felt for Keturah Burns. For the past two years he had fallen more and more in love with her, but he had not been able to elicit the same feelings toward him. Keturah was an attractive young woman one year younger than Sam. She had, of course, attracted young men, and Sam had been hard put to find a way to keep them away from her.

Now as he made his way toward the kitchen, he heard another voice, a deep masculine one, and his lips grew tighter. Stepping inside the kitchen, he saw Keturah and a tall well-built soldier wearing the uniform of the Maryland Brigade standing by the table. Keturah's hands were white with flour.

Hearing Sam's approach, the two turned, and Keturah said, "Well, hello, Sam."

"Hello," Sam said shortly and stared viciously at the sergeant. Sam Bradford had many talents, but hiding his feelings was not one of them.

Quickly Keturah said, "This is Silas Merchison. He's with the Maryland Brigade. This is Mr. Sam Bradford, Sergeant."

Merchison stepped forward and put out his hand. "Glad to know you, Mr. Bradford," he said. He had a pleasant smile and, while not a handsome man, had a masculine demeanor. His eyes were gray, and he had long auburn hair, which made him rather attractive.

Sam reluctantly put out his hand and immediately squeezed much too hard. He had been a blacksmith, had worked with iron all of his life, so he had a powerful grip.

Merchison was not prepared for such a grip, and his bones crunched. He uttered a small grunt and then tried to match Sam's strength. Few men could do that, however, and Sam took a perverse pleasure in seeing the discomfort of the taller man. Sam, being only five ten, resented the sergeant's great height and added even more pressure.

Keturah had seen Sam do this before, and she said sharply, "Sam, you stop that!"

At once Sam caught the displeasure in Keturah's voice and, avoiding her eyes, released the sergeant's hand.

"Quite a grip you've got there," Merchison said slowly. He flexed his fingers and gave Sam a careful examination.

"Sam's been a blacksmith most of his life, among other things. He's got a good grip, and he likes to show off."

Stung by her words, Sam said without thinking, "I've got to talk to Keturah, Merchison."

Instantly Keturah said, "Go ahead and talk!" She was irritated by Sam's attitude. She had a great fondness for him, and there was no one more fun to be around than Sam Bradford, but she was tired of his possessiveness and had been enjoying her conversation with the tall sergeant. Now she turned and wiped her hands on her apron and waited for Sam to speak.

"What I have to say is private."

"Well, I'll just go along, then," Merchison said quickly.

"Stay right where you are, Silas. Anything Sam has to say to me, he can say in front of you."

Anger rushed through Sam. He knew that Keturah was fond of him, but not nearly fond enough in his opinion. The bad humor and the discouragement that had plagued him for days now suddenly brought his temper to the surface. The best of humor belonged to Sam Bradford at most times, but occasionally his anger would flare up out of control, as it did now. "You heard what I said, Sergeant. I need to talk to the lady alone."

Merchison glanced quickly at Keturah and saw that she was angry. Looking back to Sam, he said crisply, "I'll let Miss Keturah make that decision. If she asks me to leave, I will."

And then it happened as it had only once or twice in Sam's life. A red curtain seemed to come down over his eyes, and with a cry of anger he lunged forward. His large hands slapped the sergeant on the chest and grabbed him by the uniform. He lunged backward, hauling Merchison after him, intending to throw him out.

Merchison, caught off guard, lost his balance. He was dragged forward into the next room before he recovered his balance. He heard Keturah crying out, "Sam—Sam, you stop that! Do you hear me?"

Merchison managed to reach up and grab Sam by the wrists to stop their outward progress. "Now look," he said, "there's no need for—"

The sergeant had no time to finish his sentence, for Sam had wrenched his hands back. He had very strong arms and broke Merchison's grip easily. Then without pausing he struck out with a short, wicked blow that caught Merchison squarely in the mouth. The sergeant reeled backward, his arms pinwheeling, and in doing so was thrown directly against Keturah. She was driven backward and fell sprawling. She stared at Sam with her eyes flashing. "Sam—!" she cried out, but by this time Merchison was in action. He had long arms and this was not his first fight. He stepped forward and caught some of Sam's blows on his forearms and hands. They were all hard blows and stung, but Merchison saw his chance and looped an overhead left that caught Sam high on the chest. It was a hard blow delivered by a strong man, and Sam was knocked back. This did not discourage Sam, for he was in a blind rage now. He threw himself forward and grabbed Merchison, pinioning his arms. He began dragging him to the door, but the big sergeant broke Sam's grip and caught him with a short blow directly over the right eye. It cut Sam's eyebrow, and the blood immediately began to flow, but Sam was totally unconscious of it.

"Get out of the house or I'll beat you to a pulp!" he roared.

The two fought and careened around the room. They passed out into the hallway and fought the length of it. When they reached the door that led to the foyer that fronted the house, Merchison grabbed Sam and began to spin him around. Sam was beating at the sergeant with short, powerful blows with his right hand. Then both men went reeling into the foyer. The force of their motion thrust them into a glass-covered bookcase, and the glass shattered noisily. Somehow the bookcase fell forward, taking both men down with it. Sam kicked it away and was on his feet by the time Merchison got up. Both men were bloodied by now and were panting hard. Neither of them heard Keturah, who had followed them in and was crying out, "You two stop that, both of you!"

In all truth, Merchison would have been glad to stop, for Sam's powerful blows hurt, and one of his teeth, he felt, had been loosened. Blood filled his mouth, and the salty taste of it was not pleasant. Still, he was a man who had been in fights before, so he continued to strike out. His reach was much longer than Sam's, so he often landed some powerful blows. But there was no driving Sam out of the fight, and the two went around the room striking and ducking, grunting, the sound of their heavy breathing filling the air.

Sam was running short of air. He was a tough young fellow, but it was a brutal fight, and the two had been at it long enough to sap his breath. Blood now dimmed his vision, for the cut over his eyebrow was serious, and the eye was closing. A fierce desire to finish the fight came, and he lowered his head, and his powerful legs pumped as he threw himself forward. He struck the abdomen of Merchison, who uttered a loud "*Oomph!*" and then was driven backward. Sam held on to him and the back of Merchison's knee struck the window seat framing the bay window. Then the force of Sam's drive carried them both into the window itself, and with a terrible smashing, grinding noise, both men went through the glass, tearing the whole window loose.

They turned a half somersault and landed in the snow. Sam was the first on his feet, blood streaming down his face, gasping for breath. "Now, get out and don't come back!"

But Silas Merchison was not going anywhere. He got to his feet and struck Sam in the mouth with a mighty blow. Sam, for a moment, could see nothing but blinding stars, yet he refused to give up. Moving forward, he rained fist after fist on Merchison. Merchison returned them as best he could.

Keturah had run out the door, crying their names, and now she rushed forward to throw herself between them. She was furious at Sam, and as she stepped forward, Sam threw a roundhouse right.

Merchison moved his head back so that it merely grazed his chin, but the arch of the blow continued and caught Keturah Burns in the temple.

Keturah went down as if she had been struck by a club and lay still in the snow. Both men suddenly stopped as Sam looked down at the still body. "Now look what you've done!" he yelled.

"Me! You're the one who hit her!"

Sam could hardly see for the blood that covered his face. He shoved Merchison back and turned to Keturah. As he was kneeling down beside her, he heard someone say, "What in the world are you two doing?"

Sam looked up and saw his brother's wife, Jeanne, who had come outside. She had not taken a coat, and her face was pale. She had her baby in her arms, and the baby began to cry. "Are you two crazy?" she demanded and knelt in the snow awkwardly. She touched Keturah's face, and already a knot was beginning to form on her forehead.

Sam began to regain his sanity, and as he looked at Keturah lying so still, a terrible guilt rushed over him. He came forward at once and said, "Jeanne, it was an accident."

"An accident! You've wrecked the house, you oaf! What were you thinking?"

Merchison came forward and said, "Let me carry her into the house."

"I'll carry her into the house!" Sam said angrily. "Haven't you done enough?"

Merchison clamped his teeth together. He knew there was no arguing with Sam, and he turned to Jeanne and said, "I'm sorry, ma'am. It was none of my doing. This young man jumped me, and I had no choice."

"All right, Sergeant. Come back later."

"Yes, ma'am. I'll do that."

Jeanne gave Sam a withering look and rose to her feet. "Sam, pick her up and take her inside!"

Sam quickly picked Keturah up and followed Jeanne inside the house, where Jeanne directed him to put Keturah on her bed. He laid her down carefully, and she said, "Now, get out of here."

"But she's got to have somebody to take care of her."

Jeanne Corbeau Bradford had a temper herself. She still had a trace of French in her accent, for she had been raised by a French Canadian father. Her high cheekbones and wide lips gave her an attractive appearance, but the cleft in her chin made her look very stubborn. She said angrily, "Sam Bradford, do you wake up every day and think 'What can I do to cause trouble?' You must, because everything that goes wrong in this household can be traced to your door! Now go! I'll take care of Keturah."

Sam moved quickly away. He had seen the wrath in Jeanne's eyes, and he knew that he had been wrong. Moving to the door, he snatched his coat and fur cap and stepped outside. His head was down, but he looked up when a tall figure approached. "What do you want, Merchison?"

Merchison was hurting all over from the fight. His mouth was cut, and he knew the stout blows to his body would give him pain for several days. He was, however, not a quarrelsome man, and now he asked cautiously, "Are you two bespoken, you and Miss Keturah?"

Sam glared at him. "Not yet—but we will be!"

🔔   🔔   🔔

Daniel's office upstairs at the foundry was quiet. As a partner in the business, he always had a seemingly endless pile of work on his desk. However, he stopped what he was doing when he looked up and saw Sam standing awkwardly outside his open door. Bradford knew his son well and could tell that something was wrong. He said at once, "Come on into my office."

Now as he sat there and listened to Sam's tale of woe, he finally sighed deeply and shook his head. Daniel Bradford was a patient man and had a special fondness for Sam. All of his sons were loved, but this one, because of his impulsiveness, his quick wit, his cheery good humor, and just because he was the youngest, was a favorite. He looked at the bruised and battered countenance of his youngest son and knew he should be angry.

"Let me see if I can get this straight, Sam," Daniel said slowly. "You found a young man calling on Keturah, so you picked a fight with him in the kitchen, then you wrecked the house, including breaking up my favorite bookcase, you broke out the bay window, and you then knocked Keturah unconscious. Is that about the way it is?"

Sam could not say a word. His father had a way of getting right to the heart of things. He had a fierce love for this man, and of all the individuals in the world he hated to disappoint, his father topped the list.

Knowing he could make no defense, Sam finally cleared his throat and in an unsteady voice said, "I guess that's about the way it happened, Pa."

Daniel Bradford admired the way Sam shouldered the responsibility. No one knew better than he what a good heart Sam had, but he could not afford to let this pass by. Sam was nineteen years old now, a man, strong and as intelligent as any man he had ever known, but he was impulsive to a fault, and it had taken all the persuasion Daniel Bradford could summon to keep Sam from joining the army. Since he had two sons already serving, Daniel Bradford had a deep desire to keep this one son at home. He had convinced Sam that his presence at the foundry making equipment for George Washington's troops did more for the cause than being in a line regiment. Up until now it had worked, but there was no telling when Sam would kick loose the traces and simply enlist.

"Sam, you've had infatuations about young women before, if I remember correctly."

"This is different, Pa."

"It's always different. Each time was different," Bradford smiled faintly. "I guess I was the same when I was your age, but you're right that this is different—because of Keturah."

"You like her, don't you, Pa?"

"I think very highly of Keturah. I always have. But you have to remember, son, her upbringing. She didn't have the privilege of growing up with a good family as other young girls have. She had to fight for survival. Her mother was a camp follower. It's God's mercy that Keturah has kept her pure spirit."

"I know it, Pa. I know all that. But I don't care about her past."

"That's not the question. I'm sure you don't, but you have to be gentle with her. She can't be rushed. Remember, Sam, all of her life men have been at her."

"Well, I'm not like they are! I want to marry her."

"She has to learn that for herself," Bradford said firmly. "She's likely to be spooked by any man. She's had to fight to keep herself pure, and the men she's known up until now have been a threat."

"Well, she can't go through life like that. Besides, I think she loves me."

"She may very well, but she hasn't discovered it for herself. And that is something that only she can do, Sam. It can't be rushed."

As the two sat there talking, Sam finally cooled off. He had been afraid that his father would jump on him with both feet, but the gentleness and the patience of his father brought a lump to Sam's throat. Finally he said, "I'm going home, Pa. I'll fix the bookcase, and I'll fix the window. And, Pa . . . I'm sorry."

"I know you are, Sam. Don't go rushing in and overwhelm Keturah. Just tell her you're sorry. That's all. Then clean up the mess you made."

"All right, Pa, but I'll tell you this. I love her, and I'm going to marry her sooner or later!"

🔔   🔔   🔔

Giles Abercrombie, the bookkeeper for Daniel's foundry, opened the door and stepped inside. He was a tall, thin individual with a morbid countenance that concealed a cheerful heart underneath. "Mr. Bradford," he said. "There's a man to see you."

"Who is it, Giles?"

"His name is Bunch."

"Bunch? I don't know anybody with that name. Never heard of it before."

"No. He's some sort of a sailor, I believe. Has the air of one. Walks as if the room were not quite steady, if you know what I mean."

"Well, send him in, Giles."

"Yes, sir."

Daniel Bradford rose from his desk where he had been drawing a diagram for a new cannon that he was anxious to try to build. There were few enough munitioners in the Colonies. In addition to making swords and bayonets, he had been working for several years now putting out small cannons called Napoleons. Washington was anxious for bigger guns and had been urging Sam to see if he could produce them. The door opened, and the man that came in was a stranger to Bradford. He was short, thickset with a pitted face and a pair of hazel eyes. He had the walk of a sailor, rolling slightly, and the dress of one. He took off his cap instantly and said, "Mr. Bradford?"

"Yes. I'm Daniel Bradford."

"My name is Alfred Bunch. I'm the boatswain of the *Monarch*. We just tied up in the harbor."

"Glad to make your acquaintance, Mr. Bunch. What can I do for you?"

Bunch shifted his cap around in his hands with a nervous motion. His mouth twitched, and he gnawed on his lower lip for a moment, then said in a rush, "I've got some bad news for you, sir. Very bad news indeed."

Instantly Bradford grew tense. "What is it?" He could not imagine

90

what a sailor would have to say, for none of his people were in the navy.

"We took on a passenger in London a month ago. Had bad weather and the young man took sick. I found a letter in his things from you, sir, and so I figured that since he had your name, he was probably your kin."

Instantly Daniel knew it had to be Matthew and asked, "What is it? What's wrong with him?"

"Well, sir, we didn't have no doctor on board. We did have the first officer, Mr. Evans. He started out to be a doctor, you see, but he changed to the sea. What he says is the lad's got pneumonia. Very bad he is, sir. Fever so high you wouldn't believe it."

"I'll come with you at once, Bunch."

Bunch hesitated. "Mr. Evans said to tell you, sir, that you shouldn't have too much hope."

"I'll come right away. How did you get here?"

"I walked, sir."

"Come along, Bunch."

Daniel rushed out of his office and said, "Giles, get hold of Dr. Masters. Tell him to be at my house as quick as he can get there."

"What is it, sir?"

"It's Matthew. He's just come in on a ship and he's very sick. If you can't get Masters, get Pettigrew. Get both of them if you can."

Daniel moved quickly, commandeering a covered wagon. He hitched up a team of matched bays, leaped into the seat, and said, "Come on, Bunch."

Bunch quickly climbed aboard and then endured one of the most hair-raising rides of his life. Bradford drove like a crazy man, taking corners on two wheels and running several buggies off the road. Bunch held on to his seat with one hand, his hat with the other. "Won't do no good to get us both kilt, sir," he protested.

But Daniel Bradford said nothing. His face was a mask and his lips were tight. He had a special love for Matthew. He was so different from Daniel's other sons. Matthew was sensitive and gifted artistically, and right now Daniel somehow knew he needed love and acceptance more than he ever had.

When they reached the dock, Bunch directed Bradford until he drew up, pulling on the brakes and hauling back on the lines so that the horses protested and stamped their hooves. Without hesitation he jumped out and hailed a young boy, saying, "Hold these horses, son!" and threw him a coin. "Come along, Bunch."

Bunch said, "Aye, sir," and took him aboard the *Monarch* at once. He led him down some stairs to a small cabin and stepped back as Daniel rushed inside.

Daniel looked down at the pale face of his son. He hardly recognized him, for his face was gaunt and sunk in, almost like a skeleton. Bradford put his hand on Matthew's pale forehead and felt the heat of his fever. "I'll take him home right away. Can you fix up some kind of a bed?"

"Aye, sir. I can do that. We'll take plenty of blankets. I'll take care of it, sir."

"Do it now, Bunch."

Bunch left at once, and Daniel sat down beside his son. There was no use speaking to him, for he was unconscious. He prayed and tried to grab hold of God as he always did, knowing this was their only hope. It was God or nothing.

Bunch came back quickly, it seemed. "I've got a nice bed for him, sir, and more blankets to put over him. Can I help you with him?"

"No. I'll take him." Daniel Bradford was a powerful man, six feet one, and years at a forge had muscled his body. It shocked him how little Matthew weighed, but he carried him up the steep steps effortlessly, down the gangplank, and placed him gently in the bed Bunch had made in the wagon. He covered him up, then reached into his pocket, pulled out two gold coins, and said, "Thank you for your trouble, Bunch."

"Why, you don't have to do this, sir."

"No. Go on and take it," Daniel insisted.

Bunch took the coins in his hard hand and said quietly, "I hope the young gentleman comes through, sir. He's a fine young man. Anyone can see that."

"Thank you, Bunch."

Climbing onto the wagon, Daniel spoke to the team, turned their heads, and made for home.

🔔　　🔔　　🔔

"I think you'd better prepare yourself for the worst, Daniel."

Dr. Theo Masters finished his examination of the still figure and turned to say, "He's got double pneumonia, both lungs."

Daniel shook his head. "I'll never give up hope."

"Tell us what to do," Sam said. He had been working on the broken window when his father had driven up. He had a special affection for Matthew, for the two of them had been very close.

Dr. Masters shook his head. "You can do nothing but see that he's cared for. Get him to drink all the fluids you can and pray."

Sam nodded and said, "I'll do everything I can." He left the room while his father and the doctor continued to talk. As soon as he stepped outside, he saw Jeanne and Keturah standing there waiting. Jeanne was holding her baby, and Keturah stood beside her. Sam could not keep from looking at the dark purple bruise on her forehead, and he noted that she didn't speak to him. "He's bad," Sam said quickly. "Double pneumonia. All we can do is take care of him and pray, the doctor says."

Keturah listened, then turned and walked away without a word.

Sam watched her go. He had been depressed ever since the fight with Merchison. He had apologized to Keturah, and she had simply said, "You were a fool, Sam, but I forgive you."

Now he said, "I reckon it's all over with me and Keturah. She hates me."

"No, she doesn't hate you. Look, we've got a battle here, and you can't go moping around. We've got to do the best we can for Matthew. Keturah doesn't know yet what she wants. You can't build a fence around her. Now, go over and tell Abigail about all of this."

"Tell Abigail? Why?"

"Because she loves him! Don't you see anything but your own nose?"

"All right. I'll go."

Sam left the house at once, glad to have something to do. Proceeding to the house where Abigail lived with her mother, he knocked on the door. When she opened the door, Sam pulled off his hat and said without preamble, "Miss Abigail, I got some bad news."

At once Abigail assumed either Micah or Dake had been hurt or killed in the war. "Is it one of the boys?"

"Well, not Dake or Micah. It's Matthew."

"Matthew! What about him?"

"He came in on a ship today, Miss Abigail. He's got pneumonia. The doctor says he's going to die. You may want to come over, but he won't know you. He's unconscious."

"All right. You go on, Sam. I'll come as soon as I can."

When she closed the door, Abigail turned and leaned back against it. She pressed the back of her head against the wood and prayed, "Oh, God, don't let him die. Don't let him die—please don't let him die."

8

"You Have God—And He's Enough"

DURING THE FALL OF 1779 the war seemed to have ground down to a halt on both sides. Sir Henry Clinton, in charge of the British forces, sat in New York and thought up excuses for not winning the war. His great objective was to lure Washington out into an open battle, but Washington, though angered by the constant raiding of the British, refused to budge.

During this period Washington sent General "Mad" Anthony Wayne to raid a fort at Stony Point. This was done successfully and then White Horse Harry Lee made a small raid also, with little loss. But these were small victories, and for the most part, the army sat quietly as the fall turned into winter. Finally Washington pulled his tattered remnants of an army into Morristown, and almost as soon as they were settled, one of the most terrible episodes in the country's history began.

None of the trials of the Continental Army, not even the ordeal of Valley Forge, could be compared to this winter. It was a bitterly cold crucible, so cold that the New York harbor froze over. Howling blizzards lashed Morristown, and the officers as well as the enlisted men were practically buried by the deep drifts of snow after the screaming winds had blown their ragged tents away. Many of the soldiers who had neither tents nor blankets, but were barefooted and half-naked, struggled to build crude huts out of the trees that had survived.

George Washington wrote to a friend, "We have never experienced a like extremity at any period of the war. We have not at this day one ounce of meat, fresh or salt, in the magazine."

As the food supplies dwindled to nothing and the Continentals were practically dying of starvation, the country around waxed fat. The harvest that year had been bountiful. Washington's only choice was to commandeer supplies, and he was hated for it. Alexander Hamilton summed it all up when he wrote, "We began to hate the country, for it neglected us. The country begins to hate us for our oppressions of them."

Dake Bradford and his brother Micah were two of those who endured the bitter cold at Morristown. Dake was a sergeant, and Micah was a chaplain, an officer in name.

A pale, harsh sun lit up the barren Morristown landscape, with the snow broken only by trees and crude huts. Inside one of these so poorly built that the wind whistled through cracks an inch wide from the shrunken logs, Micah and Dake sat on boxes toasting bread over a small fire. The two of them wore thick beards, for shaving was impossible.

"I wish I were home," Dake said mournfully. "I miss Jeanne and the baby."

"I wish you were too," Micah said.

"I guess you'd like to be home yourself. Awful to have to leave a new bride."

Micah Bradford ordinarily weighed a hundred and eighty pounds, but like all the others, he was down to a scrawny frame and weighed no more than one fifty-five. He had straw-colored hair and hazel eyes and was slow to speak. Dake had the same colored hair and the same eyes but was tougher. He was impulsive, outspoken, and fiery tempered. Though the two were very different, they were also very close.

Micah suddenly lifted his head. "Somebody's coming."

The two men were both too tired to get up. Finally the door opened, and they managed to stand to their feet. "General Von Steuben!" Micah said with surprise.

"Yah," Von Steuben said. "I bring you a visitor. Come in, Lieutenant."

Jacob Steiner stepped in the door. He was wearing a tattered uniform from what he had pieced together and was as unnaturally lean as the Bradfords. Von Steuben was chubby as always. No one could figure how he stayed fat on the slender rations, but he and Henry Knox seemed to be able to live on acorns or something, for they both were heavyset men.

"General, have some toast."

Von Steuben knew that food was scarce, but he also knew how to win men's confidence. He sat down on the box that Micah offered and took a fragment of toast and chewed on it thoughtfully. "When spring comes it vill be better, yah?" His English was better now, but he still used Jacob to translate his more complicated orders. When he had first arrived at Valley Forge to help Washington train his raw, starving troops, he had spoken almost no English. He had cursed, it was said, in four languages, but he had been glad when Jacob Steiner had appeared speaking perfect English and German.

"What's happening, General? When are we going to fight again?" Dake asked.

"I vish I could tell you, but who knows what those Englishmen are thinking." He swallowed the morsel of toast, then said, "I tell you vat I think. I think they go south to fight."

"South! Why do you think that, General?" Micah asked quickly.

"Because they cannot seem to win any battles in the north," Von Steuben said cheerfully. "Besides, we haf information that has come. The English always think that there are so many loyalists that are faithful to the king that they vill rise up and vin the war, but it vill not happen!"

"No, it won't," Micah said. He looked over and grinned at Steiner. "Well, Lieutenant, we're a pair of new bridegrooms with no brides."

Jacob Steiner was a tall man with blond hair and blue eyes and a cheerful spirit. Now he said, "It was hard to leave Rachel, but she understands. This war must be won."

He reached into his pocket and said, "That is why I came. A letter has come for both of you."

Micah took the letter and opened it. He scanned it and with a startled voice said, "It's bad news!"

"What is it? Somebody sick?" Dake asked quickly, thinking of Jeanne and the baby.

"It's Matthew. Rachel says he's back in Boston."

"Back in Boston! I thought he was in England."

"He was, but he evidently came home and got pneumonia on the ship. He came back two weeks ago according to the letter, and the doctor doesn't give him much hope."

Dake's lips tightened. "Poor Matthew. He just can't make it, can he? I thought he was all set when he got a title and all that money and land."

"That doesn't buy happiness. You know that, Dake," Micah said. He looked up and said, "General, we're going to have a prayer meeting for our brother. You can join in if you please."

"And you, Jacob, you're part of the family."

The general pulled off his hat. "I am not a praying man, but I vill stay. We need all the Bradford men we can get."

The soldiers all bowed their heads and Micah led in prayer. In the coldness of the tent, Jacob Steiner seemed to feel a warmth. He had given up on life when he had been snatched up and thrown into the war as a Hessian soldier, but now he knew he had found his place. In Rachel Bradford he had a wife that was better than any woman he had ever seen, and although he did not know Matthew Bradford well, he prayed along with the rest.

When the prayer ended, Von Steuben said, "Good. Now God vill have to do it."

"Yes, He will, General," Micah said. After the general had left, he said, "It's going to be a battle, according to what Rachel says."

"Well, he'll make it. We'll just bombard heaven until God has to make Matthew well."

🔔　　🔔　　🔔

The darkness that had surrounded him seemed to break apart and shatter. A bright light came to him, and he opened his eyes just a slit. He closed them again quickly. His throat was as dry as dust, and his tongue felt thick. Opening his eyes a bit more, he saw a face, and after a moment, it swam into focus.

"Jeanne," he whispered.

Jeanne Bradford had been dozing in the chair, but she came awake instantly. Rising, she bent over and studied the pale, drawn face. "Well," she said. "You've come out of it." Satisfaction was in her voice and she put her hand on his head. "Your fever's down." She saw that his eyes were clear, and quickly she poured a cup of water. "Here, drink this." She had been giving him all the fluids she could, simply moistening his lips at times with a damp cloth. Now he took several gulping swallows, and then she put his head back. "You've got to drink all you can, Matthew."

"Where am I?"

"You're home in Boston. This is your old room."

Matthew tried to turn his head, but the effort was too much. He simply closed his eyes and fell back into a deep sleep.

Jeanne, however, knew that a crisis had passed. She left the room at once and found Keturah in the kitchen. "Keturah, go to the foundry and tell Father that Matthew is conscious again, that he's better."

Keturah exclaimed, "That's wonderful! I'll go tell Abigail, too. She's about worn herself out as much as the rest of us taking care of him."

"Yes, you do that. She'll want to hear."

🔔　　🔔　　🔔

When Matthew awoke for the second time it was easier. He simply opened his eyes and stared around the room. The events came flooding back to him, and he saw a woman with her back to him standing across the room at a window. "Jeanne," he said, "I'm thirsty."

Then when the woman turned around, he saw that it was not Jeanne. "Abigail . . ." he whispered.

Abigail came over at once and poured a glass of water. She lifted his head and said firmly, "Drink this."

Matthew drank several swallows, and then when she laid his head back, he said, "I didn't expect to see you here. As a matter of fact, I didn't expect to see anybody."

"You've been very sick, but you're going to be better now."

"I thought . . . I'd die on that ship."

"It was a very close call," Abigail said. Her eyes were gentle as she laid her hand on his forehead. Her hand was cool, and she said, "Your fever is practically gone. We've had to fight, keeping it down with wet cloths. I've never seen such a fever, and neither has the doctor."

Matthew licked his lips and said, "I'm hungry." There was surprise in his voice, and he added, "I haven't been hungry in so long."

"You be still. I'll go get you something light."

Matthew lay there, lifted his arm once, and was shocked at how thin it was. He clasped his fingers and thought back over all that had happened.

Soon Abigail was back with a bowl of steaming broth, and she said, "You will have to sit up."

Matthew tried, but he was too weak. Firmly she reached down, put her arms around his chest, and with one motion straightened him so that he was sitting up, his back against the headboard. She put a pillow behind him and said, "Here." He tried to hold the spoon, but his hand was trembling.

"Here, let me do that. You're as weak as a baby," Abigail said. Carefully she took a spoonful of the broth, blew on it until it was cool, then fed it to him.

"I hate to be fed like a baby," Matthew protested.

"Don't say a word. God has done a miracle in bringing you through, and I just thank Him for it."

Matthew ate all of the broth, and then when she asked him if he wanted to lie down again, he said, "No. Let me sit up awhile."

Pulling a chair close, Abigail sat down beside him. He was still light-headed, and there was a dreamlike quality to her as she sat there. The pale sunlight came through the window, making a halo of light around her hair. He had always loved her hair, and now he studied her face. He finally said, "I don't know how to thank you, Abigail. There's no reason why you should do this for me."

She did not answer, and the memory of the recent past leaped into his mind. It was the first time he had been awake enough to think about it, and a deep regret gripped his spirit. He dropped his head and was silent for a long time.

"Are you feeling worse?" Abigail asked. She leaned over and put her hand on his head again.

"No. I think I'm over the worst of it." He hesitated, struggling with the weight of his failure. He knew that he was going to have to explain it all to his family, which was going to be hard. He remembered how close he and Abigail had been at one time, and suddenly he knew that he had to confess to her what an utter fool he had been.

"I've got to tell you something, Abigail. You're always good at keeping a secret—not that it matters. Everybody will find out sooner or later."

Abigail studied his face. "What is it, Matthew?" she asked quietly. "Is it trouble?"

"The most trouble a man can have. I made a fool out of myself in England."

"I can testify that most of us have done that," Abigail said. Her voice held no bitterness, however, and an encouraging light shone in her eyes. "Whatever you've done, your family will still love you. You know that."

"I don't see how they can. I've been crazy."

"Do you want to tell me about it?"

Slowly Matthew dropped his head. "I guess I do." He began haltingly, and the shame that weighed so heavily turned like a knife inside him. He told her the whole fracas, how he had fallen prey to a pair of sharks and lost his inheritance. He did not leave out his infatuation with Stella Aumont. By the time he had finished, his voice was a whisper, and torment filled his eyes as he finally lifted them to hers. "I thought I'd done every fool thing a man can do, but I underestimated the stupidity that's in me."

The silence in the room was broken only by the sound of faint voices, outside and far away, that came through the closed window. And from somewhere in the house came the sound of Jeanne's voice as she sang a lullaby to the baby.

Abigail knew that this was a delicate moment. She had loved this man for a long time, and he had utterly rejected her. Since she had come to know the Lord, she had learned to pray and to give the Lord time to speak to her and through her. Now, after a lengthy silence in which Matthew said not a word, she said firmly, "You're alive. Soon you will be healthy. You have a marvelous talent, Matthew, for painting, that I think is a gift from God. You have the best family that I have ever known in my life. You have what many men would die for."

"But I've lost my entire inheritance."

"And do you think that would matter to God? He's not interested in your wealth or your title but in *you*, in Matthew Bradford. He loves you, Matthew, and He knew all this was going to happen before it happened."

Matthew was shocked by that. "I never thought of that," he muttered. "Why didn't He stop me?"

"Because He made you with a free will. He pleads with us and sends the Holy Spirit to speak to our hearts, but He will not stop us if we're determined to sin against Him. But I know one thing. God is merciful and forgiving. He's far closer to us than we know, Matthew. Whatever you've done, it didn't disappoint God. You can't disappoint him. You can grieve Him, but that's a different thing."

For a long time Abigail Howland sat there talking to Matthew about the Lord. She herself had gone through a dark night of the soul much like Matthew was enduring right now. She knew what a breaking heart was, and she knew what a misery it was to realize that sin had yielded its harvest. As she spoke, she studied his face. It was such a sensitive face, not roughly handsome like Dake's or dignified like Micah's, but aristocratic, as she knew his father's had been. She knew the devastation would hurt Matthew Bradford far more than it would hurt Dake or Micah. They were stronger and tougher and did not have Matthew's sensitivity.

Finally he looked at her with misery and said, "I'm such a mess, Abigail."

Abigail suddenly reached forward. She put her fingers on his lips and whispered, "It doesn't matter, Matthew. All that matters is that God has spared your life, and He still wants all that you have."

🛡   🛡   🛡

Clive Gordon arrived at Daniel's house, pulling up in front with a wagon that seemed to be loaded. When he jumped out and tied up, he went at once to the door. The snow had melted somewhat, but he knew another storm would bring more soon. He knocked on the door, and Keturah answered. He reached out and took her hands, his face touched with the cold, but healthy looking and strong. "Keturah, you're getting prettier all the time."

"Mr. Gordon, I'm so surprised to see you! What are you doing here?"

Clive stepped inside as Keturah stepped back. He pulled off his coat and cap, and she hung them on the peg on the wall. "I came back from Morristown to get some supplies. I've got a wagonload of food out there, and some medicine. But I heard about Matthew and I want to see him."

"Come along. He's in the parlor."

"How's he doing?"

"Much better. He's sitting up now. He's very weak, though."

Clive followed Keturah into the parlor, and Matthew said at once, "I saw you out the window, Clive. What are you doing here?"

Clive came over and shook hands, noting the thinness of Matthew's hand. He explained what he was doing and said, "I want to give a report to Micah when I go back. You're looking good."

Matthew laughed shortly. "If a corpse can look good, I guess I look good. I bet I don't weigh a hundred and thirty pounds."

"You're on the mend, though, and you've got some good cooks here. You'll get your strength back and some pounds with their good food," Clive said. He sat down and spoke cheerfully to Matthew, storing it all up so that he could give a good report. "Why don't you write to Dake and Micah? I'll take the letter back."

"All right." He raised his voice and said, "Abigail!"

Abigail Howland appeared at the door and said, "Hello, Mr. Gordon."

"Why, hello, Abigail. It's so good to see you. Have you turned nurse?"

"The best nurse in the world," Matthew said. "I've got three women waiting on me here hand and foot. Not bad, eh?"

"Not bad," Gordon smiled. He was well aware of the checkered history of these two and wondered what would become of it. "Matthew is going to write to Micah and Dake. Would you get him a paper, please?"

"Yes, I will. I'll even write it for you if you want me to."

"That would be good. Your writing is better than mine."

"I'll just go on in the kitchen and see if I can find something to eat, if you don't mind," Clive said. "I'm saving everything on the wagon for the fellows back in Morristown."

Going into the kitchen, Clive found Keturah peeling potatoes. She got up at once and her eyes lit up. "Mr. Gordon," she said.

"Oh, come now. You can call me Clive. We're practically family, aren't we?"

Keturah said, "I'd like to think of it that way. I just made some donuts. Would you like some?"

"Would I! Try me." Clive sat down and proceeded to fill himself up on donuts and tea. He listened as Keturah spoke, and finally he said, "You're a good cook, Keturah."

"Thank you, Clive."

"I came by to see Matthew, but mostly I came to see you."

"Me! You came to see me, Clive? Why?"

Clive shifted in his seat and ran his hand over his thick brown hair. "We've got a problem. It's my sister, Grace."

"Is she ill?" Keturah asked at once.

"Well, she's having a baby, and evidently it's not a good pregnancy. She's having a hard time of it. I wish I could go be with her, but I can't get leave. She's not one to complain much, but she wrote me asking if I could help her."

"Oh, what a shame! But surely they'll let you go if she's in danger."

"I tried, but General Greene says I'm going to be needed, and I guess he's right. We've got so many sick men at camp, I work at it from dawn until dark."

Keturah was studying him carefully. "Why did you want to see me?"

"Well, I'm going to ask a favor, Keturah," Clive said simply. "And you say no if you please. It won't make any difference. I won't be upset."

Keturah said, "I'll do anything I can for your sister."

"I don't know. You haven't heard what I'm going to ask yet." Clive hesitated and then said, "She needs a woman there with her, Keturah. Someone who will take good care of her. She's evidently unable to do many things for herself. I'd like to hire you to go and stay with her."

Keturah was taken aback. "You mean all the way to South Carolina?"

"I know it's a long way, and it's asking a lot, but I couldn't think of anyone else. All of the Bradfords talk about how you practically run this house, so I just thought I'd come and ask."

"Well, I'm no nurse. You know that, Clive."

"I think she needs someone to talk to more than she needs a nurse, although there's that too. I'd be glad to pay you well for going, Keturah."

"It's not a matter of money. I'd have to ask Mr. Bradford."

"Well, you won't like this, but I've already asked him."

"What did he say?"

"He said the decision is yours. He's very fond of Grace. He doesn't have many relatives, you know, and he's worried about her. So are my parents."

Keturah did not hesitate. "If Mr. Bradford says it's all right, then I'll be glad to do all that I can."

Relief washed over Clive's face. "You don't know how good that makes me feel, Keturah. I'll arrange for your trip down there. It'll be a hard one in winter, but it'll all be taken care of. You start getting your things together, and whenever you say, I'll make the arrangements."

"I can be ready anytime. I don't have many things to take."

"Would tomorrow be too soon?"

"Not at all."

Still Clive hesitated. "I feel rather awkward about this. Are you sure you can do it? I know you have a comfortable place here, and the family loves you."

But Keturah Burns was ready for a change. She did not say so, but the constant pressure of Sam's courtship was becoming oppressive to her. She had actually been thinking of leaving anyway, and here was a perfect opportunity. With a bright smile, she said, "It's just what I need, a little change. And maybe I can help your sister."

Clive then slapped his leg and got up. "Wonderful!" he exclaimed. "I'll go make the arrangements. You get ready to go, and I'll be back later to tell you what they are."

Keturah watched as the tall physician left, and then she turned and stood still for a moment in the middle of the kitchen. "Sam will be terribly disappointed, but it will be good for me to be away for a time."

9

MISSION OF MERCY

THE WINDOW OF DANIEL BRADFORD'S OFFICE looked down on the open yard beneath where the supplies consumed by the foundry were stacked. It was crowded now with stacks of material and bars of iron to be used in the manufacture of equipment for the Continental Army. As Daniel moved over to look down, he was surprised to see his son Sam sitting on a barrel and staring down at the ground.

"Well, that's a peculiar thing," Daniel murmured. "I don't see Sam that still very often."

For a few moments he stood there expecting that Sam would get up and throw himself into the work, for he was an energetic young man. Instead of that, Sam sat like a statue, his hands clasped before him. His son's strange behavior troubled Daniel, and he abruptly turned and left the office. Passing through the foundry, he stepped outside into the bright sunlight. The new year had come, bringing warmer weather, and now the sun shone brightly and had melted away the snows of winter. The yard was muddy from the melted snow, and he picked his way carefully, avoiding the worst of the spots until he came to stand directly in front of Sam.

"Well, Sam, what's going on?"

Sam was startled, for he had been deep in thought. He blinked, shoved his hat back on his head, exposing his auburn hair, and muttered, "Nothing, Pa. Just thinking."

Studying the young man who was so different from the rest of his children, Daniel did not plunge at once into the matter by asking questions. He began talking about a new project Sam had been interested in, a new type of machine that would turn out buttons for the Continental Army at a tremendous rate of speed. Sam had been working on it, and now for a time, Daniel spoke of the invention. But he saw that

Sam's eyes did not light up as they usually did when his inventions were the subject of conversation. Finally he hesitated, then said, "You seem a little down in the mouth today, son."

Looking up, Sam did not speak for a moment, and then he shrugged his broad shoulders. "I guess we all get that way from time to time."

A thought came to the older man. *It must be that he's pining over Keturah. He hasn't been the same since she went to South Carolina.* Carefully he said, "Anything I can do?"

"I guess not, Pa." Sam heaved a big sigh and said, "I guess I'm worried about some things."

"I'd like to hear about them if you'd care to tell me."

"In the first place, I miss Keturah something terrible," Sam said.

"Well, I guess I knew that. We all do. She brings a light into the house. It seems like it's not the same with her gone, but she's doing a good work there with Grace."

"Oh, I know that, Pa. I just miss her, I guess."

"Well, maybe after the baby's born she'll come back," Daniel said.

Sam did not answer. His mouth was pulled down into a frown, and he shook his head, saying quickly, "It's not only that. I feel terrible about Jubal. He got himself captured so the rest of us could get away, and now he's wasting away in one of those hulks."

For a moment Daniel did not reply. He balanced in his mind how much he could tell Sam, for ever since Jubal had been captured, he had been working on a plan to get him released. He had said nothing of this to Sam because it was not at all certain that he could do it, and he did not want to raise false hope. But now he thought the plan had gone far enough that he could share it with Sam.

"I haven't said anything about this," he said carefully, "but I've been working on a plan to get Jubal exchanged."

Instantly Sam's face lit up and his eyes brightened. "Exchanged! You mean traded for another prisoner?"

"Yes. It happens all the time, but I wasn't too familiar with the mechanics of it. I asked some of my friends at Washington's headquarters to look into it, and I've written a couple of letters. I don't want to get your hopes up, but it looks as though there may be a chance to get Jubal exchanged."

Sam came down off the barrel with a bound and grabbed his father's arm. "Do you really think so? When could we get him out? What can I do?" He peppered his father with questions and finally said, "Come on, Pa. I want to do something."

"Well, as a matter of fact, I think you might be a help. The way this business works is there are two boards of exchange, one for the British and one for our side. Each of them has a list of all the prisoners that the other side has. What has to happen is you have to trade even."

"What do you mean trade even, Pa?"

"Well, I mean like you trade a lieutenant for a lieutenant. A colonel for a colonel. Like that."

"But Jubal wasn't really in the army or the navy."

"I know, but he was captured by a naval force, and they treat privateers the same as if they were in the Continental Army."

"Well, what have you found out?"

"It's been very tricky, Sam. I asked Clive if he had any friends in that department, and it turned out that before he left, he had become fairly well acquainted with the officer in charge of their prisoner exchanges. His name is Maurice Devon. So I had Clive look into the matter. He didn't go directly to Devon because, as you can imagine, since Clive left the British army and came over to our side, he's not in the best of favor. But he has a good friend there that still thinks a lot of him, and he's handling it."

"What did he say?"

"He said it wouldn't be any problem, but it would cost money."

Sam stared at his father. "You mean they sell the prisoners?"

Daniel smiled frostily, a cynical look in his eyes. "I guess men are swayed in all nations at all times by money. This fellow Devon is a corrupt fellow, so Clive tells me, but for fifty guineas in gold, he'll exchange Jubal for one of their sailors."

"Have we got the money, Pa?"

"Yes, I think so, and I believe we owe it to Jubal. He's a fine fellow and was doing a good job."

Sam was almost hopping with excitement. "Let's do it, Pa! I'll take care of it if you'll just give me the money."

"Wait a minute! Hold on! It's not that easy," Daniel protested. "We have to work through our exchange board, and someone will have to take a prisoner to New York—and the money. It's a touchy business, and I'm not sure you're the one to do it."

"Why not, Pa?"

"Sam, you're a great inventor, but you're not the most patient fellow in the world. This Captain Devon is probably going to be hard to deal with, and whoever goes will just have to bite his lip and take whatever insults he hands out. He could trick you, you know. He could take the money and then not let Jubal go."

Sam grew serious at once. "Let me do it," he said quietly. "I know

I've acted a fool in so many ways, but Jubal's my friend, and I feel responsible for him. I promise I'll put my feelings in a box. I'll do whatever this captain says, and I'll stay there until I get Jubal out. Trust me, will you, Pa?"

Suddenly Daniel Bradford saw a new side to his son. Sam had always been a helter-skelter young scamp who was into everything and always out to have fun. But lately he had seen some changes, and it pleased him. "All right, Sam," he said. "I think you can do it. It will take a while to get it all arranged, but just as soon as we get the ends tied up, we'll do it."

Sam knew that his father was putting a trust in him that he never had before. He felt determined to carry out this mission at whatever cost. Quietly he stood there for a moment and nodded. "I'll do it, Pa. It's time I grew up."

🔔   🔔   🔔

The last of the afternoon light was flowing over the garden where Matthew stood before a canvas. Molly, the calico cat, lay sleeping in front of him, her front paws dropped over the stone wall that surrounded the small garden, and her tail dropped over the other side. Matthew carefully added a touch to the canvas, then studied the animal carefully. Her coloring was so unusual that it had been a real challenge for him to paint. She was a mixture of gray, red, tan, and orange all blended together and yet standing out separately. A look of frustration swept across his face, and he gnawed his lower lip, muttering, "I'll never get it right."

"Yes, you will."

Matthew turned around to see his father standing behind him. He had been so intent that he had not heard his footsteps on the stone walkway. Now grinning sheepishly, he said, "I didn't hear you. You shouldn't sneak up on a fellow that way."

"I like to sneak up on people," Daniel said cheerfully and came over to stand squarely in front of the canvas.

The two men made a contrast in almost every way. Matthew was slender, especially since his illness, his face almost delicate and aristocratic with a thin nose and pale complexion. Daniel was thickened by years of hard labor, weathered by the elements, and the inner strength showed in the rugged features of his face. His hands, unlike Matthew's, were toughened and scarred by labor, and now as he stroked his cheek, he said, "I'm no judge, but it looks good to me. I just don't see how you do that, Matthew. I'd spend a lifetime and not be able to draw a picture."

The praise warmed Matthew. His father had always been supportive of his talent, and now for the first time since coming home, Matthew knew that he had to speak his heart. "I've been wanting to talk to you, Father," he said. He cleaned the brush out carefully, put it down on the table beside the easel, then turned to face him. "I can't tell you how stupid I feel over the way I've behaved. A child could have made better decisions. I don't think I'll ever be able to get over it. . . ."

Listening patiently until Matthew finally finished and ended with his head hanging down, Daniel Bradford said quickly, "I suppose we all feel as you do when we've done something foolish, but you're young and your whole life is before you, Matthew. You've got a great talent, and God has given you something in your hands and your eyes that other men don't have. It's a great gift to be able to share things like this." He motioned toward the painting, and his voice grew warm with enthusiasm. "Why, that picture you painted of Marian, I can't tell you what a blessing it's been to me. Almost every day I stop and look at it. Somehow you've captured the essence of her spirit, and not only her outward beauty, but what's inside. And it just does something to me. You should feel good about that."

"Do you really mean that, Father?"

"Of course I do. Tell me, Matthew, are you really sad about the loss of the title?"

"No!" Matthew said almost explosively. "That title didn't mean a thing to me. As a matter of fact, from the moment I decided to take it I knew I was wrong. I'm Matthew Bradford—not Matthew Rochester. I'm sorry I ever got involved."

"Well, is it the money, then?"

"No. Not even that. I know that I'm not going to starve, and I saw enough people burdened down with money who were miserable and unhappy. No. It's just that I made such bad decisions."

"We all do that. Living is making decisions, and some of them are bad. You might as well get used to it." Daniel hesitated for a moment and said cautiously, "You know, I've seen your unhappiness since you've been back and even before you left. Can I ask you a very personal question?"

"Why, certainly. Go ahead."

"I don't know your heart, but I just wondered if somehow your unhappiness isn't tied to your feelings for Abigail."

Instantly Matthew dropped his head. He fidgeted and picked up a brush and twirled it around his fingers. His silence ran on so long that Daniel thought he was not going to answer. Finally, however, he lifted his eyes and met his father's. Shrugging his shoulders, he said, "I think I've been a fool about Abigail too."

"I think she's become one of the finest young women I've ever known, Matthew," Daniel said. "She made her mistakes when she was younger, but as the Scripture says, 'If thou, Lord, shouldest mark iniquities, O Lord, who shall stand?' I'm glad God doesn't hold all of our sins and indiscretions before His eyes and constantly look at them. I'm glad He puts them away from us. He says He puts our sins as far away from us as the east is from the west."

Matthew listened as his father spoke of Abigail, and finally he nodded and said, "In all that you're right. I've had bitterness against Abigail, but I think it's gone now. It took getting knocked flat on my back and nearly dying in order to see some of the things that were in my life."

"Well, 'Whom the Lord loveth he chasteneth,' the Scripture says." Daniel put his arm around Matthew and squeezed his shoulders. "We have to go from where we are."

"I feel that my life has been a total failure."

"Well, it hasn't been. No son of mine can be a total failure." Daniel squeezed Matthew again. "I won't put up with it. Come on, now. Paint that cat."

Matthew suddenly laughed. "All right. I don't know where in the world I'm going with my life or what I'm going to do. I don't have a dime, and I'm living off of your charity, but I'll paint that cat."

🛡   🛡   🛡

The sun was warm on his back as Sam stepped out of the carriage and paid his fare. The driver, a thickset individual with a mouth full of gold teeth, grinned broadly, the sunlight catching his display. "Thank you, sir. Very generous of you, I'm sure."

Sam nodded and turned to look at the large, insignificant gray building that occupied a space between two larger ones. There was no sign, but the driver had assured him that this was part of the British army headquarters. A tall man dressed in a crimson jacket of His Majesty's forces was passing by, and Sam stepped toward him. "Pardon me, sir. Could you tell me, is that the Department of Prisoner Exchange?"

"Yes, that's it." The soldier nodded and said no more but went on his way.

Sam reached to his chest and touched the heavy weight of gold coins

110

that occupied his pocket. It was the cash that he had brought to effect the delivery of Jubal Morrison. It had taken several weeks, but his father had persevered, and having friends in high places, he was finallly able to obtain an exchange. It had been a rather delicate operation, for it amounted to bribing an officer of His Majesty's service. Captain Devon was a crafty man, but all had been arranged by James Smith, the friend of Clive who was in a regiment—the Royal Fusiliers—stationed in New York.

Now all was done, however, and Sam turned to the prisoner, a short stocky man named Holmes with short-clipped black hair and a pair of muddy brown eyes. "Come along, Holmes," he said.

"Aye, sir."

Holmes followed obediently half a step behind Sam. "Can't thank you enough, sir, for getting me out of that jail."

"Well, I'm glad you're out, Holmes. What will you do now? Enlist in the navy again?"

"Never enlisted in the first place," Holmes said mournfully. "I was a pressed man."

"Is that so?"

"Oh yes, sir. I had no dogs in this fight over here. I'm a printer, or an apprentice at least. I was on my way home to my family when I was snatched up. Next thing I knew I was on a man-o'-war. It was downright miserable, I can tell you that, sir. Not much better than the prison."

Sam listened as Holmes continued to speak, and then the two entered the building. They looked around the room where a sergeant sat at a desk with a stack of papers before him. Moving in front of the desk, Sam said, "I'm here on the business of exchanging a prisoner."

"You have the papers?"

"Yes. Right here."

The sergeant took them and ran his eyes over them in a bored fashion. "You have to see Captain Devon."

"Where will I find him, Sergeant?"

"Down that hall. Third door to the right. Is that the prisoner?"

"Yes."

"You can leave him here. I'll take his papers."

Sam surrendered the papers, nodded to Holmes, and then moved down the hall. When he reached the door indicated by the sergeant, he knocked and a voice said at once, "Come on in!"

Entering the office, Sam found himself confronted by a corporal who stared at him and said, "What is it!" in a gruff voice.

Sam said, "I'm here to talk to Captain Devon about a prisoner exchange."

"You'll have to wait. He's busy. You can take that seat if you want to wait."

Sam did not answer. He had determined before leaving home that he would not lose his temper under any circumstances. Now he took the seat and for the next hour forced himself to remain still. Several people came and went into the office, but he was not called. Finally the corporal stepped inside and after a few moments exited. "You can go in now," he said, gesturing toward the door.

"Thank you, Corporal." Sam got up with alacrity and hurried into the office. Once inside he found himself facing a pale-faced man of medium height with gray eyes and gray hair to match. He was in his midfifties, Sam estimated, and had a sour look. His mouth was twisted like a fishhook, and his eyes scanned Sam in one contemptuous motion as he picked up a paper and dipped his pen in ink.

"Well, what can I do for you, sir?" he asked gruffly.

"I'm here to effect the exchange of a prisoner, Captain."

Devon looked up. "What's your name?"

"Sam Bradford, sir."

"You're not in the army."

"No, sir, I'm not. I was asked to take care of this exchange because there was no one else."

"What's the prisoner's name?"

"Jubal Morrison, Captain."

"What was his unit?"

"He was not in the regular forces," Sam said carefully. It would not do to tell Devon that he himself had been in the privateering affair with Morrison. "He was an operating privateer of what we call a spidercatcher and was captured by one of your gunboats."

"There's nothing I can do about it. You'll have to go through proper channels."

"But, Captain Devon," Samuel said quickly. "If you would just hear me out, I think you might want to consider it a little bit more carefully. I believe Lieutenant Smith might have mentioned this exchange to you."

A light suddenly touched the cold eyes of Captain Devon, and Sam knew that it was greed. "Smith? Let me see. Oh yes, he did mention some sort of exchange, I believe."

Sam knew that he had to behave very carefully.

"Lieutenant Smith is no relation to the prisoner nor to me, but another friend became interested. I know, Captain, that these things are tedious and that there are ... expenses involved. And, of course, I wouldn't want His Majesty's government to be out any money on this affair."

"These things do cost money," Devon said smoothly. "You wouldn't believe how much. What about the man you're exchanging?"

"His name is Holmes, sir. He's a member of the Royal Navy. He's outside with your corporal."

"And they trusted you to bring him, did they?"

"Yes, sir. He's not going anywhere. I kept close watch on him. He's glad to be out of prison and back in His Majesty's service."

"Well, he should be! These rotten patriots ought to be shot! If I had my way, we'd hang every one we caught."

Sam's face did not move a muscle. He stood there while Devon raved about the Americans, cursing and calling them every name he could think of with his face growing flushed.

"Well, I'm not sure it can be done. It is expensive."

"Yes. My friend who is interested in Mr. Morrison knew that it would be. He suggested that fifty guineas would cover it, but I told him that it ought to be at least seventy-five." Reaching into his pocket he pulled out the heavy leather bag of gold coins and put it on the desk. It made a pleasant clicking sound, and Devon stared at it as if hypnotized.

Finally he looked up with a furtive glance and said, "These things have to be handled diplomatically. I can't give you any receipt."

"Oh, certainly not, Captain. That would be quite out of order."

Devon hesitated, and Sam knew that he was weighing the risk that he might be entering a trap. Sam had an innocent-looking face, and he managed to keep it so. He almost held his breath, knowing that Devon could have him arrested for bribing a king's officer. He had the evidence right before him, but that was a gamble he had decided to take.

"Very well," Devon said. He swept the bag of coins off the desk, dropped them into the drawer in front of him, then shuffled through some papers. Finding what he looked for, he ran his eyes down. "Yes. Here is Jubal Morrison. He's on the hulk, the *Marybelle*. I'll make out a release, and you will take it to the ship. Morrison will be released to your custody."

"Thank you very much, Captain."

The scratching of the pen was the only sound in the room, and when Devon had made out the form, he handed it to Sam, saying, "I want to hear no more about this matter, you understand."

"Certainly not, Captain. It's all over. You'll never see me again."

"See to it, then."

Sam turned at once, and it was all he could do to keep from shouting as he stepped outside. He sailed down the hall almost as fast as he could and said, "Good-bye, Holmes," and before the startled sailor could answer him, he asked, "Which way to the hulks, Sergeant?"

"To your right. You can't miss 'em."

The smell of the hulk announced the nature of its use before Sam got there. With five hundred men confined belowdecks, no light except for a few flickering candles, and terrible sanitary conditions, it was no surprise that many of them never lived to see the light of day again.

Sam had to remind himself, *No matter what you see, don't say anything*. He clutched the paper from Devon in his hand and ascended the gangplank. He was halted on deck by an armed marine with a musket.

"What's your business?"

"I have a release order from Captain Devon."

"Down the deck that way. You'll find Major Evanston in his cabin."

Major Evanston proved to be an old worn-out man, overweight and tired. He also seemed to be quite ill. He barely glanced at the order and said to the marine who had accompanied Sam, "Go bring Morrison out."

"Well, sir, I don't think he can walk."

"Well, carry him, then. Get what help you need."

Evanston stared at Sam, then said, "That will be all, I take it."

"Yes, Major. Thank you very much." Sam left the cabin and went back to the gangplank. It seemed to take a long time, and at any moment Sam was afraid he might be intercepted. Finally, however, he heard steps approaching and turned to see four sailors carrying a body in a blanket. He leaned over to look and would never have recognized Jubal Morrison, for the man he remembered was strong and healthy with a reddish complexion and bright eyes. The man he saw was nothing but skin and bones; he was pale and emaciated, with eyes blinking and a mouth twisted in a tight line.

"Hello, Jubal," he said.

Jubal Morrison had not been told why he was sent for. He had given up hope of getting off the hulk alive, and now he blinked like an owl in the bright sunlight until he focused on the face before him. "Sam," he croaked, his voice rusty from lack of use.

"You're free, Jubal. Just lie back and take it easy."

"I'm free?"

"You're free." Sam said no more but directed the sailors down the gangplank and to the carriage. He cautioned them as they put him inside, then thanked them. "Take us to a good inn, driver," he said.

"Aye, sir."

Sam got in the carriage and found that Jubal had barely managed to sit up. He smelled like the filth he had been confined in, and his whiskers stood out against his pale skin, but he was beginning to come to himself. "How'd you do it, Sam?" he whispered.

"I'll tell you all about it later. The first thing we've got to do is to get you settled. Could you eat something?"

"I could do with a bite," Jubal said, some of his old humor flickering in his eyes. He reached over and took Sam's hand and squeezed it. "I don't know how you did it, but I thank God for you, Sam Bradford."

Sam felt a lump in his throat. Jubal seemed to be reaching out for help, and Sam held his hand for a time, then put his free arm around Jubal and said, "It's going to be all right, my friend. We'll stick around here for a few days until you get some strength back, and then we'll head back to Boston."

Jubal could not speak. Sam saw tears gather in his friend's eyes, and then he turned his head and looked out the window to hide his emotion. Sam felt the thin body under his arm, and anger rose in him for what the war had done to his best friend.

Finally, as they rode along, Jubal asked, "Have you heard anything from my brother?"

"Yes. Grace isn't doing too well. Keturah went to take care of her until the baby comes."

This news caught at Morrison's interest. He turned around and studied Sam and managed a grin. "Lost your girl, did you?"

Sam Bradford grinned broadly and squeezed Jubal's thin shoulders. "Not for long," he said. "Not for long!"

10

A Time to Be Born

KETURAH ROSE UP FROM HER BED and shivered slightly as she dressed. She put on a white cotton chemise that was loose fitting, white undergarments, and a pair of white linen pantalettes ending just below the knee. She then slipped into a blue-and-white striped skirt, a light blue blouse, a striped cotton lawn cap, and a fuchsia muslin apron with bibbed cotton stockings. Leaving her small room on the second floor, she went downstairs and began to rekindle the fire. She had covered the hot coals with ashes, and now she raked them back and added splinters of pine until the fire caught. She carefully added to it until she had a good fire going, then went outside and filled two pails with fresh water from the well.

The sun began to peek through the windows as she started breakfast. Under her breath she softly sang a tune called "The Distressed Maiden," which told of the kidnapped boys and girls sent to the Colonies as bound servants:

> Five years served I, under Master Guy,
> In the land of Virginie, O,
> Which made me for to know sorrow, grief, and woe,
> When that I was weary, weary, weary, weary, O.

It was a mournful song, but Keturah loved songs of all kinds and was constantly singing. She had a clear voice, and when she lifted it in church, everyone turned around to look appreciatively.

In the fireplace she placed the Dutch oven, which had short legs to keep the bread above the hot coals. While the bread was baking, she heated the griddle for making johnnycakes, at which she had become an expert. She put the ingredients together quickly and then poured the

117

batter onto the griddle, using the spatula to keep them from burning.

As soon as the bread was done, she made dressed eggs. She did this by heating a salamander, a long-handled shovel, in the fire until it was red-hot. Then she cracked the eggs into a frying pan and cooked them over the fire. When the eggs were set but not hard, she held the salamander over the eggs to cook the tops.

She took the food from the kitchen to a sideboard in the dining room. It was a beautiful piece made of rosewood brought from somewhere far overseas, and she never passed it without running her hands over the smooth wood.

She went back to get the apple butter she had made the previous day. This was the one part of cooking she did not like. She had to stir a huge pot of hot apple mush over an outdoor fire until her arms ached, and she had to be very careful not to let her petticoats get too near the flames when the wind gusted.

Finally, when all was set, she left the kitchen and went down the hall. Knocking briefly on the door, she waited until a voice said faintly, "Come in."

Stepping inside she saw that Grace was waking up and struggling to get herself upright.

"Breakfast is ready, Miss Grace," she said cheerfully and went at once to help her remove the covers. She lifted Grace's feet over the side, then helped her stand up. "How do you feel this morning?"

"I can't complain."

"You never do," Keturah said. She had become very fond of Grace Morrison during the weeks she had been in the home. The work had not been too hard, and she had spent many hours reading to Grace or simply sitting with her, sewing or knitting. Keturah had been raised roughly and had learned more about childbearing from direct observation than most women of her age, and of late she had been concerned about Grace's condition. *She doesn't look well at all. I'm afraid this baby is going to get the best of her.*

But Keturah kept a smile on her face as she said, "Come along. I've got your breakfast ready."

"Oh, Keturah, I'm not hungry. I couldn't eat anything."

"To be sure you can. Don't argue with me."

Keturah held on firmly to Grace and helped her get into a light blue robe, then eased her feet into woolen shoes. "Here, I'll help you," she said and led Grace down the hall.

When she had Grace seated at the table, she went down and knocked on the master's door. The two had taken separate bedrooms since Grace was sleeping so fitfully, and Morrison opened the door at once and came out. He was already dressed, wearing a pair of plum-colored breeches stuffed down into black leather boots. He wore a white shirt and a square-cut gray waistcoat, and was, as usual, costumed for riding over the fields.

"Breakfast is ready, sir," Keturah said.

"All right. I'll be right in."

Keturah went back and got the plates from the kitchen. She kept a plate warmer there in front of the fireplace. As she opened the front of the plate warmer, she juggled the plates around, for they had become very hot from the fire.

Carrying the meals in, she set them down and waited as Morrison asked the blessing, which he did perfunctorily.

"And how do you feel this morning, my dear?" he asked.

"All right, Stephen."

Keturah gave Stephen Morrison a withering look. He had asked, but he had not listened to the answer, and he had not even given Grace more than a casual look. He began eating and paused only long enough to answer a question or two that Grace asked him. When he was finished, he rose, wiped his mouth on the white napkin, and threw it down. "I've got to go to the field over on the north section," he said. "I'll be back late this afternoon."

Grace looked up and turned her face toward him. Keturah, who was standing off to one side holding a teapot ready to refill her cup, saw the pathetic look on her face and knew that Grace was hoping that her husband would come over and say something kind and gentle to her. Keturah felt a flush of anger as Stephen stood up and left the house without another word.

She came over, poured more tea for Grace, and then poured herself another cup. She sat down and began to talk about small, insignificant things. She could not help but notice that Grace's face was puffy and pale. Having this baby was proving to be hard on her, more so than on any woman she had ever seen, and now she asked as casually as she could, "Do you think it might be good to have the doctor in?"

"No. It's a month before the baby comes. What good could he do?"

The physician, Dr. McCormick, was a rough man and not at all interested in women having babies. He had made but one visit thus far and had given her a cursory once-over before leaving without offering any advice whatsoever.

Now Grace looked up and said, "I don't like that Dr. McCormick."

"Don't you, now? What's wrong with him?"

"He doesn't care anything about me. Only his fee. He told me that a midwife was all that I really needed."

Keturah was at a loss as to how to answer this. Finally she said, "Well, we'll do fine, you and I."

Grace gave Keturah a quick glance. "Have you ever actually seen a baby born, Keturah?"

"Oh yes! Three times, as a matter of fact."

"Did you help?"

"Well, I just did things like boiling water and cutting up bandages."

"Was it very hard on the mothers?"

As a matter of fact, it had been very hard on one of the mothers, but Keturah was not about to say so. "Oh, the babies were all born fine and healthy as you'd please. And the mothers all did very well, Miss Grace. After all, it's a natural thing, and God's going to bring you through it, and you're going to have a fine baby. Do you want a boy or a girl?" She had hoped to take Grace's mind off her discomfort but did not succeed.

"I don't really care as long as the baby's healthy," she murmured. "I think I'll go lie down again, Keturah."

"You do that. I'll come in after a time and bring you some more tea, and we'll read together."

🔔　　　🔔　　　🔔

When Stephen reached the north field, he found Taws, as usual, berating the field hands. Stephen had exhausted himself trying to get Taws to change his methods, but it did not seem to do much good. The overseer was a burly, harsh, stubborn man and would have his own way. Stephen had considered letting him go, but he could not be sure of getting anyone who was as effective. At least the work got done, although it could have been much more pleasant.

Taws turned, and as the two rode along the field, Taws pointed out the harvest and the work that had yet to be done.

"Have you heard any more of Francis Marion?" Stephen asked. "There's been some raiding over to the east of us."

"He's not been around here," Taws said, "and I'm thankful for that. But he's not the only one. If I were you, I'd hire some more help. Men that can shoot. We wouldn't have a chance against an attack from Marion or Pickens or some of the others that keep pecking at the loyalists around here."

"Do you think they'll bother us?"

"Not Marion, but some of the others might."

The ever present threat disturbed Morrison greatly, and he thought about it all day. Money was short, and he did not have the funds to hire guards as Taws had suggested. It would be impossible, anyhow, for sometimes the raiders had as many as two hundred. The only security was that at the moment the Tories were in the majority, and they had several bands riding to and fro throughout the Peedee River section, too much for Marion or his fellow partisans to tackle.

Reaching the house, Stephen got off his horse awkwardly, handed the lines to a young slave boy, and without comment moved to the house. He intended to go to his room, but he was met by Keturah.

"Could I speak with you, Mr. Morrison?"

"With me? What about?"

Keturah lowered her voice and stepped closer. "It's about Miss Grace. I'm worried about her, sir."

"What's wrong? Has she been worse?"

"Not worse, exactly, but she's not doing well. You must have seen it."

"Well, that's what you're here for, isn't it, Keturah? To take care of her."

"Yes, sir," Keturah said, barely holding on to her temper. "But after all, sir, I'm not a doctor."

"Well, she's got Dr. McCormick. He promised to be here when the baby comes."

"I don't think she likes him very much. From what she's told me, he wouldn't be a very good doctor for a woman in her condition."

"Well, he's all there is," Stephen said shortly.

"I've been thinking, Mr. Morrison. Wouldn't it be better if Mrs. Morrison and I went to Charleston until the baby's born? There are good doctors there and a hospital."

Stephen hesitated and for a moment was almost ready to agree, but the finances were tight and he was pressured on every hand for money. "I don't think that would be necessary, Keturah. It's her first baby and she's a little concerned, but all first-time mothers, I suppose, have that problem. You just do the best you can, and we'll have Dr. McCormick here when the baby comes."

Without another word, he moved away and went at once to Grace's bedroom. Stepping inside, he walked over and said without preamble, "Keturah tells me you're not feeling well."

"Not . . . too well, dear."

"Well, this is probably the worst time, from what I hear. But in a few weeks it'll all be over, and we'll have our son or our daughter, and all will be well."

121

"Could you sit down and talk with me for a little, Stephen?"

Stephen moved nervously, then shrugged. "I suppose for a time. I have the bookwork to do, though." He sat down and said, "What would you like to talk about?"

"Oh, about the baby, about us, about what's going to happen."

Stephen Morrison tried to make conversation, but his mind was pre-occupied with the problems of running the plantation. It had been a far more difficult job than he had anticipated, and he had wished more than once that he had stayed with his business in New York. But it was too late now, and there was no turning back.

He studied Grace, and the thought came to him, *We married too quickly*. He was fond of Grace, but he saw now that it would have been better if he had come alone to the plantation. She was rather fragile, and although he knew nothing about having babies, he could see that she was losing more and more strength each day. "I wish your mother could have stayed with you," he said suddenly.

It was not much, but it was one of the few remarks he had made recently about her comfort. She reached out and took his hand, and he saw her eyes fixed on him and knew she was terribly worried. "Well, don't worry," he said. "It's a little hard right now, but it'll soon be over. You'll see." He patted her hand, and a few minutes later he said, "Well, I must do the books. We'll talk later."

Keturah was in the dining room polishing the silver when she glanced down the hall and saw Morrison enter his own bedroom. She put down the cloth and went to Grace's room and opened the door cautiously. She stopped abruptly when she saw Grace weeping, her face buried in her hands.

Keturah was a compassionate young woman. She had received little in her own life during her formative years. Only at the Bradford household had she learned what a comfort love could be. Now her heart swelled with indignation against Stephen Morrison but filled with compassion for Grace. She went over and sat down on the bed and put her arm around her. Grace turned and fell against her, and Keturah held her as she would a child. "Now, now," she said, "don't cry." She began to whisper comforts to her, but inwardly she was raging at a husband who would show no more concern for a sensitive, ailing wife than Stephen Morrison had.

For a long time she sat there, and then Grace said, "I declare. I don't know what's become of me. I've become a regular crybaby."

"You're not a crybaby. You're a woman having her first baby, and you're a long way from most of your family. But God is going to help you."

"You're a comfort, Keturah!"

Keturah did her work that day, but she paused in midafternoon while Grace was sleeping and wrote a fiery letter to Clive:

> Your sister is not doing well at all. I'm very concerned about her, Clive. She seems to have some physical problems that I can't explain. She has no appetite, and she's all swollen up more than she should be. Her circulation is poor, but I think her problem, Clive, is emotional. Her husband shows absolutely no concern. I've gone to him and asked him to let me take her to Charleston, where she could have better care. The doctor here is worthless according to Miss Grace. Stephen refuses, however, so there is nothing I can do. Please write and see if you can get your brother-in-law to agree to let me take her to Charleston.

She sealed the letter, but the post was slow, and she had little hope that it would get to Clive before the baby was born. Certainly there was little he could do anyway, but at least she had relieved her mind.

In the end, the letter never got mailed, for four days after Keturah had written it, Grace Morrison went into labor.

Keturah learned of it when a hand battered at her door in the middle of the night. She jumped up and cried out, "Who is it? What's wrong?"

"It's Grace. She's having the baby!"

"I'll be right there." Keturah jumped out of bed and threw her clothes on. She found Stephen Morrison pale-faced and shaken outside. "I'll ride for the doctor."

"It'll be too late," Keturah said, scorn withering in her voice.

"But what . . . what can we do?"

"Go get Annie."

"Annie? You mean the slave Annie?"

"Yes. She's helped before with birthing, and I know a little bit. Go get her."

Stephen was in no mood to question. He ran out of the house, and ten minutes later Annie came in. She was a strongly built woman of some thirty-five years with peaceful brown eyes and an air of efficiency in all she did. "Mr. Morrison say Miss Grace is birthin'."

"Yes, and there's no one to help but you and me."

Annie took a deep breath. "We'll do all right. We'll do all right. The good Lord will help us."

Indeed, the good Lord did help. The baby came after a surprisingly short two-hour period of labor. There were no complications, and as Keturah took the squalling red-faced infant from Annie—who grinned, and said, "He a fine boy"—she turned and moved to the bed.

"Here's your son, Grace," she whispered.

Grace lay still but her eyes fluttered open. She raised her arm, and when she received her infant son, she studied his face through half-closed eyes. "His name will be Patrick," she said. "That was my grandfather's name."

"He's a fine boy. Now you've got a baby to love."

For a moment Grace did not move, and then she kissed the baby's still damp forehead and gazed at him intently. She lifted her eyes then, and her voice was so soft that Keturah could not be sure that she understood. What she thought she heard was, "I can't love my husband, Keturah. I'll never love a man again."

11

A Tragic Ending

IT WOULD HAVE BEEN DIFFICULT to have found three men more different than the trio that sat around the table in an opulent drawing room: Sir Henry Clinton, Lord Charles Cornwallis, and Banastre Tarleton. Clinton had been appointed as commander to replace Sir William Howe as chief commander of the British army. Howe had been an ineffective officer in many ways. It was not that he was a poor tactician; quite the contrary. In six major battles against Washington's forces, Howe had always managed to turn the Americans' flank and position his troops in the rear. This was the approach that all armies traditionally had taken. It had never occurred to William Howe that it would take a much more aggressive grand strategy to put the final nail in the coffin of the American Revolution.

However, since Clinton had assumed command, he, too, had achieved little, except perhaps an adeptness at offering excuses why he could not pin Washington down. He was a short man, not impressive at all, when contrasted with the two officers who sat at the table with him.

Lord Charles Cornwallis was a heavyset man with a high forehead and a pair of clear gray eyes. He had been born into one of the oldest noble families in Britain and had built a successful career in the military. He had married, and upon the death of his father, he had taken his seat in the House of Lords, where he had rendered good service to his country. However, his wife had died, and her death had shattered Cornwallis. They had been closer than any couple among the royal set in England. He had asked for a commission, and Lord North had been eager to reinstate him as a major general. It was not what Lord Cornwallis wanted. He had never had an independent command, and now he sat toying with his glass thinking how much better than Henry

125

Clinton he would be at bringing the Revolution to an end.

The third man was the youngest and most impressive of the trio. Banastre Tarleton was short, powerfully built, and proud in bearing. His uniform was custom-made with a scarlet coat and a hat with a high plume on it. He had proved himself, under Cornwallis, an able commander of the Dragoons. Everyone, it seemed, in the high command understood that here was a bold young man, shrewd and quick to strike. Like many such commanders he was arrogant, insolent, and domineering, and in battle vindictive and bloodthirsty. He had made his name an anathema in the South and was feared and detested as Butcher Tarleton. Women threatened their children in Georgia and the Carolinas with "You be good or Ban Tarleton will get you."

The three men had come together at General Clinton's bidding, and now the two lower-ranked officers waited to see what their commanding officer would say.

Clinton, though he was not a man of firm decision, could give the appearance of such when he chose. He stuck his chin out and said with a firm determination, "I have decided to open the campaign."

"Indeed," said Lord Cornwallis, "I am happy to hear it." To himself he was thinking, *It's about time!* Henry Clinton could move slower than any officer in the British army.

"What will it be, sir?" Banastre Tarleton asked quickly. His bright eyes shone, for he was always anxious for battle.

"We are going to subjugate the South."

Both Tarleton and Cornwallis were not surprised at this. The situation in the North had deteriorated to such a point that absolutely nothing was taking place. Clinton had barricaded himself in New York. Washington was strong enough to take the city, and Clinton had lacked the aggressiveness to move out and run Washington into the ground.

"I agree with Lord George Germain," Clinton said, "that the South is Tory land. With Georgia, or at least the eastern half of it where the population lies, now restored to the Crown, we can use Savannah as a base to conquer the Carolinas. And from there it's a mere stepping-stone to Virginia."

"Do you think our forces are sufficient?" Cornwallis asked. He was always a man thinking of supplies, for he knew that any victory depended on sufficient food and munitions.

"Once we move in with our army," Clinton said, "the loyalists will rise up. We will see our forces swell as we liberate those who have been subjugated by these ragtag patriots."

"What is your plan, Sir Henry?" Cornwallis asked.

"I have been pondering a great deal our failure at Charleston in '76, and I think we should now have no trouble taking that city. Everything is in our favor. Our strength lies at twenty-five thousand men. That will be large enough to spare a sufficient body. Washington's army, wandering in New Jersey, will be too small to save the city and too far away, in any case, to make a winter's march through New Jersey, Delaware, Maryland, and Virginia. Then, of course, the rebels in the Carolinas are bound to be discouraged by the loss of Savannah."

"And the French are gone too," Tarleton said quickly.

"That's very true. We won't have anything to worry about there."

"I understand that General Lincoln is in charge at Charleston."

"Yes. Not a lucky general," Clinton grinned through fixed chops. "And from what I understand, his forces there are very weak."

The three men sat around the table as Clinton brought out maps. They studied Charleston's location, and the plan seemed feasible.

"I think we need not have any fears about taking Charleston," Clinton said with satisfaction. "Once we take South Carolina, you can proceed at once into North Carolina, General Cornwallis."

"You intend for me to command the forces?" Cornwallis was surprised. He had expected Clinton himself to lead the campaign.

"Yes. I must stay in New York and direct all of the operations."

Banastre Tarleton covered his mouth, concealing a grin. "That's just what Corny wants," he said. "A command of his own." He was excited, for he knew that Cornwallis depended on him extensively for striking power with his cavalry and for gathering information. He was the eyes of the British army in this strange land, which none of them knew very well.

"Very well, then. We will launch our campaign, and once Charleston is ours, the war will grind to a halt. The South will fall," Clinton said with satisfaction, "and the Colonies will be cut in two."

T　　　T　　　T

The Battle of Charleston went much as the three officers had anticipated. Clinton changed his mind and accompanied the army that surrounded Savannah. General Lincoln was indeed an unlucky general and allowed himself to be trapped in the city. It was no trick at all for Clinton's forces to pin Lincoln's men in and trap them.

The loss at Charleston was a disastrous defeat. Benjamin Lincoln simply did not fight. He sat in Charleston, allowed himself to be surrounded, and fifty-five hundred Continentals were imprisoned. Three hundred and ninety-one guns and over six thousand muskets, thirty-three rounds of ammunition, eight thousand round shots, three hundred seventy-six barrels of powder, and all of the American ships in the harbor were lost. The siege only cost the British seventy-six men killed and a hundred thirty-eight wounded. The operation was successful, and the British took satisfaction in a complete victory—or at least it should have been. But for a fact it was not. Clinton returned to New York, leaving Cornwallis with eight thousand troops in Charleston, and ordered him to move into North Carolina. He hoped for a rising of loyalists to join Cornwallis's forces, but it never happened.

Banastre Tarleton, to some extent, was responsible for this situation. Tarleton caught up with some Virginia troops, and at Waxwas a bloody massacre took place. The Americans asked for quarter but were cut down viciously. Butcher Tarleton had fulfilled his nickname.

A few Tories may have rejoiced over the slaughter, but now bands of outraged patriots were roaming all over the territory sniping at Redcoats and loyalists, cutting off couriers. Men such as Francis Marion, called the Swamp Fox, and Thomas Sumter effectively brought civil war to the land. And instead of an easy march to North Carolina, suddenly General Cornwallis found himself in the midst of a fiery, bitterly contested internal struggle. Not only was Cornwallis hard-pressed to find available loyalists to enlist, but he also had to fend off the outraged patriots, who wanted nothing more than to exact revenge on Ban Tarleton and the Tories who had swarmed in upon them, burning their homes and murdering their families. And so what should have been an easy assignment for Lord Cornwallis turned out to be very difficult indeed.

⚜   ⚜   ⚜

Stephen Morrison showed little interest in his new son. From time to time he would ask how the boy was doing, but never did he offer to pick him up. Grace had seemingly fenced herself in after the birth of the baby, and only Keturah knew that whatever love she had had for Stephen had died. Now with his lack of interest in the baby, the situation had deteriorated further.

At supper on Thursday evening, he interrupted the usual awkward silence by announcing, "I have had a letter from Jubal, my brother. He's out of prison now."

"How could that be?" Keturah said. She had always liked Jubal and had grieved over his imprisonment.

"You can read the letter, but it seems your friend, Sam Bradford, somehow engineered his release."

Instantly Keturah took the letter and read it. Her face glowed, and

128

she said, "My, wasn't that a wonderful thing for Sam to do!"

"I didn't know he had that kind of ingenuity," Grace said. She was holding the baby in her arms, looking down at him, but now she looked up. She knew something of Sam's single-minded pursuit of Keturah and now smiled. "He seems to be a young man who gets what he wants."

Keturah's face flushed, and she read over the letter again, then handed it back to Stephen. "I'm glad your brother is out. Those hulks are horrible things."

"Yes, they are. But it's just as I told Jubal. He should have stayed out of that war."

"What will he do now?" Grace asked.

"I have no idea."

"Well, if he's lost his ship, why don't you ask him to come here. He could be a help."

"That might be a good idea. I'll think on it." He got up and left the room without saying a word about Patrick.

As soon as he was gone, Grace looked over at Keturah and said, "How can a man not show any more interest in his only son?"

Keturah had no answer. She herself had learned to love the baby, and of course, she had long had a deep affection for Grace.

"I think as Patrick grows up he'll take more of an interest. Men aren't very good with babies."

"Some of them are. My father was," Grace said. "I remember my mother telling me how he couldn't leave any of us alone—Clive or me and especially David. That he couldn't wait to play with us and to hold us. She always said he was the best father that ever lived."

Keturah went over and said, "Let me hold him awhile."

"No. You go ahead and take care of the dishes. Then we'll give him a bath."

As Keturah left, Grace felt a pang. She had had such high expectations of marriage, and now they all lay in ashes about her feet. She had known very soon after her marriage that she had made a serious mistake. She was a loving young woman and she needed love in return. Stephen had never been ardent, even during their engagement, which should have told her something. She looked back now as she touched Patrick's chubby cheeks and smiled as he bubbled at her. She thought, *At least I have you.* She had closed the door on any relationship between her and Stephen, and she knew now that what she had felt for him had not been love. Many women chose unwisely when it came to husbands, but somehow she never thought it would be her.

T T T

"I wonder at Stephen being gone so long." Grace walked to the window and looked out. Several weeks had passed, but the relationship between her and Stephen had gotten no better, just as she had expected.

"Where was he going, Miss Grace?" Keturah asked. She was sewing and looked up out the window. "It's getting dark. Surely he'll be home while there's light."

"He should have been home long ago." Grace came back and sat down and fidgeted. As always, her ears were half-tuned to hear Patrick, but there was only silence in the house.

The two women sat there, and Keturah spoke of how wonderful it was that Jubal was doing better. She had received a letter from Sam and read it several times. He was not the best letter writer in the world, but despite herself, her heart felt warm that he had written to her. She did not exactly know how she felt about Sam Bradford. She knew that he was wildly in love with her, but being with Grace and seeing the poor relationship she had with her husband had made Keturah cautious. She did not want to make a mistake, and when she wrote back to Sam, her reply had been much cooler than his.

"There he comes now," Grace said. She got up and walked to the window and peered out. The darkness was falling fast and she squinted. "No. That's not him. That's Taws."

She moved toward the door and was startled when Taws banged on the door with his fist. "What's he knocking so hard for?" she asked.

Going to the door, she opened it and then blinked with surprise. Taws' face was pale and he could hardly speak.

"What is it, Taws?" she said. "What's wrong?"

Taws shook his head and looked down at the floor. He seemed to be searching for the right words.

Keturah had come over to stand beside Grace. She saw the strain on the heavy face of the overseer, and Grace asked again, "Tell me. What is it?"

"It's your husband. He's—" He swallowed hard and said, "I hate to tell you, but—well, he's dead, Mrs. Morrison."

Both women stood stock-still for a moment, and then Grace swayed. She still was not strong, and Keturah said, "Quick, come and sit down." She led Grace to a chair and quickly ran to get some wine.

Taws followed the two women in and stood twisting his hat in his hands. He watched as Keturah gave Grace the wine, and then he blurted out, "It was them partisans! They came at us and killed him without a word. Just rode up and shot him down. Then they took our slaves and burnt the barn out on the north side. I don't know why they didn't kill me too." He dropped his head again, and he said, "They said to tell you that they don't need any Tory widows around here. You'd best get out while you can."

Taws explained that a group of patriots were seeking revenge for a Tory raid in which some of their families had been killed. Fighting between patriots and loyalists was sweeping the land now, and no man or woman was safe.

Grace could not take in what was happening. She sat utterly still and listened as Taws spoke, and then she said, "Get Patrick. I want to hold him."

"All right, Miss Grace." Keturah ran and got Patrick from his bed. He began crying and did so until she put him in Grace's arms.

"Where is Mr. Morrison?"

"I left him where he fell, ma'am. I was afraid they'd kill me too."

"Go back and get him. Bring him home."

Taws nodded and swallowed but said miserably, "Yes, ma'am," then left the room.

Once Taws had lumbered out, Keturah came over and sat down beside Grace. They sat there silently, and Keturah could not think of a thing to say.

"What will you do?" she asked finally.

"We'll have Stephen's funeral," Grace said and lifted her chin. Her eyes were dry, but her hands were trembling as she held the baby. "Then we'll see."

※   ※   ※

The funeral was poorly attended. Stephen had made few friends, and no more than a dozen people were there. The pastor of the church was a strong patriot, and he came reluctantly and was no comfort.

Strangely enough, Grace got more sympathy from Colonel Francis Marion than anyone else. He did not attend the funeral, but he came two days afterward. Grace received him at the door, and he took off his hat, a man no taller than she was herself.

"I'm Colonel Marion, ma'am. I've come to offer my sympathies."

"Come in, Colonel Marion," Grace said evenly. She escorted the colonel into the room, where he sat down and did not speak for a time. Then he said, "I want you to know, ma'am, it was none of my men that did this terrible thing."

"I'm glad of that, Colonel."

Marion's intense black eyes seemed kind to Grace. He was so small that she found it difficult to believe that he was feared as he was throughout the Carolinas as a military leader without peer.

"What will you do now, Mrs. Morrison? The country's falling to pieces. My own place has been burned. The house and barn are gone. There's nothing for me to go back to. It's terrible and it may not get any better."

"It's kind of you to think of me, Colonel," Grace said. "I suppose you would advise me to sell out and to leave."

"It might be wise, Mrs. Morrison. Without a man to see to the place, you'll have little hope."

"Yes, I suppose so."

Marion sat there quietly, and then he said cautiously, "It might sound strange coming from me, but I'd like to help you."

"I thank you for your concern, Colonel, but I feel I must stay here."

The colonel rose then, bowed, and left the house at once. Grace went to Keturah, who was bathing Patrick, and told her what had happened.

Keturah ran the cloth over the smooth skin of the infant and then said, "Maybe it would be better if we left. You could go back to your family in England."

But Grace Morrison's face was set. She had made a bad mistake in her marriage, and now, somehow, an iron determination filled her with resolve. "This is all I have, Keturah, this place. I'll keep it for Patrick. I'll make a way somehow."

Keturah had not seen this side of Grace Morrison before, but it was clear that nothing she could say would change her mind. "All right," she said. "We'll do the best we can. Me and you and Patrick."

12

A Small Miracle

MATTHEW HAD FOUND HIMSELF drawn to Jubal Morrison. After his harrowing experience in the hulk, Morrison had been practically an invalid when Sam had brought him home. The family had taken him in, and Jeanne had seen to it that he had gotten good care. Sam had been a great help, and the three of them had spent many hours together. Their time together had helped Matthew, for the two were good companions, and it had taken some of the edge off of his loneliness.

Late one Thursday afternoon the post came with a letter for Jubal. Sam brought it to Jubal, who was sitting in the parlor playing chess with Matthew. "A letter for you, Jubal," he said and handed the envelope over.

Jubal had not recovered well. His right leg had been scratched in the hulk, had gotten infected, and then turned into a vicious ulcer that would not heal. He had lost a lot of weight, and even the good food and care he had received at the Bradfords' had not been enough. He took the letter and glanced at the writing. "It's from my brother, Stephen," he remarked. "I'm a little bit surprised to hear from him. He never quite forgave me for joining up with the patriots." He opened the letter and ran his eyes over it briefly, then glanced up. A smile turned the corners of his broad lips upward, and he said, "He wants me to come to South Carolina."

"What in the world for?" Sam said. "You two never really got along, did you?"

"Oh, we got along all right as long as we weren't together," Jubal laughed. "Stephen's a good fellow. Just sort of stuffy. I'd hoped that being married to a woman like Grace would change him, but I don't think it has." He studied the letter again and said, "Mostly what he says is that I made a fool out of myself, but he's willing to forgive me and save me from starvation by giving me work on his plantation."

"What a generous offer," Matthew said. He picked up one of the chessmen and spun it in his fingers, then asked, "Is that all he says?"

"Oh, he says that times are difficult there. There's a lot of shooting back and forth between the Tories and the patriots. Doesn't sound like a very peaceful place to me."

"What does he say about Grace?"

"Not a word, and not anything about the baby that's coming either. Stephen's a strange fellow. Why, if I had a wife like Grace and was expecting a baby, I'd be shouting it all over the rooftops," Jubal remarked.

"Will you go?" Sam said.

"I don't think so. I never liked that part of the South much. I spent a few months there once, and though some of it's beautiful, the weather's terrible."

Sam sat down and watched as the two men continued their chess game. Finally, out of the blue, he said, "I've been thinking. I'd like to see that part of the world."

Matthew laughed aloud. "You're a butterfingered scoundrel, Sam! Jubal and I know the attraction for you in South Carolina. You just want to see Keturah."

"Well, maybe I do!" Sam said defensively. "What's wrong with that?"

"Nothing," Jubal said. He winked at Sam, saying, "You're nineteen years old, and sooner or later you're going to make a fool out of yourself. Why don't you just do it now and get it over with?"

Sam was offended. He got up and stalked out of the house as Jubal watched him. "I shouldn't have teased him like that."

"Won't hurt him," Matthew said. "He'll be all right. He has been pining after that girl forever. I think he really does love her."

"What about her? Does she care for him?"

"Hard to say about Keturah. She's had a tough upbringing."

"So how did you like plantation life?" asked Jubal, changing the subject.

"Well, it's not easy. Mostly hot and plenty of mosquitoes, and some say the only workers that can stand the strain are the Africans. Not the kind of thing I'd like to do for the rest of my life. But I may not be the best person to ask."

They finished the game. Then Jubal leaned back and said, "I wish I could go, but in the shape I'm in, I'd just add to their problems. Stephen's the only brother I have, although we haven't been close. He didn't say much, but I can tell he's having a hard time."

"You could go when you get better," suggested Matthew.

"That's not a bad idea. I always liked Grace, and she seems lonely. And it would give Stephen and me a chance to get a little closer."

☙ ☙ ☙

Two weeks after Stephen's letter came, Jubal decided to go to South Carolina. His decision to go came as somewhat of a surprise to the rest of the Bradfords. Rachel, who had come back to stay until she could be with Jacob after he got out of the army, had always liked Jubal. It was she who said, "You're doing the right thing, Jubal. Family's important. I know you and Stephen have had your difficult times, but he is your brother."

This had settled it, and Jubal had set about building up his strength. He ate as much as he could, got fresh air and exercise, and as the days passed he grew stronger.

It was on a Thursday morning when Jubal received another letter. He was sitting in the kitchen with Rachel and Jeanne, watching them as they moved about preparing the food for the noon meal, when the post came by. "I'll go out," Jeanne said, seeing the horseman stop. She got up and moved out of the house and nodded to the horseman.

"Letter for Mr. Jubal Morrison."

"He's here."

"That'll be one guinea."

"I have it." Jeanne pulled some coins out of the pocket of her dress and handed it over, saying, "One day it'll be nice if the person that sends the letter pays for it instead of the person that receives it."

"That's right," the post rider grinned. "Most letters I get aren't worth paying for."

Jeanne turned and went back into the house.

Jubal stared at the letter and said, "I don't recognize this handwriting."

Rachel looked over. "It's a woman's. One of your old flames, no doubt."

"No doubt," Jubal grinned. "They're lined up waiting for me now that I'm stove up and don't have a penny to my name. There'll be quite a fight over me," he said.

He opened the letter and the two women watched him idly. Both of them saw his face turn very still and knew that something was wrong.

"Bad news, Jubal?" Rachel asked quietly.

"It's my brother, Stephen. He's dead."

"Oh, Jubal, how awful!" Jeanne said. She reached out impulsively and put her hand over Jubal's. "How in the world did it happen?"

Jubal answered slowly. "He was killed in that fighting down there. One of the partisan groups murdered him."

Rachel asked, "Is that Grace who's writing?"

"Yes. She's had the baby. They named him Patrick."

Rachel said quietly, "I'm so sorry. I wish I could help."

"There's no help for it," Jubal said. The light had gone out of his face, replaced by a heavy look. He glanced up with misery in his eyes. "I could have been better to Stephen. He was a difficult fellow, but I could have tried harder."

"You mustn't think like that," Jeanne said. "It's always easy to think of what we could have done after someone's gone, but don't torment yourself. What about Grace?"

He looked down at the letter and read aloud:

I know this comes as a shock to you. It was very difficult, of course, for me. It's hard to be a widow with a young baby, especially in a troubled place like this.

The serious fighting here makes things rather precarious. Keturah wants me to leave and go back to England, but I can't do that. I'm determined to stay here. This place is Patrick's inheritance from his father. It's all I have and all he has. I would be a dependent if I went back to England. No one will buy a plantation during these troubled times, so I'm determined to stay. Keturah has said she will stay with me.

I would not ask it of you, Jubal, but if you could come and help for a time, I would greatly appreciate it. It will take all I can do to hold on to this place. Stephen put a great deal of money into other lands. One of them I know was financed by Mr. Matthew Bradford. We were not able to keep up the payments, so now the land, of course, will revert to him. He owns the mortgage on it. It is a fine place, but I cannot handle this one very well, much less take on another one.

After Jubal had read the rest of the letter, Rachel said, "I never knew that Matthew financed a place inside South Carolina."

"My brother told me about it," Jubal said. "Now it seems it wasn't a good idea."

"What will you do, Jubal?"

"I'd already decided to go, and now it seems I'm needed more than ever. I've got to do what I can for Grace and her son. After all, they're family."

Later that morning, when Matthew and Sam returned from looking at some of Sam's new inventions in the foundry, Jubal gave them the news of Stephen's death. After they both expressed sympathy, Sam asked, "What are you going to do, Jubal?"

"I'm going, of course. I've got to. It's my responsibility."

Instantly Sam said, "Well, I'm going with you. You're not all healed up yet. You need somebody to look out for you."

Despite Jubal's grief he managed a smile. "That's your only motive, is it?"

Sam flushed. "Well, I'd like to see Keturah, of course, and I always liked Grace. She is my cousin, you know."

"You'll have to clear that with your father, Sam."

"I'm nineteen years old. I'm a man. I can make my own decision."

"No. You owe it to your father to talk to him," Jubal said. "He may need you at the foundry."

Sam's head dropped. "You're right," he mumbled. "I'll go see him right now."

"When will you be leaving, Jubal?" asked Matthew.

"As soon as I can. I've enjoyed being with you, Matthew. It's been a good time."

Matthew was silent for a moment. "Yes, it has, Jubal." He said no more, but there was a thought in his mind that he would not speak.

🜨   🜨   🜨

Esther Howland passed away in the most gentle way possible. Abigail had put her to bed the night before, tucked her in, and her mother had asked her to pray. After she had prayed, the older woman took Abigail's hand and said, "You've been a good daughter. God has blessed me with you, Abigail."

"Not as good as I should have been, Mother," Abigail had said. "Now you go to sleep."

"I'll see you in the morning, daughter."

That night she had slipped out from this world to the next, and when Abigail had found her, she remembered those words, *"I'll see you in the morning, daughter."* They echoed in her mind constantly through the business of the closing of a life—the arrangements of the funeral, the funeral itself, and finally the cleaning up and settling of personal possessions. *"I'll see you in the morning, daughter."* Somehow her mother's words gave her great comfort, and although she wept a few tears, she was happy for her mother, for she had been suffering greatly.

She stayed by herself a great deal during this time. Clive came by one day, once again searching for supplies for Washington's army. He had given her his condolences and had seen that she had a peace about her, so he had left and gone on to visit the Bradfords.

When he got to the house, he found Matthew and asked for Jubal. "He's gone to buy some clothes for his trip, Clive."

"Well, I have a letter here. I'm sure Jubal's talked with you about Grace."

"Yes. She's in poor shape."

"Indeed she is. It's going to be a touchy thing. I wish I could go help her. I wish she would go back to England, but she won't do that."

"Clive, you remember the property that I financed adjoining the Morrison place?"

"Yes. You'll never get your money back on that."

"But what about the place itself?"

"Why, legally it's yours, Matthew."

"Do you know anything about it, aside from how big it is?"

"From what I remember it was pretty well run-down. It would take quite a bit of money to get it up and working again." Clive turned his gaze upon Matthew. "You're not thinking about going there, are you?"

"Yes, I am. It's really the only place I have to go. I don't have any money. I've wasted everything that the good Lord gave me, and now I've got to work for a living."

"What about your painting?"

"I can paint in South Carolina as well as I can here."

"Well, I wish I had the money to finance you, but I don't. Soldiers in the Continental Army don't make very big salaries."

"I'll find a way. Sam and Jubal are going, and the three of us could do something."

After his conversation with Clive, Matthew went at once to Abigail's house. He had not seen her since the funeral, and now when she opened the door, he removed his hat and said, "I came to see how you were doing, Abigail."

"Come in, Matthew," Abigail said. She took his hat and hung it on a peg, and then the two of them went into the parlor. "Would you care for tea?"

"No, not really. Are you doing all right? You must be lonely."

"You know, the last thing my mother said to me, Matthew, was 'I'll see you in the morning, daughter.' That's been a great comfort to me. When I went to her the next morning, she had already gone to be with the Lord, but I know there'll be another morning and I'll see her then."

Matthew stood there silently. He knew she was a different woman from the one he had resented for so long. Now there was an undeniable peaceful quality about her. He stood there thinking about their relationship, and he could not help but consider himself a fool. Finally he went and sat beside her on the couch. He saw surprise leap into her eyes, but he was determined. He took her hand, held it in his for a moment, unable to speak but trying to put into words what he felt. "Abigail, I want to ask you to forgive me."

"Why, Matthew!"

"There's no reason why you should. I've treated you shamefully. But I want you to know one thing, Abigail. I've had a change in my heart. I know that I've been wrong to let bitterness cloud me and turn me against you. Will you forgive me?"

"Of course I will."

Matthew's eyes brightened, and he put his other hand on hers, holding it tightly. "Well, I may as well tell you the rest of it."

"The rest of it? What's that?"

"I guess I've always loved you, Abigail. I got off on the wrong track, but right now I want you to know that I love you with all of my heart."

Abigail Howland sat there silently. His hand was strong on hers. The marks of suffering showed in his face, and she knew that he had not yet gotten over the wreck he had made of his life. But she had loved this man for years, and now she spoke that thought. "I love you, too, Matthew. I have for a long time."

Her words brought unspeakable joy to Matthew. Many other women had touched his life, but none had ever affected him so powerfully as Abigail. He cherished the richness of character—sometimes playful and reckless, other times soft and gentle—and the passionate emotions that dwelt within this proud young woman. Intensely aware of her beauty, he felt the same stirring that he had known years ago. His lips met hers as her arms reached around his neck, holding him tightly.

The two clung together for some time, savoring the closeness that each had long desired. Drawing back, Abigail lifted her face to him and whispered, "I thought we had lost each other."

"So did I," said Matthew, his fingers tracing a wisp of her rich brown hair. "So did I. . . ."

♜   ♜   ♜

Matthew set out at once to firm up his plans, and he told his father first of all. "I'm going to South Carolina to become a planter."

Daniel Bradford was not caught completely off guard. He had seen this coming, and now he said, "It'll be quite a change for you, son."

"Yes, it will, but we're going to be happy, Abigail and I."

"I'll be glad to have her as a daughter-in-law." The wedding had been set for the following Friday, and the entire family was happy that Matthew had finally settled down.

"Will you be able to make it? I know planting is a rough life. I don't know anything about that kind of farming."

Matthew barely had enough money to get to South Carolina, but he was determined to stand on his own two feet. He had told Abigail, "I'll go first and get things started and you stay here. I'll send for you."

After Matthew left his father's office, he went to talk to Abigail. When he stepped inside she put her arms around him and kissed him at once.

"Well, that's the kind of welcome I like," he said. "You'd better store up on these kisses. We'll have a short honeymoon, and then I'll be gone a long time."

"I won't miss any kissing," Abigail said.

"Why, you shock me! I won't be here, so who will you get all this kissing from?" he teased her.

"From you! I'm going with you, Matthew."

"You can't do it, Abigail," Matthew said instantly. He held her by the arms and said, "It's going to be too hard. It'll take some time to get that plantation on its feet. We'll be starting from nothing."

"No, we won't. Come in and sit down. I've got to talk with you." She led him into the parlor and sat him down, then sat beside him. Taking his hand, she looked up at him and said, "I've been praying about this, Matthew. Once we're married we'll be one, won't we?"

"Certainly."

"And what's yours will be mine?"

"Of course. There goes my banjo," he said ruefully, "and my paintbrushes. It's about all I have."

But Abigail was not smiling. "And what's mine will be yours?"

"Well, I suppose so."

"There's no supposing about it. If we're going to be one, we can't have one little pile of things that's yours and another little pile that's mine. There's just one big pile, and it's all ours."

Matthew studied her curiously. "What are you talking about, Abigail?"

"I sold this house, Matthew. The papers will be finished, and I'll have the money in two days. My mother and I got an inheritance from Mrs. Denham. We didn't touch it. It's all intact. So with what we get from the house and from the inheritance, we'll have enough to build a good plantation in South Carolina."

"Why, I couldn't take that!"

"You're not taking it. It'll be yours anyway. Don't argue with me," Abigail said. She reached up and took his hair and playfully shook his head. "You're a stubborn man, Matthew, but I'm also a stubborn woman, and we're going to begin by letting me have my own way."

Matthew suddenly laughed. "You're going to be a hard woman to live with. I can see that now."

⚜   ⚜   ⚜

The wedding was not formal. It took place in Daniel Bradford's house and was attended only by family and the minister.

After the brief ceremony was over, there was a wedding supper. It was a time of rejoicing, and no one could remember ever seeing Matthew so happy. Growing up, he had always felt different from his brothers, and it had been discouraging to him. But then to find out that Daniel was not his real father had nearly crushed him, although he had said little about it. His recent humiliating experiences in England had only added to the weight he seemed to carry upon his shoulders. But now there was no sign of it. His eyes were bright, and he and Abigail were inseparable, holding hands the whole evening.

Sam stood and proposed a toast, saying, "Here's to the bride and groom. Left alone, you two wouldn't get anything done, so Jubal and I are coming to South Carolina to make sure that things go right."

Everyone laughed, but Abigail's eyes misted with tears. She said, "It'll be like having a family. I never had one, really. Just Mother and me." She looked around the table, then said to Daniel and Marian, "Thank you for raising such a fine son."

They all drank the toast, and Matthew looked toward Abigail and said, "We found each other."

A murmur of approval went around the table, and Matthew looked at his family. "I want to thank you all for standing by me through my troublesome period . . . which has been practically all my life. And I want to ask you to pray for Abigail and me as we begin a new life together."

There was a time of silence. They all bowed their heads, and Daniel Bradford prayed a mighty prayer for God's blessing on his son and his new daughter. As Matthew sat there, he realized that his life was new and that he could never again be the same man that he had been.

PART THREE

—

THE OPEN DOOR

13

A Distant Trumpet

"THE AORIST TENSE IS ALWAYS USED to show that an action took place at a certain time in the past—and that it was completed at a certain time after that."

Reverend Evan Drystan looked up at the face of his pupil and sympathized with the struggle he saw written across the rugged features. He said quickly, "I know it sounds difficult, but it is really very common in the Greek language. Far more common than the imperfect tense."

The textbook in Cormac Morgan's big hands looked very small. For a Welshman he was very large, only a fraction of an inch short of six feet. Hunching his broad shoulders forward, he held the book so tightly that his fingertips grew white. "What is the imperfect tense, Pastor?"

"Well, the imperfect tense shows an action that began in the past and is still going on. For example, when I say in English, 'I have been eating here for three years,' it means I started three years ago and am still eating here."

The pale sunlight that slanted down through the window illuminating the desk where the two men sat was occupied by millions, it seemed, of tiny fractions of dust. Cormac studied the swarming mites for a time, then placed the open book carefully on the table and rubbed his eyes. "I'll never learn Greek, Pastor," he said.

Weariness was in his tone, and Evan Drystan immediately put his hand on the young man's shoulder, which was smoothly muscled and hard as granite. The minister's favorite student had uncommon physical strength. There was a thickness and breadth in his torso, and his chest swelled against a thin white shirt. His thick wrists and forearms filled the sleeves of his shirt, and every move he made gave the suggestion of power and spoke of many years spent working in the coal mines in Conall.

Very few men in Wales have the power of this man, Drystan thought.

"You've got a good mind, Cormac. You just got a late start."

Indeed Cormac Morgan had gotten a late start. He had worked in the mines from the age of ten until he was twenty-two, and then, because he could no longer bear to be cooped up like a mole underground, he had hired out as a laborer on a farm. For the next eight years he had learned how to farm and now, for all practical purposes, managed one of the largest estates in the county—although he was paid only a pittance, for the owner, a drunken and brutal man, kept all of his help on the fine edge of poverty.

"You got a late start," the pastor repeated, "but you've got a good mind. You'll catch up." He thought fleetingly of Cormac's hard life, orphaned at the age of ten, passed around for a time, then put to work in the mines. He thought also of that period of Morgan's life when he had fallen in with unsavory companions, joining their drinking and carousing. He had become a bully boy, whipping any man in the valley who dared challenge him.

Cormac looked up and studied the thin, wiry aristocratic face and steady gray eyes of Pastor Evan Drystan. "I don't see why you waste your time on me, Pastor. How long have we been at this now?" He knew very well, for it had been Drystan who had befriended him and given him an education. It had been hard, for the only time Morgan had to study was after all the farm work was done, which was often near midnight.

But Drystan had done more than educate Cormac Morgan. He had witnessed to him of the grace of God, and although Cormac had resisted for a time and even insulted the pastor, he had been impressed. Three years ago Cormac had finally agreed to attend an open-air service where the Reverend George Whitefield was preaching. It was in that open field that the Spirit of God had broken Cormac Morgan so that he had fallen on his knees begging God for mercy—and had received it. Since that instant he had been the most faithful member of the small chapel where Drystan was the pastor and had become known as a fine lay speaker.

Cormac rubbed his eyes, which were gritty from lack of sleep. "I remember the first time I told you that I felt God was calling me to do something special."

"I remember it too. It was the greatest thrill I had ever received in the ministry. You're going to make a fine preacher someday, Cormac."

"I have grave doubts about that, Pastor." Thinking back, that call from God was like a distant trumpet, very far away, very hard to understand. He ran his hands through his thick auburn hair, slightly curly, and slumped forward, his elbows on the table. "I wish God would speak a little bit more plainly."

"That's not His way. You know that from your study of the Scriptures, Cormac. He shows us only one step at a time." Evan Drystan hesitated, then said, "Have you thought any more about what we discussed last month?"

"About preaching the Gospel in America? I think of it every day, but it seems impossible."

"With God all things are possible. You know that."

"With God things aren't impossible, but with me they are. All I can see is working here until I'm an old man. I'll never get enough money to go away to university—and that's assuming I could even get in."

Drystan did not answer. He had tried everything he knew to get his young friend accepted at a university, but they simply refused to believe that any man who had had so little formal education could succeed in academic studies. Besides, it would be expensive, and Drystan, with a house full of children to support on a meager salary, was in no position to help.

"I'll be going home now." Cormac arose, dwarfing the slight frame of the pastor. He picked up the book and shook his head doubtfully. "So . . . the imperfect tense shows an action that began in the past and is still going on."

"Think of it this way, Cormac. God has been working in you for three years. He began that day when you first fell under His power, and He's still working this very moment."

"Well, I'm *imperfect*, all right." Cormac suddenly laughed, and his teeth seemed very white against his bronzed skin. Although his face had been somewhat battered during his earlier brawls, he'd been on the winning side of most of them and still looked younger than his thirty years. He put on his coat, said good-bye, and started for home. The pastor waited until he had closed the door and then began to pray for Cormac Morgan.

☙   ☙   ☙

Three days later Cormac returned to the pastor's study off the rear of the small white church. He noticed an unfamiliar horse tied outside, but that was not unusual, for many came to call on Pastor Drystan. He went inside and sat down on one of the pews, as the door to the pastor's study was closed. He thumbed through the Greek textbook, still not satisfied with his grasp of the imperfect tense. The door opened, and Drystan said, "I thought I heard you, Cormac." He came out quickly and his face was radiant. "I have a surprise for you. Come, there's someone I want you to meet."

Cormac was often introduced to various preachers. As a matter of fact, he knew almost all the pastors in the county. But when he stepped inside he saw that this man was not a local pastor. He recognized him instantly and stopped dead still.

"Mr. Wesley!" he said, stunned. He went forward at once and took Wesley's hand. "I'm so happy to see you, sir."

John Wesley had to tilt his head back to look up at the tall Welshman. "My, what a big, tall fellow you are!"

Cormac had heard Wesley preach on three occasions, but each time he had been far back in a crowd, and the famous preacher had been up on a hill. He had never gotten closer than fifty yards, and now he was shocked at how small Wesley was. No more than five six, he estimated. Thin and with a tanned face, Wesley was not at all physically impressive.

"This is my pupil I've been telling you about, sir," Reverend Drystan said quickly. "I'm very proud of him."

"Are you indeed? That's good to hear. All of us older men need a young Timothy."

"I'm afraid I'm no Timothy, Reverend Wesley," Cormac said. "Mr. Drystan does his best, but he's got poor stuff to work with, I'm afraid. I'm a late starter."

John Wesley studied the rugged face and frame of Cormac Morgan. Wesley was a famous man now, not just in England but throughout the world. He had begun as a minister by teaching at Oxford, and for a time had gone to Georgia as a missionary with his brother, Charles. But it was only on his return that he had been led by Whitefield into the open air to preach. God's power had fallen upon him, and now all the world knew of John Wesley.

"Your pastor tells me that God has called you to preach the Gospel."

Cormac hesitated and shook his head ruefully. "I wish I were as certain as Mr. Drystan," he said haltingly. "God wants me to do something, I know that—but it's very vague, I'm afraid."

"He also tells me that you have had the call to go to America."

"Well, sir, I have felt that way, but it may only be my feelings. It may not be God speaking at all."

"That's always possible, of course. But you two have fasted and prayed and sought God, have you not?"

"Yes, sir, we have."

"That's all a man can do," Wesley said firmly. "I do not know you, Mr. Morgan, but I have great confidence in your pastor. He has a sense of discernment that I have rarely encountered, and he feels this is God's leading. I want to pray for you. Mr. Drystan and I will lay hands on you and God will speak."

There was no uncertainty—at least not in John Wesley's firm voice. "Kneel down, sir."

Cormac fell at once to his knees, and the two men knelt beside him. He felt the hands of Wesley on his shoulder and also those of his pastor. The presence of God seemed to fill the room as Wesley and Drystan prayed for quite some time. Then there was a lengthy silence in the room, and Cormac began to wonder why the two men did not arise. Finally he heard Wesley say firmly, "A door will be opened for you, my son. It might not be a door that you would choose for yourself, but God's ways are not our ways. You must pass through it, and He will lead you in the way that He shall choose. You will preach His Gospel to the glory of Christ."

"Amen," Pastor Drystan said.

The three men stood up and Wesley nodded. "I must be on my way. I have a meeting to conduct. I will expect to hear from you, young man. God must be served."

As soon as Wesley was out of the door, Cormac turned and demanded, "What did he mean 'a door will be opened'?"

"I expect he meant an opportunity for you to become a minister."

"But what door did he mean? Surely there's no door about to open at Oxford."

"There will be if God ordains it. He has His ways, Cormac." But the pastor was doubtful. "I admit that that door seems to have been firmly closed, and I think it was God's doing. No," he said thoughtfully, "I think there will be a different door."

"Different?"

"You may not even recognize it. When I was a young man like you, I was firmly determined to be a physician, but then a door shut and another opened. I passed through it and have become a minister of the Lord, and I have never regretted it."

"Did you know the door was for you when you entered in?"

"No, I did not. I was in fear and trembling—and so may you be, my boy. But even if you do not recognize it, study each opportunity that comes your way. One may be the open door that you have heard prophesied by John Wesley."

🛎   🛎   🛎

For weeks after Cormac's meeting with John Wesley, he woke every morning expecting that something would change in his life—that the door that the famous preacher mentioned would present itself. Each night he would go to bed exhausted from the arduous work, disappointed that nothing seemed to have changed. He said nothing to his pastor as the weeks rolled by, but the pastor knew his pupil's heart, and after every meeting, late at night after their time of study, he would say, "We will pray now that the door will open soon, Cormac. Do not be discouraged. God's timing is never wrong."

Cormac did his work faithfully, but his mind was elsewhere. The owner of the estate, a huge man named Murdoch, eventually noticed that Cormac's heart was no longer in his work. He had always showed contempt for Cormac, but now he became even more insulting. He was a profane man, his language full of blasphemies, and he let the full weight of his disdain fall on Cormac day after day. Cormac had learned to ignore, or at least not to react to, the vile language and the constant abuse. He simply clamped his jaws together and went about his work.

The county fair, which came once a year, was an event that one and all looked forward to. The mines gave the workers the day off, and the farmers all came with their families. The hired laborers looked forward to it, for it was one of the few holidays they were given.

Cormac had always enjoyed the fair, and as he rose on the morning it began, he was whistling and combing his hair after putting on his one set of good clothing. The door opened. It was Murdoch.

"Don't waste your time, Cormac. You're not going to the fair."

Shocked and angered, Cormac turned and said, "You're mistaken there, Mr. Murdoch."

Murdoch was in an angry mood. He was also more than half drunk, and now he shouted, "You mind what I say! There's work to be done here, and until it's done you'll go to no fair!"

Something happened at that instant to Cormac Morgan. He was, on the whole, a rather even-tempered man, but suddenly his anger at all of the cruelty, the indignities, the cursings that he had endured from this vile man seemed to boil over. He felt light-headed and his muscles grew tense. "I've looked forward to this all year, Mr. Murdoch. It's in our agreement that I would have this day off, and I'm holding you to the agreement."

Murdoch's piggish little eyes glinted. He extended one arm to push the door fully ajar and said, "Be my guest. But if you step out this door now, you needn't come back! You can find yourself another place!"

At that instant Cormac suddenly remembered what John Wesley had said to him. *"A door will be opened for you."* He had no idea if this was part of God's plan. He only knew that he was going to the fair. He stepped forward and said, "I'm going to the fair and that's final."

"Then you can take your things."

"Fine. I'll have what you owe me."

Murdoch had not expected this. Cormac Morgan was doing most of the work of managing the large estate. He knew all the workers and got along well with them, whereas Murdoch himself could not get along with anyone. He was, however, a stubborn man, and the whiskey began to talk. He cursed and reached into his pocket, counted out the money to the penny, and said, "Get out! You'll come crawling back when you're hungry!"

An unexpected feeling of relief and peace washed over Cormac. He did not even answer Murdoch but turned and began to stuff his belongings into a bag. It did not take long, for he had few possessions—his clothing, a dozen books, his razor and brush. He was aware that Murdoch was watching but said nothing until he was ready to leave. "Good-bye, Mr. Murdoch."

"You'll be back!" Murdoch shouted as Cormac walked away. "Times are bad, and I'll spread the word that you're a troublemaker."

But Cormac did not even pause. He turned down the road that led to the village, where the fair would be in full swing, and somehow his heart felt lighter than it had in years. Times were hard in Wales, and work was hard to come by, but he could always go back to the mines. He hated being pinched underground in a mine, knowing that any moment the roof might come crashing in, squashing them all like bugs. But he did not think that losing his job would happen. A door had closed, and he gazed up at the sky and said, "Lord, I'm having a hard time with this, but I'm trusting you to open a door. Thy will be done. . . ."

By the time Cormac arrived at the fair he was warm, so he stopped to buy a glass of cold punch. He looked around with pleasure at the sight of the men and women from this small Welsh valley dressed in their Sunday best. The men's clothes were plain, but the women's were delightful, their multicolored silk and satin dresses mingling together as if in a kaleidoscope.

He listened to the music, which was his favorite part of any fair. He grinned suddenly, musing that no matter how much pastors might preach against fairs and their worldly goings-on, as long as Welshmen were Welshmen there would always be singing and dancing.

The fair was large, and it seemed as though everyone in the county had come to enjoy the festivities. Cormac knew a great many of them, and he spent over two hours just wandering around renewing old acquaintances. He said nothing to anyone about his trouble with Murdoch, for he had determined he would not ask for any help. If help came, it would have to come because God sent it. More than ever he was praying that God would open a door.

At eleven o'clock Cormac heard a voice urgently calling his name. He turned and saw his friend Huw Griffin. They were the same age, and though Griffin had remained in the mines, the two had remained close to each other. Griffin was not a believer, but Cormac was praying for him. He saw a troubled look on his friend's face and asked at once, "What's wrong, Huw?"

"It's Morvan Powys. He's being slaughtered!"

"Who's slaughtering him?"

"It's that bareknuckled fighter that's come here takin' on all comers. He's a big bruiser named Charlie Branwell. They call him the English Gamecock. He's beating Morvan to death. I'm afraid he's going to kill him."

Morvan Powys was also a friend of Cormac's. Instantly anger shot through Cormac Morgan. "Come along, we'll stop it!" he said without hesitation.

The two men shoved their way across the fairgrounds. Cormac had been in many fights himself but never a professional one. He had gone to two or three and had always been disgusted with them.

Cormac and Huw rushed up to the crowd of cheering people that had formed a circle around the fight. Inside, a big man in his forties with huge fists was brutally pounding a smaller man, Morvan Powys. Cormac saw that Huw had not overstated the situation. This was Branwell, the English Gamecock. Morgan had heard of him, for he had come to Wales before, taking on all comers for a purse to be taken by the winner.

"Who's his manager, Huw?"

"That fellow over there. The big Irishman."

Instantly Morgan moved over and confronted the man. "You're Branwell's manager?"

"That's right. I'm Mack Reagan. Who might you be?"

"My name's Cormac Morgan. I want you to stop that fight."

"All the man has to do is quit. He gets twenty pounds if he stays ten rounds with my man. He's been down eight times now. He can leave if he wants to."

"He's beaten," Cormac said. He looked again and saw that his friend

152

was helpless. He was practically being held up by Branwell, who was smashing him in the face again and again.

Like liquid lightning, anger and rage ran through Morgan. Without a thought, he shoved Reagan backward, wheeled around, and ran to where Branwell had his bloody fists ready to smash into Powys's unprotected face.

Charlie Branwell enjoyed beating up men. That's why he was a fighter. He certainly had not grown rich at it and was not getting any younger, but he was still able, with his powerful frame, to overwhelm most challengers likely to appear. But suddenly a band of steel seemed to enclose his right fist. He whirled and met a pair of dark brown eyes with golden glints. "Take your blasted hands off me!" He jerked at his arm, but it seemed to be imprisoned. With a roar of anger, he pulled his left back and threw a punch that would have demolished Cormac had it landed. But Cormac simply reached out and grabbed Branwell's arm, then swung the man to one side. He started in a circle, and the big fighter was swept along trying to keep his feet. But it was impossible. With a mighty heave Cormac threw him through the air, crashing into the spectators and knocking at least half a dozen of them down. Branwell got to his feet, his face crimson with rage. "I'll kill you, you filthy Welshman!" he shouted. He started toward Cormac, who smiled grimly, welcoming the challenge.

"Wait, now! Hold on, Charlie!" Mike Reagan had suddenly appeared. He threw himself in front of his fighter, shouting at him to stop. "We don't fight for nothin'," he said. "Be smart, Charlie. Be smart."

Reagan turned and said, "What about it? You got ten pounds you want to risk? Ten pounds, and you get twenty if you stay ten rounds with the Gamecock."

A cry went up from the crowd, for most Welshmen were a rowdy lot and liked a good fight.

Cormac heard his name called out. "Whip the Englishman, Cormac!"

Cormac ordinarily would not even have considered such a thing, but he glanced over and saw Huw kneeling by Morvan Powys, who had fallen to the ground, his face a bloody mess. The white-hot rage bubbled over in him again, and he reached into his pocket for the money. "There. Bring your man on."

Cries went up, but Huw came over quickly and said, "Don't do it, Cormac. He's a professional pugilist."

But Cormac hardly heard him. "Take care of Morvan," he said. "Get him to a doctor."

Mike Reagan was an old hand at taking charge when necessary. He pushed the crowd back, saying, "Make room! Make room!" He looked over and said, "Have you got a second?"

Half a dozen men shouted, and Rhys Gandwy leaped forward at once. "I'm his second, and I hope he kills him!"

Indeed, that seemed to be the prevailing hope among the Welshmen. Morvan Powys was a popular young man, and he had been half murdered by the bruiser.

"Strip off, then, and get the terms straight. This gentleman is holding the money." He turned to the mayor of the town and said, "Your Honor, you'll see that we're taken care of."

"That I will," the mayor said. His eyes gleamed, and he said, "I wish you wouldn't do it, Cormac."

Cormac did not answer. He stripped off his coat and his shirt, followed by his shoes and socks. As soon as he was stripped, Mike Reagan was taken aback. He looked at the smooth hard muscles, and as Cormac limbered up, he could see that the Welshman was not a slow man. "You've fought before," he said. "You're a ringer."

"Never professionally," the mayor responded quickly. "He's nothing but amateur."

The Gamecock shouted, "Come on, Mike, let's get at it! I'll kill him!"

The ring was quickly reformed, and Cormac stood there watching the Gamecock, who was grinning at him fixedly through his thick chops. He listened as Reagan gave the rules. "When any man goes down, that's one round. There'll be no kicking and no gouging. If the man can't come up to the mark, he loses. Ten rounds for the prize."

There was no referee in the ring. Cormac watched as Branwell shuffled forward, his fists clenched. He was a huge man, over six two and weighing probably two hundred and twenty pounds, though a good chunk of that was in his stomach. He was powerful, and a thousand battles had taught him every trick. Rules meant nothing to Branwell, Cormac understood. The Gamecock came forward with a roar and threw a punch that could have ended the fight. But it was slow, and Cormac had no trouble dodging it. He knew that he could not hit the man in the head, for most pugilists had learned to duck so that the blows fell on their skulls. He would break his fingers that way. Only a direct blow in the face, when there was no danger of hitting the skull, would do. But there was another target, the huge midsection, and he pivoted and with all the power in his body threw a right that caught the Gamecock directly in the pit of the stomach.

Everyone in the crowd heard the wheezing gasp that came from

Charlie Branwell, and a cheer went up. "That's it! Hit him in the belly, Cormac! He can't take it there, the big slob!"

Cormac, however, was more cautious. The blow he had just struck would have defeated an ordinary man, but Branwell was no ordinary man. He was huge and, if not fast on his feet, was quick with his hands. Cormac discovered this the hard way as Branwell charged again, delivering a blow Cormac never even saw. The world spun around, and he found himself flat on his back with a ringing in his ears. He heard the roar of the crowd and shook his head. He saw Branwell waiting, ready to strike him down as soon as he got up and before he caught his balance. He had seen pugilists do this before—a fallen man had little chance. He rolled to one side in an unexpected motion and hopped to his feet. His movement was so quick that Branwell was taken off guard. He shouted a curse and came forward, but this time instead of striking, Cormac slipped to one side, grabbed his opponent around the thick body, and stuck his left foot out. Branwell went sprawling to the ground, and everyone cried out. "That's two rounds!"

It was not necessary to hit a man to get him down, and Cormac was a much better wrestler, so time and again he would simply find a good grip and sling his opponent to the ground. Branwell did throw some solid punches, and Cormac's face was streaked with blood. But none of the blows had struck him squarely, and his head was clear. He saw that Branwell was wheezing.

"This ain't a wrestlin' match! It's a fight!" the Gamecock protested.

"When you go down, that's a round!" the mayor shouted. "On with it!"

There were only two rounds left for Cormac to take his prize, and the Gamecock refused to come in fast so that he could throw him. Forced to throw punches, Cormac concentrated on Branwell's midsection.

Out of nowhere, the Gamecock's beefy left fist connected with Cormac's jaw and knocked him down. Cormac felt blood in his mouth, but he got to his feet instantly, grinned, and taunted, "That the best you can do?"

The big fighter roared furiously and rushed forward, only to have Cormac smash him directly in the mouth. The Gamecock snapped backward in a spray of sweat and blood; his back slammed the ground. "That's ten rounds!" the shout went up. "You win, Cormac!"

Cormac knew he would be sore for days over the beating he had taken, but the rage had left him. He turned and picked up his clothes as his friends and neighbors pounded him on the back. They practically carried him to one of the refreshment stands, where his cuts and bruises were treated. He managed to refuse the alcoholic treats, and finally the crowd faded away. He had knelt down beside the refreshment stand to put his shoes on when he looked up to see Mike Reagan standing before him. Reagan was smoking a cigar and looking down at him rather strangely.

Instantly Cormac was suspicious. "What do you want, Reagan?"

"Just a little talk. Mind if I sit down?"

Actually Cormac did not want to talk to Reagan. He shrugged and continued to put on his shoes.

Reagan bought a drink and offered one to Cormac, who refused. "I've got a proposition for you."

"What do you mean a proposition?" Cormac said. His mouth hurt, and he wanted more than anything else to lie down. He had the extra twenty pounds in his pocket, which was more cash than he had had in some time, and he could not imagine what kind of a proposition this man could have.

"The Gamecock's getting old. He was good for a long time, but he won't last more than a year. I'm looking for a younger man. I'm thinkin' maybe you and I could do some business."

Cormac was shocked. He laughed suddenly, which hurt his bruised ribs, and said, "I'm no pug."

"You'll do until one comes along," he said.

"Not interested," Cormac said. He stretched back, felt his jaw, and said, "I couldn't take this every day."

"You wouldn't have to. You're fast as any man I ever saw and stronger than most. All we have to do is go on a tour. Most of the fights will be quick and painless. We'll make more money than you ever saw."

"Not me. It's no way for a man to live."

For ten minutes Reagan tried to persuade Morgan. Finally he said regretfully, "Well, too bad. I'll have to go without you."

"You're going back to England?"

"I am for a while, but I'll be going to America in six months. Lots of folks over there would pay to see a good fighter, and I know how to spot, and sell, good fighters."

Cormac had stood up and was preparing to leave, but he suddenly, at the Irishman's words, stopped dead still. He turned back and said, "America? You're going to America?"

Mike Reagan was a rough one but very sharp. He had finally caught the interest of this young man who had more potential than he had ever seen. "That's right," he said.

156

"Tell me again about this proposition, Mr. Reagan. . . ."

🐾   🐾   🐾

Pastor Drystan stared at his young friend. "A prizefighter! I can't believe what you're saying, Cormac!"

Cormac had found the pastor over at one of the booths. The minister always came to the fair, but he spent most of the time chatting with the villagers, encouraging them to attend the gospel service he held annually at the fairgrounds, which was often better attended than many of the attractions.

"It won't do, Cormac. It just won't do," he said after listening to what Morgan had to say.

"He's going to America. I can get there that way."

"But to become a pugilist!"

"I won't stay one forever. I hate the idea, too, but I hate more the prospect of going back to slave in the coal mines, which is what I'll have to do if I stay here. My calling is stronger than ever, Pastor. Even now I feel it, but I've got to go to America to preach the Gospel."

"Come with me."

Cormac was puzzled. He followed the pastor until they cleared the fairgrounds. They found a small grove of oaks and moved into the shade. "Kneel down. We'll ask God," the pastor said, and the two men knelt there. They prayed for some time, and finally the pastor said, "I can't answer. It's your life, your calling. But you do have a place here in Wales."

"No. I lost that this morning," Cormac said.

"You have no job?"

"No. The door shut."

The pastor lowered his head and stood in thought. "It will have to be your decision. I have always held that we should go forward as Christians until we get a strong warning. You don't have any such feelings in your spirit about this, Cormac?"

"No, I don't. I think, for now, that this is a door that God is opening."

"A door to become a pugilist!"

"I can't explain it, but I feel I must go. I've got to leave Wales, and I've got no other way to get to America."

Reverend Evan Drystan sighed deeply and paused for several moments before speaking. "Very well. Go with my blessing. I'll be praying. You can always walk away from it if God gives you a warning. Promise me that, Cormac. If God comes to you and warns you, you'll walk away from this."

"I can promise that. I take no pleasure in it. I hate fighting, especially for money, and I don't understand why God would put me into this situation. I don't even know for certain if it is God, but I believe it is, and I've got to try it."

As the two men walked back, the pastor said, "The one thing I fear is that you'll be successful as a fighter."

"Why is that?"

"Because success is dangerous. Money has killed more people than guns or swords, Cormac. It kills the spirit, not the body. It's much more dangerous. More people have left God to follow after money than for any other reason, I fear."

Cormac paid close attention to Drystan's words of caution, and then he said, "Let's say good-bye here, Pastor. I'll be leaving. I've got what few things I have with me. I was going to go back to work at the mines, but now I'm going to England with this man. Thank you for all you've done for me. I wouldn't know the Lord Jesus if it hadn't been for you."

It was a painful parting, but one that both men knew was inevitable. An hour later Cormac was in a carriage sitting beside the Gamecock headed for England.

He said nothing to the Gamecock for some time; then to his surprise Branwell began to talk. "Going to become a pug, are you?"

"It looks that way."

"It ain't a good life," he said. "What's your name?"

"Cormac Morgan."

"It's a hard life, Morgan. A young fellow like you shouldn't get involved."

"Shut up, Charlie, you'll scare him off!" Reagan said roughly.

"He won't do that, Reagan," Cormac said with a grin. "In fact, I think God has sent you both my way."

The two men suddenly stiffened up. Reagan turned around and pulled his cigar out of his mouth. "I didn't know you was crazy. Just a good fighter."

Neither man spoke again for a long time, and finally Cormac settled back. His body and face were sore from the pounding he had taken at the hands of the Gamecock, but his spirit was at peace. He felt that whatever was happening was because God had ordained it.

As the carriage rolled on and darkness began to fall, Cormac had some doubts. He could not see the future, but it seemed dark and somehow ominous. He was ready for adversity, however, for the pastor told him that the ways of God would often be difficult and beyond our understanding. Now he simply sat there, his eyes closed, as the carriage rumbled on toward London and the Welsh countryside faded into the night. He prayed, *Lord, I don't know about tomorrow, but to you it's already happened. So if you want me back in the mines, just let me know.*

London lay ahead, and the mines of Wales lay behind him. But somehow Cormac Morgan knew that he would never go down in a mine again.

14

THE *LEOPARD*

A SICKNESS ROSE IN CORMAC MORGAN'S THROAT as he stared across the open space at the man he had just destroyed. The sight of the man's broken features and the blood streaming down his face were disgusting to him. He had had three bouts and had won them all, but he hated what he was doing a thousand times more than he had hated going down into the coal mines. He stood there listening to the screams of the crowd and watched as the poor fellow he had beaten almost insensible struggled to get up. He got to his knees and made a terrible effort to rise, but his eyes were blank, and he simply collapsed face forward and lay still.

Hands were beating Cormac on the back, as they always did, and he hated this also. To him the crowd was a pack of beasts yelling for blood. He knew they would scream for his blood just as quickly when he was defeated.

"A fine fight, Cormac, my boy!" Reagan had come to him and now cleared a path through the crowd that called his name and reached out to touch him as he passed.

"You're going to be a good one, Morgan. You're going to be a champion. We're going to have it all."

The words did not comfort Cormac, and the sickness in his throat threatened to choke him. His face was set in a mask, and he ignored Reagan's excitement as he made his way out of the crowd.

🐾 　　　 🐾 　　　 🐾

London had become a familiar place to Cormac. As he walked along the streets late that afternoon, he dodged to avoid being flattened by a coach and four horses driven by a haughty driver in livery. He had

161

grown adept at dodging the vehicles and pedestrians that filled the great city.

As he moved along the streets of Cheapside, he took a deep breath and tried to force the memory of the battered man out of his mind. Back in his younger days he had never felt bad after a fight, but those fights were not for money and not in front of a screaming crowd. Those times it was often to defend himself or the honor of another. He knew something was different about what he was doing now, and a constant guilt nagged his conscience each time he stepped into the ring. He could not help but remember the many scriptures that warned against violence, and the one that came into his mind as clearly as if it were carved in marble was: "The servant of the Lord must not strive; but be gentle unto all men."

Lowering his head, he continued on his way. Carts and coaches made such a thundering it seemed that the world went on wheels in London. At every corner he encountered men and women and children from all walks of life—some in the sooty rags of the chimney sweeps, others arrayed in the gold and satin of the aristocracy gazing languidly out of their sedans borne by lackeys with thick legs. Porters sweated under their burdens, chapmen darted from shop to shop, and tradesmen scurried around like ants pulling at the coats of those who passed by their shops.

He had walked all afternoon, and finally the shadows were falling. He stopped to look at a ditch about a foot wide and six inches deep containing a slow stream of putrid slop and garbage in the center of the cobblestone street. He was wondering about it when an old man with a grizzled beard stopped and grinned at him.

"That carries it all away quite nicely. What a change modern improvement made, wouldn't you say? Why, most cities just let it pile up, but not London. No, siree."

He paused in admiration of the open sewer and then moved on. On and on down the crooked winding streets of London Cormac wandered. He had no place to go but the room that he shared with his manager and the English Gamecock. They were, he knew, out drinking and carousing, which he wanted no part of. Since he had been in London he had attended services twice, both times in a traditional church. They had been strange services for him, so formal and without the passion of Pastor Drystan's congregation back in Wales.

The street lighters came out, and Cormac watched as they lit the whale-oil lamps. The light from them cast a flickering illumination over the few passersby. Few people wanted to be out in London after dark,

162

for that was the time when thieves and robbers were about. Cormac turned and headed down toward a wharf. He liked to stand beside the Thames and watch the ships come and go with the tide.

He was already sick of fighting, and he longed for the company of the pastor who had mentored him for such a long time. Most of all he was filled with doubt and worried that he had made a terrible mistake. Even now as he moved along, he was thinking, *God could not be in this. Surely He wouldn't have me fight like a beast to please the passions of a crowd! I can't believe it!*

He lifted his head as he heard footsteps coming and suddenly became alert. There before him a group of men walked down the middle of the street. He saw at once that they were sailors, and all of them carried short clubs in their hands. Immediately behind them was an officer who called out, "There's a likely one! Get him, men!"

Cormac had no time to run, for the sailors had rushed him. They were all wearing shirts with horizontal stripes, and each man's hair was tied back in a pigtail. He knew instantly what this was: the press gang! *I'm in trouble now!* he thought.

The British navy was always in need of sailors, for in wartime manpower always presented a problem. Not nearly enough men volunteered, so in port a ship would send out a press gang, usually a group of eight to twelve men. It was their job to try to persuade seamen they met onshore to join the navy. If a sailor didn't want to join, the press gang simply took him and pressed him. That is, forced him into the navy, and they did not confine their prey to sailors. Any man they could grab was fair game.

The first man that reached Cormac was knocked senseless by a blow to his head. The next two were almost leveled, but then Cormac was simply overpowered. Their clubs descended on him, and though he struck out again and again, a crack to the head suddenly turned his world into a brilliant orange light and he knew no more.

The lieutenant, William Simms, who was in command of the press gang, stood staring down at Cormac. "Well, he's a tough one. Look at the damage he's done." He stared at the men who were down nursing broken faces and one who did not stir at all. "We'll soften him up. Take him aboard the ship."

The sailors gathered up their injured companions, and four of them seized Cormac and hauled him down the dark streets toward the ship. When they got to the ship, they turned him over to another part of the crew and then turned and went back in search of more men.

☫   ☫   ☫

The first thing Cormac noticed when he came out of the darkness that had enveloped him was the terrible smell—a mixture of human bodies, human waste, and rotten food that almost gagged him. He sat up and a sharp pain bolted through his head. He lifted his hand and found that one of the clubs had opened a cut and the blood had stiffened on his hair. He took several deep breaths, and the throbbing eased somewhat.

The scene before him was like something out of Dante's *Inferno*. It was so dark he could barely make out the forms of the men who were all around him. A few lamps threw dim, flickering illumination over the deck, and Cormac, who had never been on a ship in his life, knew indeed that another door had opened for him—but not one he had walked through willingly. He rolled over, coming to a sitting position and gasping with pain. Then he looked around at his fellow prisoners. None of them were speaking, but he could hear the laughter of the sailors as they moved around on deck.

He saw that he was in a low-ceilinged area with great cannons behind windows of some sort that were closed. He was to find out later the windows would be opened to admit air, but when new pressed hands came aboard they were closed to prevent escape.

Stunned and wondering what would happen next, Cormac sat still for a long time. Years ago in a tavern he had overheard a sailor, home from the sea, describe the horrors of life on board one of His Majesty's warships. He had determined then and there that the one thing he would never be was a sailor.

Time passed and nothing happened. He could hear the moans of the other pressed men, most of whom, like Cormac, were recovering from brutal beatings. Cormac himself did not utter a sound but simply sat there, and as always when he could not sleep or when there was nothing to do, he prayed.

But prayer did not come easily on the gun deck of the ship. Cormac had been depressed enough by his life as a bareknuckle prizefighter. But now to be thrown into a life that he knew he would hate brought black doubt rushing through him. The devil seemed to be telling him, *You see, you should never have left Wales. You were a fool to think you were following God! Now you see where it's gotten you. You'll spend years in this place and probably will be killed!*

Being killed was a very real possibility, for England was at war with France as well as with America. Her ships were fighting battles all over the globe, and the mortality rate among sailors was astronomically high.

Finally a sailor bearing a lantern appeared, followed by an officer. "All right, you men. Get up. You are sailors in His Majesty's navy now. We're going to make you look like it."

Getting to his feet, Cormac joined the lines of men being driven along the deck toward a set of stairs. He stumbled as he moved upward, for it was still dark belowdecks. He was later to learn that darkness characterized life aboard a man-of-war. When he stumbled out on the deck with the others, the sun was just beginning to appear over the horizon. He blinked like an owl as the lieutenant barked, "Stop right there." He turned and said, "I'm Lieutenant Simms, and you men now are all sailors aboard His Majesty's ship the *Leopard*. It is my job to make sailors out of you men, and sailors you will be."

At that moment a man wearing two epaulets appeared behind Simms. Simms turned and said, "Captain, these are the pressed men."

Captain Reginald Stokes looked at the men before him with a cold eye. "A poor lot, Mr. Simms."

"Most of them are just out of prison, sir."

"Well, they'll do to pull a rope. Delouse them and put them to work."

"Aye, sir."

Cormac Morgan had known hard work. He had known poverty, but his introduction to the Royal Navy was something altogether different. He was treated as if he were an animal. He and his fellows first had their hair shaved off. When one of them protested, he was knocked to the deck, and a grinning sailor who wielded the shears said, "Got to get rid of that lice, mate. It'll grow back again."

Cormac had never been a vain man despite his rugged good looks, but somehow when the barber was through with him, he felt ugly and stripped of his humanity.

The men then were stripped naked and hosed down with cold seawater, which was pumped up by sailors who laughed at their discomfort. "The first bath you've had in many a year, I'll wager!" cracked one of the marines.

After the bath was over, the miserable men were taken to a small dark section of the ship where the purser issued them new clothes. "It'll all come out of your pay," he grinned, showing great gaps in his teeth, "though most of you won't live to wear 'em out."

The purser's attitude was typical of the crew of the *Leopard* toward the pressed men. They seemed to take delight in telling them how terrible life was going to be for them.

Lieutenant Simms surveyed the lot of them, then said, "All right. Hack, show them where they're going to sleep."

Sleeping aboard the man-of-war was a considerable problem, as Cormac was to discover. There were almost seven hundred common seamen on board, which, along with the officers, made a total of nearly eight hundred men. Cormac could not imagine how that many people would sleep in such cramped quarters.

The seaman who led them downstairs said, "Come along. My name's Hacker. Everyone calls me Hack." He took the men belowdecks and said, "This is where you'll sleep—fourteen inches apart."

"Fourteen inches!" one man cried out. "I'm bigger than that."

"Well, half the crew will be on watch, so that'll double it to twenty-eight inches. Here, unroll your hammocks." Hack showed them how the hammocks were attached on hooks on the beams overhead. "Now," he said, "it's quite an art getting into one of these. I'll show you how." He stepped up to Cormac and said, "You're a big fellow. You'll have more trouble than most. Here's the way you do it. What's your name?"

"Cormac Morgan."

"All right, Morgan. Here. Here's the way you do it." Hack balanced on his left leg, put his right leg over into the hammock, and held on to the top bar of the hammock with his left hand. With one quick spring and a twist, he fell into the hammock. "There it is. Nothing to it. Now you try it, Morgan."

Cormac stared at the hammock. He had never seen such a contraption in his life. It was nothing really but strands of rope tied together with a canvas to form the middle. There was no padding except for the blankets. He grasped the bar that had been placed at the top to spread the hammock and tried to imitate Hack's motion. He did manage to land partially in the hammock, but it twisted and he felt himself falling. He hit the deck with a thump and Hack laughed.

"Don't worry. You'll get the hang of it. Now, when you get out of your hammock for your watch, you roll it up like this." He skillfully rolled Cormac's hammock into a very tight roll, tied it with ropes, and said, "You see this?" He held up an iron ring. "Your hammock's got to pass through there, or you'll get a taste of the cat. When you get it together, you all take your hammocks upstairs and place them around the edge. They come in handy to hide behind when the firing starts. Now, I'm going to assign you all to a mess."

"A mess? What's that?" Cormac asked.

166

"It's seven men that eats together. I'll put you in my mess, Morgan. The rest of you, I'll find a place for you."

And so life began for Cormac Morgan aboard His Majesty's ship the *Leopard*. It was a new world and a hard one. The *Leopard* departed two days after Cormac had been pressed, and he had to learn through hard trial and error. The watches were staggered so that no man ever got more than four hours sleep at a time. And Cormac did not sleep well in a hammock to begin with, for it was impossible to lie in any position except flat on your back, sagging down in the middle. When the ship hit the open sea, he discovered that he was susceptible to seasickness, as were several of the other men.

And then there was a nasty little instrument called a "starter." This was a short piece of rope that the bosun, a man named Thomas, carried. Any sailor not moving fast enough to suit the bosun was struck sharply across the back of the neck. All the new men received their share of cracks, and at times anger consumed Cormac Morgan. But he knew that to survive in this world, he would have to control himself.

The food on board the *Leopard* was terrible. It was a monotonous diet: Sunday and Thursday was dried peas and salt pork; Monday, a bowl of oatmeal, butter, and a piece of cheese; Tuesday and Saturday, salt beef; and Wednesday and Friday, oatmeal, butter, a piece of cheese, and dried peas.

The dried peas were usually made into soup. They also received two pints of beer and a portion of rum every day. Cormac drank the beer, since it was better than the water, but he had sworn off hard liquor and gave his ration to Hack, who had become a good friend after several weeks on board.

The meals were also served with biscuits, which were often home to maggots and weevils. Cormac would never forget the first time he picked up a biscuit. He started to bite it, then suddenly stopped and stared. "There's a worm in this biscuit!" he exclaimed.

"Nothin' to that. Just tap it on the table. It'll crawl out."

A shiver ran up the length of Cormac's spine. He had been rather fastidious about his eating and shook his head. "I think I'll just exchange it."

"You've got to eat it, Cormac," Hack said. "That's all there is."

Another of the sailors, an old hand named Peters, said, "They ain't bad. The black-headed ones are fat and cold but not bitter like the weevils."

Hack grinned and said, "There's an easy way to get rid of 'em. Put a dead fish into a sack of the biscuits, and the maggots will crawl out to eat it. When the maggots are on the fish, you throw the fish in the sea. Keep doin' that until there ain't no more maggots."

"I'll be glad to do that," Cormac said quickly.

"Well, you're a finicky eater, lad. I can tell that you've been brought up right."

The work was hard and endless. There was always something to do. Cormac was utterly confused by the hundreds, even thousands, of ropes that controlled the various sails that billowed overhead. All he could do at first was simply to pull on a given rope when he was told to do so. Slowly he began to learn that each sail had a name, as well as each rope, and by his second month on board the *Leopard*, he was speaking almost a different language. He had become part of a six-man gun crew, and his job was helping to move the gun back. His great strength impressed Hack, who told the lieutenant that the new man was doing good work.

As the weeks passed, Cormac survived. He learned that a man-of-war was like a small city afloat. There were all sorts of men, from wealthy landowners, who were invariably officers, right down to common laborers and former convicts. Ruling like a king over the whole ship was Captain Reginald Stokes. His word was absolute law, and when the captain was in bad humor, everyone suffered for it.

Several of the men received floggings, being tied up on a grate and struck by a cat-o'-nine-tails, which was a whip made of nine knotted lines fastened to a handle. All the crew had been assembled to watch these punishments, and Hack had whispered, "You want to stay away from the cat. It scars a man for life."

Matthew Hacker had become a good friend to Cormac. He had listened sympathetically as Cormac had told him his story and had been interested when he had heard that Hack's desire was to get to America.

"I'm an American," Hacker said when Cormac finished.

"An American! What are you doing in the British navy?"

"I was pressed in Savannah. Went down on business and they caught me in the street just like they caught you."

"I didn't think the British would press Americans."

"Yes, they do, and they stop American ships and take their sailors off. Press them right out into their own navy."

"What part of America are you from? New York or Boston?"

"No. I'm from down south. We've got a farm close to Charleston. Wish I was there now."

From that time on Cormac encouraged his friend to talk about his home. He still knew deep down in his heart that God was going to use him in America, and finally he mentioned it to Hack.

"Well, we're headed for America. This ship's takin' supplies to His Majesty's forces there. We'll either land in New York or down south in Savannah or Charleston."

Hack said nothing more about it for several days, but finally as the ship approached the coast, he said, "I heard the officers talking. We're landing at Charleston, and I'm jumpin' ship."

"You're gonna escape?"

"Right."

"But I've heard them say they shoot deserters."

Hack was a small man with warm brown eyes. His mouth twisted now in a sour grin. "I'd rather be dead than live like this." He hesitated, then said, "Come with me, Cormac."

Cormac Morgan did not have to be urged. "All right," he said. "I'll go with you. I can't stand this life either."

From that moment on the two talked about nothing but escape. By the time they anchored in Charleston's harbor, they had their few belongings in small bags. They knew they could not wear their uniforms for long, as they would be easily spotted. Cormac had miraculously managed to hang on to some of the money he had when he had been pressed. They had missed discovering it, and he was grateful. It was in gold coins, only a few, but at least it would buy them some clothes.

"For the first few days they'll be watching for men trying to get away," Hack warned. "We'll have to wait a spell."

They waited for four days. In the middle of the night Hack, who was in the hammock next to Cormac, whispered, "Come, lad."

Cormac crawled out of his hammock, fully dressed, and slipped on his shoes and picked up his bag, which he kept ready. The sleeping quarters were manned, usually, by marine guards, but many of them had been granted leave ashore, and the way was clear. The two waited until the one guard on the upper deck moved to the other side of the vessel, and then they were on deck.

Clouds covered the moon, and the ship rose slightly with the swell as they crept toward the rail. "We can't make a splash, so we'll have to let ourselves down slow, you see," Hack whispered.

"Right. Can you swim?"

"Not much."

"Well, I can. Give me your bundle. I'll take care of it."

"I can dog-paddle. It ain't far to shore, you see. There it is."

Cormac looked through the night, and he could see the faint lights of the city. His heart suddenly burned within him, for he knew that God had brought him to this place. "I'll go first, Hack. You can follow me down."

He tied the two bags to rope and slipped them over his shoulders, then tossed a longer rope down to the water, securing one end to the rail. He lowered himself hand over hand until he entered the water, keeping silent. He waited until Hack slipped in beside him, and then the two started for the shore. It was not a long swim, and they moved as quietly as possible. There was no sound of alarm from the *Leopard*. Finally Cormac's feet touched the bottom. "Right," he whispered. "We're here."

The two men waded ashore, and Hack said, "We've got to get out of here into the country."

"What about clothes?"

"We'll worry about that when we get out of Charleston. There's too many British officers and soldiers here. They'll be on the lookout for sailors jumping ship."

The two walked along the shoreline, and finally, when they had cleared the main part of the city, Hack pointed. "We go that way. That's where my home is, on the Peedee River."

Cormac looked into the darkness and said, "My pastor told me a door would open. I think this is it, Hack."

"Maybe it is," Hack nodded. "It's a good country, Cormac. A man could make a place for himself here."

As Cormac trudged alongside his friend, he thought back to the words of John Wesley. He could not help but believe that somehow God had brought him to the New World. It had been a rugged, terrible route, but he looked up at the stars twinkling faintly between the clouds and breathed a prayer, "Thank you, Lord. You opened the door, and I'm walking through it."

15

TWELVETREES

HEARING THE SOUND OF A CARRIAGE APPROACHING, Grace put Patrick down on the floor and immediately went to the front door. Any movement outside made her cautious, for the word had spread that the partisan battles that were wrecking the countryside were moving closer to the Peedee River area. It was September, and the hot weather had not mitigated, so the door stood open. She peered at the carriage coming down the dusty road, a plume of fine dust thrown behind it, and then smiled. "Keturah!" she called out. "It's them! They're here!" She hurried out at once without waiting for Keturah to come out of the kitchen. Descending the steps, she waved as the carriage pulled up, and as soon as it stopped, she cried, "Get out and come into the house!"

Matthew had been driving. He leaped out, secured the lines, then went around to help Abigail out. From the rear seat Sam leaped out, but Jubal did not. He sat there, his face pale and his lips a white line.

"Well, we've descended on you, Grace," Matthew said. "That's what relatives are for—to come almost without warning and eat you out of house and home."

Grace smiled and took his hand. "I'm so glad to see you, Matthew. And this must be Abigail."

"Yes. Abigail, I want you to meet my cousin Grace."

"I've heard so much about you, Grace," Abigail smiled. She was wearing a peacock blue dress with a round neckline edged in white lace, three-quarter length sleeves, a tight-fitting bodice with black buttons running down the front, and a full skirt. She looked fresh despite the heat.

Abigail greeted her, then turned to Sam, whose eyes were on Keturah. The young woman had come to stand just behind Grace, and she

171

was very conscious of Sam's gaze. He moved at once past Grace and said, "Hello, Keturah."

"Hello, Sam."

The greeting lacked some enthusiasm, and Sam's face dropped. He had been hoping for at least some small encouragement on her part.

Grace's eyes went to Jubal, who had not gotten out. "Why, Jubal," she said, moving over, "how are you?"

"Not very well, I'm afraid, Grace. That prison just about did me in. I can't even get in and out of a carriage by myself."

Sam came at once and said, "Here. Let me give you a hand." Grace and Keturah watched as Sam had to practically lift Jubal down. "I got an infection in my leg that just won't go away," Jubal said. He shook his head, and his eyes held a bitter glint. "I wanted to come down and help you, Grace, but instead I come down to add to your burdens."

"It's no trouble at all," Grace said quickly. "We'll take care of you, and you'll be as good as new in no time. Keturah, we'll put Jubal in the blue room downstairs."

Sam and Matthew immediately got on each side of Jubal and helped him into the house. He held on to them ashen faced, and Grace whispered to Abigail, "I didn't realize he was in such poor shape."

"Those prison hulks are terrible. He got an infection in that leg. It's a bad ulcer. Your brother Clive was there and looked at it. He said he's going to need care for a long time."

"Well, I'm glad you've come," Grace said. "Now, let's go into the house, and we'll fix something to eat."

They went inside and at once Abigail spotted Patrick, who was lying flat on his back wearing only a nappy. She walked over and knelt beside him. "Oh, what a fine boy! This must be Patrick."

"Yes. Watch out. He may be a bit damp. He's a little fountain, that boy," Grace said. She watched with pride as Abigail smoothed the baby's hair and touched his fat cheeks with her finger.

"He's so handsome, and he looks like you, Grace. I can see the resemblance."

"Do you think so?" Secretly Grace was glad that Patrick resembled her. He did have some of the traits of his father, but he surely had her eyes and hair. "Well, Keturah's been a godsend helping me take care of things here. I know you'll want to wash up. Come along, I'll show you your room."

They went down the hall, and when Grace opened the door and stepped aside, Abigail exclaimed, "Why, this is a lovely room!" It was a medium-sized room with dark blue carpet and walls with large designs in blue, white, and green. Pictures of peacocks and trees hung in dark wooden frames on the walls, and the two small windows, which were covered with lace curtains, let in the sunlight. A small pine fireplace, elaborately carved, was flanked by two mahogany chairs covered in blue-and-white silk damask. It also had a mantel with candlesticks and vases of paper spills in order to light fires. There was an oak tester bed with a paneled canopy, a dressing table with a porcelain bowl and bottles decorating the top, a mahogany washstand, and a small wardrobe with molded cornice.

"I've worked hard on the house," Grace said. She did not add that her husband had spent practically no time with her, and she had had nothing else to do. "Keturah has also done a great deal," she said. "She's a fine young woman."

Abigail turned and smiled. "I know. I'm very fond of Keturah. Not as fond as Sam is, of course."

"Keturah doesn't mention him much."

"No, but Sam mentions Keturah a lot. I'm afraid the attachment's fairly one-sided."

"Well," Grace shrugged, "Keturah's a fine young woman."

"So she is, but then Sam is the most stubborn young man I've ever known in my life. He's determined to win her, and I wouldn't bet against it."

"You stay here and lie down and rest. When you get up we'll have something to eat."

An hour later they were all gathered around the table in the large dining room. "We were all grieved to hear of Stephen's death," Matthew said.

Grace nodded but did not dwell on the subject.

The room was an airy place with windows along two sides of the room. The open windows let in a breeze, but with it came plenty of flies. Grace said, "We need to put gauze or something on the windows. It's hard to keep the flies out."

"I thought we'd go on over to our property tomorrow," Matthew said. He was eating the food that had been set out, which was plenty: salted pork; butter beans; mashed potatoes with cream, butter, and parsley; homemade bread with fresh apple butter; and sweet potato pie for dessert.

"Oh no, you must stay here and rest up. I know Abigail's tired and you must be too. That's a long trip all the way from Boston."

In truth they were all tired from the journey, and Matthew agreed without any resistance. Sam was seated down the table from Keturah and could not see her face, but he was alert when she spoke. Several times she got up to replenish the glasses of sassafras tea they were all drinking, and he thought he had never seen her look so pretty. She did not meet his eyes, however, and he was depressed, saying little.

"Well, have the politics changed, Grace?" Jubal asked. He had been helped to the table and was now nibbling at his food. The sickness edged lines in his handsome face, and everyone could see he was uncomfortable.

"No. Not really. This war has wrecked the country. In a way," Grace said thoughtfully, "it would be better if either the British or the Americans controlled the country. As it is, right now the British have control, but that could change. If they pull their army out, the patriots will come rushing back, and then we'll see more fighting."

Abigail listened quietly as Grace went on to explain the political difficulties. She saw that Grace was suffering from tension and knew some of the story. Jubal had once confided to her his feelings on the situation. *"Grace should have never married my brother,"* he had said. *"Stephen was a good man in many ways, but he wasn't thoughtful. He was all business. He wasn't the kind of man Grace needed at all."*

Now as Abigail studied the face of their hostess, she saw great beauty but also something in Grace's eyes that troubled her. She had heard much of Grace's softness and tenderness from Clive and others of the family who knew her. She could see traces of this, yet there was a distinct hardness in Grace's expression—as if she had drawn herself inside a protective fence and would let no one in.

The South Carolina night was hot and oppressive. Sam and Matthew had gone outside to look around the plantation. Jubal was extremely tired and had gone to bed early.

Abigail sat in the spacious parlor with Grace, and the two women talked, mostly about Patrick. Grace was pleased at how fond Abigail was of the child. "You love babies, don't you, Abigail?"

"Well, in the abstract I do." Abigail smiled and then held Patrick high in the air. When he squealed with delight, she gently lowered him. "I've never really had much to do with them. If they're all as handsome as this young man, I want to have at least six just like him."

Grace laughed. "They don't come that easy, Abigail, I'm afraid."

"Was it very difficult?"

It was as if Abigail's question had crossed an invisible line, for Grace's eyes at once assumed the hardness that Abigail had noticed before, and she answered vaguely, "I suppose all deliveries are difficult."

As the conversation moved on, Grace relaxed and soon asked about Abigail's marriage.

"It was a very troublesome road for Matthew and me," Abigail said quietly. "It is no secret that we had an affair once when we were younger. I was a sinner then, very much so, and I hurt him terribly."

"What brought you two back together, Abigail?"

"I think it was when Matthew lost absolutely everything. I'd already lost everything," she said ruefully, "years ago when I came to know the Lord, but Matthew hadn't."

"I heard he lost all of his inheritance and his estate in Virginia."

"Yes, and he gave up the title. It never meant anything to him anyway. In any case, he stumbled home sick and penniless, but God spoke to his heart. He found the Lord, and from that time on God has been the center of our relationship."

From outside far off a dog howled mournfully. Abigail saw that Patrick was getting sleepy. She held him in the crook of her arm and rocked him back and forth, studying his soft features. "Why do people have to reach the bottom before they discover the truth?"

"I can't say," Grace said. She had not been able to talk candidly with Keturah, for the younger woman would not have understood. But she knew that Abigail would, and she soon found herself confiding how unhappy her marriage had been. She said finally, "I can't even grieve over him, Abigail. Isn't that terrible?"

Abigail listened closely. She had already found out some of the truth from Jubal and from Clive, and now she knew she must be very careful. "You mustn't punish yourself over that," she said. "From what you say, you two, despite being married, were never . . . close."

"We never were," Grace said bitterly. "I had such high expectations of marriage. I was going to marry the perfect man, and we were going to love each other and have a wonderful life together."

Abigail studied Grace's face. The lovely lines were now marred with strain. Gently she said, "All we can do is pray for God's grace and His guidance. You can't do anything about Stephen, but you have a son, and you're still a young woman."

Grace dropped her head. She did not speak for a long time, and then she said, "I always wanted tenderness in a husband. I wouldn't have cared if he had nothing as long as he loved me—and told me so." She looked up, the tears glistening in her eyes. "That's all I wanted to hear, but Stephen couldn't say it. I suppose he never felt it either. . . ."

Abigail knew more about this side of men than Grace. "Some men are selfish. They think only of themselves, but not all men are like that.

Besides, I think men can learn to show tenderness."

"I don't see how. I tried everything I could with Stephen. You can't train a man like you do a dog."

Abigail had no answer. Her own brief marriage had been a source of constant joy to her, but she could not express this to Grace, for it would only hurt her. Finally she said, "God has a plan for you, Grace. In the meantime, you just simply be faithful."

When the men returned a short while later, Sam managed to find Keturah alone. She was sitting on a wooden chair out in the backyard watching the huge moon as it shed its beams down. Sam approached her and said, "Keturah, I need to talk to you."

"About what, Sam?"

Sam sat down on the swing that was suspended from the branches of a giant oak tree. "About us, of course."

"Sam, didn't you learn anything back in Boston? Back when you had that awful fight with that corporal? Can't you see that I don't want to be pressed?"

Sam, however, had built up some high expectations, and now as he sat there he saw the beauty of Keturah's face. He suddenly stood up, reached out, and tried to kiss her.

She jumped to her feet and said, "Sam, don't paw me like that!"

"Keturah, I'm going to marry you, and that's all there is to it!"

As soon as Sam had uttered the words, he knew he had done the wrong thing.

Keturah's eyes grew small, and she said harshly, "Nobody is going to tell me who to marry, Sam Bradford!" Then she turned around and rushed away.

Sam stood there and looked up at the moon. He was upset and angry at himself. He went at once to the bedroom he was sharing with Jubal, who had already gone to bed.

"Going to bed this early, Sam?"

"Yes," he snapped.

Sam's curtness drew Jubal's attention. He felt very weak, for the journey had been hard, but he was concerned about his old friend and suspected what was happening. "You have a fight with Keturah?"

"What does she want out of a man, Jubal? Here I've come halfway across the country just to be with her. You'd think she'd appreciate it."

Jubal closed his eyes. He had taken some of the pain medication that Clive had provided and was so drowsy he could hardly murmur. "You can't rush her, Sam. . . ."

Sam shook his head and began to undress. His face was set and he

176

did not answer, for Jubal was already asleep. When he finally lay down, he tried to calm himself. *I'll have to do better than this*, he thought grimly. *But I meant what I said. She's got to marry me!*

🃏   🃏   🃏

Breakfast the next morning was a huge meal, prepared mostly by Keturah, although Abigail had come into the kitchen to help her. They had set the table with biscuits, fresh butter and jam, pork gravy, slices of thick ham, hot oat cereal with currants, eggs, and cup after cup of hot tea. After the breakfast Grace said to Matthew, "I asked one of our neighbors, Mr. Greer, to find someone to help you with your plantation. He says he knows a good man who's available."

"That will be helpful," Matthew said. "We're anxious to get started."

"I hope you don't expect too much," Grace cautioned. "The place hasn't been kept up."

"That's why we came," Abigail said quickly. She squeezed Matthew's arm and smiled at him. "We're going to have a fine home there."

They met Simon Taws as soon as breakfast was over, and Grace was terse as she introduced him. "This is Taws, my overseer. Taws, I want you to take these people over to Twelvetrees."

"I'll see to it." There was a curtness about Taws and a lack of politeness, Sam thought. Always ready to take offense when a woman was slighted, he narrowed his eyes and thought, *That fellow needs to be taught a lesson. I may have to see to that.*

As Grace returned to the house, Taws led Matthew, Abigail, and Sam outside and beckoned to a huge slave who was working in the garden. "Leo, come here."

The man came over. "Yes, Mr. Taws."

"Take these people over to Twelvetrees. Then you get right back."

"Yes, sah, Mr. Taws. I will."

Taws left with a curt nod, and Matthew frowned. "Not a very pleasant fellow."

"Just lookin' at him makes me want to punch him in the eye," Sam said. "I don't see how Grace puts up with him."

A light glowed in Leo's eyes when he heard them speak of Taws in this manner. "I'll get me a mule and lead you over," he said.

"Could you also hitch up our carriage, Leo?"

"Yes, sah, I'll do that."

They made the trip down the dusty road with Leo riding alongside. He was a pleasant man, huge and muscular with a terrible scar down his right cheek. It gave him an almost sinister look on that side, but he

177

was polite enough and spoke very well. "Twelvetrees. Is that the name of the place?" Abigail asked as he rode alongside.

"Yes, ma'am. Don't know why they call it that. They's more than twelve trees on it, but it's always been Twelvetrees."

"Do you know the place, Leo?" Matthew asked.

"Oh yes, sah. It belonged to old Mr. Hugo Ramsey. He done passed some years ago. I think there was some kind of fuss over who would get the place, and finally it went back to the county for taxes. Mr. Morrison, he bought it back for the taxes, and then I reckon he sold it to you."

"Yes. We bought the place," Matthew answered. "Is it a good plantation, Leo?"

"It could be, sah. Yes, indeed! It been let go down, but what goes down can sho come up."

The trip took only an hour, for it adjoined the Morrison plantation. When Leo informed them that they were now on Twelvetrees' property, they began to see what the slave had meant. The fields were filled with weeds, and most of the fences were broken down. The whole place had a general air of decay, and Matthew's jaw tightened as his eyes scanned the property. But he was determined not to complain and said nothing.

"And there's the house, Mr. Bradford. Right there."

They pulled up in front of a large two-story house with broken windows and peeling paint. Part of the roof was fallen in, and chickens wandered in and out of the front door.

"Welcome home, Mrs. Bradford," Matthew said, trying to put a good face on it. He jumped out, helped Abigail to the ground, and then, along with Sam, they went inside.

It was a disaster! They went from room to room and saw that vandals had been at it. A terrible odor permeated the whole house. They soon traced it to a chicken that had died in one of the upstairs bedrooms.

Finally Matthew said gloomily, "We can't stay in a place like this!"

And then Abigail Howland Bradford proved what she was made of. She laughed and reached out and hugged Matthew. "This is Twelvetrees, the home of Mr. and Mrs. Matthew Bradford. Of course we're staying here."

"But it's such a mess!"

"It's our home, Matthew," Abigail said, "and I can see it all painted, with new carpets and wallpaper, these hardwood floors refinished, everything shiny and beautiful. And outside there'll be green grass and white fences and a garden, with flowers everywhere."

Matthew stood there listening and could not believe what he was hearing. He finally glanced at Sam and winked. "I married the right woman, Sam. Make sure you do the same. It means everything."

"I plan to," Sam said. "Now, I guess we'd better get to work."

Going outside, Matthew said, "Leo, do you know anybody we could hire to help us clean the place up?"

"Sho do. How many you need, Mr. Bradford?"

"Well, at least half a dozen. All you can find."

"People hard up around here. They could sho use a little money. I'll have 'em here sooner than you think, and I'll come over and help myself when I get through with my work for Miss Grace."

There seemed to be no place to begin, but as Leo rode off, his legs raped over the sides of the rawboned mule, Sam said, "Well, I'll start haulin' stuff out and make a trash pile."

"I'll start sweeping," Abigail said. "Come along, Matthew. Time to go to work. . . ."

🏛   🏛   🏛

Two bedrooms had been cleaned out by the day's end, and Matthew and Abigail were preparing to go to bed in one of them. Filthy from their exertions, they had managed to take baths with water hauled from the creek. They were both exhausted, and Matthew had crawled into bed first. The window was open, and the full moon dappled the room with its silver beams. He watched Abigail as she brushed her hair. She was wearing a graceful white nightgown, translucent in the moonlight.

"Come on to bed, wife," he said. "I'm lonesome."

Abigail laughed and turned. She came over and slid into the bed beside him. At once he took her in his arms and whispered, "You are the most beautiful woman in the whole world—or anywhere else for that matter."

Abigail kissed him. "Tell me more," she whispered.

"I'm never going to let a day go by without telling you how lovely you are and how much I love you."

"What if you forget?" Abigail said.

"Hit me with a broomstick!"

Abigail laughed. She thought how much it would have meant to Grace Morrison if her husband had loved her the way Matthew loved Abigail. But there was no more time for thought as he pulled her close and she nestled against him.

16

A New Hand

THE FALL HAD BROUGHT COOLER WEATHER to South Caro-
lina. The ridges around the fields were beginning to lose their bright
greenery, and already the sweet gums were dotting the countryside
with yellow, gold, and red leaves. The woods were entangled with
brambles and wild vines, and along the swamps and rivers cypress
trees lifted themselves like stately sentinels, their knees bare and their
features hidden by long, flowing Spanish moss.

Keturah had learned to like the landscape, although it had been hard
to adjust from the bracing New England climate to the sultry semitrop-
ical swamps and lowlands along the Peedee and Santee Rivers.

Now as she hung out clothes on a line, she welcomed the coolness
of the breeze and laughed suddenly at the love bugs that flew in front
of her. The tiny insects amused her, and as she finished hanging out the
bed sheets, she picked up her basket and turned to go into the house.

From her right came the sound of a horse approaching, and she
turned and narrowed her eyes until she recognized Sam approaching
on his bay mare. As usual he was coming at a dead run, and as soon as
he pulled up and roughly dismounted, she said, "Sam, you're going to
ruin that horse."

"Ruin Nellie? I don't reckon so." Sam patted the horse on the steaming flanks, and she suddenly nipped at his hat, grabbing the brim and
snatching it off. Sam laughed and made a grab for it. Securing it, he held
it in his hand and stood before her, his blue eyes excited. "I think we're
going to go out on a raid soon with Colonel Marion."

"When?" Keturah asked. The news did not please her, for she knew
that the raids led by Colonel Francis Marion were often bloody and dangerous affairs, and a sudden fear shot through her as she thought of
Sam lying dead in some field somewhere.

"I don't know, but it'll be soon, I think. Ban Tarleton's been burning houses all along the riverbanks. I'd like to get close enough to get a shot at him. I'd put a stop to his raiding!"

"Everyone speaks of him as an awful man."

"Well, he *is* awful! He's a fop, for one thing. Dresses with a fancy uniform and a feather in his cap, but the worst thing is," Sam said, his eyes flashing, "when men try to surrender, he just orders his legion to cut them down. 'Tarleton's quarter,' everybody's starting to call it. If we ever catch him, we'll show him how to give quarter."

"Come on in and have some lemonade."

"I can't stay. I'm on the way to the village. Do you need anything?"

"We need some salt."

"Who doesn't?" Sam said. Salt was in short supply in the southern colonies, and people had resorted to all sorts of dealings to get it. "I'll see if I can find some," Sam said.

"I suppose you'll stop at the Green Lantern."

The Green Lantern was a tavern in the small village of Fairdale that lay ten miles away.

Sam suddenly stared at Keturah, then averted his eyes. "I hadn't thought of it," he mumbled.

"It'd be the first time. I hear you're spending a lot of your time there."

"I've been once or twice. What about it?" Sam said.

"I hear you and that Polly Brown are getting thick as thieves."

Sam flushed. He had indeed flirted some with Polly, but then everybody had. His ears grew red with embarrassment, as they always did, and he said, "I wouldn't think you'd care. You won't have anything to do with me. A man's got a right to talk to a woman, hasn't he?"

Keturah had really been meaning to tease Sam, but she saw that he was serious. Now she grew irritated with him. "You followed me all the way down here from Boston, or so you say, and now the first chance you get you're carousing with some wench at a tavern!"

Sam stared at Keturah. "I wasn't carousing," he said. "And I haven't had anything to do with Polly Brown except just to flirt with her a little bit when we stopped for ale."

"You think I don't know how men get after women? I've had to see enough of it in my day."

Sam was embarrassed but at the same time very defensive. "Well, I noticed you're seeing a lot of Charles Dixon."

Charles Dixon was a neighboring planter, a man in his late thirties who had lost his wife. He had been attracted to Keturah, as had several of the other single men in the area. Keturah had never once thought of him as a possible husband, but now her eyes flashed and she said, "If you can see a tavern girl, I suppose I can be pleasant to a respectable man like Charles Dixon."

Sam was totally frustrated. He slapped his hat against his leg and said, "I don't know what you want of a man, Keturah. I've told you I love you, and that's all I can do."

Keturah at that moment felt very sorry for Sam Bradford. Her life had been so terrible before the Bradfords had taken her in, and she was filled with gratitude to all of them—especially to Daniel. The whole family had accepted her as a member of the family. It had been obvious to everyone that Sam had strong feelings for her. But Keturah had vivid memories of fighting off men when she had been under her mother's charge in the army camps. She had kept herself pure by a driving determination not to become like her mother. Her resolve had developed in her a protective suspicion of any man, even Sam.

Sam studied Keturah for a moment and then said, "Well, I've got to go."

"Go on and see your Miss Brown, then!" Keturah was sorry the moment she said it, for it was obvious that Sam cared nothing for any woman but her. She saw the hurt flood his eyes and was about to apologize. But without another word he swung into the saddle and spurred Nellie until the mare gave a startled cry, reared up, and then shot off down the road in a cloud of dust.

Now, why did I have to say that? I had no call to be so mean to Sam. Keturah was highly displeased with herself, and she determined to make it up to Sam the next time she saw him.

☫   ☫   ☫

The day had been a disaster for Grace. Patrick had developed a rash the day before, which made him fussy all day long and had kept her up half the night. She had been gritty eyed all morning, and it was one of those times when nothing seemed to go right.

Early in the afternoon, Simon Taws had come by, as he did almost every day. He had become especially attentive since Stephen's death, and Grace had known that sooner or later he would try to make advances. So she was ready for it.

She and Taws had just finished going over the books. She had closed the account book firmly and risen to her feet. Taws rose with her. He suddenly brushed against her, and she grew rigid. He put his hand out to touch her, but she stepped back at once, saying, "That'll be all, Taws!"

Taws had not been intimidated. He grinned, saying, "It's hard for a woman to get along without a man."

"You get out of this house!"

"Oh, I'll be going now, but you and me are going to be a lot closer before too long."

"I won't have this kind of talk!"

Taws grinned. "You can't run this place without me." His eyes narrowed, and he seemed to be considering moving toward her. But she was blazing with anger, and he merely said, "We'll talk about this again."

The overseer's constant attentions had intensified a deep depression that had been attacking Grace. Usually she managed to fight it off by busying herself with work and by spending time with Patrick. Now, however, she could not shake it off, and after an early supper, she said, "I've got to take a walk and get out of here for a while, Keturah. Would you clean up and take care of Patrick?"

"Of course. We'll have a fine time, won't we, Patrick?"

Grace put on her woolen coat and bonnet and left the house. The South Carolina autumns were nothing like those in New England, but still the wind was growing brisker, and she did not want to risk catching a cold. She walked down the path that led to the dirt road, then turned east and made her way along the line of large oaks that lined it. They formed a canopy, giving a cathedral-like appearance. She had always loved this beautiful stretch of road. The Spanish moss hung down in long, tattered bunches, some of it like lace. Grace had discovered that many people stuffed their mattresses or their pillows with this, although she herself preferred goose-feather pillo...

As she continued to stroll down the lane, looking up from time to time at the pale sliver of a moon that had been visible all afternoon, she tried to give thanks for the blessings of God. It was something her parents had taught her. Her father's favorite Scripture was "In everything give thanks: for this is God's will for you in Christ Jesus." She, David, and Clive had had this verse drilled into their heads since childhood, and she remembered her father saying, *"It doesn't say give thanks for every-thing. For instance, if you break your leg, you don't thank God for that. But it says in everything give thanks. So while your leg is broken, give thanks to God that you didn't get it chopped off!"*

A smile fleetingly touched Grace's lips, and then sadness returned. She missed her father and her mother a great deal. She had been very close to them since childhood, and now more than ever she longed for her father's steadying influence and her mother's sweetness and love that she expressed so freely.

Thoughts of her parents and her brothers made her black mood even more stygian. She fought it by thanking God for the baby's health, for the food they had to eat, and for other blessings, but it was a forced, seemingly empty prayer, for she felt nothing.

From far off came the sound of hunting dogs yelping, some of them high-pitched and others deep and tolling like a bell. She had learned that South Carolinians loved their hunting dogs almost as much as they loved their children.

Time passed but she was not conscious of it. She stopped and sat down on the trunk of a huge fallen oak. It was at least three feet in diameter, but time and weather had trimmed it of branches and bark. It was not a comfortable seat, but she remained there and again tried to pray as the darkness of the night descended swiftly.

Grace Morrison was not a weepy woman as a rule, but suddenly she found herself overcome by the enormity of the problems that confronted her. Tears leaped into her eyes, and she put her fist up to her mouth to block off the emotion that rose to her throat. It would not be repressed, however, and she suddenly lowered her head and began to sob. The pressures had built up within her, and for the first time since Stephen had died, she allowed herself to weep.

She sat there crying for a long while until suddenly she was startled by a voice saying, "Can I be of some help, ma'am?"

At once Grace leaped to her feet and peered through the twilight. The trees overhead shaded the man who stood before her, but she saw at once that he was a stranger and fear gripped her. The intense fighting in the Carolinas had brought many dangerous men into the area, and quickly Grace stepped back, saying, "No. I'm all right."

She nervously scanned the stranger who stood large in the gathering darkness. She could barely make out his face, but he appeared to have dark eyes and light brown hair. He was a big man, six feet tall and bulky under the gray jacket that he wore.

"My name is Cormac Morgan, ma'am."

"Where are you going this time of the night?"

"I've been walking all day." Cormac studied the woman before him. She was not tall, but he could see that her features were well formed and that she was attractive—in her early twenties, he supposed. "I haven't been in this country long. I got off the ship a few days ago and thought I had work with a family called Hacker, but their plantation's been burned out, so there was nothing there for me to do."

185

He and Hack had discovered that the family home and the barn had been burned by Ban Tarleton. Hack had chosen to stay there and help his aging parents put the place back together, but there was really nothing Cormac could do, so he had said good-bye to Hack and gone on the road looking for work.

"I've been stopping at every place asking for work. Would you know of any, ma'am?"

The fear had left Grace; for some reason she instinctively trusted this man. "I'm not sure," she said quickly, then asked, "Are you hungry?"

"I could eat a bite." Cormac laughed, and his teeth flashed white against his tanned skin. "As a matter of fact, I could eat a lot."

"Come along. I'll see that you get something to eat, and you can stay in the barn for the night."

"That would be good of you, ma'am. What might I call you?"

"I am Mrs. Morrison."

The two made their way back without speaking. Grace was not at all sure that she was doing the right thing, but as they walked back she recalled how often Taws was gone, sometimes for several days. She herself could not control the workers, and often the work ground to a stop. *If we just had another man here to direct the workers,* she thought. *But I know nothing about this fellow.*

They reached the house, and she walked around to the back, entering the kitchen. Keturah was not there, and she assumed that she was getting Patrick to bed. "Sit down. There's plenty of supper left over." She did not take him into the dining room but sat him down at a large pine table that was used for preparing meals in the kitchen. Without speaking, she fixed him a plate of ham, potatoes, greens, and rolls.

She made a pot of tea and heated it up on the stove. When she set the meal before him, he smiled and said, "It's grateful, I am." He bowed his head without warning and said, "Thank you, Lord, for this blessing and for this kind lady who has been good to a stranger on his pilgrimage. In the name of Jesus."

Grace was taken aback by the prayer. Somehow it confirmed her feelings about the man. He had taken off his coat, and now as he ate, she noticed that he had good manners. His hands were very large, and beneath the light chambray shirt that he wore, his muscles appeared to be quite powerful.

"Where did you say you were from?"

"From Wales, Mrs. Morrison."

"What did you do there?"

"I was a miner during my younger days, and later on I started farming."

This caught at Grace's attention. "What kind of farming?" she asked, refilling his plate as soon as he had emptied it. Obviously he was famished, and she listened as he told her of his experiences.

"So you actually managed a large farm?"

"Yes, ma'am. It's not exactly like the farms here, mind you, but farming's farming."

Keturah suddenly came in the door and halted abruptly upon seeing the stranger. "Oh, I didn't know you had company!"

Cormac had risen and turned to face the young woman. He bowed slightly and smiled, saying, "Mrs. Morrison took me in and has fed me, for which I am very grateful."

Keturah glanced at Grace, and Grace replied, "We'll let him sleep in the room out in the barn. He's looking for work." She turned to him and said, "Suppose I try you for a week."

"It's grateful I'd be for any work at all, Mrs. Morrison."

There was a pleasant lilting quality to Cormac Morgan's speech. Similar to rural English but richer, and the words were always slightly poetic, it seemed. "Very well, then," Grace said. "Ask for one of the slaves named Leo. He'll show you to the room out in the barn."

"Yes, ma'am, and I thank you for your kindness."

When Morgan left the room, Keturah said, "You don't know anything about him, Grace."

"I know we need someone here who can hold things together while Taws is gone."

"Taws won't like it. He likes to be in control."

Grace smiled then. "I'm not afraid of Simon Taws," she said. "I won't be asking him. I'll be telling him."

☩   ☩   ☩

Taws stared at Cormac and shook his head. "We can't use you!" It was early in the morning, and Taws was considerably worse for drink after having spent all night in the village of Fairdale. When Grace told him that she had hired a new man, he instantly protested. "I do the hiring around here, Mrs. Morrison! You wouldn't know anything about that."

"I know that you're gone half the time, Taws, and somebody has to take charge when you're out carousing. Morgan stays!" There was a sharp edge in her voice as she stood between the two men, her back stiff and her eyes fixed on the huge overseer.

187

Cormac studied her, admiring her dark honey hair and gray-green eyes set in an oval face. He had learned from Leo that she was a widow, her husband having died a short time before. He had also ascertained that the place was going downhill fast. Leo had been cautious not to mention Taws, but Cormac had drawn the obvious conclusions. Now he turned his attention on Taws and waited to see his reaction.

Taws wanted to argue, but something about Grace's attitude told him that this was not a debatable matter. A crafty look came into his eyes, and he said, "You're some kind of a Limey. Well, I never knew a Limey that could work this land. You can stay as long as you do your work, but no longer. Now, come with me."

Cormac followed Taws, who mounted his horse and without even a backward look rode off at a fast pace. Cormac knew that this was meant to humiliate him, but he was determined to do the best he could even with a man like Taws. He fell into a trot and kept pace with the big stallion. Taws pulled up in a large field where quite a few hands, some fifteen or so, were digging what appeared to be a large ditch. "Get a shovel and start in!" Taws said. He turned with a grin and looked up at the sky. It was going to be a hot day. "I've got business. When I come back tomorrow, I expect that ditch to be dug. You're responsible. If it ain't dug, you can be on your way."

Without another word, Taws laughed crudely and spurred his horse away.

Cormac watched him go, then walked over to where Leo was standing. The big man was stripped to his waist, and his physique was equal to Cormac's own. "Well, it looks like this ditch has to be dug. How long you been at it, Leo?"

"Nigh onto two weeks now. It's mighty hard ground. You have to use a pickax."

Cormac studied the ground thoughtfully. He had dug many drainage ditches on the farm back in Wales. He said, "I'm going to talk to Mrs. Morrison. Why don't you all take a rest."

"Take a rest!" Leo's eyes flew open with astonishment.

"Yes. Go get some water. Take a couple of hours off."

Leo stared at Cormac as if he had told him to jump over a house. "We ain't never had nobody tell us nothin' like that, Mr. Morgan."

"Well, you can't dig that ditch the way you been goin'. It'll take you a year. I've got an idea. You just take it easy."

Cormac returned to the house. Stepping up on the front steps, he knocked on the door. Grace Morrison appeared at once, and he said, "Could I speak with you, Mrs. Morrison?"

Grace stepped out in the bright morning sun and said, "What is it, Morgan?"

Cormac explained Taws' ultimatum, and a smile touched his broad lips. "I think it's a test for me. If the ditch isn't dug, I'll be on my way."

"Can it be done?"

"Not the way he's doing it. It'll take two months to do it. But there is a way. It'll cost a little bit—we may have to pay your neighbors for some extra equipment—but in the long run it'll be a lot cheaper. You can use the hands for something better."

Grace stood there listening as he explained his plan. "You say you've seen this system work in Wales?"

"Oh yes, ma'am. It's not at all difficult. I think I can have it done in two days."

"Very well. I'll get the money."

Cormac stood there until she came back with some coins. "How do you know I won't run off with this, Mrs. Morrison?" he said.

Grace stood there and studied the man before her. He seemed to exude masculine strength, yet there was a sense of honor about him. She could not put the two together. She had never met anyone quite like him before. "It's worth that to find out if you're honest or not."

Cormac laughed and said, "Well, devil fly off! If you're not a woman of sense as well as beauty!" He turned without another word and left at a quick run. She watched him saddling up a horse, and he rode out quickly with purpose in his attitude.

Grace was anxious about the project, but she did not go out to where the ditch was being dug until late in the day. Taws was not there, and she knew he would stay away long enough to give Cormac Morgan a chance to fail so he could use it as an excuse for running Morgan off.

When she arrived at the field she was amazed at the activity. There were at least half a dozen yoke of oxen busy, and she rode over to Cormac, who came to meet her. He pulled his hat off, wiped the sweat off his face, and smiled.

"It's going fine, Mrs. Morrison."

"How does it work, Morgan?"

"Very simple. That first yoke of oxen pulls a steel-tipped plow that breaks the ground. The second yoke comes right behind them and they widen it. The third yoke has a board that shoves the broken dirt up to one side, and then we have three more yokes doing exactly the same thing to make it double width. The dirt thrown up on the side forms a sort of a dam that holds the drainage water in for a while. It'll flatten out eventually."

Grace watched as the oxen plodded along, powerful beasts cutting straight furrows across the long field. Her own workers, she saw, simply followed behind with shovels, throwing the loose dirt out on the side.

"We'll be through sometime tomorrow, I think."

"Why, it's marvelous!" Grace cried. She shook her head, then asked, "Why didn't Taws think of such a thing?"

Cormac did not answer. He had his suspicions about the overseer, but to state his real opinions about Taws would be offensive to Grace Morrison. He had never been much of a man for women—for good women at least. With a woman of honor and integrity like Grace, he had little experience. He studied her there, her beauty unavoidable. Her shoulders were petite and square in the light green smock that she wore, and he admired the lovely turning of her throat. The light that danced in her eyes revealed that she was pleased with his work. There was a hint of pride in the smile that slowly emerged from her delicate features.

"You've done so well, Cormac," she said, using his first name.

"Not much of a job, Mrs. Morrison." He looked around and said, "Got a fine place here. Very fine indeed. Much better than the one we had in Wales."

"Taws says the workers won't work."

Cormac glanced over at the industrious men and said, "Look at them. They just needed a little encouragement."

"Instead of beatings?" Grace said bitterly.

"I never knew a beating to make a better worker out of anyone. It was tried on me, and all I became was more stubborn."

The two stood there talking for some time, and finally Grace said, "I'll be going now."

Quickly Cormac said, "I'd like to do something special for the men. They've worked hard, and I'd like for them to think that they're appreciated."

"What were you thinking of?"

"Maybe a fine supper. They don't get much meat, Leo says. If we could butcher a yearling, it would cost a little perhaps, but it would mean a lot to them."

"I'll see to it. That's a fine idea."

🔔   🔔   🔔

As Grace stepped out onto the porch and crossed the yard holding Patrick in her arms, the smell of roasted meat filled the air. She had given orders for one of the hands to slaughter a yearling, and now she came to the huge barbecue pit, where the meat was roasting on spits. Mary, the wife of Leo, came to her and said, "Oh, Miss Grace, it's so good of you to feed us all like this!"

"Well, actually it was Mr. Morgan's idea."

"Yes, 'um, I know, and I appreciate that man. I do hope he stay on around here." The flickering light of the fire highlighted the planes of Mary's face, and Grace suddenly realized she had never seen an expression like this on the features of the slave. All of the slaves wore masks, she thought. They sometimes smiled but it was empty. But now she saw pure joy overflowing in this woman's warm brown eyes.

"Will there be enough food, Mary?"

"Oh yes, 'um. Plenty of food."

Grace moved around, speaking to the workers. All of them were slaves, and she was uncomfortable with their demeaning lot in life. Slavery existed throughout the British Empire, and the Carolinas and Georgia had drawn heavily on the African trade to do the hard work in the fields.

"Well, Mrs. Morrison, you've given a fine dinner for all of your hands."

Grace turned to find Cormac standing beside her. He was wearing a pair of light blue trousers and a thin cotton shirt. His chest swelled against the fabric, and his neck looked strong as an oak. He was smiling now and said, "Come over and sit down."

"Oh, I just came out to visit."

"Of course you'll have to join in the festivities. After all, you're the hostess. Here, let me have the old man."

Before Grace could protest, Cormac had reached out and taken the baby. He held him up high and said, "There's a fine old man, you are."

"Old man! He's not even six months old."

"Looks like an old man to me—not much hair and no teeth."

"Well, he's cutting teeth right now."

"He's a fine boy. Sit here, Mrs. Morrison."

Grace sat down, and Cormac held Patrick, who seemed fascinated with the buttons on his shirt. She was amazed to hear Cormac's conversations, if they could be termed such, with her son. "There's a handsome old man, you are!" he'd say. Or, "My, you're just full of sweetness, aren't you, Patrick?"

Grace had never heard a man talk to an infant like this. It was what she had always wanted Stephen to do, but he never seemed to have time for Patrick.

"You love children, I take it?"

"Who wouldn't love the little ones? I'd like to have a house full of them. Of course they'd have to be handsome like the old man here."

Grace laughed. "I've heard that Welshmen were charmers. I'm beginning to believe it."

"Me! I'm a charmer? Well, devil fly off. I've never been called that!" Cormac laughed freely, and then they began to listen, for the slaves had started singing. The two of them sat there quietly for a time. The songs were not in English, and Cormac said slowly, "We have singing in Wales, but nothing like this. It's as if their hearts have been torn right out of them."

"What a strange thing to say."

"Well, listen to it. There's a sadness there." He leaned back and held Patrick up and examined him. "The old man here will never be a slave, will you, now?" The baby chortled, and Cormac lowered his head, allowing Patrick to grab at his hair. Finally he leaned back and said, "Now you're going to scalp me." He turned to Grace. "It's kind you are to take in a stranger like me. I'm thanking you for it."

Grace looked at him with surprise. "You don't have to thank me. If you can do other things around here as well as you're digging that ditch, I'll be in your debt."

"It's a lovely lady you are," Cormac said.

It was a chance remark, but the words touched Grace. It was the sort of thing she never heard from her husband, and the big Welshman uttered it so naturally, so simply, that a sadness swept over her. "You mustn't say things like that to me."

"Like what?" Cormac said with surprise.

"Why, that I'm lovely."

Cormac shook his head. "If I spoke out of turn, I'm sorry. It just seemed natural. Like saying the old man here is handsome."

Grace could not answer, for she could see that this man had a special quality in him. He spoke from his heart.

The two listened to the slaves' singing until Leo came up and said, "Mr. Cormac, why don't you ask God's blessing on the food?"

Cormac handed the baby back to Grace and then stood up. His voice was clear as he thanked God fervently for the food. He ended by saying, "And we thank you for our gracious lady, Mrs. Morrison, who has provided this meal. In the name of Jesus."

"He's eloquent, isn't he?" Keturah said as she came over to sit beside Grace and took the baby.

"Yes, he is."

"I like a man who speaks well, don't you, Grace?"

Grace Morrison did not answer, but the complimentary words Cormac Morgan had spoken about her lingered in her mind, and she knew that she would not soon forget them.

17

LOVE IS STRONG AS DEATH

THE TROUBLE STARTED AS SOON AS Simon Taws rode back onto the place. Grace had taken the morning off and was riding over the fields. She had found that riding was a good exercise for her and gave her time to clear her head and to think. Now as she rode past the savannas that marked the edge of the swamp that bordered her land, she discovered that she had developed a strong affection for the plantation. She had hated it when she first arrived, but now she had adapted to the climate, and Patrick was thriving. What the future held she did not know, but the determination to cling to this place and build a heritage for Patrick beat strong in her heart.

When she rode back toward the house, she saw a group of workers gathered, and she recognized Simon Taws' big stallion. She spurred her horse forward, and as she approached, she heard Taws' angry voice shouting. As usual he had been drinking, and his bulbous face was red with anger.

She heard Cormac say, "But I tell you, Taws, they finished the drainage ditch."

"Don't lie to me, Morgan!" Taws said.

At that moment Leo made the mistake of saying, "He's tellin' the truth, Mr. Taws. We done finished that ditch this morning."

Instantly Taws stepped forward and struck at the slave. Leo turned his head and caught the blow on his cheek, but it drove him to the ground. Taws turned back to his horse, where he always kept his bullwhip over the saddle horn. "I'll teach you to sass me!" he shouted.

Grace said quickly, "They're telling the truth—both of them. The

195

ditch is finished. Stop this nonsense!"

But Taws was beyond reason. He grasped the whip and snaked it out behind him, and with a strong motion he struck Leo. The whip curled around the man's skin and left a pale mark.

Cormac glanced quickly at Grace and saw her face turn pale. She seemed helpless, but he knew she hated what was going on. He stepped forward and directly in front of Taws. The other man was taller than he by a good two inches and outweighed him, but he said quietly, "There'll be no whipping of anybody. You can't whip a man for telling the truth."

"They're not men! They're nothing but animals! Get out of my way, Morgan!"

"I won't do that. Put your whip up and act like a man!"

Taws was not accustomed to having his will thwarted. He reached out and tried to shove Cormac away, but Cormac's hand closed around his wrist. "Don't shove me," he said. "I don't take kindly to it."

With a roar Taws dropped the whip and struck out at Cormac. Cormac easily avoided it. He released Taws' wrist and stepped back. "Let's stop this thing right here," he said.

"Yes," Grace said. "There's no point. I won't have any more trouble over this."

But Taws was past reason. He threw himself forward cursing and aimed a blow that would have half torn Cormac's head off if it had landed. Cormac simply moved his head and allowed the punch to go by. He could have struck Taws to the ground, but he said instead, "Don't be a fool, man!"

But there was no reasoning with Simon Taws. He came forward throwing blows, which Cormac easily warded off. He tried to speak but took a glancing blow on the cheek. Knowing that Taws would not listen to reason, he suddenly planted his feet, avoided a wild right, and struck Taws in the pit of the stomach right where the ribs divide. It was a fearsome blow, and he knew that he had not broken a rib, but Taws reeled backward. His face was pale and he could not speak.

It was the effect that Cormac wanted. He had learned in the ring not to hit men in the head because you could break your hands, but a blow in the pit of the stomach would render a man just as helpless as if he had been poleaxed.

"We'll have no more fighting," Cormac said quietly, and he stood waiting for Taws to respond. Taws gasped for breath and was aware that the slaves were all staring at him and at Cormac with awe.

When he got his breath, he turned to Grace, saying, "I won't have this man . . . on the place!" He was still reaching for his wind and shook

196

his head. "I'll leave if he doesn't go."

Grace instantly said, "Pack your things and go! I'm sick of you! Now, get out!"

"I'll take what pay's comin' to me."

"You've overdrawn your pay for the last two months. Get your things, and I want you off the place at once!"

Taws was livid. His hands were shaking, and he reached down and picked up his whip. Cormac watched him carefully, for he knew that if the man had had a gun, he would be dangerous. He stepped forward and said, "Do you need help to get on your horse, Mr. Taws?"

Taws stared at him, cursed, and then got on his horse. As he wheeled the animal around cruelly, he shouted, "You'll be sorry for this! You'll be burned out! You're nothing but a Tory!"

Grace watched him ride off and then turned to Cormac. She was silent for a moment and then finally took a deep breath. "It looks like you're the new overseer."

Cormac blinked with surprise. "But I don't know this kind of farming," he said mildly. Then he smiled and winked at Leo. "But Leo and some of the other hands do. I think they can teach me a few things."

Leo smiled brilliantly, and a murmur went around among the slaves. They had already decided that this man had a feeling for them that no white man had ever shown them, and Leo had sung his praises. "Between us, we'll make this place the best in the county, Mr. Cormac. You'll see." He turned and said, "Miss Grace, you done good. You done right gettin' rid of that man. He's worthless. We'll make this a fine place."

Drained by the confrontation, Grace rode back to the house. She found that her hands were trembling. She had seen instantly that Cormac Morgan could have literally beaten Taws senseless, but he had not. The control of the strength he possessed pleased her. *He has great strength,* she thought, *but there's a gentleness with it.*

When she arrived at the house, she said at once to Keturah, who was peeling potatoes, "We've got a new overseer." She explained what had happened and then said with a gust of relief, "I'm glad Taws is gone."

"Do you think Cormac can do the job?"

"Yes. The hands think so much of him already after just a couple of days. He did in that time what Simon Taws couldn't do in a lifetime. He's the kind of man that inspires loyalty."

Keturah suddenly giggled. "And he's handsome, too, and has fine manners. If he comes courting me, I might have to watch out."

"Keturah, don't talk foolishness!"

Keturah put her hands on her hips. "Well, la-di-da!" she said. "What if he came courting you?"

"That's impossible."

"Why?"

"Why . . . I've only been a widow a few months."

Keturah stared at Grace and shook her head. "A woman like you needs a man. I guess we all do, but you more than most."

Grace was angry. "What do you mean by that? You think I'm so desperate for a man I'll take anybody?"

"No. I just think some women are made for marriage—and you're one of them. You didn't get the love you needed from your first husband, but that doesn't mean another man couldn't provide it."

"You're talking foolishness," Grace said huffily and swept out of the room.

As soon as she was gone, Keturah picked up Patrick and said, "Well, your mama can't take the truth very well, but she just had a dose of it."

🔔   🔔   🔔

Matthew pulled his horse up and reloaded his pistols. He had learned to do this on horseback, and his mare was steady enough that she provided a good platform. He had just finished loading both of them, a matched set, when Colonel Marion came up, his face beaming.

"We gave them a good thumping that time, Matthew."

"Yes, we did, Colonel. Have you seen Sam?"

"Yes. He's coming." Marion shook his head. "He's a firebrand, isn't he?"

"He always was. The most impulsive man ever. He's been that way since he was a boy."

"Well, I wish I had a hundred more just like him." Colonel Marion gnawed his lip and then shook his head. "We lost two men back there, and three got wounded, but we've captured enough supplies to keep us in fighting trim for a time."

"What's going to happen, Colonel Marion? Will the British throw more troops into the South?"

"They might do that. Cornwallis is a stubborn man and a firebrand himself. He's not at all like Clinton."

"How's that, Colonel?"

"General Clinton is cautious. He sits in New York afraid to move. That's why he's given command of the southern armies to Cornwallis and Banastre Tarleton. He thinks the two of them can take the Carolinas like they did Georgia."

The two men sat there talking about the problems that beset them. Matthew had agreed to join Colonel Marion's band and had been strangely pleased with his decision. He had been the lone holdout in the Bradford family to join in the fighting, but now he knew that he wanted this country to be free as much as Dake or Micah or even Sam himself.

Sam came rushing back on his mare, his face flushed with excitement. "Let's go after them, Colonel. We can take them all."

"No, Private Bradford. We'll wait for a better time. We don't have an army, but we can do a lot of damage by cutting Cornwallis's supply line. That's his weakness, you know."

"His supply line?" Matthew asked.

"Certainly. His soldiers have to have food and ammunition and equipment. The farther he comes away from New York and the coast into the interior of South Carolina, the thinner that line will be. So we'll just keep cutting it until we starve him to death."

"What about Ban Tarleton?" Sam said. "I'd like to get a shot at him."

"So would I," Colonel Marion said. He frowned. "I don't think we'll have to wait long."

"What do you mean by that, Colonel?" Matthew asked.

"I mean sooner or later General Cornwallis will send Tarleton and his legion to root us out of these swamps. I've already heard rumors from our informants that he's thinking that way."

"He won't succeed," Sam laughed. He was excited from the action and said, "Let him come. We'll show him Tarleton's Quarter!"

♜   ♜   ♜

Reverend John Dowrimple sat across from the tall man who had come to visit him. He had met Cormac Morgan a month earlier and had welcomed him into the church each Sunday morning. Morgan came with the Morrisons but usually sat apart from them. Dowrimple had heard of how he had simply appeared from nowhere and how Simon Taws had lost his place as overseer. Taws' dismissal had not displeased the minister, for he disliked Taws, as did most people in the community.

"I'm interested," Reverend Dowrimple said, "in what you say about your conversion. You know Whitefield has also turned this country upside down with his preaching."

Cormac shook his head with wonder. "There's nothing like him. Have you ever heard Whitefield, sir?"

"Yes, I have. Twice. He has a power from God. There's no question about it. How does his teaching compare with Wesley? I've never heard John Wesley preach."

"Oh, he's a much better preacher than Wesley. Actually, I think Wesley learned open-air preaching from Mr. Whitefield."

The pastor listened carefully, and when Cormac related how it had been Wesley who had laid hands on him and, more or less, prophesied he would preach in America, Dowrimple slapped his thighs. "Well, that's a wonderful thing to have in your memory, Mr. Morgan!"

"Yes, it is. I took a roundabout way to get here," he said ruefully. He went on to tell the pastor how he had become a prizefighter and then had been pressed as a sailor and finally had escaped. "If I had had my way, I would have come straight here without all of that."

"Well, our ways are not God's ways, and the important thing is you are here now. What I would like to ask you is, will you preach for me next Sunday?"

Cormac was astonished. "Me, sir? Why, I'm not certain I can."

Reverend Dowrimple grinned abruptly. "That's what God told you to do, isn't it? Preach in America. Well, here's your chance. John Wesley said a door would open. I'm opening the door."

Cormac ran his hand through his thick brown hair, but then he smiled. "Well, if you'll risk it, sir, I'll do it. I'll get a few thoughts on paper and have you look it over, if you don't mind."

"No. I'd like to hear it as it comes from the pulpit. I believe God's put His hands on you, son, and we're going to see what He makes of a fellow like you."

Cormac rode home from the village where the church was located, and as he dismounted, he was met by Charles Dixon, who was just leaving. "Hello, Mr. Dixon," he said. "I take it you've been calling on Miss Keturah?"

Dixon grinned ruefully. "Yes, I have, but I'm wasting my time."

"Why, don't say that. She's a fine young woman."

"Yes, but strong-minded and strong willed."

"Well, I sort of like that in a woman," Cormac grinned. "No point being married to a dishrag, is there?"

Dixon shook his head. "I suppose not, but she's got some romantic ideals. Those things are bad for people."

Cormac, who had as many romantic ideals as any man alive, disagreed but did not say so. He said good-bye to Dixon and went up to the house. He knocked, as usual, and Keturah met him.

"I met your suitor, Mr. Dixon, leaving here. He was not encouraged, Miss Keturah."

"Oh, he's wasting his time. He needs to marry a widow with three children and a lot of money, qualities that I am clearly lacking."

Cormac laughed. He liked this young woman and said, "Is Mrs. Morrison here?"

"Yes. I'll get her for you."

Cormac waited in the foyer and Grace came at once. She was wearing a honey-colored dress with a scooped neckline edged with ruching and covered with a white muslin inset. The sleeves ended just below the elbow, and the skirt was worn open to reveal a matching petticoat.

She smiled at Cormac and said, "Come into the kitchen. I've just been making some apple cake."

"I see no harm in it," he grinned, "as long as there are no women or children present."

As he walked into the kitchen, Patrick was on the floor playing with a spool. He popped it in his mouth, and Cormac swooped him up, saying, "No, old man! You don't eat the spool." He removed it and offered his finger. "Here, let me see if you've got a tooth going there."

Patrick bit down with all the force of his jaws on Cormac's finger and gnawed with his gums.

"There's a good old man. You're just like a snapping turtle."

As always, Grace was fascinated at how well Cormac got along with Patrick. Patrick had learned to know him in the short time he had been here and often cried when Cormac had to leave.

"You're spoiling that child," she said as she put the cake on the table and cut a healthy piece.

"Of course I am. That's what babies, and wives, and grandchildren are for. For a man to spoil."

Grace laughed. "I like that theory," she said. "But you'll never make it work."

"That's what you think," he said. "I don't have any of those right now, but I can tell you, Mrs. Morrison, the Cormac Morgan plan for raising children and grandchildren and making wives fall madly in love will definitely work."

"I'd be interested to hear this plan." Grace sat down and brushed a strand of hair back from her face. Cormac always brought cheer with him when he came, and now she leaned forward and said, "So. . . ?"

"Why, it's simple," Cormac said. He smiled, which always made him look younger, and the tiny dimple in his right cheek seemed more pronounced. "Wives, children, and grandchildren—you give them anything they want, and then they will hush and be quiet and love you to death."

Grace could not help laughing at his romantic ideas on life. "You ought to write a book about it."

"Maybe I will. Then I'll get rich and buy me a new suit."

The two sat at the table, Cormac eating the cake and drinking fresh milk. Finally he said, "I hope this won't come as too much of a shock to you, but I'm preaching in Reverend Dowrimple's church next Sunday morning."

Grace was surprised. She knew that Cormac was a rather outspoken Christian, that he had preached for the slaves more than once. Now she studied him carefully. "Is that what you want to do? Be a preacher?"

"God's got something for me," he said, and he grew serious. "I don't know what it is. I led a sinful life when I was a young man, but the mercy of God has taken all that away. Now all I want to do is serve Him with all my heart."

Grace was impressed with this side of Cormac's character. She said quietly, "I think that's a noble calling. You're like my cousin, Micah. He's a chaplain with General Washington's army."

"You may want to stay home Sunday," Cormac said, picking up a morsel of cake and carefully feeding it to Patrick, who slobbered and drooled over it and opened his mouth for more. "I don't think I'm much of a preacher."

Grace suddenly smiled. "I'll make up my own mind about that, and after the service I'll tell you everything you did wrong."

"Will you, now?" Cormac smiled. "Just what I need."

The two sat for a long time at the table, and finally Grace said impulsively, "I thought love lasted forever, but sometimes I think it doesn't."

"Do you tell me that?" Cormac said. "What makes you say such a thing, Mrs. Morrison?"

"I see so many people who claim to love, but it runs away from them."

"One of my favorite Scriptures is in the Song of Solomon."

"The Song of Solomon. You like that book?"

"Very much."

"I suppose you would. You're a poetic sort of man. What's the scripture?"

"It's in chapter eight. It says: 'Set me as a seal upon thine heart, as a seal upon thine arm: for love is strong as death.' And then in the next verse it says: 'Many waters cannot quench love, neither can the floods drown it.' " He sat back and thought for a moment, then looked directly at her. "Many waters cannot quench love. It's stronger than death."

202

"You really believe that, Cormac? That a man can love a woman no matter what happens? Or a woman a man?"

"I've seen it a few times. And if it can happen once, it can happen twice. As for me, I won't settle for less. If God ever blesses me with a wife, my love will be stronger than death."

Grace could not think of how to answer him. She was puzzled by this big man, so strong and yet so gentle, able to destroy a huge opponent with a single blow yet hold a tiny baby as softly as a woman, whose lips always seemed to have something poetic and gentle and good coming from them.

"I don't understand you, Cormac," she said.

"I don't understand myself, but I know one thing. The love of God is unfailing, and He's able to make a man and a woman have a love that doesn't fail."

Grace sat there as Cormac Morgan played with the baby and continued to speak of the plantation, and she said no more about his sermon. But as Cormac said good-bye, she thought, *I'll go hear that sermon. It will tell me a lot about what kind of a man has come into our lives.*

18

THE RAID

HISTORIANS WHO SET OUT TO TRACE the fortunes of the Continental Army during the years 1880 and 1881 have always found it difficult to account for the catastrophe known as the Battle of Camden. After the fall of Charleston, when Benjamin Lincoln surrendered the city with all of its stores and supplies and twenty-five hundred Continental troops, one would have thought that a greater catastrophe could not have happened. Leaving Cornwallis with eight thousand troops in Charleston and ordering him to maintain control of South Carolina, Clinton returned to New York, where he did little but stare across the river at George Washington.

Cornwallis, however, pursued a more aggressive strategy and assigned "Bloody" Tarleton to conduct a series of terrible raids—burning, murdering, leaving a trail of disaster across South Carolina. During this time the infamous colonel made himself more hated than before, if that were possible.

The results of this course of action on the part of Cornwallis were not at all positive for the British. Little bands of outraged patriots led by Thomas Sumter and Francis Marion began to effectively strike back. And the lack of order in their resistance greatly assisted Washington's forces in South Carolina.

But any advantage the Americans had established in South Carolina was seriously jeopardized when Congress ignored the advice of George Washington—who had recommended Nathaniel Greene to command the beleaguered army in the South—and instead chose Horatio Gates, the "hero" of Saratoga. In fact, Benedict Arnold had been the real hero of that battle, but nevertheless, Gates had received the credit and had become known as a hero.

When Horatio Gates arrived to take up his army, he found only thirteen hundred half-starved men. He named this group the "Grand Army" and at once proceeded to lead in a bullheaded fashion, rarely taking advice when he could have used it. It took his little army a full two weeks to get to the site of the Battle of Camden, leaving a trail of sick, starved soldiers over the one hundred twenty mile march.

When he met Cornwallis at Camden, Gates had close to three thousand Continentals and militia. The British numbered twenty-two hundred. Gates put his army under eight different generals and set them on a night march through unknown country covered with brush and woods with orders to attack at dawn. As if that were not enough foolishness, he fed his men green corn and molasses—resulting in half his army getting sick.

The battle was a rout. Cornwallis opened the attack, and the starving, disorganized Americans fled at the first sight of the Redcoats. They threw down their loaded guns and took off as fast as they could retreat.

General Kolb, one of the eight generals who had come from Germany to fight for the American cause, struggled valiantly to hold his little band together but eventually went down, his eleven wounds testament to his perseverance and bravery.

In contrast, Horatio Gates fled the scene of the battle at the height of it, racing the sixty miles to Charlotte, North Carolina, and barely stopping before reaching Hillsboro two days later.

In three weeks Gates had practically ruined the American cause in the South.

The one positive aspect of such a defeat was that Washington was permitted to appoint a new commander, and he chose, of course, Nathaniel Greene. Greene moved at once to assume his command, and though he had practically nothing left to fight with, he began a campaign that was to be without parallel. With a small group of Continentals and the help of militia and partisan groups, he proceeded to confound Cornwallis's forces with a strategy based on the guerrilla tactics perfected by the likes of Francis Marion.

Realizing his vulnerability, one of the first things Cornwallis did was to send Banastre Tarleton out to capture Marion. He had barely known who Francis Marion was a few weeks earlier, but by January 1781 Marion became the scourge of the British.

Speaking to Tarleton in an emergency meeting, Cornwallis said, "This fellow Marion seems to be ubiquitous. He's everywhere!"

Ban Tarleton only laughed. "He's nothing but a bandit," he said.

"Well, he's wrecking havoc with our supply lines. Our wagoners are afraid to cross at Nelsons'. They have to go around by way of Camden."

"I'll go out and bag the old boy," Tarleton said.

"Do so."

Tarleton camped his Green Dragoon troop by the Broad River, where he was poised to strike at any enemy that showed itself, but particularly Francis Marion. He was fully recovered now from the yellow fever that had prostrated him and more eager than ever to inflict damage on the colonists. His motto was: "Swift, vigilant, and bold." Finally, acting on information gained from one of his Tory spies, he led his troops across the Wateree at Camden and headed out to erase Marion's threat once and for all.

When Francis Marion learned of the rapid approach of Tarleton's Dragoons, his own force was down to less than thirty men. He was not afraid of Banastre Tarleton, yet he was not foolhardy. He quickly gathered his men and at once pulled out of camp.

Tarleton pursued for seven hours. His written report to Cornwallis was: "The core under my command made a rapid march of twenty-six miles through swamps and woods toward Black River without a halt. The enemy, being all mounted, have been difficult to catch."

Tarleton did his best. He pursued Marion and his men as well as any officer could have done. Finally, however, at Ox Swamp he pulled up. Ahead of him lay a roadless bog. His Dragoons were tired and hungry; their horses were winded and heaving. Slowly Tarleton reined his horse around, and he shook his head. "Come on, my boys. We'll go find Sumter!" he cried in a thick Lancaster accent. "But as for this old fox, the devil himself could not catch him!"

Tarleton's words were heard by one of Marion's men who had lingered behind to give a report. He had chortled gleefully at the description of Marion as an old fox, and when he reported back, the name stuck, so that forever afterward Francis Marion was known as the Swamp Fox.

Tarleton continued his campaign to punish the patriots. One typical raid occurred at the home of the recently widowed wife of a general named Richardson. Tarleton ordered his troops to dig up the corpse of General Richardson, who had lain in the plantation graveyard for a mere six weeks. As the Richardsons wept anew, the Green Dragoons plundered their home. Tarleton forced Mrs. Richardson to fix dinner, and after he had dined, he ordered his troops to drive all the cattle, hogs, and poultry into the barn. He then set the barn on fire, killing all the animals and destroying the building.

Tarleton's cruel raids called for action on the part of the patriots, and it soon came. Cormac Morgan was standing outside the house speaking with Grace when he heard a distant noise, turned, and said, "Look, there's Sam."

Grace looked up and saw the rider coming at full speed. "There must be something wrong for him to punish his horse that way."

Sam pulled up and dismounted. His eyes were bright, and he said with excitement, "Colonel Marion's calling all of the band together. We're going to get some of our own back on Tarleton and the Tories."

Keturah had come up holding Patrick and seemed shocked at the news. She had heard from Matthew how rash Sam was in battle, and as he finished talking, she found herself wishing he did not have to go.

"And so," Sam concluded, "we need every man we can get. Will you come, Morgan?"

Cormac Morgan had thought much about the battle that was taking place for freedom here in the land of his calling. He had made up his mind only recently, but he nodded without hesitation. "Aye," he said. "I'll be with you."

Sam slapped the bigger man on the shoulder and said gleefully, "Great! We'll have a fine time!"

Sam moved over to speak to Keturah, who at once began cautioning him to be careful.

As the two walked away, Grace was upset. "Do you really have to go, Cormac?" she asked. It was one of the only times she had used his first name, and it did not pass unnoticed.

A light came into Cormac's eyes and he smiled briefly. "Yes, I do."

"But this isn't really your fight."

"I think I'll have to make it mine. I'm going to make my home in this place, and I want to be a free man—not under the thumb of some king who doesn't care a thing of who I am or my rights. I had enough of that in Wales."

Grace bit her lip and shook her head. "I don't like to see you go."

The admission surprised Cormac. "Why, Miss Grace," he said, "I'll be back. These things never take long. Come with me now. I'll have to borrow one of your horses."

Grace went down to the stable, where Cormac saddled his horse. When he had finished tightening the cinch, he patted the animal and said, "Would it be all right if I borrowed one of the muskets?"

"Take what you need, Cormac."

They were standing in the shade of the barn, and Grace made one more plea. "Please, Cormac, you don't have to go. Stay here."

Cormac studied her intently. She was wearing a light green dress made out of cotton with a rounded neck, a tight bodice, three-quarter-

208

length sleeves, the long skirt covered with a white apron. He had learned to admire this woman greatly. He did not understand her, for he knew that beneath her stern exterior was a woman warm and loving. He understood, somehow, that it had to do with her husband and her marriage, and he suspected she had not been happy.

He said, "You wouldn't have me be a coward, would you, now, Miss Grace?"

"It's not cowardice."

Cormac stroked the back of the horse for a moment and then turned to her. She had to tilt her head back to look up at him, and she did not know at that moment how lovely she was in his sight.

"Look, Miss Grace," he said. "I could stay here and be safe, but in the years to come, what would I tell my children when they asked me what I did to fight in the war? What would I tell them?"

Grace had no answer for that, and then almost without meaning to, he reached out and put his hand on her arm. "You know what? I was thinking only last night about the possibility of having to leave here and go off and fight like this, and I thought of a poem that I once memorized. It was about a man who had to go to war."

"What was the name of the poem?"

"I forget, but the poet's name was Richard Lovelace. An Englishman."

"What was the poem?"

"It was about a man who had a sweetheart and had to leave her. And she was begging him not to, just like you're begging me now." He smiled gently and said, "These things never change, do they?"

"I suppose not."

"Well, the poem was like this:

'Tell me not, sweet, I am unkind,
That from the nunnery
Of thy chaste breast and quiet mind
To war and arms I fly.

True, a new mistress now I chase,
The first foe in the field;
And with a stronger faith embrace
A sword, a horse, a shield.

Yet this inconstancy is such
As thou too shall adore;
I could not love thee, dear, so much,
Lov'd I not honor more.' "

He spoke so well that Grace was unable to speak for a moment. She remembered the poetry that her husband had written, but it was all about flowers and trees—never anything about the passions of the heart. Now she looked up and found it difficult to believe that she had become so fond of this man. He stood looking down at her, and she suddenly reached up and put her hand on his chest. "Go with God, Cormac," she whispered, then turned and left the barn.

Cormac stared after her, then he reached up and touched his chest where her hand had lain. He said nothing, but many thoughts swirled in his mind.

He led the horse, tied him up to the rail, and made the rest of his preparations.

Twenty minutes later he and Sam rode out as the two women stood staring after them. Keturah fretted, "I'm worried about Sam. He takes such awful chances."

Grace did not speak, but somehow a specter of fear had touched her. She knew that it was the same emotion that came to women all over the world who watched their men ride out to war, and she remembered the last two lines of the poem:

> I could not love thee, dear, so much,
> Lov'd I not honor more.

And somehow she knew that whatever else Cormac Morgan may be, he was a deeply honorable man.

🔔   🔔   🔔

"What could have happened to them?" Keturah said. The men had been gone now for five days, and they had heard reports of bitter and violent fighting over to the east. Keturah went to the window and looked out for what seemed the hundredth time. "I'm worried about them. They should have been back by now."

Grace had said little all day. She had gone about her work and had been relieved to find that Leo was able to handle all the affairs in the field. He came every morning for instructions, but actually he knew the place much better than she did.

"We'll just have to wait, Keturah," she said.

"I'm going out for a walk. I'll be back soon," Keturah said.

Leaving the house, she crossed the backyard and went out into a small copse. She did not stop until she came to the creek that bubbled over the well-worn stones. As she made her way alongside the clear water, she remembered the time Sam had come with her. She reached the arching live oak, and it brought back the memory of how he had kissed her here.

Leaning back against the oak, Keturah took a deep breath. She simply stood there thinking about Sam. She was shocked at how the possibility of his death had affected her. She had known she was fond of him, but now a thought hit her hard. *What if he's dead?*

She could not bear the prospect of losing him, and she pressed her hand against her lips and shook her head violently. "No, he can't be dead! He can't be!"

She slumped down against the tree where the leaves had fallen and made a cushion. The wind was keen, and overhead a gray squirrel suddenly appeared, chattering angrily at her, but she did not notice.

Keturah had not realized how much Sam Bradford had come to mean to her. When she had first come to the Bradfords, she was so ill she could not walk. She thought of how he had come every day laughing and entertaining her with his wild stories. She remembered how he had escorted her all over Boston. And how, when she had grown angry with herself at not being able to do the lessons that Rachel laid out for her, it had been Sam who had sat beside her patiently helping.

The winds whistled through the trees overhead, and a gentle rain of leaves settled down on the forest floor. She knew they would lie there and go back to the earth again. "He's not dead!" she whispered. "I won't let him be dead!"

And then Keturah felt her throat begin to thicken. Sam was so full of life, always laughing, always sharing his fun with everyone around. He could brighten up a room just by coming into it, and she suddenly discovered she could not imagine a world without Sam Bradford.

"I shouldn't have come here," she said. "He wouldn't be here if I had stayed in Boston. He's followed me, and now he may get himself killed."

She rose up, unable to bear the thought, and walked for more than two hours in the woods. Finally she went back, and as soon as she walked in the house, Grace said, "Where have you been, Keturah? I've been worried about you."

"Just walking."

Something in Keturah's tone caught Grace's attention. "What is it?" she said.

"Nothing, I say." Then Keturah, to her horror, felt tears gathering in her eyes. They ran down her cheeks, and she groped for a handkerchief.

"Keturah, come and sit down. Tell me what it is."

Keturah sat down, and as the tears rolled down her cheeks, she whispered, "It's Sam. I'm worried sick about him."

"I knew that you would be."

"I . . . I guess I love him, Grace."

"He's a fine man. I've never known anybody that could bring as much cheer as Sam Bradford, and he loves you so much, Keturah."

"Oh, Grace, what if he's dead! I'd die too!"

Grace comforted her for a time, and then Keturah went up to her room to be alone. Grace started for the kitchen, where she found Jubal sitting peeling an apple. "What's the matter with Keturah?" he said.

"She's worried about Sam."

"So am I," Jubal said. He shook his head with disgust. "I should be there with him."

"You're not able to do such things as that, Jubal. You still haven't got all your strength back."

The two sat there for a time drinking tea, and finally Grace said, "Jubal, I want to tell you something, and I'm ashamed."

"What is it, Grace?"

"It's about . . . it's about Stephen." She hesitated, then said, "I didn't love Stephen as I should have."

Jubal carefully sipped his tea and considered his answer. "He wasn't an easy man to love. I didn't show him enough affection either. He didn't welcome closeness. Even as my brother, I never understood him, Grace."

"You're different from him. But a woman should grieve for her husband, and I do—but not as deeply as I should."

Jubal, who had always suspected that Grace had made a bad choice in marrying Stephen, said, "We can't order our hearts, Grace. We love not because of reason but just because it's love."

Grace spoke for a long time and found relief in telling Jubal how hard her marriage had been. Finally when she stopped, Jubal said, "Grace, I've met many women, but never one with your capacity for love. When you marry again—"

"Marry again! Why do you say that?"

"Why, you'll marry again. You're a young woman. You'll find a man, and your heart will go to him, and his will come to you. I thought at one time I'd be that man," he said. "But things didn't work out that way."

"You're a good man, Jubal, but I can't stop feeling guilty. And I don't plan to marry again."

" 'The heart has reasons that the mind knows not of.' Some Frenchman said that." Jubal had studied this woman for weeks now, ever since he had been there. He had seen the capacity for love in her and knew that she was miserable. He had also seen the difference in her since Cormac Morgan had arrived. He almost said something about Cormac but did not. *I can't speak it aloud. She'll have to find her own love*, he thought.

🔔 🔔 🔔

"They're back! They're back!"

Grace had just finished changing Patrick, but her heart lurched and she at once left him lying on the floor where she had knelt to do the job. She raced outside, where Keturah was already standing in the yard.

She saw indeed that the two horsemen were coming slowly along. She was surprised, for Sam always came at a dead gallop.

"Something's wrong," she whispered.

Indeed, when the two men got to the house, they could barely get out of the saddle.

Cormac dismounted first and then reached out and practically pulled Sam to the ground.

"What is it, Sam?" Keturah cried as she came to him.

Sam's face was pale, and his arm was bound tight in a sling. He could not speak for a moment, but then he whispered hoarsely, "Not a thing. We showed those British what a real fight was like."

"We'd better get him inside," Cormac said wearily. He himself had a shirt that was crusty with dried blood across the front and torn and ripped.

"Quick, come in, both of you!" Grace said.

The two men had to struggle to get up the front steps. Grace took over at once. "Here, Sam, lie down on the couch."

"I'll get . . . blood all over it."

"That doesn't matter. Tell me what happened. Let me get water and bandages."

The two men were almost past the point of exhaustion. All Cormac could do was slump in a chair and put his head back. It had been a bloody, brutal battle, and both he and Sam had been in the thick of it.

"We ambushed the British," he said. "We won, but then Tarleton circled around. They caught our band, and we had to hack our way out of it. There was no question of surrender. We know well Tarleton kills anybody who tries to do that."

Sam's arm had a long cut from shoulder to elbow. It was deep and had been roughly sewn together by an amateur doctor. "He's lost a lot of blood."

Keturah was bathing the arm, and when Sam opened his eyes, he said, "Better take care of that arm, Keturah. It's the one I hug you with." Then his eyes rolled upward and he passed out.

Keturah swallowed hard. "Is he going to die?" she whispered.

"No," Cormac said. He straightened up and said, "He just needs food and lots of care."

"I'll do that," Keturah said.

"What about you, Cormac?"

"Oh, just a slight cut."

"Come into the kitchen. I'll see to it," Grace said.

When she got him to the kitchen and sat him down on a high stool, she said, "Here. Take that shirt off."

Cormac was so stiff that she had to pull the shirt off herself, for he could hardly move his arms upward. He had a rude bandage, stiff with brown, dried blood, but there was fresh blood bubbling out from underneath it. "I'm going to change that bandage. How old is it?"

"Two days now. No, three."

"Where have you been?"

"We had to hide out in the swamps, Sam and I. We got cut off from the others."

Quickly Grace looked up and saw that his face was pale. "You've lost a lot of blood too," she said. "Be still." She peeled off the bloody bandage, and her heart lurched when she saw the slashing cut from the top of his shoulder going crossways down to his side. She said, "I've got to stop that bleeding. Here, drink this."

He drank tea, hot and comforting, while she fetched bandages and began to work on him. Her hands were not steady as she washed away the old blood, then carefully applied the new bandages, held together with sticking plaster.

Cormac studied her expression as she worked on him. Her touch was soft and gentle, though he had been in so much pain that he was almost numb by this time.

As for Grace, her heart was in a storm, or so it seemed. She realized that this man, who had come into her life so abruptly, had come to mean more to her than she could ever have imagined.

"You could have been killed," she whispered as she attached the rest of the sticky plaster. She put her hand on his chest lightly, and suddenly he reached out, took it, and kissed it.

"There is kind, you are!" he exclaimed.

As he held her hand and smiled at her, for some reason that she could not explain, all the sorrow and grief and pressure of the past

214

weeks and months came to the surface. She had been more concerned about Cormac Morgan than she had realized, and now as he held her hand, she could still feel his lips impressed on it. She did not move for a time. Then she looked up and whispered, "Thank God you're back, Cormac."

"Aye, God is good." He was still holding her hand, and since she did not pull it away, he squeezed it and put his other hand over it. His hands were big and hard and very strong, and hers seemed small and fragile. "You are a caring woman, Grace Morrison," he said. Then his eyes drooped, and she pulled her hand back.

"Come. You'll sleep here until you're better. There's plenty of room for you in with Jubal."

He hesitated only for a moment, but he was not through yet. "When I thought it was all up with us, when we were surrounded by Ban Tarleton's Dragoons, do you know the last thought that came to me?"

"What was it?"

"I was thinking about the poem that I recited to you. About the young man who loved honor more than he loved his sweetheart."

"Is that what you were thinking?"

"Partly that," he said. "But I was thinking that fellow was a fool."

"Why so, Cormac?"

"Because any man should love a woman more than anything, even his own foolish honor."

Her eyes met his, and for a moment they did not move. She was very conscious of her hand held in his as she said, "Come along, Cormac. You've got to get well and strong again."

"Yes. I've got a lot to do," he said. He released her hand and then smiled crookedly. "Fine fellow I am, spouting poetry! I never thought I'd see the day."

But Grace Morrison had a smile of her own. It was not much of a smile, rather tremulous, but she said, "I liked it, Cormac." Then she led him away out of the kitchen toward Jubal's bedroom.

PART FOUR

THE VICTORS

19

A Very Merry Christmas

WHIRLING FLAKES OF SNOW were falling outside the window as Grace and Cormac sat at a table going over piles of papers. South Carolina did not have snow often, and after a while Cormac got up and walked to the window. He stood there looking out silently, and Grace, surprised at his movement, rose and came to stand by him. "What is it? Did you hear something?"

"No," Cormac replied briefly. His eyes were fixed on the myriad of flakes as they fluttered down out of a steel gray heaven. A faint gleam of sunlight from time to time gave the flakes the appearance of tiny flashing diamonds as they descended to rest upon the earth. The ground itself was now coated with snow, and a pristine whiteness reigned over all the scene.

"Nothing so beautiful as snow," Cormac murmured.

"Yes. I miss that down here," Grace replied. "There's something about snow that has always delighted me. It makes everything so beautiful."

Cormac studied the flakes as they swarmed, turning into tiny cone-shaped whirlwinds as the winds swept across the flat grounds that surrounded the house. "Ever notice how every one of them is different," he murmured.

"Every snowflake, you mean?"

"Yes. Try catching a few on your glove sometime. Each has a slightly different shape."

"I don't see how you could know that. Surely some of them have the same shape."

"Maybe so, but I like to think that they are all different—like people," he murmured.

Caught by his odd remark, Grace turned to look up at him. "Does that please you? That people are different?"

"It pleases God." Cormac smiled suddenly. "Just think of how different the people in the Scriptures were. There was Absalom, a fool of a man who took so much pride in his appearance and in gaining power that he betrayed his own father. How different from David he was!"

"That's true. And think about how different Jezebel was from Mary."

He turned to look at her and was pleased by her face, as he always was. It was beautifully shaped, all of its features generous, capable of robust emotion. Her smile was a small lightness around her mouth. Her lips now were long and composed and held back some hidden knowledge that he could not fathom. Her skin was smooth and held a lingering tan from the heat of the summer sun. Her blouse fell away from her throat, revealing the smooth ivory roundness of her shoulders. Her hair was dense and the color of dark honey, and it shone gently as a faint light came in through the window. Cormac was overwhelmed by the sheer womanliness of Grace Morrison.

Grace saw him looking at her, and for a moment she was not able to fathom the expression of his eyes. "What is it, Cormac?"

"Nothing."

"It must be something. Why were you looking at me so strangely?" Her lips made a small change at the corners, soft with the caught interest of a woman.

Cormac wanted to express himself but could not. Ever since he had come to Carolina, he had known that he must be careful, for this woman held a strong attraction for him. Even now her soft fragrance slid through the armor of his self-sufficiency, and he could not speak what was in his heart. She had a loveliness about her, born of a nature more complex and unfathomable than any he had ever known.

Color ran freshly across her cheeks. "What is it, Cormac? Why are you staring at me?" she asked.

Suddenly, without meaning to, he let his heart speak. "There's a sweetness in you, Grace, that I've never seen in another woman."

For a long moment Grace Morrison stood there, the words falling on her spirit like sweet rain. They were the sort of words she had longed to hear from her husband, that she had expected to hear, but they had never come. Now that they had been said she knew without a doubt that her desire for love and goodness and gentleness from a man had not perished. She had been terribly hurt by her marriage, and the coolness of Stephen had scarred her. But now she felt new hope as she replayed Cormac's words in her mind: *"There's a sweetness in you, Grace, that I've never seen in another woman."*

"You shouldn't . . . you shouldn't say things like that," she said, her voice trembling.

"I know I shouldn't." Cormac suddenly grinned, and his long lips twisted in self-derision. "It seems I've made a career out of doing and saying things I shouldn't have." He looked back out the window and said nothing more but watched the snow as it continued to carpet the earth. Finally he was aware that she was waiting, and he said, "Look at that, Grace. Only yesterday the earth was brown and dead and barren and ugly, and now look how beautiful it is." He struggled to find the right words, then said finally, "That's the way I felt when I was converted. Everything in me, my heart and my brain, everything was ugly. And then when the Lord Jesus came into my heart, it was as if God covered me with a whiteness and a goodness. Not mine, you understand," he said quickly. "I well know there's no goodness in me, but somehow I believe the Scripture when it says 'Christ is our righteousness,' and I thank Him that despite my misspent life and sins, He nonetheless has clothed me with His righteousness." He turned to her and shook his head. "There I go preaching at you again. Sorry."

"No. I like the way you put that."

For a long time the two stood there silent, watching the snow fall, and there was a closeness that both of them experienced but could not express. The silence, however, was not uncomfortable. The heavens were sending innumerable tiny flakes to blanket the earth, bringing a peace upon it. And inside the warmth of the room, Cormac Morgan and Grace Morrison knew an inner peace that both of them had desperately desired and finally found.

Finally Grace whispered, "Well, we must finish the work."

"All right, Grace." He suddenly realized what he had said. "I've been calling you Grace. I'm sorry."

"It's nothing."

"That's a wonderful name—Grace," Cormac said as they seated themselves. He smiled then broadly and said, "You wouldn't be nearly as attractive if you were named Jemima."

His spontaneous sense of humor always pleased Grace. "And you wouldn't be nearly so handsome if you were called Melchizedek."

"You could call me Mel," he grinned. "And I'd call you Jemmy."

The lantern threw its yellow light across the two as they bent together, their heads close as they worked on the books. Somehow Grace wished that this moment, this peace or whatever it was that had driven the bitterness out of her, could last forever.

☙   ☙   ☙

Jake Huger lived not ten miles from the Morrison plantation. He was a huge man with a broad, brutal face. His strength was proverbial all over the county. He had been known to wrap his fist in a heavy jacket and break a two-by-six with one single blow of his huge fist. His politics were as brutal as the brawls he had often engaged in, which had become rare, since no man cared to stand up to him.

Huger rode up to the Morrison house, tied his horse, and came up the steps. When he knocked on the door, Grace answered almost at once. He pulled off his hat and said, "I'd better talk to you, I think, Mrs. Morrison."

"Why, yes. Will you come in?"

Huger nodded and stepped inside the house. He seemed to make the place smaller, for his shoulders were enormous and his legs were thick and meaty. He gave everything about him an air of fragility, and when he stood in the middle of the drawing room, refusing the seat Grace offered, his words were thick and short and curt. "I hope you'll listen to what I have to say, Mrs. Morrison. I don't mean to be unneighborly, but I think it would be best if you would consider selling your place and moving out."

Grace was taken aback by the man's blunt words. "What are you talking about, Mr. Huger?" She was well aware that Jake Huger was a leader of a small band of partisans. He rarely joined himself to Marion or Pickens or Sumter or any of the other men who led partisan bands in a military fashion. He had some twenty men who would follow him, and the rumor was that he had led some of the brutal murderous raids against Tories in retaliation for the actions of Banastre Tarleton.

"You Tories are about finished here," Huger said. "The war ain't over, ma'am, but it's going to be soon, and then there won't be room for any king lovers here."

"What makes you think I'm a Tory?"

"Your husband was, and I guess that makes you one too."

A feeling of weakness suddenly ran through Grace. He was such an enormous man, and according to what Leo and others had told her, he was absolutely merciless and cruel when he attacked. And now there was a warning in his muddy brown eyes that silenced her.

"I think you could maybe get a good price for your place."

"But I don't want to sell."

Ignoring her protests, Huger said, "Better to lose a little money on a sale than to lose it all. When this war's over and complete, the government will take over all the Tory property and divide it up among those who fought for liberty." He stared at her for a moment, and there was a cruelty in his lips that belied his words. "I'm going around to all the Tories and putting the same word out. Mrs. Morrison, you'd be wise to leave before you lose everything. I bid you good day."

Huger's visit disturbed her greatly, and she was quieter than usual the rest of the day. When Cormac came in to eat dinner before going back to the fields, he noticed her silence, and as the two were cleaning up, he said, "What's bothering you, Grace?"

For a moment Grace said nothing, but her heart was so troubled she finally said, "It's Jake Huger. He came to pay me a little visit today."

Cormac listened as Grace told him what Huger had said. He dried the dishes and put them up and finally said, "It's tragic that neighbors can't get along."

"I'm afraid of Huger. He's an evil man. According to all the reports, he's capable of murder. He burned out a Tory family, from what Leo tells me, and killed them all just two months ago."

"What are you going to do?"

"I don't know. I hate the thought of selling out. I want this place to be Patrick's heritage. If we left here now, Stephen's death would have no meaning, but if we stayed here and built a life, it would belong to Patrick, and I want him to have it."

Cormac offered no suggestions, but after he left the house, instead of going back to the fields, he rode directly to the plantation that belonged to Colonel Francis Marion. He found the small leader out in the field surveying as his men slaughtered a hog and cut it up.

Marion listened intently as Cormac explained what had happened; then he shook his head, displeasure in his eyes. "I can control my own men, but there are hotheads who want to take things into their own hands. Huger doesn't do the cause any good. The only way we're going to win is to unite and fight military actions. I admit we're small, but the end is coming quickly now." A light of amusement suddenly came into his eyes. "Did you know that I'm a general now? A brigadier general, that is."

"I didn't know that."

"It makes no difference to me," Marion said quietly, "but all I want is to see this war over and for everyone to go back to life as it should be."

"Do you think Mr. Huger will attack the Morrison place?"

"He's capable of it. He's a hard drinker and has a temper like a forest fire—just takes over and there's nothing anyone can do." Marion walked slowly along with Cormac, and the two spoke of possible solutions. "I'll have a talk with Huger. Mrs. Morrison is no danger to the cause. Her husband wasn't either. He wasn't really a supporter of the king. He just wanted to have a plantation and make a life."

"That's right. Do you think you can make Huger listen?"

"I'll do my best, but he's an independent, stubborn fellow." Marion suddenly stopped and stroked his chin thoughtfully. "If Mrs. Morrison would marry again, a good American with no ties to the Crown, that would shut Huger up, I think."

"I don't think she has any plans to marry."

"Too bad. Well, in any case, I'll see what I can do with Huger."

Cormac thanked General Marion and left at once, headed back for the plantation. He went to the fields and was surprised to find Jubal mounted on a gray horse. "Well, you're doing much better, Jubal."

"Yes, I've decided I can carry some of my weight around here. I've been nothing but a parasite."

"I wouldn't worry about that. Grace doesn't think of you that way."

"I know she doesn't, but I can't stand to not pull my own weight. Where have you been?"

For a moment Cormac hesitated, then said, "I've been over to talk to General Marion."

"*General* Marion? I thought he was a colonel."

"Not anymore. Washington has had him made brigadier general."

"A general right here in our own county! Well, he's a fighter. I'll bet Washington wishes he had a hundred more just like him."

"I'm sure he does."

"What did you go to see Marion for? You going to join his band?"

"I might, but that's not why I went. Maybe Grace will tell you about it, but Huger came for a visit."

"What did he want?"

Cormac explained quickly and then said, "I thought Marion might be able to control him, but he says that would be difficult."

"A bullet through the head would control him."

"Now you sound like Huger himself."

The two men sat there talking quietly, watching the workers as they worked on a new drainage ditch. The system had been so successful that they had bought oxen of their own, and now fields that had previously been useless because they flooded would soon be fruitful.

"General Marion said a strange thing, Jubal. He said that if Grace married a loyal American, it would solve her problems."

"That's probably true," Jubal said. "I worry about Grace. She needs help. She hates the idea of going back to England and losing this place." He looked over the fields and then murmured, "You know, I think I might marry her myself."

Jubal's words took Cormac off guard. "Marry her! Why, Jubal, I didn't know ... I didn't know you cared for her."

"Oh, I've always admired Grace. When Stephen was courting her, I thought I'd be a better husband to her than he was."

Cormac found himself deeply disturbed, and finally he said, "But does she care for you?"

"I don't think she does. As a matter of fact, I think marriage to Stephen has spoiled her taste for the institution. But she respects me, I think, and I respect her. No one would suspect me of being a loyalist, so if we were married, she wouldn't have any trouble with losing this place."

Cormac stared at the tall man across from him. Jubal was handsome and would be very strong once he had fully recovered. Cormac, however, shook his head. "I can't think that she'd marry just to save a plantation."

"I don't know, Cormac. Women put a lot of store in a place. They want a nest, like a mother bird, I suppose. We men can wander endlessly and not think twice about it. In any case I'm going to offer myself."

Cormac could not answer, and he watched, nonplussed, as Jubal rode off toward the house. A part of him wanted to go after Jubal, to argue, to persuade him not to do such a thing, but finally with a sense of gloom, he said, "It's none of my affair."

🔔 🔔 🔔

"Marry you! Why, Jubal, what in the world are you talking about?"

Grace Morrison stared at Jubal, who had simply come into the house and quite cheerfully said, "I heard about Jake Huger, and I think we ought to get married. That would save the plantation."

Jubal saw Grace's shock and went on to explain. "I know you don't really love me, but I respect you. I think you're one of the most beautiful women I've ever seen, and I think we could make a good couple."

Suddenly Grace laughed aloud. Her eyes sparkled and she shook her head. "Jubal, you are a—you are a ridiculous man!"

Jubal blinked. "What? Here I make you an offer of marriage and you say I'm ridiculous!"

Grace came over and put her hands out. He took them and she squeezed them. "You are a dear man. You have a good heart, Jubal, but it wouldn't do."

Jubal stared at Grace, and then she laughed again, and it was an infectious laughter. "I suppose you're right," he admitted. "In any case, if you change your mind, I stand ready to be a dutiful husband."

"It's kind of you, Jubal, but it's no solution, I'm afraid."

Jubal was a sharp fellow in many ways, and suddenly a thought came to him. "I might have known you'd refuse me."

"Of course you should have known."

Jubal hesitated, then said, "You had a hard time with Stephen, but now I think there's someone else, isn't there?"

"What are you talking about?" Grace said with alarm. The laughter left her, and her eyes flew open with surprise. "Of course there's no one else!"

"You tell me that?"

"Yes, I tell you that! Now be on with you, Jubal."

Jubal smiled, squeezed her hand, and said, "Your secret is safe with me."

Grace watched with some consternation as Jubal Morrison left. She went about her work, but her mind was preoccupied. The idea of marriage with him was preposterous, of course, but her heart warmed as she reflected on the offer. *We'd have a good marriage*, she thought. *He's kind and considerate, and we respect each other.* But then as she continued throughout the morning, she could not imagine being married to Jubal. *He does not stir me as ...* She could not complete that thought, for the image of Cormac Morgan had leaped into her mind, and her cheeks flushed as she remembered his words: *"There's a sweetness in you, Grace, that I've never seen in another woman."*

Grace Morrison was an honest woman, and she could not deny what had happened when Cormac had said this to her. The simple words had stirred her emotions as few things ever had. She shook her head and bit her lips. "Don't be a fool, Grace," she cautioned herself and went about her work as best she could.

🔔   🔔   🔔

Christmas had always been a happy time for Matthew, but somehow this Christmas seemed particularly special. Although not fitted for it, he had worked hard to become a planter. The money that Abigail had received from her house and her inheritance had gone a long way. They had hired a good man named Seth Devaney as overseer, and Devaney had proved to be a godsend. He was not a tall man but was sturdy and knew farming as Matthew could never know it. He also knew how to work men, and with a minimum expenditure, Devaney had transformed Twelvetrees into a presentable place.

"Wait until next year, Mr. Bradford. We're going to have a great year. You'll see!"

Devaney's encouraging words had taken root in Matthew, and now during the Christmas season, he was filled with a sense of peace he had never known in his whole life. He had gone to great trouble to get special gifts for Abigail and for Sam and smaller ones for the workers.

A fire was crackling in the fireplace as he came in on Christmas morning with another load of wood. He dumped it beside the fireplace, added a few chunks, and then came over to where Abigail was standing looking out the window. "Beautiful, isn't it?" he said. He put his arm around her and drew her close. She turned to him and lifted her face. He kissed her and was stirred by her caress. "Merry Christmas," he whispered.

"Merry Christmas to you."

"I got this for you last time I was in the village," he said. He reached inside his pocket and pulled out a small package.

"A Christmas gift from my husband."

"I hope you like it."

Carefully Abigail unwrapped the paper and removed a small box. When she opened it she was absolutely silent for a moment. She did not move nor did she even breathe.

"Don't you like it, Abigail?"

Abigail lifted her eyes, which were damp with tears. "I love it." She pulled the golden locket out and held it up to the light. It was delicately made, and the gold chain caught the flickering of the fire. "Help me put it on," she said.

She lifted her hair, and Matthew fastened the catch in the back. She turned around, and it fell on her throat. Reaching out he touched it, saying, "It's not so beautiful as you are, sweetheart."

"I have a present for you too."

"Well, I should think so. What is it?"

Matthew knew that Abigail had always treasured Christmas. She had told him how she had spent long hours looking for presents, and he was very curious as to what she had selected for him. Whatever it was, he knew he would treasure it.

"I can't give it to you today, but I will after a while."

"What?" Matthew said, pretending to frown. "What do you mean?

227

It's Christmas! I want my present now!"

Abigail's lips were tremulous. "I can't give it to you right now. You'll just have to wait."

"How long?"

Abigail took his hand and suddenly placed it against her body. She looked up and whispered, "About seven and a half months, I think."

Matthew, for a moment, could not imagine what she meant. Then looking into her eyes, he saw the joy there and said, "Abbey, you mean it?"

"Yes."

Matthew put his arms around her and said, "What a gift! Thank you, Abigail, and thank you, God!"

Abigail stood there in the security of his arms, and she knew a happiness that had escaped her all of her life. She felt complete. She drew back and studied his face. Some men did not want children, the responsibility and the burden of them, she knew, and she desperately wanted Matthew to want this baby. He was smiling, and finally she said, "Will it be a boy or a girl?"

The impish humor leaped out of Matthew, and he said innocently, "Why, it would have to be, wouldn't it?"

Abigail suddenly laughed with delight. "You crazy fool!" she said. "I mean, which one do you want?"

"Whichever one it is, I hope he or she is just like you," he said as he took her in his arms and kissed her.

Abigail knew then that life for her was a gift from God. Indeed she had been faithful for years, and now this man had come to know God himself, and the two of them were secure in each other.

🔔   🔔   🔔

At almost this same instant Sam was standing beside Keturah. He had brought a large package inside, and now as she came to him, he said, "Merry Christmas."

"Merry Christmas to you, Sam. Wait. I'll get your gift."

"No. Open this one first."

Keturah saw his eagerness and smiled. "What is it? Surely you didn't buy me a dress."

"I could have," Sam said. "Everyone knows that I'm an expert in women's clothing."

"I'd hate to see the dress you'd pick out for me," Keturah laughed. She untied the string that held the package, and as it fell open she caught her breath. She let the paper fall and held up a beautiful fur coat with a high collar and a belt. "Sam!" she exclaimed. "I never saw anything so beautiful! What is it?"

"It's mink. Before I left Boston, I traded some of my belongings for all these skins and had them made up into a coat for you. Try it on," he said.

Keturah slipped her arms into the sleeves of the coat that had been lined with rich, dark satin. The fur was smooth, smoother than anything she could have imagined, and as she held it around her, she exclaimed, "Sam, it's so warm and so beautiful! How do I look?"

"Like an angel in a fur coat," Sam grinned.

"I never got a gift like this."

"I wanted it to be something that you didn't have."

"Well, I don't have anything as nice as this, and I've never seen anybody that did," Keturah said. She came to him and suddenly pulled his head down and kissed him. It was a rare gesture for her, and she would have moved back, but he wrapped his arms around her, fur coat and all. "I hope you like it well enough to believe that I'm the sweetest man that ever lived."

Keturah suddenly felt the strength of his arms around her. She had been abused in her youthful years and had become so leery of men that physical affection had been difficult for her, but now she put her arms around his neck and knew suddenly that this man would never hurt her. "You are the sweetest man that ever lived. You're crazy sometimes, Sam, but you are sweet." She pulled his head down and kissed him firmly. Sam held her for a time, enjoying the softness of her lips.

He drew back, lifted her chin gently, and said, "I reckon I'll never be able to say how much I love you, Keturah. I wish I were better with words. All I can say is, you're the sweetest girl I've ever known, and the prettiest, and I'll love you all of my life."

"Will you, Sam?"

"Yes, and I want you to marry me."

At that moment Keturah knew that this was the man for her. "Maybe I will," she whispered.

"Maybe! What kind of talk is that?"

Keturah put her hand on his chest and laughed up at him. "You're too healthy looking. All the novels talk about how men in love become pale and can't eat. You eat like a horse, Sam. Go get pale and skinny and come around singing love songs to me and write poems, and then we'll talk about marriage."

Her talk was jovial, but Sam knew this girl. He had cared for no other woman as he did for this one, and he suddenly caught her up and swung her around. He was very strong and she protested, but he would not let her go. Finally he put her down and held her imprisoned in his arms. "I'll always love you, Keturah," he said simply. "Other things may change, but my love for you never will."

"Won't it, Sam?" Keturah put her hands on his cheeks and held them for a minute. "All right. I'll marry you, then." She lifted her lips and he kissed her, and she knew his love would protect her for the rest of her life.

🔔   🔔   🔔

Christmas had been a pleasant time for Cormac. The Bradfords had come over with Sam. All of them were full of the good news about the child that was to come. They had sat around the living room singing, and Cormac's fine voice had been a surprise to them all. They had eaten a scrumptious meal, and finally when it was all over and Sam and the Bradfords had gone home, and Keturah had gone to put Patrick to bed, Cormac and Grace began cleaning up the table and discussing Sam and Keturah. "They're going to be so happy," she said. "They're just perfect for each other."

"I think they are."

Cormac fell silent then, and Grace knew that something was troubling him. She said, "What's the matter, Cormac?"

"I guess I'm wondering about what's to come."

She turned to him and said, "You mean about this place?"

"Yes. Jubal said he offered to marry you and you refused."

"Oh, that was foolish of Jubal. He should have known better."

"He meant well."

"I know he did. He's such a good man, but it wouldn't do, Cormac."

Cormac suddenly dropped his head, and she came to stand beside him. "What is it you're troubled with?"

"I'm a poor man and you're a rich woman. . . ." He hesitated, then said, "If it were the other way around, I would offer to marry you myself. But I have nothing to give you."

Grace stood stock-still. She could not think for the life of her of a single word to say. Finally she stammered, "Why, Cormac . . ." and could not add another word.

"Another thing. I'll probably be a pastor, and that's not a life that a well-to-do woman could take." He suddenly smiled wistfully as he said, "I don't have anything to offer you but my affection. It's not enough, but it seems right to tell you that I feel for you in a way that I never expected to feel about a woman."

Grace was so rattled she could not think. She was a woman who needed affection, and she loved the way he spoke to her.

Now he simply put his hands on her shoulders and leaned forward and kissed her on the lips. It was a kiss of regret, for he knew that he would never have this woman. Her lips were soft under his, and he had to restrain himself from throwing his arms around her and crushing her to his chest. Still, he could not hide his passion from her. Yet she did not move away but put her hand up suddenly on his neck and added the pressure of her own lips.

For Cormac she was all he could ever hope for in a woman, and a fire seemed to burn within him and a wind rush through him as he held her kiss. When she moved back, her eyes were gentle and warm. She smiled. He saw the quick rise and fall of her breathing, and the moonlight through the window whitened her throat.

Grace knew she could not prolong this moment. Faint color stained her cheeks, and she held him with a glance, half possessive and half frightened. She whispered, "Good night."

As she left, her fragrance lingered in the air like a melody coming over a great distance. Cormac was shaken by her beauty, so fresh and turbulent and strong, and a great sadness came over him for that which he knew could never be.

20

AN AMERICAN VICTORY

"I'D LIKE TO FIX MATTHEW something special for when he comes in for dinner."

Abigail and Keturah were in the kitchen, and as they had talked, they had put together a fine meal. One of Matthew's favorite dishes was chicken pudding, and Abigail had grown adept at making it. Now as it was bubbling in a pan over the hot coals, she turned to Keturah, who had come over for a visit, and said, "You have any ideas for something special for a brand-new husband?"

Keturah took off her mobcap and handled it for a moment, then replaced it. "What about raspberry flummery?"

"What's that?"

"Do you have any raspberries?"

"Yes, we do," Abigail said. "Is it hard to make?"

"No. It's real easy. Get the raspberries and I'll show you."

The two women busied themselves, and Keturah did most of the work as Abigail spoke of her marriage and of the baby that was to come. Her cheeks were flushed, and there was a happiness in her that Keturah loved to see.

Keturah washed the raspberries, put them into a pan along with water, and cooked them for about ten minutes. While they were cooking she measured out a cup of sugar, a half teaspoon of salt, and six tablespoons of cornstarch and stirred them with a fork. She quickly added the sugar mixture to the cooked berries and stirred them before sitting down on a small stool in front of the fire. She studied Abigail for a moment, then blurted out, "Abbey, what's it like being married?"

Abigail blinked with surprise and looked over toward her young friend. "Why, whatever do you mean?" She laughed and said, "I've been telling you how happy I am."

"I know, but I . . . well, I worry about it sometimes. Especially now that I've agreed to marry Sam." Keturah was wearing a simple gray dress with a white muslin inset in the low-cut bodice. Her long sleeves were rolled up to her elbows, and a white cotton apron covered the long skirt. She shifted uneasily on the three-legged stool. Reaching out she picked up a splinter of wood, stuck the end of it in the fire that crackled under the flummery, and waited until it caught. She held it up like a candle and said, "I've been so independent for so long I don't know anything about being married. I don't know what Sam will expect."

Abigail leaned back on her rocking chair as her heart went out to Keturah. She had formed a real affection for this young woman and prayed that God would give her wisdom.

"Keturah, you love Sam and he loves you, and when the two of you are married it will be wonderful, but you will have to deal with small problems. One will be adjusting to each other's ways. You can be sure that Sam will do things that irritate you—maybe he will eat an apple in your ear and it will drive you crazy. And you'll have your own peculiar ways that will irritate him—maybe singing when he doesn't want to hear it. It doesn't matter. There will be things like that, and you two will have to learn, as all couples do, to lovingly discuss them and to adjust."

"What bothers you about Matthew's ways?"

"Let me see. There aren't too many, but he does have the bad habit of grinding his teeth sometimes in his sleep. First time it happened I thought he was sick, and I woke him up. He didn't even know he was doing it, Keturah. And, of course, since it's something he does in his sleep, he can't quit, so I just have to take that as part of who Matthew is. I'm sure some of my ways drive him up the wall at times."

Keturah listened intently as Abigail spoke, but still there was a worried frown on her face. Finally she said, "It sounds like marriage is a lot of work."

Abigail reached over and squeezed Keturah's shoulder. She smiled gently and said, "It is, but Sam loves you and you love him. It takes a lot of love and forgiveness to make a worthwhile marriage, but believe me, Keturah, it is the most wonderful thing in the world when you can do that."

By this time the flummery had thickened. Keturah got up and said, "Now we'll put it in glass dishes." The two women poured the mixture out into glasses, and Keturah asked, "Do you have any butter molds or jelly molds?"

"Yes."

"Then we'll put some in those too."

Abigail came up with a mold in a fish shape, and Keturah poured in some dark blue syrup. "Now," she laughed, "you can tell Matthew he's having blue fish for supper. I bet he won't know what *that* is."

"What do we do with it now?"

"We'll put it out in the snow. It'll freeze there and will be just right for supper."

Keturah turned then and said, "I guess you think I'm silly asking all these questions."

"Of course not. I think most young women have some fear about getting married. But when two people love each other, it'll work out." Abigail smiled at Keturah's face as it seemed to grow peaceful and thought, *I know she and Sam are going to be happy. How wonderful it is to see a young couple starting out without going through all the bitter ups and downs that Matthew and I did.* She had managed to put her past behind her now and hardly ever thought of it. The prospect of the child to come always brought a rush of joy to her, and as the two women continued preparing the meal, Abigail Bradford was content.

⚜   ⚜   ⚜

Grace and Cormac were riding over the fields, the sound of the horses' steel-shod hooves muffled by the two inches of snow that had fallen. Overhead the luminous sky was a clear, pearly gray. Not a cloud marred its surface, and a pale sun looked down on them as they made their way across one of the fields.

This ride had become customary for these two, something that Grace looked forward to. Her cheeks were glowing, and she had donned a dark green riding-coat dress that had a close-fitting bodice with pointed revers in the front. The neck was encircled by two falling collars, and the neckline of the dress was low with a white neckerchief wrapped around her neck and tucked in. The dress had a full skirt, fastened with buttons down the front, and the sleeves were long and tight and fastened at the wrists with small buttons.

Now she glanced over at Cormac, admiring secretly the strong planes of his face, noting the strength of his neck and the easy seat he had on his horse. He was wearing clothes that molded themselves to him—dark blue woolen breeches, a pair of knee-high black boots, and over his waistcoat a gray jacket of fine wool. He wore a tricorn hat that was pushed back on his forehead, and now as she studied him, she saw a thoughtful look on his face and suddenly realized that he had not spoken for some time.

"I think it's going to snow some more," Grace said, mostly to attract his attention.

"It might." Cormac looked up and tested the skies for a moment. "I think it's good for the fields. It soaks in slowly and nurtures the little seeds that are hiding there."

Grace loved the poetic side of Cormac. He never wrote formal verse, but he had a wonderful knack for giving a phrase a colorful turn, for providing unique, evocative descriptions, quite unaware of doing so. She had come to treasure his company. She knew that the slaves all adored him and would do anything in the world for him. Few days passed that she didn't give a prayer of thanksgiving to God for sending him. Indeed, she did not know what she would have done if he had not come when he did. The memory of Taws was fading, and as long as Cormac was here, she knew things would be well.

Cormac suddenly gave her an odd look. "The fighting seems to be winding down. I think the war will be over soon."

"Do you really think so?"

"That's what General Marion says. He says the British Parliament is keen to end the war, and the British people are sick of it. And I think he's right."

"It's been a hard time, especially for General Washington," said Grace. "It must have broken his heart to discover that Benedict Arnold turned traitor and betrayed his cause and his country."

"I understand that Washington had a fondness for Arnold, but it wasn't well placed. He's a scoundrel."

Benedict Arnold had indeed sold his country out, and his name was and would ever be the symbol of treason and betrayal. Arnold was probably the best fighting general on either side during the entire war. Men would follow him anywhere, it seemed, and his quick mind was able to see a situation and immediately take effective action. But Arnold was fighting for the British now, and Washington grieved, as did the country.

Suddenly Cormac said, "Did you hear about the mutiny?"

"Mutiny! You mean at sea?"

"No. It was close to Morristown. The soldiers of the Pennsylvania line just threatened to walk out."

"How terrible for General Washington!"

"From what General Marion says, they felt they had been tricked by Congress. They thought they had signed up for only three years. They were unhappy with their treatment."

"What happened?"

"Well, General Washington was able to put it down, but it was a close thing."

The two rode on, and Cormac spoke of the coming spring and the time of planting. He had soaked up knowledge from Leo and the other hands, and since he was a man who could take advice, they willingly and eagerly poured themselves into educating him.

"What about General Greene? I understand he's the commander now over all the forces in the South."

"General Marion thinks the world of him. He says that Greene, though his forces are small, will be able to defeat Cornwallis."

General Nathaniel Greene was facing a difficult time. He had been defrocked as a Quaker because they did not believe in fighting. Greene walked with a pronounced limp and had a rough charm that could win both men and women to his way of thinking. He had learned his trade as a soldier the hard way, fighting all the way from Lexington to Concord as a private, rising to become the most prominent general in Washington's army. He had been sent to do whatever could be done in the South, to salvage the mess left by Horatio Gates, and he had pulled together his small forces to face the mighty British.

"General Marion tells me that Greene makes no secret of the fact that he'll never be able to fight a full battle against Cornwallis and the British. He doesn't have the men for that, and he can't gamble his army. But I heard now, as small as it is, he's divided his army into two parts—half for him and half for General Daniel Morgan. As a matter of fact, I wouldn't be surprised but what General Marion pulled all of his men out to join in that battle."

"Will you go, Cormac?"

"I expect I will. If I'm going to live in America, I'll have to fight for her."

The two rode along, and after a time they pulled up at a stream. It was cold, but the horses lowered their heads and drank, then blew their breaths, forming small geysers of steam.

"Cormac, do you think you'll ever become a pastor?"

"I don't know. If God calls me, I will, but it's a hard life. Especially for—" He broke off, then sat there for a while.

Grace knew that he had intended to say, "It's a hard life especially for a woman." She did not answer. Something had joined her and this man that neither of them was certain about. He had brought richness and hope into her life, and as the two turned back, she wondered what it would be like if he lost his life. And she found the thought intolerable.

🍺　　　🍺　　　🍺

Jubal burst in to where Matthew and Abigail were eating breakfast. His eyes were bright, and he said, "Matthew, General Marion's calling for all men!"

"What is it, Jubal?" Matthew said, getting to his feet at once.

"General Morgan is in trouble. Ban Tarleton is after him, and General Marion says we've got to give him all the help we can."

"Where is he?"

"A place called Cowpens."

"Where's that?"

"North of here, but we're all going. General Marion's sending every man he possibly can."

"Is Cormac going?"

"Yes. He's getting ready now."

"Then I'll be ready as soon as I can."

"Right. We'll meet Cormac at the crossroads."

As soon as he left, Abigail came over and stood beside Matthew. He turned to her and said gently, "Don't be afraid."

"I'll try not to." She threw her arms around him and pressed her face against his chest. "But I can't lose you now, Matthew. I just can't!"

The two stood there clinging to each other, and Abigail knew that all over South Carolina women were praying for their men, fearful as they rode away, trying not to think that they might never see them again.

I can't send him away like this, she thought. She lifted her head and touched his cheek and said quietly, "You've got to come back. We've got a daughter on the way."

"You sure it's not a son?"

"I think the Lord has told me it is to be a girl."

Matthew held her tightly, then took a deep breath. "I'll come back. God will take care of me."

At almost this same time Cormac was leading his horse out of the stable. Sam was already mounted and urging him to hurry up. Sam leaned over and took a kiss from Keturah, and she whispered, "Come back to me, Sam."

Grace had come over to stand beside Cormac. She did not know how to say what was in her heart, and when he turned to her, she could only whisper, "Come back, Cormac."

She put out her hands, and when he held them, he saw they were trembling. "Never take counsel of your fears, Grace."

238

"I'll try not to, but, oh, be careful!"

He suddenly leaned forward and kissed her, then whispered, "I'll come back." He threw himself into the saddle, and the men left at a full gallop.

As Grace and Keturah watched them ride off, Keturah said quickly, "They'll come back. They just have to."

Grace Morrison put her arm around Keturah as the cloud of dust from the horses became smaller and smaller. "We'll have to pray mightily for their safety, Keturah," she whispered.

🛡   🛡   🛡

As the party from the Peedee River basin arrived at the camp of Daniel Morgan, near the Broad River, Matthew looked around and said, "It doesn't seem like there are very many of them."

At that moment a lieutenant came over and said, "Where are you men from?"

"We're part of General Marion's force," Matthew said quickly. "He sent us to see if we could be of any help."

The lieutenant, a tall gap-toothed man, grinned and spat tobacco juice on the frozen ground. "Come along. General Morgan will be glad to see you."

The lieutenant led them to a campfire, which in the early morning air was blazing cheerfully. As they approached, a huge man dressed in some semblance of a Continental uniform turned to them. He had a roughhewn face and looked old and tired.

"General Morgan, General Marion has sent thirty men to join us."

"Has he, now!" Morgan's voice was rough and coarse, and he came forward and put his hand out.

Matthew took it and found his hand swallowed in the huge grasp of the other. General Daniel Morgan was over six feet two and weighed probably two hundred twenty pounds. He had served with George Washington during the French and Indian War, and once when an officer had struck him with the flat of his sword, Morgan had knocked the man down. He had been court-martialed and sentenced to five hundred lashes, which would have killed some men, but Morgan had survived.

Matthew studied the huge figure of Morgan and remembered that General Marion had said, "Morgan is old but he's a fighter, and that's what we need in these days."

Morgan questioned the newcomers carefully and then said, "Ban Tarleton's on his way. Do you fear him?"

"No," Sam said quickly. "I've been wanting to get a shot at that man for a long time."

"Have you, now? What's your name, young man?"

"Samuel Bradford. You may know my father, Daniel Bradford."

"Indeed I do," Morgan said. "Wish he were here with us. He's a fighting man himself, and that foundry of his has been invaluable."

"He'd like to be here, sir." Sam was twitching with anxiety and said, "Do you think Tarleton will catch up with us?"

"Yes. He'll be here in the morning with all of his Green Dragoons."

Cormac had said nothing thus far, and now he introduced himself. "My name is Cormac Morgan, sir."

"Oh, you're a Morgan too, are you!" The general grinned and came over to shake Cormac's hand. He found the young man's grip impressive and said, "We need more Morgans in this fight. I see by your speech you ain't from here."

"No, I'm from Wales, but I'll be here from now on."

"Good man," General Morgan said.

Cormac nodded his head toward the river and asked, "What river is that, General?"

"It's called the Broad River."

Cormac looked to the opposite direction and said, "And Tarleton's coming from that way, if I understand it?"

"That he be." Morgan's rough face broke into a grin. "You're thinkin' this is a bad place to fight."

"Well," Cormac grinned suddenly. "We'll *have* to fight, won't we? The river's at our backs."

General Morgan studied Cormac. "You're a bright lad. All us Morgans are that way. Look, let me tell you what's going to happen. I'm going to do something with the militia that's never been done. Usually the commanders put the militia far to the back. I'm putting you boys right in the front line."

"Good!" Sam exclaimed. "Just where I want to be!"

"Militia have a bad habit of running, I understand," Matthew said. "Aren't you afraid we'll do that?"

"You've only got two ways to run. You see the river's behind us, the woods on each side. Tarleton's ahead of us up there, so if you turned you'd run right into the guns of your own men. You'd most likely get shot. They don't like militia that run away, these Continentals don't."

General Morgan studied the faces of the men and said, "I sure wish General Marion were here."

"He would be if he could, sir," Jubal spoke up for the first time. "But

240

he had to leave someone there for the defense of the country."

"Well, he sent some fighting men and that's important. Now, here's what we'll do." He took a stick and began to draw in the frozen ground. "Here comes Tarleton. You see down here? What will he meet? He'll meet you men and Pickens' militia. All I want you men to do is to get in two shots."

"Just two shots?"

"Yes. Two shots, and I want both of those shots to knock a man down. Be best if it was an officer. As soon as you do, you cut around to the side and go to the rear, where you'll be the reserve. Ban Tarleton will meet the Continental line then under General Howard."

"What about support?" Cormac asked.

"General William Washington and his cavalry are at the very rear right by the river. When we get the British engaged, the cavalry will ride out along the side. Then we simply tighten the pincers."

The men listened carefully, and finally General Morgan said, "Cook yourself something to eat now, if you can find anything. We'll be having some action come morning."

Cormac and the others stayed together and were given a more detailed plan of attack from Pickens, who would command the militia.

All that night General Morgan, huge and rugged, moved cheerfully among the men. He went from fire to fire speaking to every man, his deep voice filling them with courage.

Just before dawn all of the men ate their breakfast rations and quietly took their battle positions. Sam, Cormac, Jubal, and Matthew were all shoulder to shoulder in the front line. Sam grinned at Jubal, saying, "Don't you try to run, now. Maybe I'd better tie a rope around your leg."

Jubal, accustomed to Sam's teasing, looked down through the fields through which Ban Tarleton would soon come. "I'm going to get two officers, Sam."

Cormac was calm, and turning to Matthew, he said, "Don't be a hero, Matthew. You're a husband now and are going to have a little one."

"Do you think this will work? The militia's never been put on the front line of any battle that I know of."

"I've got confidence in General Morgan. I think this is the way to beat Tarleton. We've got to surprise him."

Someone cried out, "There they come!" and Cormac strained his eyes. He saw the red coats of the British as they emerged from around a stand of trees. They came marching in perfect order, three light infantry companies. Ban Tarleton knew only one tactic of attack—full merciless force. They heard Tarleton's cry, and then Morgan's voice came floating on the breeze. "Old Morgan was never beaten! Give them two shots and we'll win!"

Pickens came along saying, "Wait until they're within fifty yards, and aim at the men with the epaulets."

Cormac watched as Tarleton came on. He picked his target, and when Pickens screamed, "Fire!" he pulled the trigger. He saw his target throw his hands at the sky and fall off his horse. Still Tarleton pressed on, and Cormac loaded his musket quickly. He picked another target and shot but suspected he had missed.

"Come on," Cormac said, pulling at Sam, who was trying to get in a third shot.

"Just one more shot," Sam pleaded.

"No. It's time to obey orders."

Morgan's plan went exactly as he had foreseen. The militia faded around the two wings of the main army, and the British marched, their ranks decimated, into the deadly fire of the Continentals. While they were engaged, Tarleton's cavalry came pouring in, but they were met by the cavalry of General William Washington, and the fight became bitter and fierce.

Morgan was everywhere, it seemed, shouting, "Old Morgan was never beaten! Give me one more fire and I'll charge them!"

Finally the British knew they were whipped. Tarleton rode back to try to gather up what was left of his feared legion for a final counterattack, but it was impossible. Tarleton started to flee, but Washington was hot on his trail. Tarleton snapped his pistol and fired, and though the ball missed Washington it wounded his horse and Tarleton was able to get away. The battle, which had lasted little more than an hour, was over.

"We won! We won!" Sam cried.

Indeed, the Battle of Cowpens was won. It was soon called the Bunker Hill of the South. The casualties among the British officers were shocking—thirty-nine killed and twenty-seven wounded. Six hundred of Tarleton's forces were captured unwounded, and the spoils of war included one hundred horses, eight hundred muskets, and thirty-five wagons. The total American loss was twelve killed and sixty wounded.

The Battle of Cowpens was the most perfect battle ever fought by the Americans in the Revolution. With little more than creativity and sheer confidence, General Morgan, an unlettered American frontiersman, and his ragtag battalion defeated the best of the English army.

The victory at Cowpens made the battle for the South much simpler for General Nathaniel Greene. Banastre Tarleton had been the main

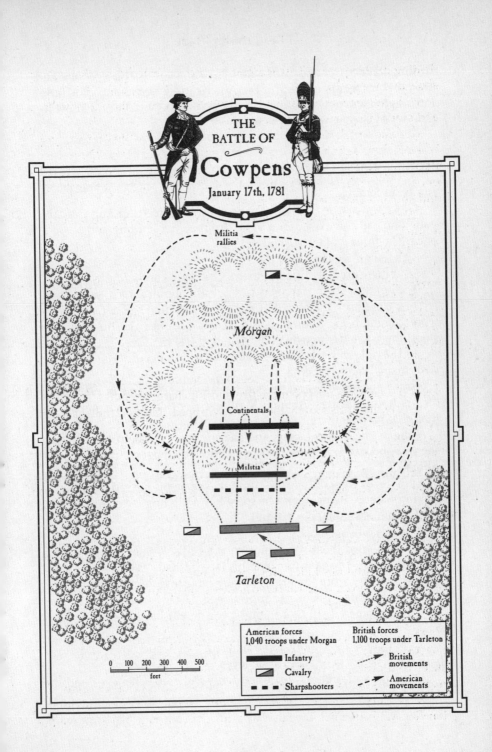

THE BATTLE OF
Cowpens
January 17th, 1781

Militia
rallies

Morgan

Continentals

Militia

Tarleton

American forces	British forces
1,040 troops under Morgan	1,100 troops under Tarleton
▬▬ Infantry	⇢ British movements
▨ Cavalry	⇠ American movements
▪▪▪ Sharpshooters	

0 100 200 300 400 500
feet

striking force of General Cornwallis. He had also been his eyes and had brought him regular reports of the Americans' whereabouts. But Tarleton's legion was now destroyed, and Cornwallis would never know for sure when Greene would appear.

🔔　　🔔　　🔔

Keturah suddenly rose up out of the chair, holding Patrick. "I hear someone coming."

Grace was startled, as her hearing was not as keen as Keturah's. Abigail, who had come over for a visit, dropped her knitting and stood at once. The three women rushed outside.

"It's them," Keturah said.

"But there are only three of them. One's not coming."

The horses were too far away to see, but Keturah, Grace, and Abigail felt fear close in on their hearts. Of the four men that had left, only three were coming back. Keturah could hardly breathe. The three women stood there wondering which of them had lost her love.

As the riders approached, Abigail's heart went cold. "Matthew's not with them," she whispered.

Grace put her arm around her, but as the men came in, Sam piled off his horse, saying, "Abigail, Matthew went on to your house. He thought you'd be there."

Abigail's heart was racing, and she suddenly felt light-headed, as if she was about to faint. Grace said quickly, "You must go to him at once, Abigail."

Sam's eyes were only for Keturah. He came off his saddle, his eyes blazing with excitement, and he gave her a big hug, sweeping her off her feet and swinging her around.

"Put me down, Sam!"

"We whipped them! We whipped the British!" Sam exclaimed. He savored the kiss she gave him, and his face flushed. "Well, if that's what happens when I whip the British, I may have to do it more often!"

Grace hesitated as Cormac approached. His eyes were fixed on her, and she stammered, "I . . . I thought you might have been hurt, Cormac."

"No, I guess I was born to be hanged." He smiled then and stood before her with a gentleness in his eyes.

"I'm glad you're back." Tears suddenly gathered in her eyes, and she dashed them away.

Cormac was touched. "It's good to be missed," he said quietly. For

244

a moment neither knew what to say, and then Cormac asked suddenly, "How's the old man?"

She laughed and said, "Come and see."

The two went into the house, and he picked Patrick up and tossed him into the air, grinning broadly. "Here's the old man!" He kissed him on top of the head, then turned and saw Grace watching him.

She came over and suddenly reached up and laid her hand on his cheek. "I prayed for you, Cormac, all the time."

"Did you, now? That was mighty thoughtful of you." He put his hand over hers and gently held it until Patrick began to clamor for attention. Cormac began walking him around, talking to him, teasing him.

As Grace watched the two of them, she knew that this man had made a place in her heart.

21

"A Man Needs a Woman"

A CLOSE RELATIONSHIP HAD SPRUNG UP between Cormac and Leo. The black man had proven to be not only physically strong, but shrewd and knowledgeable in all of the affairs of running a plantation. He seemed to know by instinct what to do, and the two made it a habit to ride over the fields late in the afternoon, talking over any problems and making plans for the future.

Cormac twisted to glimpse the profile of the big man who rode beside him. Leo's skin gleamed like black ebony, and the strength of his body showed through the thin gray coat that covered his shirt. His mother, Cormac had discovered, had been brought over from Africa when Leo was only three years old. The horror of the slave ship still haunted him, and once he had told Cormac about how the slaves had been packed so tightly belowdecks that they had to lie in "spoon" fashion, each one fitted between two others, in long horizontal lines. Hundreds of them had died and had simply been thrown overboard without ceremony.

Now as they walked their horses along the outlines of a field they planned to open up in the spring, Leo, who had been silent for some time, suddenly turned and said, "It was a good day, Mr. Cormac, when you came to this place."

"I'm glad you think so, Leo. It's been good for me too."

"Yes, sah. You the first white man that ever cared anything about me—as a man, I mean."

Cormac did not know how to answer, and finally he shrugged and said, "I hate this whole business of slavery. It's a disgrace to the human race and especially to the British Empire. The British are supposed to be enlightened, and yet they're involved in this abominable slave trade."

Leo lifted his eyes and watched a hawk sail lazily around the sky before he answered. When he did speak his voice was almost harsh. "There ain't very many white men who feel like you do, I guess."

"More than you think, Leo."

"Not in South Carolina."

Unable to answer this Cormac suddenly pulled his horse up. "I've got something to tell you," he said, and a smile tugged at the corners of his lips.

Instantly Leo turned to face him. His dark brown eyes were intent. He had never been brought before a white man, prior to Cormac's arrival, for anything good, and old habits were strong. "Have I done something wrong, Mr. Cormac?"

"No, not at all. Just the opposite, Leo." Cormac's horse shied, and he reached up and slapped her on the nose. "Stop it, Daisy! You've got better manners than that." The horse snorted and settled down, tossing her head. "This horse has got too much pride," Cormac commented. He turned to Leo and said, "I've been talking to Mrs. Morrison about you."

"About me, sah?"

"Yes." Cormac had been saving this for the proper time, and now it seemed just right. He grinned as he said, "I've convinced her that you would be a better worker—if you were a freeman."

"Me free? That ain't hardly likely, Mr. Cormac."

"Oh, I know you don't have the money, but I've worked it out with Mrs. Morrison." He reached into his inner pocket and pulled out a paper and opened it up. "You see this?"

"Yes, sah. What is it?"

"It's a paper stating that you will work one more year for Mrs. Morrison, and then you'll be free. After that you'll do some work for her to pay part of the price, but basically what it means, Leo, is that you're not going to be a slave any longer."

Leo sat utterly still on his horse. It was as if he had been stricken dumb. His throat moved convulsively as he swallowed, and he reached out timidly and touched the paper. Cormac waited for Leo to speak and wondered what it would be like to belong to another human being—not being able to leave and go where you please, at the mercies of an overseer that could be as cruel as Simon Taws.

Leo had lowered his head and seemed to be staring at the ground.

248

Now, however, he lifted his eyes and met Cormac's gaze straight on. "Thank you, Mr. Morgan."

"It's Mrs. Morrison you want to thank, Leo."

"Yes, sah, I knows." He suddenly reached out and extended his hand. Automatically Cormac took it, and his hand was crushed from the mighty grip. "All the same, sah, I know where it come from. Mrs. Morrison, she'd never think of a thing like this. It was all you, Mr. Morgan. I know that, and I ain't never gonna forget it."

"I'm glad for you, Leo, and of course we'll work on getting Mary and your children free too. Why don't you go tell her?"

"I'll do that." Leo suddenly released Cormac's hand and grabbed the lines. He kicked the gelding into a run and, yanking off his hat, uttered a loud cry in a tongue that Cormac could not understand. It was a glad burst of speech that had been tied up in the big man all of his life, and now as he raced along yelling and crying out for sheer joy, Cormac laughed aloud.

"Well, I guess some stories have a happy ending." He felt all good inside, and as he turned his horse back, he said aloud, "I wish I could free every slave in the world just like that."

♦   ♦   ♦

"Look out, you got a bite!" Sam said. Keturah and Sam were fishing down beside the creek. It was July, and summer had come, bringing a warm breath over the land. The fields had been plowed, and both Twelvetrees and the Morrison place had burst into activity.

Sam had come over late in the afternoon and insisted that Keturah go fishing with him. She had protested but actually had been happy to get away. Now she watched the cork as it dashed madly along in zigzag patterns. "Just another fish," she grinned.

Sam could not stand seeing her doing nothing when it was obvious a fish was on her line. He threw his own pole down and went over to where she was standing and jerked the pole from her hands. He pulled the fish out, a rather small bass, and threw it back. "You're not much of a fisherman," he said. "My heart just beats wildly every time one of those things gets on my line."

Keturah smiled mischievously. The warm weather had brought a new happiness and contentment to her. Sam had ridden over almost every night after the workday, and the two of them had grown very close. Now she reached out and suddenly gave him a shove that almost pushed him off the bank.

"Why, you imp!" he cried. Throwing the pole down he reached out and picked her up, wading thigh deep in the water.

Keturah screamed, "Samuel Bradford, don't you dare throw me in!"

"I won't," he said, "if you promise to marry me."

A sprightly reply came to Keturah's lips, but then she paused and said nothing. Their faces were very close together as he held her in his arms, and somehow she felt very safe and secure. Sam, like all the Bradford men, was physically strong and powerful. He had worked at the forge, and she could feel the sinewy, tough muscles of his arms under her. She had one arm around his neck, and with the other she grasped his shirt. "Do you really want to marry me, Sam?"

Sam Bradford stared at her. "Well, I'll be dipped!" he groaned. "Do I really want to marry you? If that's just not like a question a woman would ask! Here I've thrown up everything and followed you from home to this swamp. I've been every night proposing over and over, and now you say, 'Do you really want to marry me?' "

Keturah suddenly realized that she had loved Sam for a long time, and now she put both arms around his neck and said, "All right. I'll marry you."

Sam was speechless. She pulled his head forward and kissed him soundly and then said, "Now take me back to the bank."

Sam walked back to the bank and put her down. "I can't believe it," he said. "You just throw a man sideways."

Suddenly Keturah giggled, reached out, and shoved Sam with both hands.

"Hey!" Off balance, Sam fell backward and then fell full-length into the creek. His head went under, and he came up sputtering and grabbed his hat, which was floating downstream. "What'd you do that for?"

"I'm not going to marry you! I just didn't want to get wet."

Sam came out of the water, and Keturah said, "Sam, don't you dare!" But he caught her, walked to the edge, and then waded out. Then with a mighty heave he threw her into the air. She hit the sparkling, translucent water, sank down, and then came up gasping. "Sam, I'll kill you!"

"No," Sam said, "you won't do that. You'll marry me."

Keturah laughed. "Yes, I will. Oh, Sam, I love you! I can't imagine life without you."

"Do you really love me, Keturah?"

"You know I do."

For young Sam Bradford the world was now complete. He put his arms around her and held her close. She put her face on his chest, and he stroked her soaking hair. "It's going to be great," he whispered. "We're going to have the best marriage anybody ever had!"

"That youngest son of mine is the most boastful rascal I've ever heard of." Daniel Bradford laughed aloud several times as he read a letter from Sam.

Finally Marian demanded, "Well, what does he say?"

"Why, he's boasting that he knew all the time that Keturah wanted to marry him. He says he knew from the very time she came here that she was in love with him and he just had to fight her off."

"That Sam!" Marian laughed. "I got my letter from Keturah. Says she's going to keep him on his toes."

"Sam says he won't marry her until the war's over."

"That may be wise."

"But it won't be long now. Washington, for once, has had everything come together. He's got twenty French warships under General De Grasse and has trapped the British at Yorktown—seven thousand of them, plus Cornwallis himself. And Washington has seventeen thousand troops mobilizing. It's just a matter of time."

"What does that mean, Daniel?" Marian asked.

"Always before, the British could never be penned in. If they did get any kind of a licking, they'd just go to the coast, and the big guns of the British navy would blow anything that challenged them into smithereens. But now De Grasse has whipped them, and it's the French, our allies, who are there. Washington has got him penned down, and I think it'll be over soon."

The two talked about the war for a while, and finally Daniel picked up Enoch and sat him on his lap. The infant stared up at him soberly, then widened his lips into a big grin. "There's my boy," Daniel said. He ran his hand over the silky hair and said, "It's wonderful to have another son."

"It is for me too. God was so good to send Enoch into our lives."

"And I'll have another grandson soon, or a granddaughter. Abigail's baby is due next month."

"Would you like a granddaughter?"

"It would suit me fine as long as she didn't look like me or Matthew. I hope she looks just like Abigail."

One month after Daniel's wish was made, Bonnie Esther Bradford was born to Abigail and Matthew. Matthew was wild with happiness, and Abigail noted with some asperity, "You act like you're the only man who ever had a baby."

"Well, I feel that way," Matthew said. "Only trouble is she won't stay still long enough for me to paint her." He had been trying to paint a portrait of the baby and had given up in despair.

Cormac, who had come over to visit, laughed at this. He reached out and took the baby from Abigail and said, "Well, here's a fine old lady you are."

"An old lady! She's only a week old," Matthew protested.

But Cormac paid no heed. He cuddled the tiny morsel of humanity in his arms and walked around for a while saying sweet things to her.

Grace, who had come over with him, sat beside Abigail. She leaned over and whispered, "He's the only man I ever saw who doesn't mind if anybody hears him make sweet, silly remarks and talk baby talk. He does it all the time to Patrick."

"I think a man who's afraid to do that is not quite sure of his manhood," Abigail said. "Matthew's the same way."

After the visitors had left, Matthew said to Abigail, "I like Cormac. Do you think he and Grace might ever make a match of it?"

"I'm not sure. Grace was hurt very badly by her first marriage."

"Well, she'll have some scars, but we all have those." Matthew knew only too well.

"Yes, we do, but they fade in our memory, don't they?"

Matthew picked up Abigail's hand and squeezed it. "Yes," he said gently. "They do."

🔔　　　🔔　　　🔔

As usual, Sam came tearing down the road at a breakneck speed. Cormac and Grace were seated on the front porch along with Keturah, the three of them watching Patrick as he sat on a quilt and played solemnly with a few toys that Cormac had made for him.

"Well, here comes Sam again," Cormac grinned. "He always acts as if the world's on fire and he's got the only bucket of water."

The three did not rise, but Sam practically fell off his horse and came running up to the porch. His face was alive with excitement, and he cried, "Washington's heading for Virginia! He's got Cornwallis penned up at Yorktown. One strike and that'll be it! The war will be over!"

"Oh, is it true, Sam?" Keturah said, going to him at once.

"You bet it's true!" Sam said. His eyes sparkled and he could not keep still. He practically did a little dance and said, "I'm going to get in the fight. It'll be the last battle."

"Will Matthew go?" Cormac asked quickly.

252

"No," Sam replied. "He says he's got to stay home and take care of Bonnie Esther and Abigail."

"That's just right. That's what he should do."

"You don't have any business going either, Sam," Keturah said.

"But I've got to go! It'll be the last of the Revolution. I want to tell our grandchildren how I was there when that old Cornwallis and Ban Tarleton got what was coming to them. I've got to go, Keturah!"

The argument went on for some time, Keturah leading Sam away. Cormac and Grace sat there alone except for the infant playing on the quilt. "Will you go too, Cormac?" Grace said, and a sudden fear ran through her.

Cormac looked over, thought for a moment, and then said slowly, "No. I don't think so."

"Don't you want to go?"

"No, I'm no young man in search of adventure."

"What are you in search of, then, Cormac?"

Cormac Morgan got to his feet. He came over and reached out his hands. Grace took them with surprise, and he pulled her to her feet. "I can't tell you, for I'm not sure. But one thing I know."

"What's that?"

"I've learned that a man is not whole without a woman." He suddenly squeezed her hands and then lifted them to his mouth and kissed them ever so gently. Then without another word he turned and walked off.

Grace's hands seemed to burn where his lips had touched them. Once again she was struck by how demonstrative Cormac Morgan was. A thought drifted into her mind: *Stephen would never have kissed my hands. He never did.* But she felt disloyal and shoved the thought aside.

Sam left, promising to return before he set out for Yorktown. Keturah came to stand beside Grace. "I'm afraid," she said. "There'll be fighting, and just think of how awful it would be if Sam got killed just when it's almost over."

"I'm sure the Lord will take care of him."

"Is Cormac going?"

"No. He said not."

Keturah had a lively curiosity. "What about you and Cormac?"

Grace did not answer but leaned over and picked up Patrick, who gurgled and pulled at her hair. "I can't say, Keturah."

"Do you love him?"

Grace did not answer, but Keturah's question echoed in her mind all day and still touched at her consciousness when she went to bed that night. She lay quietly, and the mild breezes of early October came through the window, stirring the mosquito netting that hung over her. She reached up and touched it and whispered aloud, "Do I love him?"

In the cradle across from the bed Patrick rolled over onto his stomach, tucked his knees up under him, and sighed deeply. She watched for a moment, but he drifted off back into a sound sleep. As she lay there, she thought, *I made the wrong decision once. I can't go through that again....*

22

THE WORLD TURNED UPSIDE DOWN

IT WAS A MILD OCTOBER DAY with cool breezes flowing off the Chesapeake when Sam and Jubal set out for Yorktown. They had joined a regiment of Continentals from New York. It had not occurred to either of them to bring food or supplies, and they were fortunate to meet an old friend of Sam's, a private named Joseph Martin. Sam had met him at Valley Forge, and Martin was glad to see him.

"Where are your two brothers?" Martin asked. He was a small man with bright blue eyes and a weathered complexion. He had fought in every battle, it seemed, since Lexington and had a lively, inquiring mind.

"I'm hoping I'll see them at Yorktown, Joe," Sam said.

"And your good father. Will he be there too?"

"I wouldn't be surprised," Sam laughed. "You know how my father is. He wants to be in on everything."

Martin nodded stately and said, "I hear tell that everything's looking up if we can just get to Yorktown before the French fleet leaves."

Jubal asked quickly, "Who's in charge of the fleet?"

"Some admiral called De Grasse."

"I've heard of him," Jubal said quickly. "He's about the best the French navy has."

"Well, if he can pin Cornwallis down until we get there, we'll make hash of him," Martin said.

The march went on all day long, and although both Sam and Jubal rode horses, they moved along at the same pace as the infantry. That night Martin, as usual, had to do some scrounging for food. It had been

255

that way, he had told Jubal and Sam, since the war started. "It ain't so much that I'm good at shootin' the British, but lots of boys went home because they couldn't get nothin' to eat. But I'll find us a bait." And sure enough, he managed to find some fresh meat, although it was late at night before they actually were able to eat.

The next morning they started out again, and Sam and Jubal were amazed at the large body of men moving toward Yorktown. Washington's army of about eight thousand men was on the move. Martin was a part, and a French general named Rochambeau had at least an equal number. The roads were filled with marching men, and when they passed through villages, it was easy to tell who were the patriots, for they stood along the side of the road and cheered, offering ale and cider and food to the soldiers. Those who stayed in the background were obviously Tories.

"I think we're going to have more men than they have for once," Martin said with satisfaction.

"I hope Ban Tarleton's there," Sam said grimly.

"So do I," Martin agreed. "Tarleton's got to have a taste of his own medicine before this is over."

🔔   🔔   🔔

In New York General Henry Clinton knew that he was in a precarious position. He had one force there in the city. Cornwallis was holed up in that town, and there was a smaller force in the South trying fruitlessly to catch Nathaniel Greene, that elusive general that no British force ever managed to catch.

As the possibility of disaster opened up before him, Clinton knew he had to do something besides make excuses. He sent Benedict Arnold, who had returned to New York after ravaging Virginia, to strike at New London, Connecticut. The place was a hornet's nest of privateers and inveterate rebels.

Arnold led a force of seventeen hundred men. Regulars, Germans, and Tories sailed up Long Island Sound and landed. Much of the town was burned. The Americans said it was deliberately, but the British said it was by accident.

The raid itself turned out to be rather gruesome. A few men, mostly militia under a Colonel Ledyard, made a good resistance. They drove the British back several times, but the Redcoats pushed back. There was a great deal of confusion, and Ledyard finally offered to surrender. He turned over his sword to a Tory officer, who then stabbed him with it, whereupon one of the Americans stabbed this officer, and the British came roaring in. Since most of the Americans had thrown down their arms, it was another massacre. Within a few minutes eighty men were killed and another fifty shot or bayoneted before the slaughter stopped.

This New London raid was, in fact, the last major operation of the Revolutionary War in the North. It was no more than a senseless waste of life and property, and the people of that country hated Arnold even more than the rest of America for many years.

🛡   🛡   🛡

Lord Cornwallis had at last begun to fortify Yorktown. He did not choose a place of defense very wisely, for the area would be difficult to defend against a larger force. A great many of his small army were ill in the hospital, and he was anxiously awaiting the arrival of reinforcements and ships, without which Cornwallis knew the defense of Yorktown would be doomed to failure. He considered the possibility of breaking out, but General Henry Clinton had at last promised that he would send support down from New York, and Cornwallis rather foolishly rested himself in that promise.

Cornwallis went out and spoke with his officers. One of them, a Major Forest, said, "You know, my lord, this is not a good place to defend. It's a pretty little place, but there are few advantages of terrain."

"It will have to do, Major."

"Yes, sir. I'll do the best I can, but the field works are only about three hundred yards deep and a thousand yards long. I think we're in a trap here, sir. Couldn't we make an attempt to get away?"

Cornwallis shook his head. "We'll wait for General Clinton to send support."

The major risked a snub by his officer. "Sir, General Clinton has not been known for his quick movements. I think we ought to at least consider leaving."

"And where would we go? We've just come back from the Carolinas, where we wore ourselves out chasing Marion and Greene. We can't go back there. We can't leave because that blasted French admiral has driven our fleet off." He stood looking moodily out over the ocean, where the French fleet of De Grasse made an ominous curtain through which it would be impossible to pass.

"We'll just have to fortify the town."

"Yes, sir," Major Forest said. "I'm seeing to that now."

While the defenses were being constructed, Cornwallis tried to convince himself that he held all the cards. First, he told himself that Clinton was coming with reinforcements. Second, he tried to make himself believe that the British navy would, as always, make short work of the French fleet. And third, as he told his officers, "These French and the Americans are simply incapable of maintaining a siege, since they have no heavy artillery."

This latter assumption was the biggest mistake Cornwallis made, for rather than having only the usual small American field artillery, which would scarcely damage the redoubts, Washington arrived at Yorktown with Rochambeau and the might of the French artillery.

And so Cornwallis sat and waited in vain for help from Clinton while Washington's force of over seventeen thousand men closed in.

🔔　　　🔔　　　🔔

Sam had little trouble finding his brothers. He came upon Dake and Micah in their camp to the right and rear of the line. He yelled at them, so excited he practically fell off his horse, saying, "Hey, I'm here!"

Dake got up at once and grinned. He was a strong, powerfully built man and six feet tall. He still walked with a slight limp from a battle wound but had come back to join Washington for the last few months of the Revolution.

"Well, the battle's all but won now that Sam's here to take over." He pounded Sam on the back and said, "I hear you're going to get married. May the Lord help that poor girl."

Micah, wearing an officer's uniform, smiled and took Sam's hand. "I'm glad to see you, Sam," he said. "Congratulations on your engagement."

"Jubal's here. Here he comes."

Jubal Morrison was a favorite with all of the Bradford brothers, and they greeted him warmly.

"What's going on? When does the fight start? I'm ready to go," Sam said.

Dake shook his head in mock disgust. "I guess you forgot to tell His Excellency to begin," he said, using the soldiers' affectionate name for Washington. For a time the four men stood there talking and catching up on everyone's news. Sam listened eagerly to the news from Boston, and Dake and Micah were anxious to hear of Matthew and also of Grace.

The talk suddenly broke off when Micah said with astonishment, "Look, there's General Washington, and Pa's with him!"

All four men turned at once, and sure enough Washington and several of his staff, including Lafayette and Henry Knox, were moving through the lines. Sam called out, "Hey, Pa!"

Daniel Bradford looked up and laughed. "That's my son Sam, General," he said.

Washington turned. His eyes were alive with excitement, and he waited as the men came forward. He knew Dake, and of course, Micah was one of his favorite chaplains. He shook Jubal's hand and welcomed him to the force.

Henry Knox, the huge commander of artillery, said, "Well, Sam, I hear a wedding's in store."

"Yes. Keturah finally persuaded me to marry her."

Everyone laughed, and Daniel Bradford said, "You'll have to excuse Sam. He's somewhat given to overstatement."

Washington was in a good mood. "It's good to have all of you Bradfords here to witness the end of the Revolution," he said.

"Do you really think it is the end, sir?" Dake asked quietly.

"I do, Sergeant. We've got them this time. The Lord God has been good to us."

"I'll just stay here with these sons of mine, Your Excellency, if it's all right," Daniel said.

"Of course. We'll begin operations tomorrow. I intend to fire the first gun myself."

As the officers passed on, Daniel shook his head. "There's never been anybody like him and probably never will be." Then he turned and said, "Now let's go somewhere quieter, and you can catch me up on that new granddaughter of mine. Is Matthew a good father? Tell me all about it."

🔔   🔔   🔔

The siege itself was not what Sam thought it might be. He still thought of a battle as two forces running into each other shooting and slicing with sabers or thrusting with bayonets. He had expected the excitement of Cowpens, but it was not to be. The first order of business was digging a flying sap, a trench to provide cover for the infantry, so Sam and most of the other American solders found themselves wielding not sabers but shovels—decidedly unexciting.

"I could have stayed home and dug a ditch," Sam complained.

"I declare, Sam! I've never heard such griping," Dake laughed.

"Well, this ain't war. This is more like farming!"

But it was the way siege warfare was conducted. The soil made easy digging, and in one night the Americans had a position that would allow the bombardment to begin. The French generously took the left flank, ceding the place of honor to the Americans. The heavy guns were moved in, and George Washington himself fired the first gun of the siege of Yorktown. With the explosion ringing in his ears and his eyes blazing, Washington is said to have turned to his close friend General Marquis de Lafayette, removed his hat, and yelled, "It's the last act of the play, Marquis!"

"Yes, my general," said Lafayette, smiling at Washington's rare display of boyish exuberance. "We will overcome."

This shot fired by Washington was the beginning of an intense bombardment. On the first day alone nearly four thousand balls smashed the British line, and Cornwallis soon realized that he was in a lot more trouble than he had originally thought. With scarcely more than three thousand men fit for duty, he was facing an allied army of almost seventeen thousand.

By October 11, the American artillery had advanced to within three hundred yards of the British inner defenses, and by the fourteenth, two British redoubts had been captured, one by the French, the other by Alexander Hamilton, secretary to General Washington.

Inside the British camp food supplies were running so low that slaves were driven out to save on food. The number of sick rose quickly, as did the number of the dead. Corpses lay haphazardly about the town, some with arms and legs shot off, and many horses had to be killed because they were so weakened by starvation they could hardly stand.

Cornwallis grew desperate and made up his mind to try to get his army across the York River, where there were British reinforcements. He sent out three hundred and fifty men on a desperate mission to spike the enemies' guns, but it was a failure. He tried to move the men by ship, but a storm blew up, and the boats were scattered. Any hope of escaping Yorktown was rapidly fading.

On October 17, the artillery further intensified their bombardment of the British, and the whole peninsula trembled under the roars of these mighty cannons.

Finally on the far side of the British line, a drummer boy in a shabby bearskin hat appeared, followed by an officer who was waving a white handkerchief.

Washington could not move for a moment; then he turned to Lafayette and said, "I think they have had enough."

One of Washington's officers went forward, and the British officer, blindfolded, was brought before Washington. When the blindfold was removed, he said, "Sir, General Cornwallis asks for a twenty-four-hour armistice."

Washington's face was grim. "You may tell the general he has two hours."

The officer stared at him and swallowed hard. "Yes, sir."

He was taken back to his own lines and released, where he reported to Cornwallis. Despite the two-hour limit that Washington set, it was noon of October 20 before all the details were worked out. The terms were, in fact, generous. Arms and military equipment were to be surrendered and the soldiers held captive. But officers were allowed to keep their sidearms and were paroled. For all intents and purposes, the American Revolution was over.

🪶　　　🪶　　　🪶

The bright sunlight shone down, and at noon the two allied armies, French and American, were lined up facing each other along the route by which the British would march out to surrender.

Micah and Dake stood alongside Jubal and Sam as they eagerly awaited the procession.

The scene was solemn but impressive. All of the French wore white uniforms with white-colored facings. They all looked neat and proper with their regimental colors flying.

Washington, every inch the Virginia gentleman, would have loved to have managed an equal show, but his troops were not up to it.

The American soldiers had cleaned and polished as best they could, but nothing could disguise the patched knees and ragged breeches, the jackets riddled with holes and tears. Only the commander in chief, his staff, and a number of the regimental officers had new uniforms.

Daniel Bradford stared down the line of bedraggled, rawboned Americans, men who had fought as much of a war against starvation as they had against the British. "It's just as well they didn't have new uniforms," he said quietly to Major Griffith, who stood beside him. "They look like what they are, the best soldiers I've ever seen."

Finally music was heard and everyone seemed to freeze. George Washington rode up on a great bay horse and stood and waited. Across from him the French officers lined up. The British drums were beating, and their fifes played a sad tune.

"I know that tune," Sam whispered to Dake. "It's 'The World Turned Upside Down.' "

That the British were defeated soldiers was obvious to all. They were disorderly and their step was irregular, their ranks frequently broken. Many were drunk and angry, and a few were actually weeping as they marched out of their fortifications at Yorktown. They looked away from

261

the Americans and stared at the French. It was as though they were saying, "We are surrendering to the French, true soldiers, not to this American rabble."

Observing this, Marquis de Lafayette ordered the band to play "Yankee Doodle" and noticed with satisfaction that the British turned their heads at the sound of the tune.

Washington was waiting for a glimpse of Cornwallis, but it became obvious that he was not there. An officer appeared and identified himself as General Charles O'Hara. He said in a chastened voice, "General Cornwallis is indisposed." O'Hara tried to surrender his sword to Washington, but the American general turned aside, refusing to accept it from an underling. Bewildered, O'Hara stood there until Washington nodded at General Benjamin Lincoln, after himself the senior American officer present, who took the sword and called for the surrender to begin.

It was a supreme irony. Benjamin Lincoln, the fat champion of lost battles, a political general who squandered the lives of thousands of men, took the surrender. But Washington was a stickler for protocol. He would have preferred to have Nathaniel Greene, but Greene was still keeping the British armies pinned down in the South.

On they came then, the scarlet-coated British and their Hessian allies, brilliant in blue and green. The German mercenaries walked quickly, stacking their arms neatly, but the British threw their arms down in a disorderly crash. Drummer boys stove in their drums, infantrymen smashed their musket butts and stopped their cartridge cases, officers pouted like schoolboys and made a sorry sight.

As the emasculated British band played on, it occurred to Samuel Bradford as he stood there watching the remarkable scene that indeed the world had been turned upside down.

23

As Long as the Sun Is in the Sky

A BLEAK NOVEMBER DAY HAD COME to reign over the earth, and as Keturah walked along the road shielding her face from the cold biting winds, she looked up often into the sky. A wisp of dirty white clouds scudded along the horizon to the north, and directly overhead a lone buzzard made a wheeling vigil. The great birds, hideous up close, were beautiful from a distance as they sailed through the air with such graceful power. Keturah stopped and watched it for a time, then turned back toward the house.

Her heart had been heavy since Sam had left, and she had made a habit of taking long walks to clear her head. Ever since she had left her old life, so grim and terrible, and had joined herself to the Bradford family, her cynicism and bitterness had gradually been replaced by joy and a belief that life could be wonderful. Knowing little of God when she had first arrived, Keturah had been drawn by the warmth, the faith, and the love of the Bradford family. She had seen in Dake and Jeanne how beautiful a marriage could be, and this had been echoed in the marriage of Daniel Bradford and Marian. Later she had observed Micah's happiness with his bride, Sarah. And now, so close to such fulfilled happiness herself, Sam's absence was more painful to Keturah than she ever could have imagined possible.

When she reached the house, she found Grace seated in the parlor reading a book. Patrick was sound asleep on the carpet. Keturah paused to look down on him and smiled. "I never saw a child sleep so soundly."

"Except sometimes at two o'clock in the morning," Grace smiled. "Then he wants everybody's undivided attention."

Keturah moved over to the bookcase and studied the titles. Most of them were books of poetry, for Stephen Morrison, a poet himself, had been an avid collector. She finally shrugged and said, "I can't understand poetry. I don't know why people don't just say what they mean."

Grace looked up from her book. "Some things can't be said like that, Keturah."

"What do you mean?"

"Well, I mean you can say two plus two equals four. Everyone understands that. And when you tell the shopkeeper you want two pounds of flour, you don't want to put that into poetry. You want to be clearly understood. But some things aren't as easy to pin down with words as sugar or numbers."

Keturah plopped down in the chair across from Grace. It was her favorite chair, intricately carved of mahogany with smooth arms, a high, padded back, and blue and gold silk damask upholstery. She curled herself up in it and studied her friend. "I don't understand what you mean."

"Well, sometimes, Keturah, I'm walking outside at night and I look up at the skies. You've seen those nights when the sky is dotted with literally thousands of bright stars. I could tell you there are, say, one million, three hundred thousand stars in the sky, but that would never express the feeling that's in me as I look up and know that God has made every one of them and given each its own name. Something powerful stirs in me, and I can't put it into words. But a good poet can."

Keturah considered Grace's words for a time and then said reluctantly, "I know what you mean about that. Sometimes I can't put into words the way I feel either."

The two talked for a long time, for they had become close friends. Finally Keturah straightened up and turned her head. "Someone's coming." She got up and looked out the window and said, "It's Harley, the post carrier."

"I hope I have a letter from my parents," Grace said. "I miss them a lot."

Keturah went outside, being careful to take some coins, and Harley Simpson said, "Three letters, Miss Keturah. Two for Mrs. Morrison and one for you."

"Thank you, Harley." Taking the letters, Keturah paid the postrider and turned back into the house. She looked at the three letters and recognized Sam's large, bold, rather careless handwriting, and her heart quickened. "He said he'd write, and he didn't forget."

Moving inside the house, she handed Grace her two letters and exclaimed, "I got one from Sam!"

The two women opened their letters at once, and when Keturah had scanned hers quickly, she said, "It's from Sam, and there's a note in there from his father!"

"Read it to me, Keturah."

Keturah read the letter aloud:

> We welcome you into the family, Keturah. You always seemed to me like a daughter, anyway. From the first time Micah brought you into the house, I knew that you were going to be more than just a visitor. Now that you're going to marry Sam, you'll become my real daughter. I hope you'll look on me as your father and Marian as your mother. I want to encourage you to come home at once, as soon as Grace can do without you. Sam wants to be married on Christmas Day, and we all think that would be wonderful. If you need money to buy your passage home, borrow it from my niece and I will repay her. Welcome to the family.

"What a nice letter!" Grace exclaimed. "Mr. Bradford is a wonderful man!"

Keturah's face was filled with excitement as she said, "I never had a father, but I've got one now."

"And what does Sam say?"

Keturah read the letter and was somewhat taken aback. "I can't read it to you. It's very personal."

"Does he tell you how much he loves you?"

"Yes, he does. Sam's always done that, though. He's not a poet, but he's very emphatic in what he says." She smiled and said, "I like it that way too."

"So when will you go, Keturah?" Grace asked.

"As soon as I can."

"I think it would be best if I took you to Charleston. You could catch a ship there. Many of them make the trip to Boston. Will that suit?"

"Oh yes, Grace!" Keturah got up and walked around muttering something under her breath. When Grace asked her what she was saying, she flushed and laughed aloud. "I was saying 'Mrs. Keturah Bradford—Mrs. Keturah Bradford.' Doesn't it sound wonderful?"

"Yes, it does. Come, now. We must get your things packed. I'll ask Cormac to get the carriage ready. We can leave first thing in the morning."

The trip from the plantation to Charleston had been rapid enough. Cormac was a good driver and the team was first-class. The weather had been snappy and cold but invigorating, and when they had arrived at Charleston, they proceeded to the dock at once. Cormac had gone inside the office to arrange a passage and had come back in short order. "We're in luck," he said. "There's a ship leaving for Boston late this afternoon. I got you a place on it, Keturah. It's an old ship and perhaps won't be too comfortable." He laughed then and said, "But a young woman in love won't mind a thing like that. Why, you'd probably walk barefooted all the way just to get to Sam."

"Oh, don't tease her, Cormac!" Grace laughed. "Look how she's blushing."

"I am not!" Keturah exclaimed. But indeed her face was rosy, and she said, "Can I go on board now?"

"Well, I suppose so. Come on. We'll get you settled down."

Getting Keturah settled took little time, and afterward the pair took her out to eat a good meal. They got back just as the ship was ready to depart, and Keturah hugged Grace and whispered, "I'm going to miss you so much—Patrick too."

"Make Sam bring you back for a visit after you're married."

"I will. I will," Keturah promised, then turned to Cormac and put out her hand. He took it and smiled.

"May you have a hundred years of happy marriage, and may all your children be as beautiful as you and Sam."

Keturah suddenly threw her arms around Cormac. He hugged her for a moment, then released her, saying, "There's one hug Sam won't get. Better hurry, now. They're getting ready to weigh anchor."

The two stood there and waited until the ship sailed slowly out of the harbor. It grew smaller and smaller until they could no longer see Keturah waving to them from the stern rail.

Finally they turned aside and Cormac remarked, "The old man's going to miss Keturah. He's very fond of her."

"Yes, he will, and so will I."

"I expect we'd better stay the night. We'd get caught somewhere halfway home."

"All right, Cormac."

It was growing late in the afternoon, and for a time they walked along the quay, saying little. Grace somehow felt awkward now that Keturah was no longer there—she had always filled the silence with her talk about Sam and the life she was about to enter into. But now Cormac seemed distant and far away. He kept his eyes down a great deal, and when she made a comment, he would answer as though he was preoccupied.

Finally they went into the Green Dragon and ate a light supper. They lingered for a while, saying little, and Grace finally said, "I think I'll go to bed."

"Yes, we'll need to get an early start tomorrow. I guess it's the first time you've been separated from the old man, isn't it?"

"Patrick will be all right. Mary's come over to take care of him. She has a baby of her own, so feeding's no problem."

The two made their way upstairs to their bedrooms without saying a great deal more, and Grace quickly went to bed. She was tired physically from the long trip, but her mind would not stop moving about from point to point. She tried to will herself to sleep but could not.

She finally half dozed off and had some sort of a dream that frightened her. She woke with a start and could not remember what it was except that she seemed to be all alone in some strange place. Her heart was still pounding as she recalled how in the dream the fear, the loneliness, had stricken her.

Fretfully she tossed and turned, afraid to go back to sleep. When she did manage to sleep, she would dream part of the dream, awaken, and then go back to sleep and continue the same dream. Finally she couldn't face any more repetitions of the awful nightmare that had taken her.

She knew that it was still too early; the night was dark outside and the room was cold. But she got up and stumbled over to a shelf on the wall and made out the figures of the numbers on the face of the clock. Four o'clock—still two hours until daylight. Still, she was up. She lit her candle, dressed warmly, and got her things ready to go. There was still an hour and a half before breakfast would be served, but she was restless. An impulse took her, and she left the room, tiptoed downstairs, and passed out into the night. A hazy fog lay over the harbor, which was just across from the Green Dragon, and there were enough stars out, faint though they were, that she could see her way along the shore. She walked along the quay, the only sounds the sibilant whispering of the waves as they came ashore and the sound of her own footsteps on the wooden dock.

For a long time she walked and was more troubled than she could remember. It was not just the dream but something more, and when she tried to identify it, it was as fleeting as an early morning mist burned off by a hot sun. Finally the light began to break in the east.

As she turned to cross the street and go back inside the Green Dragon, she suddenly was aware of three sailors who evidently belonged to one of the British warships at anchor offshore. Their voices were loud and quarrelsome, and Grace knew they had been drinking. She turned to go in quickly and avoid them, but one of them said, "Hey, look. There's some company for us."

Grace moved quicker, but they ran after her and surrounded her. They were wearing heavy coats and brown woolen hats, some sort of uniform, she supposed, and she said quickly, "Let me pass."

"Ah, now, just a minute, missy." The largest one of the three was speaking. He put out his hand and took her arm suddenly. "You need some good company. A pretty gal like you don't need to be alone. Why, some of these landsmen might give you problems. Ain't that right, mates?"

The other two men were grinning broadly. One of them was a short, thickset man with several missing teeth. He laughed aloud hoarsely and took Grace's other arm. "Righto, Bob. Now, come along, pretty. We know how to show a gal a good time."

Grace was frightened but was determined not to show it. "Let me go," she cried, "or I'll scream."

"Ah, now, you wouldn't want to do that." The third speaker, a tall, lean man with a full reddish beard, moved in so that she was completely surrounded. "Come on. We got us a bottle, and we knows how to share. Ain't that right, mates?"

The three began pulling Grace along, and at once she lifted her voice. "Help!" she cried. "Let me alone! Help!"

Instantly a dirty, hard palm was clapped over her mouth, and the taller one, the biggest of the three, whose name was Bob, said, "Keep her quiet, there, Raben. Come on. There's an alley down the street where we can entertain her."

Grace kicked and tried to free herself, but the hand that was on her was too strong.

She had heard of women being abducted in seaport towns and terrible things happening to them, but it had never occurred to her that it might happen to her. She fought and kicked until one of them, she could not see which, slapped her sharply in the temple.

"Quiet down, there," a guttural voice said. "Keep her quiet, Raben. She'll wake somebody."

At that moment a voice cut crisply through the morning air. "You men let that woman alone."

It was Cormac!

The hand loosened from Grace's mouth, and she managed to open her lips and bite down hard on one of the fingers.

"Ow! She bit me!" the man called Raben exclaimed, but the other two were paying him no attention.

"You fellows move on and there'll be no trouble," came Cormac's reassuring Welsh brogue.

Bob said, "Hang on to that woman. There's only one of him. Take care of him, Raben."

The tall, thin man laughed and moved forward. He reached under his coat and pulled out a wicked-looking knife. It had a thin blade, and the man looked as if he knew how to use it. He held it out toward Cormac and said, "I'll cut your gizzard for you if you don't pull out of here."

"I wouldn't do that if I were you," Cormac said flatly.

He had appeared so suddenly that Grace could not believe it, but now she was afraid, for the other two probably had knives as well.

And sure enough, one of them, the shorter, thicker one, also produced a knife, and he and Raben moved forward while Bob held Grace in an iron grasp. "Cut him up a little bit," Bob laughed hoarsely.

As the two advanced, both holding knives in a practiced fashion, Cormac said, "You don't want to do that."

"Don't tell us what to do!" Raben said. "I'm going to cut your gizzard open!"

Cormac did not answer, but his hand slipped inside his belt. He came out with a pistol and held it high, aimed directly at Raben's heart. "Let the woman go, and we'll say no more about it," he said.

The short, bulky man stopped dead still at the sight of the pistol. He did not move, but the lean one named Raben said, "You only got one ball there."

"That's right. Do you want it?"

The sight of the pistol had changed things, and Cormac took advantage of it. He advanced now and came face-to-face with Raben, who stood there with the knife in his hand.

More swiftly than any of the sailors had thought possible, he raised the pistol and brought it down on the sailor's wrist. The knife fell clattering to the wooden quay, and Cormac instantly struck out with his left hand, catching Raben high in the throat. He fell to the quay gagging, and Cormac paid him no attention. Turning to the short, burly sailor, he advanced and said, "You want the same, or do you want this ball in your brain—if you've got one?"

The short sailor shook his head quickly. "No! I don't want none of that."

"Drop that knife, then."

The knife made a clattering sound, and Cormac turned at once toward the larger of the three men, who had dropped his hold on Grace's arm. He was a bold scoundrel and said, "I'm not afraid of your gun!"

He was a huge brute, and Cormac knew the sailor was speaking the truth as he came forward, his fists raised. Cormac had no wish to kill him. But left with little choice, he lowered the pistol and pulled the trigger. The sound of the explosion shattered the dawn and Bob simply collapsed.

"You . . . shot me!" he said with shock as he went down. He was holding on to his right thigh, where Cormac had planted the musket ball.

Cormac shoved the pistol back in his belt, wheeled quickly, and picked up the two knives. "You'd better get him back to your ship and have someone take that ball out," he said to Raben. "It may have hit a bone." He stepped forward and said quickly, "Come along, Grace."

Grace hurried to him at once, and Cormac's eyes were watchful as the two helped Bob to his feet. Bob was cursing him, but the blood was leaking out of him. The other sailor said, "We've got to get you back to the ship before you bleed to death."

Cormac and Grace watched them as they hobbled off, and finally Cormac said, "Well, it's a good thing I was up early."

"Where did you come from?" Grace whispered. She was still shaken from the experience, and her knees felt strangely weak.

"I couldn't sleep. I've been up a long time. Didn't expect to find you out here, though."

"I couldn't sleep either." She suddenly shivered and said, "If you hadn't come, it would have been awful."

Cormac saw that she was still frightened and said, "They're gone now. Come on. Let's take a walk. It's going to be a beautiful day."

As they walked along, Grace slowly felt the fear pass from her. She held to his arm, marveling at the strength of it.

He stopped once and said, "Don't let those sailors bother you."

She did not answer for a time. The sun was peeking over the horizon now, but very few were stirring. Only a single cart rumbled along the street in front of the Green Dragon. They moved farther down past some warehouses and seemed to be all alone in the harbor. They came to a jetty, and Cormac guided her out to the end of it. They were surrounded by the water, which was now a brilliant red in the light of the early morning sun.

"You seem sad, Grace. That must have been terrifying for you this morning."

"It was, but I didn't sleep well either. I had terrible nightmares, and I feel all out of sorts."

"Anything I can do? Is something wrong?"

Grace turned to him and studied his face. The clear plane of his jaw was so definite and clean-cut, and his cheekbones radiated strength. He was a roughly handsome man, and now she was more than ever aware of his physical power. She suddenly said, "I don't know what's wrong with me. I've been unhappy, and I don't know why."

He said nothing for so long that she studied him more carefully. "Is something wrong, Cormac? You say you couldn't sleep either?"

"I can't say whether there's something wrong or not." He hesitated, took a deep breath, then expelled it. "Not until you tell me something."

"Until I tell you something?"

"Yes." Cormac locked his hands behind him as if to put some restraint upon himself. He had indeed been up almost all night thinking of Grace and his feelings for her. If she had been a poor woman with nothing, he would not have hesitated. But he was the one who was poor, having only the clothes on his back and a few coins. Still his heart told him that this woman was for him, and he said suddenly with a demanding force that almost took her breath, "Where is your heart, Grace?"

Grace was taken aback by the directness of Cormac's question. She did not pretend to misunderstand him, and her eyes were locked with his. The forcefulness of his words were matched by the intensity of his gaze. She felt small and helpless as he stood before her, tense and waiting for her answer.

What can I say to him? she thought almost wildly. And suddenly she knew that she had come to a time in her life when she had to make a decision. Somehow she knew that this man loved her deeply, although he had never said it in so many words. She was a woman who could understand such things, and she had seen him as he had watched her these many months. She also knew that she had a longing for security, and she saw a strength in this man that she admired. But it was much more than that, she realized as he stood waiting for her answer. He had the qualities that she had always longed for in a man—he was gentle and he would speak his feelings.

Grace hesitated for a long time, and then she began to speak of her marriage to Stephen. She saw his surprise as she touched on this subject, but she told him very simply how much she had looked forward to a close and happy marriage and how it had never happened. She spoke at length, for she wanted him to know all that was in her heart. Finally she said faintly, "Cormac, I made a terrible mistake marrying Stephen. I can't make another one."

Cormac put his hands forward and took her upper arms. His grasp was firm, and he felt her trembling. He said in a low, intense voice, "Grace, I can only tell you what's in my own heart. For me, you are the only woman on earth. I love you for your incredible beauty, but that's not who you are. That will fade sometime as it does for all of us, but I tell you this: When this beautiful dark hair is white, I will love you still, and when this strong figure is thin and bent with age, I will love you even more. After you've lost the bloom of youth, I will love you, Grace, for it's you that I love and not your outward beauty."

Grace listened closely, for these were words that she had never heard but had always longed for. She was speechless, and tears welled in her gray-green eyes.

Then Cormac said, "Will you have me, Grace?"

Time seemed to stand still, and the sun was like a huge red wafer as it cleared the horizon. Grace Morrison suddenly knew what she had to do. A sense of peace and certainty and quiet enveloped her as she looked up at this big man who, for all his strength and bulk, was tender and gentle in his spirit.

"Why, of course I'll have you, Cormac!"

He opened his arms then, and she came to him at once. He bent to catch a better view of her face and saw the welcome in her eyes, the vulnerable trembling of her lips. He knew that she was the one woman on earth that God had made for him, and they momentarily stood there on the edge of the age-old, precipitous mystery known only to lovers, unsure what would come of it, but certain that they had to have each other. He kissed her, and she responded with passion. The deep longings that had been in her for love and for gentleness and for strength were powerfully satisfied, and as his arms tightened around her, she knew that she was safe with him, that she would be with this man for the rest of her life, and she clung to him firmly.

When Cormac lifted his head, Grace looked up at him. She was not quite crying, but her eyes were misty with tears. She quietly asked, "Will you be a pastor?"

The question took Cormac aback. "I don't know. I think so. Will that displease you?"

She said, "No. Not at all."

He studied her face, then smiled. "Come along. We must go tell the old man he's going to have a handsome father."

As they moved away, a happiness filled Grace Morrison that she had never known. He looked at her and said, "I'll have to write to your father and ask for his permission."

Grace smiled mischievously. "What will you do," she teased, "if he says no?"

"Find me another woman."

"You won't!" She suddenly laughed and struck out. "You're stuck with me!"

He caught her hand, kissed it, and said, "There is lovely you are, my darling Grace!"

He put his arms around her again, and she closed her eyes and put her face against his chest. "Never stop loving me, Cormac—and never stop telling me that you do."

Cormac held her gently in his solid arms. "Not as long as that sun is in the sky," he whispered. And then they turned and hurried toward the inn, anxious to get home.

24

A Surprise for the General

GENERAL LESLIE GORDON left his headquarters on Christmas Eve of 1781, saying to his adjutant, "I will see you after the holiday, Lieutenant. And a merry Christmas to you."

"A merry Christmas to you, General Gordon."

Leaving the office and stepping out into the open air, Leslie Gordon thought wryly, *I wonder if I'll ever get accustomed to being called 'General.'* His promotion had come almost at once as soon as he had returned from America and had caught him off guard. Of course he was only a brigadier general, but still that was higher than he had ever expected to get in the ranks of His Majesty's army. He was pleased with his promotion, mostly for his wife's sake. Lyna Lee had been proud of him, and he had seen tears in her eyes for the first time in years when he had worn his new uniform.

He went to the stable, where he found Colonel Henson arriving, and he spoke to him pleasantly enough. "A fine Christmas Eve it is, Colonel."

Henson was a tall, burly man, British to the core. "I don't see how you can say that, General. Not after our loss at Yorktown."

"Well, we'll have to live with it."

"I can't see how that rabble in arms beat the best of His Majesty's forces. You were there, General Gordon. How do you explain it?"

Gordon shook his head. "They were fighting for their homes. We were fighting for political reasons. Men will always do better under situations like that."

"We could still win."

"No. As soon as Lord North heard of the loss at Yorktown, he threw himself back in his chair and cried, 'It's all over!' And so it is. Merry Christmas, Colonel."

Cheerfully mounting his horse, not wanting to prolong the conversation, Gordon rode out into the street. He had become commander of the Royal Military Academy at Woolwich, and it was an assignment that pleased him. He had hated every day of his service in America, for he, along with many other officers in His Majesty's army, had felt that England was in the wrong. They were not alone, for many in Parliament and the huge majority of citizens in England had not countenanced the war against America. It was easy enough to get Britain stirred up to fight the French or the Spanish, but to fire on Englishmen, which is what the colonists were, was another thing entirely.

As Gordon made his way down the streets of Woolwich and along the south bank of the Thames, he was greeted by many of the villagers. "Merry Christmas, General!" the cries came. The villagers were as proud of the Military Academy as they were of the royal dockyard, established by Henry VIII himself, for the two institutions formed the backbone of the economy of the small London borough.

It was cold, and Gordon shivered and wondered what it was like in America. He had had a great fondness for his wife's brother, Daniel Bradford, and his son, Clive, had joined the forces of George Washington. It had not grieved him in the least; indeed he had felt rather proud of Clive.

He reached the house, the first he had ever owned, and looked at it for a moment. It was narrow, built of dark red brick with black mortar. It was two stories high, was very deep, and had long windows with six-over-six panes in each. The entryway had a massive wooden door and was flanked on each side by a single white column supporting a small balcony coming off the second floor. This small balcony had black iron fencing around it and a windowed door, through which could be seen the soft glow of a lamp. A warm sense of possession took him. As a soldier Gordon had served in many lands, and Lyna had never complained about moving. Now he was happy that she was in a home she could call her own, and he fully intended to live there for the rest of his life. He loved the busy little borough and had already made many fast friends there. Lyna was happier than he had ever seen her. David was home for the holidays from Oxford, where he was enrolled and well settled.

"Come on, girl." He touched the mare with his heels, and she obediently circled to the back of the house, where a small barn kept the team used for the carriage and the two riding horses. He dismounted, and at once Barkley came to him. Barkley was a wizened little Cockney who had served under Gordon for years. He had been wounded severely, and now one leg gave him constant trouble. Still he was a fine hostler and workman of all trades, able to fix anything, and he considered himself the general's keeper.

Barkley was usually a rather sober individual, but as Gordon stepped off the mare, he saw that a wide grin illuminated the Cockney's face. "What are you grinning about? Have you started early on your Christmas cheer?"

"There ain't a drop in me, sir," Barkley said, but the grin remained. "But it's Christmas Eve, ain't it?"

"I suppose it is. Yes, it is," he said. "And a merry Christmas to you."

"And to you, sir. The best Christmas you ever 'ad. And it will be. Don't you doubt it, sir."

Somewhat puzzled by Barkley's unexpected exuberance, Gordon stared at him sharply, half suspecting that he had, indeed, been imbibing some of the ale that he loved so well. He reached into his pocket and handed a large gold coin over. "That'll give you something to grin about."

"Thank you, indeed, General! You'll get the best Christmas present you can imagine."

Gordon laughed and said, "I hope so, but it's present enough just to be settled here. You take good care of me, Barkley. You're a good man."

"Thank you, sir. Thankee."

Still wondering at the unexpected show of hilarity that seemed to be clinging to his servant, Gordon walked around and entered the front door. As he stepped inside, he was greeted by Lyna, who came to him at once and threw her arms around him.

Caught off balance, he staggered back and said, "Whoa! What's all this?"

"Merry Christmas. There's the mistletoe. Give me a kiss."

"I don't need a mistletoe for that," Leslie Gordon grinned. He had loved this woman for so long, yet her beauty still excited him. He kissed her thoroughly and then looked up as David came down the stairs. He was smiling broadly and came over to greet his father.

"Well, everybody's grinning like Cheshire cats," Leslie said. "I never saw Christmas bring such cheer."

"You go wash up," Lyna said.

Both Lyna and David laughed at him, and David patted him on the shoulder. He had grown as tall as his father now, though not as strongly built. "Hurry up, Father. We're going to have guests for dinner."

"Guests! What guests?"

"Just go wash up. It's a surprise for you."

Gordon stared at his wife and son. "Everybody's giggling like a bunch of schoolgirls. I think you've all been down to the pub for a few drams of punch."

"You just go wash up." Lyna pulled at his arm. "I've got a fine supper prepared for you and for our guests."

"Who is it?" Gordon demanded. "What's the big secret?"

"Go on. Get ready."

Gordon shrugged and entered the bedroom. He pulled off his heavy coat, hung it in an armoire, and then washed his face and hands in the basin. The water was cold, but he was used to that. At least soldiering did that for a man. It made him able to endure hardship. *But this is no hardship*, he thought as he looked around the bedroom. After living in every sort of outlandish accommodation in the world, the house, which Lyna had furnished herself, was indeed comfortable. He loved the bedroom with the heavy walnut furniture and the pictures of battle scenes on the wall. An oil painting of Lyna by Patton, one of the foremost portrait painters in England, was his prize. He stopped and looked at it where it hung on the wall beside the outside window and murmured, "Oh, girl, it was a happy day for Leslie Gordon when he got you."

He hurried out thinking, *Who's for dinner? Probably the preacher. He's made this a second home, but he's a good fellow.* He could imagine no other visitor on Christmas Eve, and as he went downstairs he was prepared to meet the minister.

"Our guests are in the parlor," Lyna said, taking him by the arm. "Come along."

"I know who it is. It's Reverend St. Ives."

"Is it, now?"

Lyna laughed up at him and then pulled him into the large parlor. As Gordon stepped inside, he glanced over, expecting to see the tall, spare form of the minister dressed in black.

Instead, there stood his daughter, Grace, holding an infant in her arms. Over to one side stood a tall, well-built man with a roughly handsome face who was watching him out of a pair of steady, dark brown eyes.

"Father!" Grace ran forward.

Leslie took her in his arms and saw that her eyes were damp with tears, and his own voice was unsteady. "Grace," he said. "What in the world. . . ?" At that moment the infant reached up and grabbed at the decoration on his chest. It was a medal he had won, and the infant held on to it firmly.

"And who is this? This must be my grandson, Patrick."

"What do you think of him? Isn't he a beautiful boy?" Lyna said. She came over and proudly stroked the silky, light honey-colored hair. "Here. Let me hold him."

"Wait a minute! I'm not through yet. You'll have to take your turn."

"Do you like him, Father?"

"Indeed I do. He takes after me. You can see those handsome features."

Grace laughed. "You haven't changed a bit." She was proud of her father, who was one of the handsomest men she had ever seen, and she saw the joy in his eyes as he held his grandson. "Father," she said quickly, "may I introduce you to Mr. Cormac Morgan."

Gordon had not forgotten the large man who stood quietly beside him. He was simply dressed, and his powerful frame was evident. "I'm happy to make your acquaintance, Mr. Morgan."

"I've heard so much about you, General Gordon. It's a pleasure to meet you."

Gordon waited for Grace to make some explanation to identify this fine-looking strong man who had suddenly entered his home. He half expected her to say, "This is my husband," but she said no such thing. Gordon had it on the tip of his tongue to ask her who this fellow was, but he knew that would not do. "When did you arrive? What are you doing here?"

"You can talk over the dinner table," Lyna said. "Here, give me my grandson. Come along. Dinner's on the table."

It was a fine meal. The dining room was midsized with green carpet, and the walls had been painted pea green with a wallpaper border around the windows. The furniture was made of oak and very tasteful. The meal included roast goose, chestnut stuffing, cooked spinach with cream sauce, boiled potatoes, fresh rolls, and cups of steaming tea.

All during the meal Gordon's eyes kept going back to Cormac Morgan, who said but little. It was obvious that he and Grace were connected, but how? They had traveled across the ocean together alone, with only his grandson for a chaperone, but who was he? Gordon saw at once that Cormac was very much attached to Patrick, and the youngster clung to him firmly, obviously delighted with the big man.

"The war is over, Father. Are you unhappy because England lost?"

"You know better than that, daughter. I'm as pleased as I can be. It was never a just war in the first place."

"I'm so happy that Daniel and his boys made it through safely."

"That is rare—with three sons in the army and not a one of them lost. Dake did get wounded but not a scratch on the other two."

The talk went on for some time about the Bradford family, and then Gordon learned that Cormac Morgan was the overseer of the plantation. He obviously came from Wales; he still had a strong accent. There was a quietness about the big man, but also a warmth. Gordon was surprised when Grace said, "Mr. Morgan is a fine preacher. I hope he has an opportunity to preach in our church."

"A minister? Well, I'm doubly glad to have you, sir," Gordon said.

Cormac smiled. "I'm not much of a preacher, I'm afraid. I do my best to declare the glories of this great Gospel of ours."

Lyna Lee watched as the two men talked. She had spoken with Grace, and the two had so wanted Cormac to be accepted by Leslie Gordon. Now both saw with some relief that the two men did get on well.

After the meal the party broke up. David left on business of his own, the two women went off to talk, carrying Patrick with them, and Gordon invited Cormac to his study. "Not much of a study," he said as he sat down. "But then I'm not much of a studying man."

"It's a fine study, sir, and you have collected some good books here."

"I'm not as much of a reader as I should be. Now, tell me more about yourself. What's this about being a minister? I thought you were the overseer at the plantation."

Cormac hesitated only for a second. "I must say one word to you first, and then I'll answer any questions you have, General Gordon." The two were standing, and Cormac looked directly into the eyes of the tall soldier. "I've come to ask for your daughter's hand in marriage."

Leslie stared at him, then said, "Well, I must say, I had been wondering what brought you here."

Cormac laughed, and saw that he was on firm ground. "I don't doubt it, sir. If a strange man came into my home with my daughter, I'd want to know more about him too. Now, ask me anything you like."

"Sit down, Cormac. I suppose I may call you that?"

"Certainly, sir."

"Well, tell me all about yourself. Everything."

Cormac began to speak. He spoke of his early days in the mines, of when he fled from God and did not serve the Lord. He traced his life through the time he left Wales, and then spoke more slowly as he finally said, "I firmly believe that God has sent me to America to preach His Word, and I intend to do that. But I must say this. I'm a poor man, General Gordon. I have only the strength of my hands and a trust in the

280

Lord. I know your daughter is used to better things than I can provide."

Gordon admired the simple way that Cormac Morgan put the matter. He said at once, "I was a poor man when I married Grace's mother, and we've never had much. All these trappings that come with being a general, that's all new. Can you support a wife?"

Cormac said, "I trust that God will provide the means. You are aware that ministers do not grow wealthy."

"What about the plantation?"

"I expect to be able to do both, General. I love farming, and we have good hands there. Very fine men, indeed, who can take care of things while I'm gone out to preach. It's a beautiful place, and I hope you and your wife will come again, and David also, to visit."

The two men talked for a long time, and eventually Grace appeared with her mother, who was carrying Patrick.

"Put that boy down, Lyna. You're not going to let his feet touch the ground."

"You mind your own business, Leslie. I'll hold my grandson as I please."

"Well, Mr. Morgan has asked for your hand. Shall I give it, Grace?"

"Yes, Father, if you please."

Gordon turned and then put his hand out. "Why, I give it freely enough, and I count Grace fortunate to have found such a good man."

Relief washed over Cormac's face. "Thank you, sir. She'll never know anything but love from me."

"And when is this wedding to be?"

"Christmas Day," Grace said.

"A big church wedding? Tomorrow? Impossible!"

"No. Just a minister here in our home will be what I would like," Grace said quietly.

"Well, I imagine Reverend St. Ives would do it for us, but why Christmas Day?" Gordon said.

Cormac suddenly laughed. "It's more economical that way." Everyone stared at him, and he explained, "That way I will only have to get her one present a year instead of both a Christmas present and an anniversary gift."

Grace laughed suddenly and went to Cormac. She reached up and grabbed his hair and gave it a pull. "We'll see about that. I'll have two presents, thank you very much, you Welshman you!"

The rest of the evening went very well, but after Lyna and Leslie had retired and gotten into bed, she turned to him at once and exclaimed, "Isn't he wonderful!"

"You mean Patrick?"

"Well, of course, he's wonderful! He could be nothing else with such a handsome grandfather. But I meant Cormac."

"He seems to be a fine man."

"Grace is happy for the first time in years. She was never happy with Stephen. Even before she married him she had doubts and fears."

"I know."

"But he'll be a good husband to her."

Gordon reached out and swept her into his arms and pulled her up tight. "As good as I am?"

"Oh no!" Lyna whispered. "No one could be that, but he'll be almost as good."

Leslie held her tightly and said, "I'm glad for Grace and that grandson of mine. We're going to have to make a visit right away to America."

The two lay there whispering, and finally Lyna said, "I'll have to get up early in the morning, and you'll have to go see Reverend St. Ives."

"It'll give the borough something to talk about."

She put her arms around his neck and kissed him. "God has been good to us, Leslie."

"Indeed He has. 'Whoso findeth a wife findeth a good thing, and obtaineth favour of the Lord.' That's always been my favorite verse." He kissed her and she clung to him, and both knew that Grace, in more ways than one, had come home.

🔔   🔔   🔔

Sam's face was pale as Micah looked at him. "You look like a ghost, Sam. Do you want a drink of water?"

The two were standing in the minister's small office along with Reverend Ramsey. Ramsey was a tall, well-built man who smiled now and said, "Don't worry. I've never lost a prospective bridegroom yet."

As for Sam, for the first time in his life, perhaps, he was utterly speechless. Up until the time they had entered the pastor's study he had been laughing and joking, but now somehow the enormity of what he was about to do struck him.

"I don't know about all this, Micah. Maybe I'm not ready to get married."

Micah blinked with surprise. "What are you talking about? For the last year, you've done nothing but scream that all you've wanted was to get married! That's all I've heard out of you, and now you're wondering!"

"Well, I know, but it's a big responsibility."

"I never in my life heard such a thing!" Micah exclaimed. "I've known you since you were a baby, and I never heard of you doubting your ability to do anything. And now you're getting weak in the knees over a little thing like marriage."

"It's not a little thing," Sam said. "I mean, how do I know I can make her happy?"

"I'm sure you will," Reverend Ramsey said. He was almost laughing. Sam Bradford, indeed, was a forward young man bold as any in the Colonies, and it amused the minister to see his uncertainty. "Don't worry, Sam. She's a fine girl. She'll make you a good wife. Come on, now. I hear the music."

"Do I have to carry you out, Sam?" Micah said fiercely. "Come on! Brace up and be a man!"

Sam could not answer. He swallowed hard and nodded faintly. As he moved outside, the thing that was most in his mind was turning and running away. As Micah had said, he had wanted nothing so much as to marry Keturah. But he had always been such an independent young fellow, and now it was coming home to him that he was trading his independence for a wife. True enough, the wife was Keturah and he loved her dearly, but still, as he took his place beside the minister and Micah, he could not think straight.

The music swelled, and everyone turned to see Keturah coming down the aisle. She was wearing a beautiful dress made of fine white silk with lace covering the bodice. The neckline was high, the sleeves long, and each of these was decorated with tiny delicate pearls sewn onto the lace. The skirt itself was a plain, smooth white, but the lace petticoat that peeked out of the open skirt had been ornately stitched and was beautiful indeed. Keturah's face was radiant. She came down the aisle and took her place beside Sam, and in total contrast to the groom, who could barely speak, Keturah was calm and smiled as she whispered, "Hello, Sam."

Sam could not answer, and it was Micah who nudged him, saying, "Wake up, Sam. You're getting married."

Sam Bradford was not afraid of anything, and now he suddenly knew he was acting like a child. He took one look at Keturah's face, at her clear beauty, and realized that this was what he wanted more than anything in the world. "Hello, Keturah," he whispered.

The wedding ceremony went on smoothly until the minister said, "Do you have the ring?"

"Right here," Micah said, taking it out of his vest pocket and handing it to Sam.

Sam fumbled the ring and dropped it. His face flushed and he bent over and said, "I can't find it."

There were several giggles coming from the auditorium, and Keturah said, "You've got your big foot on it, Sam. Move it over."

Sam moved his foot, and Keturah bent over and retrieved the ring. "Now," she said, "put it on my finger and don't drop it again."

Dake leaned over from where he was sitting in the second row and whispered to Jeanne, "She's giving orders, and they're not even married yet."

"You hush, Dake! It's a beautiful wedding."

Sam was flustered but managed to regain enough composure to announce loudly, "Well, I've never been married before, so stop laughing!"

This brought even more giggles, and Keturah said fiercely, "Sam, be quiet!"

Keturah and Sam spoke their vows, and by the time they were through, Sam was back to his old self. When it came time to kiss the bride, he did so with such enthusiasm that another round of laughter arose.

Keturah said, "Sam, there's nobody like you."

"That's right," he grinned. "There's not."

As the two walked out down the aisle of the church, the minister leaned over and said, "Well, they made it through, Micah. I wasn't sure about it for a time."

"I never saw Sam so shook-up. Somehow I think Keturah will keep him that way, and it'll be good for him."

🕯   🕯   🕯

The large dining room of Daniel Bradford's home was filled. He looked around the table that was loaded with food, but he was not thinking of that. He was studying the faces of the family that had gathered. To his right sat his wife, Marian, holding Enoch in her lap as usual. Beside her Dake and Jeanne sat with two-year-old Jonas. Across from them sat Micah and Sarah. Sarah was expecting and was radiant. Micah had his arm around her.

On the other side of these two sat Rachel and Jacob Steiner. Steiner was wearing a fresh new uniform, and Rachel looked at him proudly.

And at the far end of the table the bride and the bridegroom glowed with happiness.

"Make a speech, Daniel," Marian said.

"All right. I will," Daniel said. He got up and looked over the faces that turned toward him. He was silent for a time, and then he began to speak. "When I came to this country years ago, I came as a bond servant, as you all know. I didn't have a shilling in my pocket and not much hope." He went on to trace the hard days of his early life. He spoke of his first wife briefly and the birth of all of his children. Finally he turned to Marian and said, "God has given me a wife like none other and a brand-new son, who I must confess is my favorite."

"Even over me?" Sam interrupted, grinning broadly.

"I'm afraid so, Sam. You'll have to get your spoiling from Keturah, but Enoch and I—well, we have a very special relationship."

Marian beamed, for this new son had tied the two of them together, and she thanked God in her heart for sending this fine boy.

Daniel spoke for some time, and finally he said, "All of the Bradfords have served in the army, and it is God's mercy that not a one of us has died. And I thank the Lord for it right now. I would like for each one of you to say a word of thanksgiving. We are here and God has blessed us. And I want everyone in this room to express out loud their thanks to the Lord."

One by one the Bradfords spoke up, all of them briefly, but as Daniel listened his heart swelled within him. He reached down and took Marian's hand, and finally, when all had spoken, he prayed a simple prayer. "God, you have spared my house and my family. I thank you for every good thing you have sent our way, and I pray that in this new land of ours the Bradfords will always cling to the things of God and refuse those things that are displeasing to you."

Marian's hand was swallowed up by Daniel's, and she squeezed it hard as he said, "Amen."

"Amen," she said. "Let everyone say amen."

The Bradfords all echoed her amen, and at that moment Enoch let out a piercing cry and Daniel laughed. "He's got a loud enough voice. I suspect he'll become an evangelist."

🔔　　🔔　　🔔

The house was quiet now; everyone had either gone to bed or gone home. Daniel was standing looking out the window, and Marian came to stand beside him. She put her arm around him, and he turned and embraced her. "What are you thinking, Daniel?"

"I was wondering," he said softly, "what kind of a country this will be in a hundred years. It's dearly paid for; the blood of Americans has darkened its soil, and God has given us freedom. I'm just wondering if we'll measure up to it."

Marian did not speak for a time, and then she said, "We can only be faithful to our own day. Isn't that true?"

"Yes, it is. Dake and Micah and Sam and Matthew, they'll have to keep the lamp lit. And their children will have to carry it on." He turned to her and took her in his arms. "I have a family, and I have you, Marian."

"Come. Let's go to bed, husband."

With a roguish wink, Daniel effortlessly swept her up into his arms, saying, "Mmm . . . that's a wonderful idea, my dear."

Marian struck him slightly on the chest. "Put me down, Daniel Bradford, or you'll be sleeping in the stable!"

Daniel laughed deep in his chest as the two made their way up the stairs hand in hand. When they reached the bedroom door, he stepped inside, waved her in, and then shut the door firmly.

Outside the winds were quiet now, and a blanket of snow had fallen over Boston, rendering the city beautiful beyond compare. This Boston, where the Revolution had been born, the city that had suffered like no other through the years of struggle, now lay quiet. A silver moon shone overhead, laying pale, lucent beams down on the sleeping city.

The war had come and now was passing away. Many had died, and a host of the living would carry scars to their graves. Thousands of families sat down to meals where an empty place at the table cut into the hearts of those who still lived.

Yet America had passed through a fiery trial, and the republic, a grand nation of free men and women, had come to birth.

And as for the Bradfords—they endured.

NEW in
THE HOUSE OF WINSLOW

THE HOUSE OF WINSLOW is one of the best-loved and bestselling historical fiction series available today. With over twenty books to choose from, you can read the whole series or individual titles—each book is a complete story on its own. You'll enjoy every romantic adventure, rich in history and a life-changing encounter with Christ.

In *The White Hunter*, John Winslow is a restless young man who travels to Africa to visit a missionary relative. Though he is completely uninterested in religion, John loves Africa and decides to stay on as a white hunter. Meanwhile, a young woman named Anne Rogers dreams of becoming a missionary in Africa. But first, she faces a treacherous voyage aboard the Titanic. Will she survive the Titanic only to find danger in Africa? Or will John intervene in time?

Available from your nearest Christian bookstore (800) 991-7747 or from Bethany House Publishers.

From Bestselling Author Gilbert Morris!

★ ★ ★ ★ THE HOUSE OF WINSLOW / BOOK 22 ★ ★ ★ ★

THE WHITE HUNTER
GILBERT MORRIS

Three very different lives separated by a dark ocean as foreboding as the Dark Continent.

The Leader in Christian Fiction!
BETHANY HOUSE PUBLISHERS
11400 Hampshire Ave. South
Minneapolis, MN 55438

www.bethanyhouse.com

GILBERT MORRIS—
With a Contemporary Twist!

WHAT WOULD YOU DO IF YOU LOST ALL MEMORY OF WHO OR WHERE YOU ARE? Gilbert Morris proves just how versatile a writer he is by turning to a modern setting and developing a unique plot in this meticulously crafted thriller. A page-turner with heart, *Through a Glass Darkly* holds a powerful message of the indelible image of God on the soul of man.

A man wakes to unfamiliar walls, unfamiliar faces, and no memory of who he is or how he has come to be in this place. Fleeting images race through his mind, but he doesn't know whether they hold the secrets of his past, his present, or his future. An unlikely group of people gather around him and try to help him back into life, but it is a woman who touches his heart and emotions in a powerful way. Can he trust that she is part of his unknown past, or will she only further complicate his life?

Available from your nearest Christian bookstore (800) 991-7747 or from Bethany House Publishers.

THE LEADER IN CHRISTIAN FICTION!
BETHANY HOUSE PUBLISHERS
11400 Hampshire Avenue South
Minneapolis, Minnesota 55438
www.bethanyhouse.com